IDIOT FARM

Also by
Susie Mattox

Fairly Strange

Idiot Farm
Copyright © 2020
Susie Mattox

ISBN: 978-1-952474-20-0

Cover concept and design by David Warren

Published by WordCrafts Press
Cody, Wyoming 82414
www.wordcrafts.net

IDIOT FARM

Susie Mattox

WordCrafts

In memory of my mother, Joyce West,
the first reader of *Idiot Farm*,
and my father, Don West,
who grew up on a farm very much like this.

abandoned like a three-legged dog

If I'd been in Vietnam instead of stuck on my grandmother's rundown crap of a farm in the summer of '72, I would've known what to do with the monster in her cellar. I would've nuked it.

The scariest thing about being dumped on Ida Mae's farm, if you could call twenty rows of corn and a tumbling-down barn a farm, wasn't the creepy foster kids she took in—it was the roar of torment rising up out of her root cellar.

Mama dropped us off on a Saturday in June, barely a week after school let out, and Willie cried for days. He ran along the dusty driveway after her car, his face sweaty and streaked with the dirt her Buick kicked up. Then he sank to his knees and commenced to bawling.

"Cut it out," I called from the front porch. "Nobody likes a crybaby." Least of all, me.

He sat in the dirt, blubbering toward the road where Mama's car disappeared. As the sun sank behind the trees, I thought, *Dang, that's bad when your mama leaves you*. Especially with somebody you scarcely know.

A hard woman. That's what Mama called Ida Mae Bolenn. My daddy's mother. The same daddy who'd volunteered for the war after his buddy got shot up, even though he was way too old to be drafted.

As we clamored out of the car, Ida Mae eyed us from the front porch. The first thing out of her mouth was, "Lord, Martha June, what've you done to your hair?"

"It's M.J., Ida Mae," Mama said. She skirted the hood of the car patting her newly-dyed curls, the color of hot tamales. "I done told you that on the phone."

She clunked up the crooked steps in four-inch platform shoes as Willie and I followed. Mama stopped shy of the old woman and propped her manicured fingers on her hips. "You know I changed my name," she said.

Ida Mae folded her arms over a raggedy white t-shirt like Daddy used to wear and pressed her lips until they were swallowed in a face that looked like a peach gone to rot. In faded jeans, the old woman wasn't much to look at. Her wiry gray hair was pulled in a bun so tight I was surprised her head didn't squeak when she turned it. So tight it should've straightened out some of the wrinkles in her collapsed cheeks.

Her eyes were blue chips of winter broken off and embedded among the wrinkles. They reminded me of that story about the Snow Queen, where the piece of glass broke off and stabbed the boy in the eye and then he viewed the world different. Colder, you know, and somehow meaner.

I was glad Mama had not worn her go-go boots and mini skirt because Ida Mae was already eyeing her up and down like something that just crawled out from under her porch.

"You remember the boys," Mama said, her expression a little too bright. She grabbed me by my collar and yanked me up the last step and squeezed me against her side. "This is Flynn, the oldest." She let me go and pulled Willie beside her and kissed the top of his ratty head. "And Willie."

Ida Mae stared at us.

"Say hello to your grandma, boys." Mama dug her nails into my arm until I was forced to cough up a hello.

"Flynn's just turned fourteen," Mama said, "and don't have any idea what to do with it. He should be interested in girls by now, but it's war all the time. Mooning over grenade launchers and other crazy shit. Got us all to worrying, don't you know." She reached out to ruffle my hair, and I ducked out of range, feeling my cheeks torch three shades of red.

"Lord," Ida Mae murmured, "if he ain't the spitting image of his daddy. One tall drink of water and hair sticking out in every direction."

"Ain't that the truth," Mama said. "Now Willie, he's your man. A real sweetheart. He'll do anything you ask. Won't you, sweetie?" Willie let her muss his hair, his expression lit bright as a Christmas bulb.

"That the girl?" Ida Mae nodded toward the car. Our sister crawled out of the back seat, even though Mama told her to stay put. Sunny stood beside the door I left open and smiled, shielding her eyes from the sun. Decked out in a pink polyester pantsuit with fringe, she could've been a rodeo princess. When she realized she had our full attention, she waved like crazy, a doll wound a bit too tight.

"That's Sunny," Mama said over my shoulder. "That's my girl."

"Tell me again why you're leaving the boys here," Ida Mae said and fixed her flinty stare on Mama. A flash of white caught my eye. A dark face above a stained white t-shirt darted behind a scrubby azalea bush at the edge of the house.

"I done told you," Mama said. "During the summer, the boys need a place to roam. They can't be cooped up with Sunny and me in that hot ol' car traveling to these pageants. Why, they'd be positively stifled."

"Stifled," Ida Mae said.

"You know, with all their energy. The road ain't the place for growing boys."

"Nor growing girls," Ida Mae said.

"Listen, Ida Mae," Mama dropped her voice as she sidled closer, "with Jimbo running off to join the army, we've got no income coming in except his piddling military check and my hair styling business. I got to make some extra money to keep this family afloat while Jimbo's off at war trying to *find himself.* I'm doing the best I can for this family, but I need help. And the boys ain't old enough to do much yet in the way of assistance. So, if you could just find your way to help me out…"

Another face appeared around the corner of the house. A girl this time. No, another boy, with blonde hair nearly to his shoulders and pretty enough to be a girl. His shirt was neat enough, but his jeans were frayed around his ankles. His feet were bare. He fingered the edge of the weathered wood as he inched toward us. His free hand groped the air in front of him.

"Look, boys," Mama said, "you got somebody to play with. Hello." She wiggled her fingers at a girl who pushed her way past the boy. The girl was as pretty as any girl I'd ever seen. She was maybe a few years older than me, and just as tall, with a fluff of white dandelion hair. The uneven hem of her dress sagged below her knees. When she stuck her thumb in her mouth and sucked, a tiny bell at her wrist tinkled.

The dark-skinned boy returned and edged toward me, thinner than Willie. But as everyone stared, he dove back out of sight. After him, a big white belly in a shrunken t-shirt poked out from behind the spent azaleas.

"Okay, boys, got to go." Mama planted a hard kiss on top of our heads and hurried down the steps. Motioning for Sunny to get in the car, she popped the trunk.

She struggled with Daddy's battered suitcase before banging it in the dirt. She dropped my knapsack beside it. The one Daddy bought me in an Army surplus store where they guaranteed it'd seen action in 'Nam. She slammed the trunk shut and gave a last wave in our direction before sliding behind the wheel.

"Mama!" Willie ran down the steps. "Sunny!"

Sunny appeared confused, half in the car, half out. She glanced between Mama, who was already leaning over the front seat tugging her inside, and Willie barreling toward her.

"See you later Willie, Flynn," Sunny waved. "I'll call you when we get settled." Mama grabbed the back of her shirt and yanked so hard Sunny banged her head on the edge of the window.

"Wait!" Willie yelled as Mama ground the car into gear. "Don't go!"

But Mama tore out of there in a spray of gravel with Sunny's head hanging out the window, her blonde curls bouncing with the ruts in the road.

Willie chased the car along the dusty lane until the blue Skylark screeched onto the main road and rumbled out of sight. Then he crawled to a patch of scrubby grass and cried his heart out.

My eyes stung a bit. But I was fourteen. So, I let Willie do the bawling for both of us.

Ida Mae stood on the porch, arms crossed, staring at Willie puddled on the ground. I fetched my knapsack and the suitcase, which thumped behind me as I climbed the porch steps.

I stood beside the grandmother I hadn't seen since I was too little to remember much of anything except drinking well water out of a tin cup, a bathroom that smelled of raw sewage, and throwing corn cobs at a pig in a barn.

"That's your Uncle Marshall's suitcase," she said, staring into the distance.

"No," I said, "it's Daddy's."

"Jimmy took it after he finished college. He filled it with his brother's things. He didn't think I knew."

"Daddy's brother who died in Korea? He never talks about him."

"No," she said. "I don't imagine he does." Her voice was flat, and the brooding look on her face discouraged any further questions.

She and I stared straight ahead until Willie finally crawled out of the grass, got to his feet, and shuffled toward us, sniffling and wiping his runny nose against his shoulder. His face was red and splotchy and grass stuck out of his hair. Ida Mae turned to go in the house.

"Who're them others?" Willie said, all trembly. He pointed to the kids creeping out of the bushes again and climbing the stairs, their faces full of curiosity. The dark-skinned boy, the pretty blonde boy, the redhead who was as pale and round as a frog's belly, and the girl, as beautiful as an angel, but still sucking her thumb.

I backed toward the front door as they crept toward us. The black boy hung behind the others. But the pretty boy fingered everything, the porch railing and the steps all the way up. He stared straight ahead as he made his way.

"Creepy," I said staring at his dead eyes. I turned to Willie. "Does it appear everybody here might be running a quart low?"

Ida Mae heaved a sigh. She returned to the porch and let the screen door slam behind her. "We're all family here," she said.

"Family of what," I said, "freaks?" Willie scooted closer to me.

"The black boy is Delbert," Ida Mae said. "He don't speak. The blonde one is Pretty Boy. He can't see. The redheaded kid with the freckles is Jimmy. He lost his mama and daddy in a car accident up north and somehow landed in Alabama. But careful if you sleep with him. He sometimes wets the bed."

Willie squeezed my elbow hard.

"The girl's Delilah. She's the oldest. In years, at least." With a dopey grin, Delilah lifted her dress and scratched along the lace of her white panties, tinkling the bell at her wrist. "And then there's..." Ida Mae hesitated and frowned at the ragtag group. "Never mind," she said. She opened the door and let the darkness of the hallway swallow her up. I peered into the gloom after her.

Under the circumstances, being dropped on Ida Mae's farm was like being sentenced to the moon with mutant aliens and no chance of parole.

The kids crowded around us, bumping Willie into me. The pretty boy reached out and touched the edge of my sleeve, brushing fingers along my arm. His fingertips were calloused.

"Get your paws off me." I snatched away. He cradled his hand like I'd lit it on fire. The black kid stared at us with his big round eyes. The fat kid's cheeks flushed pink, with splotches of freckles popping out all over. He licked lips so puffy they appeared to be stung by bees.

"Where you guys from?" He glanced between Willie and me. "Ida Mae's always bringing kids home. I'm from Ohio.

Cincinnati. And Delbert," he pointed at the black kid, "well, I've got no idea where he came from. Delilah's been here the longest. She's from further south. And Pretty Boy's from the orphanage."

"We ain't no stupid orphans," I said, "if that's what you're thinking. "We're her grandsons."

"Ohhhhhhh," they said it together as if God himself had broken through the clouds. Except Delbert. The mute.

"So, you got family," the fat kid said.

"Yeah, we got family," I said. "Didn't you just see our mama dump us like last week's trash?" They stared at me. I blinked back. Willie sniffled into my shoulder. "Come on," I said to him and hefted our one suitcase.

Mama sprung the idea on us that very morning right after breakfast. She was in such a hissy, tossing our pajamas and t-shirts into our suitcase, she didn't give us any time to ask questions. She even rushed us so bad I left behind my 1965 war canteen, and the dog tags Daddy let me order from the JC Penney catalog. So, while I could've maybe gotten more details out of her on the day-long drive north from Peach City, I was so mad I gave her the silent treatment instead.

I did, however, have just enough time to pocket the four-blade, military pocketknife Daddy gave me before he left for the war. He got it from his buddy in 'Nam after he got himself blown up. And I managed to smuggle a handful of cherry bombs left over from last year's Fourth of July into my knapsack.

I had no idea how long we were staying. Or where all Mama was traveling. Or where Daddy was. Or nothing. He sent only a few letters and a reel to reel tape where we actually got to hear his voice before he went MIA in some skirmish we couldn't get any information about. He'd barely been there six months. I couldn't believe his rotten luck. I mean, it wasn't like I wasn't proud of him for volunteering when everybody else was bailing out. But still, we needed him. I needed him. And the not knowing what happened to him was gnawing away at my insides something fierce.

I found Ida Mae in the kitchen, peeling potatoes for supper. From the hallway, I watched the gritty brown skin curl around and around her paring knife without breaking.

"Put your things in that room there," she said with a jerk of her head.

I followed her direction into the bedroom across the hallway, past the living room. It was a small room with little light and less furniture. The headboard of an iron bed was shoved against one wall, a rickety desk and chair against another, and a dresser between the windows. The room reeked of something I couldn't quite put my finger on.

The wallpaper was faded blue with tiny white stars, yellowed by the years. Water stains spread storm clouds over the window. Hovering above the bed was a picture of a dark man slumped on a darker horse. The sky above the rider was stormy. And something about it made my gut clench.

I thumped the suitcase onto the hardwood floor next to an oval rug that might've once been blue, but was now faded to a dull gray. Its ratty fringe was chewed up in clumps. The bed was tall, nearly too high to climb onto without help, and a patchwork quilt covered it.

I stared at the scraps of faded blue jeans stitched together willy-nilly and wondered if there was anything in this place that wasn't worn out and used up. I punched a pillow and a puff of white feathers floated out and drifted onto the quilt.

"We stuff them ourselves."

The fat kid had snuck up behind me, causing me to bump my shin against the bed's wooden runner. His shirt rode over his belly again, as soft and white as the pillow I punched. I wanted to punch it, too. "We pluck the feathers," he said. "Stuff them in the pillows. Ida Mae stitches them up."

"You're lying."

"Am not."

"I didn't see any chickens out there."

"They're the neighbor's chickens, past the barn. Ida Mae had to sell them off because some critter kept breaking into the hen house and tearing them apart. We'd find chicken parts all over the yard. It upset Delilah so bad, Ida Mae finally got rid of them. But Mr. Larson lets us pluck them when the pillows need re-stuffing."

"You and what army?" I peered into the dark hallway.

"Delbert, Pretty Boy, Delilah," he said. "Delilah likes it the best. The rest of us do it because we have to. But boy, when she gets her sticky fingers into those feathers… well, I can tell you it's a big mess."

"That girl couldn't pluck her way out of a paper bag," I said.

"Who do you think works this farm?"

"Don't know. Don't care." I strolled to the desk and found a stack of coarse drawing paper, some torn brown paper bags, and a few paper napkins. The desk wobbled on spindly legs.

I flipped through the papers. On each sheet was a drawing. One showed an army tank, camouflaged and attacking a jungle of soldiers. One was an airplane, bombing the daylights out of the village below. One was a squirrel, holding an acorn in its tiny claws.

"That's Delilah's favorite." The fat kid stretched onto his

tiptoes to see over my shoulder. It caused his belly to jiggle, and I swallowed hard and glanced away.

On the next page, a trio of chickens pecked at the ground. A pig fed from a trough. Delilah sucked her thumb. I let the pages flutter into a messy pile.

"We aren't retarded, you know." He backed into the door-frame and scratched his back along it like a cat. "We're foster kids."

"Foster kids." I snorted. "What's that?"

"Kids who don't have a regular home. Some come from orphanages. Some come from homes busted up when the mom or pop gets taken away. When my parents died, I got sent here to live with my aunt. But she didn't want me."

"Not surprised." I studied the stack of drawings.

"Ida Mae takes us in until we can return to our families or somebody adopts us."

"Wouldn't hold my breath." I thumbed through the draw-ings again, blurring the images together. Anything to keep from eyeballing his jiggling belly.

"Delbert doesn't like people messing with his pictures." The fat kid frowned and tugged his shirt down. It simply rode back up.

"So what?" I thumped a fist onto the pile and leaned my whole body into it as if I could shove the whole mess through the desk as I stared back at him. "What's he going to do? Beat the crap out of me?"

"No," Chubbs said. "Delbert won't. He's too little. But Monty will. He hates anybody messing with Delbert."

"Who's Monty?" I lifted my fist and peeled off a scrap of paper that stuck. "Another freak?" I flicked the paper onto the desk and strolled to the chest of drawers opposite the bed. I skimmed a palm along the scarred surface. The drawers hung crooked on their runners and a streak of red paint slashed one side.

Willie pushed past Chubbs into the room. "I want to go home," he said. He struggled to climb onto the bed, but couldn't get a knee over the edge. He launched again. And again. Then he collapsed onto the rug and commenced to bawling.

I stared at his quivering back.

"It's not so bad," Chubbs said. "And anyway, what can you do? Your mom's gone. I mean, the way she hightailed it out of here—"

"Shut up." I glared at him. Poking the back of Willie's head with the toe of my high tops, I said, "Come on Willie, cut it out. It won't do no good." But he continued to blubber into the floor. Chubbs stared at him from the doorway.

"Don't you have something to do?" I said to him. Leaning down, I grabbed the back of Willie's collar and tugged him upward. "Come on, buddy." He was dead weight and flopped against the floor. "Let's check out the place." I yanked again. "There's a barn."

"You can't go there," Chubbs said.

"Says who?"

"Ida Mae."

"Why not?"

"She doesn't want anybody messing with her hogs."

"We aren't gonna mess with her stupid hogs." I bent close to Willie's ear. "You hear that, Willie? There's still hogs in the barn. Bet you don't remember seeing a real hog up close. Just pickled pigs' feet at the gas station."

"At the fair," Willie said, his voice muffled, forehead pressed into his arms.

"Not so's you could touch 'em."

"You can't touch them," Chubbs said.

I whirled around to glare a hole in him. He scratched his back on the door frame.

"What'd you care?" I said.

"You'll get us into trouble."

"How would me going to the barn get you in trouble?"

He appeared to be thinking about that hard enough to bust a gut. A pot clanged in the kitchen. "I'm telling," he said and yelled into the hallway, "Ida Mae!"

"I'm not deaf, Jimmy," Ida Mae said over the spray of running water.

While Chubbs' back was turned, I dragged Willie off the rug and onto the slick floor. "Come on," I said. "Let's go before they stop us."

Swiping his nose against his sleeve, Willie staggered to his feet. I dragged him through the hallway, and we banged out the back door before Chubbs could even get his fat butt turned around.

the cellar door

As it turned out, the hogs rooting and grunting in Ida Mae's barn weren't terribly exciting. Willie and I exhausted all efforts to pester Ed and Janine by poking straw through the wooden slats of their pen, sifting hay onto them from above, and tossing corn cobs at them. Finally, we meandered back to the house.

Ida Mae's house was a thumbnail of a dwelling amidst a sprawling yard and flanked on two sides by woods. Directly outside the back door was the well she still used, even though she finally got hooked up to city water. A tool shed leaned beyond the well, the tin roof as rusted as the barn's. The floor was dirt. And a tractor sat parked inside, looking like it hadn't cranked in years. The pickup truck beside it appeared only slightly newer.

Tools with wicked blades and jagged edges hung from the walls. Wooden barrels were stacked in a corner. Dusty mason jars lined a worktable. The old push lawn mower, an ancient contraption of wood and rusted blades, leaned against the table.

From the shed, the yard sloped downward toward the barn. But to the left of the house and sloping upward toward the woods was the corn patch, twenty or so rows, and a vegetable garden nearly as big. All I could see there were some tomato vines and ruffled heads of greens. Between the base of the garden and the kitchen window sprawled an ancient oak with an old-fashioned rope swing hanging from it. And beneath the oak and swing, was the root cellar.

The mound of the cellar rose four or five feet above the ground and its corrugated metal door was set at such an angle it barely took a second before I had me an idea. I ran to the shed and rummaged through Ida Mae's junk until I found an empty cardboard box. Tearing the sides apart so it lay flat, I carried it to the cellar door.

"What're you doing?" Willie said. "Ida Mae didn't say you could have that."

"It's a cardboard box," I said. "And anyway, Daddy says it's easier to ask forgiveness than permission."

Willie stared at the flattened box. "I don't know."

"Stop being such a scaredy cat." I climbed to the top of the door and plopped onto the cardboard.

The girl with the dandelion hair appeared around a bush, sucking her thumb. With a shove of my heel, I flew down the cellar door and landed in a tumble at the bottom.

"My turn!" Willie shouted, dancing like he had to pee. I was going to pass him the cardboard, when I noticed a small tear where it must've caught on a nail. "Gimme it." Willie snatched it from me.

"Don't wet your pants," I said.

He hauled it to the top of the cellar door, fighting to flatten it so he could ride it. With a shove of his sneakers, he flew down the door as the metal groaned beneath him. He ended in a tangle of elbows, knees, and cardboard at the bottom.

I heard a moan. "You okay?" I hovered over him. "You got to land on your feet."

"Let me go again." He scrambled back to the top. The girl crept closer and crouched beneath the kitchen window.

As Willie plopped onto the metal door, a growl erupted beneath him. "Willie, wait—" I reached out, but he was already flying down the door. He landed at my feet.

Loud clanging erupted beneath the door, and Willie jumped to his feet. The clanging stopped. A growl roared upward, staggering me backward.

"Holy crap," I said, "what was that?" The yard fell silent. The girl snuck away, leaving Willie and me to stand alone at the foot of the cellar door. Holding the tattered cardboard to his chest, Willie stared at the slant of aluminum.

He said, "Mama gets mad when you say ugly words. She'd tan your hide if she heard you talking like that."

"She ain't here." I balled my fists at my sides. "In case you hadn't noticed."

"And stop saying *ain't*." Willie glared back at me.

"I'll say ain't all day long if I want to."

A howl split us apart. The screeching of metal sounded unearthly, like something desperate to claw its way out.

Willie backed away, but I grabbed his arm. "Ida Mae's got something in there," I said. "She's caught some critter." I leapt to grab the door handle, a black strip of leather.

Willie cried, "Don't!"

I tugged anyway. The door groaned and the metal squealed, but it didn't give. It was locked. I tugged again, just to be sure.

"I wouldn't be doing that if I were you," Ida Mae said. She strolled into the yard with a dishtowel flung over her shoulder, brandishing a small, wicked paring knife. She stopped a few feet on the other side of the cellar door.

I stared at the sharp blade pointed at us. "What's in there?" I said. "Some wild animal?"

"A monster?" Willie asked.

"Nothing for you to worry about," Ida Mae said and turned to go.

"That's it?" I slapped my thigh and raised a puff of dirt. "There's growling and banging and lord knows what in there and it doesn't concern us?" I glanced around. Where were all the other kids, anyway?

"Well, if it's down there," Ida Mae fixed me with her flinty gaze, "then it ain't up here. So, you don't have to worry." She stalked back to the house.

"How come the door's locked from the inside?" I called after her. She yanked the rag from her shoulder and cleaned the knife all the way to the back door.

"This place is crazy," I said as her silver bun disappeared into the house.

"I want to go home," Willie said.

I rounded on him. "Don't start that again. I've got enough to worry about already."

"I want Mama."

"Well, what we want and what we got are two entirely different things right now." I tugged on a fistful of hair stiffened with dried sweat and stared at the cellar door.

"You think it's a monster?" Willie said and sank his teeth into his bottom lip.

Through the kitchen window, Ida Mae's head bent over the sink. "Lord knows I wouldn't be surprised at anything. More likely it's a wild animal."

"Wild animals don't scream."

"Good point."

"Maybe it's some crazy young'un she took in."

"You can't lock kids in the cellar," I said. "That's illegal. They'd put her in jail." I searched the yard for Chubbs, the fat know-it-all. He hadn't been able to keep his yapper shut yet. And where were the other kids? Shadows crept into the corners of the yard as the dying sun left a bloody smear across the sky.

"Let's talk about it inside," I said and Willie and I hurried into the house before the thing in the cellar could get us from behind.

The phone rang. I found Ida Mae in the hallway, hovering over a small table and talking into the shiny black receiver. She wasn't actually doing any of the talking, but gripped the receiver so hard her wrinkled knuckles were stretched smooth.

"Is it word about Daddy?" I said. She half turned to eye me. "Is it him?" I stalked toward her. I needed to tell him about the thing in the cellar. She turned her back on me, but I heard Mama's excited voice.

"Mama," I said. "Let me talk to her." But Ida Mae ignored me. I reached for the phone, and my grandmother blocked me with a narrow shoulder.

"I got to go now," she said. Mama stuttered something before Ida Mae slammed the phone into the cradle.

"What'd you do that for?" I said. "I needed to talk to her."

"You can talk to her later."

"I don't even know where she is."

"She didn't say. Maybe when she calls back." She strode past me through the hallway.

"*If* she calls back!" I yelled as she slammed out the back

door. What kind of crazy old lady was she? I picked up the receiver. "Mama?" The line buzzed, angry as bees. "Mama?" I stood like that for a long time, though I couldn't say why, as Mama was clearly no longer on the line.

trouble begets trouble

I might not have minded being dumped on a farm for the summer if it hadn't come from out of nowhere. Well, not exactly nowhere. With Mama hauling Sunny all over the countryside to enter those danged pageants, and Daddy losing his job at the mobile home plant, and his buddy losing his leg in combat, it wasn't totally shocking that he just up and signed up.

Mama said he'd started mumbling in his sleep about his brother dying in the previous war. When his best buddy got his leg blown off on his first tour, it got a bit prickly around the house.

But even with them arguing over the cost of Sunny's pageant dresses, and Mama and Sunny spending most weekends away from home, and Daddy worrying about staying home doing nothing until he finally got called up, I still couldn't predict my entire summer would be turned upside down. I mean, good gravy, spend three months with some old lady I didn't even remember and those crazy kids she took in?

When Daddy finally signed up, Mama barely said a word. She bit her tongue until ladies appeared on the back porch for her to fix their hair. And then she let loose. At first, I thought it simply meant more reasons for her to gab about nonsense while she teased up their beehives. But for me, it actually meant more macaroni and cheese and Hamburger Helper, with not so much hamburger any more. And worrying about Daddy facing the Viet Cong.

Most evenings, ladies with their hair teased to kingdom come sat around our house gossiping, their little girls dressed as fine as Sunny's Barbies. With the war going on, and American grunts getting blown to smithereens, and the jungles getting nuked to hell, and Daddy getting dropped into the middle of it, all them women talked about was hairspray and shoes and fancy dresses while their little girls practiced their runway walking and fake smiles. It made me want to puke.

Sunny wasn't like those girls. Not in the beginning. She loved catching fish and toads and turtles. She'd be the first to squish her toes in the sucking red mud along the creek running through the property behind our house. She loved big dogs, lazy cats, and practically every other critter imaginable.

At first, Mama only entered Sunny in a pageant once in a while. But then they commenced to spending every weekend at those dang contests, and Sunny didn't have time for frog gigging or trucking through the mud. When Daddy finally left, that's when I started getting into trouble at school.

I don't see what the big deal was. So, I shot off a firecracker outside the lunchroom. I found one in a crumpled paper bag in Daddy's toolbox. Joe Bob Harper dared me to pretend I was bombing the Viet Cong.

It was right after recess and it didn't hurt nobody. Just scared old Mrs. Prattlewhite, the chemistry teacher, so bad she thought her class had blown up the lab. She insisted on taking to her bed for the rest of the week.

And then there was the tiny gray bat Stevie Sims and I caught flying around his house one evening a few weeks before school let out. If Sunny hadn't been practicing for another dumb pageant, I bet she would've adopted the critter. We took it to school to show our science teacher, Miss Frankling. Except the bat got loose and flew to roost on the ledge above her door.

It was a fruit bat, not much bigger than a ping pong ball with wings. But the way Miss Frankling carried on, you'd think it was king of the vampires. Beating at her hair, she screamed her way to the closet and came charging out with a broom. She nearly pounded the daylights out of Principal Hecke when he came to investigate the screaming.

The math teacher finally snatched the broom from Miss Frankling, and Principal Hecke climbed onto a chair and plucked the shivering bat off the ledge. He took it outside and let it go.

Stevie and me got to spend the next five days of recess sweeping the gym floor and washing sweaty baseball uniforms. What was it about science teachers that made them so squirrelly, anyway?

Mama had to come to school and talk to the principal. And while he was suggesting that perhaps Daddy being off at war, and her being gone from home so much was causing me to act out at school, she studied a painted nail. I'm not sure she listened to half of what he said.

On the way home she said, real serious-like, "We're going to have to talk to your father about this." And I reminded her that Daddy was gone. Then we both fell silent, listening to some man on the radio singing about people hanging down in the boondocks.

I stared out the window trying to figure out what in the heck *the boondocks* was. I bet Daddy knew. I bet he could've told me. If he'd been there.

monster dreams

The first night we stayed at Ida Mae's, dinner was a disaster. Every time Willie thought about Mama, he sniveled, which upset the dandelion girl. In the end, both of them cried buckets into their mashed potatoes.

Pretty Boy asked what was going on, and Delbert stared straight ahead, ignoring his food. I lost my appetite too and pushed my plate away. The mashed potatoes weren't bad, but some slimy green things Ida Mae called collard greens bled into them. Mama was rarely a threat to serve up any sort of a vegetable. Especially a green one. So I settled on nibbling a buttered biscuit.

The fat kid cleaned the mashed potatoes and rest of the biscuits off of everybody's plate he could reach. But when he reached for Pretty Boy's, Delbert slapped his paw away.

For some reason, Ida Mae fixed a plate of food and left it on the counter. When I headed to bed, it was still there.

To be on the safe side, having no idea what kind of creature was in the cellar, Willie and I shoved the spindly desk in front of the door to the hallway. We propped our suitcase full of clothes in front of the door to the living room. It probably wouldn't hold, but at least if it scraped across the hardwood floor, we'd wake in time to escape being eaten alive.

We tied the window shut, wrapping Willie's bathrobe belt around the latch and then tying it to the knob of the dresser drawer. Willie said we'd be in a world of hurt if there was a fire. We'd made sure nothing could get in, but we'd also made plenty sure nothing could get out, either. I said we'd have to take our chances.

I lay in bed beside Willie and attempted to ignore his huffing and snoring. The only reason we got the good bedroom was because we were new, not because we were family. Blood relatives apparently held no more sway with Ida Mae than any of her other rejects.

As I stared at the ceiling with the bare bulb hanging from the center of it, I finally realized what the room smelled like. Piss.

Like when you're desperate for the bathroom, but you're riding along the highway and there's no bathroom in sight. So your daddy pulls onto the side of the road and tells you to run over to the bushes and it's so hot when your piss hits the ground it rises like steam. And you nearly gag from the smell.

That's what I lay thinking; my hands folded beneath my head. That and how much I hated Chubbs for making my bedroom smell like piss.

As I stared at the ceiling, I discovered another water stain spreading around the light bulb in the center of the room. Together, they appeared like a giant eyeball studying me. I closed my eyes, but the eyeball seemed to close in on me in the darkness. My eyes flew open.

Even with Willie rustling in the covers like a burrowing hamster, I heard the muffled voices of the television in the den.

When Willie and I headed to bed, Ida Mae was shelling peas in front of the flickering screen, watching the news.

President Nixon had placed mines in North Vietnamese ports, and the air force started bombing Hanoi again.

Back home, Mama wouldn't let me watch much about the war. She said it was depressing. But I had this crazy notion that I might actually see Daddy on some of the footage. So, I had to be sneaky about getting information.

When we told Ida Mae we were going to bed, she nodded, eyes on the tiny screen, peas dropping into the bowl, shells dropping into a paper bag. She seemed to forget I was even there.

And that's how I found out that Governor Wallace lay paralyzed in a hospital bed somewhere up north because some crazy person shot him while he was campaigning for president. Mama was right about one thing. The world did appear to be in an awful big mess.

~

"Daddy, Daddy," I called, "it's me, Flynn."

If only Daddy knew how much we needed him. His old mama waits and watches. Her gray head's bent over a sliver of knife flashing in the moonlight as she stands at the kitchen window and stares into the darkness at the cellar door.

"Fatten 'em up," she whispers, polishing the blade.

"This ain't no gingerbread house, Willie," I say. I shake him, but he won't wake up.

What does she want? My legs are trapped so I can't move. What does she need? Two more boys to feed the creature? And why didn't Mama call back? How could she leave us here, alone, at the mercy of that old woman?

The fat kid said Ida Mae's been taking in young'uns since my daddy left for college. Young'uns nobody wanted. Reckon what

*happened to all those kids? They grow up? Move away? Go back
to their drugged-out mamas and daddies who didn't want them
to start with? Or did they just disappear? Fattened up and fed to
the creature in the cellar? I try to move, but my legs are tangled
in the covers.*

The creature calls to me. It whispers outside the window.

*"Free me," it pleads. "I don't even like kids that much. Too
salty. Especially when they're blubbering. Their hair sticks in my
teeth. The eyeballs aren't bad, though. Gummy and fruity. Sweet
as candy."*

I shot straight up in bed, my head tight, like a basketball
squeezed between two giant hands. I pressed fingertips into
my eye sockets. Blood pounded in my ears and my hair was
wet with sweat. I flicked my tongue across lips dry as dust.

Willie slept curled next to me, whistling through his nose.
Moonlight streamed in and lasered across the floor. The creature was outside the window. He moaned through the trees
as the wind eased bony branches back and forth across the
moon. I thought I caught a glimpse of him peering through
the window. I wished I had my firecracker right then. I could
at least blow a claw off. Or put out an eye.

But all I brought was the pocketknife Daddy gave me and
those dang cherry bombs, which wouldn't do nothing but
smoke the monster out. And he was already on the loose. I
searched the shadowy room for a bigger weapon, but there
wasn't anything of use.

I swiped my pajama sleeve over my face. Willie continued
sleeping, oblivious to the creature moaning and groaning in
the moonlight.

My heart *ka-thumped,* and I cursed Mama for leaving us
with Ida Mae and that thing. I clutched the covers to my chin

and struggled to go back to sleep. I closed my eyes. But they popped open again and again. So I lay there, hating Mama, hating Ida Mae, and hating the creature in the cellar. And I plotted how many different ways I might blow that thing to kingdom come.

night terros

It was not my first nightmare. Truth is, I've been having nightmares as long as I can remember. The earliest was when I was about five or six, and Willie was barely old enough to crawl into bed with me.

The dream was about him. I don't remember the beginning, but I remember this.

Willie toddled into the closet. I tried to stop him because a strip of light shone beneath the door and Mama had clearly flicked the light off when we climbed into bed. And because nothing good ever comes out of a closet at night.

But before I could stop him, the door closed behind him. I twisted the knob, but it was locked. Snarling and snapping and growling and screeching erupted from behind the door. I covered my ears and scrambled onto the bed and pulled the covers over my head. Then I peeked out and watched the door.

The room fell silent and the light beneath the door went out. I gripped the bedspread around my head and clenched my teeth. The doorknob turned. The door eased open. Nails scrabbled across the hardwood floor.

An animal clicked its way into a beam of moonlight. A dog. A tiny one. A Chihuahua. I sighed and let the bedspread fall from my shoulders. Nothing scary about that.

Then the dog cocked its head. It was Willie. Willie's head on a dog's body grinning razor teeth.

I screamed. I screamed and screamed and screamed until light swamped the room so bright I blinked—and stopped screaming.

Mama's tired face leaned over me, her hair straggling around the orange juice cans she'd rolled it in. For a second, I thought she was an alien come to eat me. I screamed again until she shook me hard enough to rattle my teeth. I stopped and glanced around. Willie was curled in a ball at the foot of the bed bawling and looking at me like I was the alien.

Daddy appeared in the doorway, scratching through raggedy underwear. "Lordamercy, Martha June, can't you shut that young'un up?" he said, before staggering back to bed.

Mama pressed a palm to my sweaty forehead and eased me back into my pillow. "Just a bad dream," she said. She smelled of orange juice and baby powder. I sighed as she stroked my cheek with the back of her cool, silky hand. She made Willie lie next to me, even though he was still sniffling and staring at me like I was the boy-faced dog.

After it was over, neither of us entered that closet for like, a year.

The nightmares came and went. But after Daddy left, they came more often. Mostly, they were a blur of monsters chasing me around dark, jagged corners, aliens kidnapping me from my bedroom, or the Viet Cong dragging me from a foxhole. There was a lot of slashing and hacking and stabbing. More than once, I snatched awake as I was about to get split wide open—or eaten.

I would spend the rest of the night staring at the ceiling, wondering where my Daddy was and studying a way to kill the monsters in my dreams without anything too terrible happening to me or anybody I cared about.

Sometimes, it actually worked.

know your friendly freak

I don't know what awakened me the next morning. I lay in bed and blinked at the ceiling until I realized my headache was gone. I smiled and sat up and picked the grit out of the corners of my eyes. I glanced around the room. Something was wrong.

The desk was shoved into place against the wall. Our suitcase rested neatly beneath the window like a step leading into the room. Willie's blue bathrobe sash we used to tie the window shut was missing.

The others denied having anything to do with the rearrangement of the room. And truthfully, I had no idea how they could've moved things without waking Willie or me. When I mentioned it to Ida Mae, she muttered something about safety hazards and stalked out to the garden to pick tomatoes.

As we sat shucking corn outside the back door, Chubbs eyed me. "How old are you?" he said.

It was mid-morning and already miserably hot. Between us, a basket contained the produce picked the day before. Beneath the corn was a layer of green beans.

Chubbs occupied the only chair. Rusted and tilting on a bent leg, it threatened to give out any minute beneath his considerable weight. I sat on the edge of the concrete landing, my legs sprawled in the grass. Willie and Delbert picked tomatoes in the garden with Ida Mae. They made a game of it. Willie tossed one to Delbert, who let it drop through his fingers until Willie showed him how to catch it with his knees bent. I eyed the cellar door.

Delilah knelt in the grass beneath the mighty oak, plucking dandelions, her bell tinkling from the dirty strings braided into a bracelet. She was supposed to be helping with the corn. Instead, she blew on a velvety yellow head. The dandelion danced between her fingers. She shook the stem, then tossed it. She plucked another one and did the same thing. The petals clung to the stem. Frowning, she tossed it and picked another.

"You got to wait until they're white and puffy," I called to her. But she continued plucking little yellow heads, blowing on them, then tossing them away. I shook my head. *Idiot.*

I stripped husks the way Ida Mae showed me. I dropped the husks into a brown grocery sack at my feet. Silky threads covered the yellow kernels, as soft as Sunny's blonde hair.

I wondered where she was and hoped she was having more fun than me. The silk clung to my fingers, and I flung it into the bag with the husks. Many of the threads remained caught in the teeth of the corn. The cellar door remained quiet.

"When's your birthday?" Chubbs said as I ripped husks from the cob. "You're fourteen, right? When were you born?"

I heaved a sigh. "May third."

"Ha! My birthday's in August. I'll be fifteen then. Which makes me the oldest."

"I thought the girl was the oldest."

Delilah continued to pick dandelions.

"She doesn't count," Chubbs said. "She acts like a four-year-old. So I'm the oldest."

"You're definitely the fattest."

"Hardy har har," he said. "It's not my fault."

"Being fat?" I cocked my head. "Whose fault is it? I haven't seen anybody cramming food down your throat."

"I've been on diets." He frowned and picked at his ear of corn. "All kinds. They just don't seem to take."

"Ever hear of exercise?"

"Ever hear of minding your own business?"

"You started it."

"I was trying to be friendly."

"Lalalalalala!" Delilah knelt in the grass, hands covering her ears, her jangling bell only adding to the noise.

"What's she doing?" I said.

Chubbs turned to yell at her, "Knock it off, will you?"

The screen door slammed, and Pretty Boy tapped his way toward us with a long stick, a nice piece of smooth blonde wood swirled to a knob in his fist.

"It upsets her when people fight," he said and stopped beside me.

"Well, make her stop," I said. "She's making my teeth hurt."

He tapped his stick to the edge of the concrete. Easing into the grass, he tapped his way to the girl and leaned over her. "It's okay." He patted the air, then her head, then her skinny arm. "They're not fighting." He jiggled her arm. "Not fighting, just talking. Shhhh."

The girl stopped and dropped her hands to her lap. She commenced to rocking and humming.

"Good grief." I rolled my eyes. "She always carry on like that?"

Chubbs squinted at me. "You think you're such a hot-shot," he said. "I haven't seen you out here tearing around the yard."

"I get plenty of exercise." I dropped the corn cob into the bowl Ida Mae gave us. "Ever hear of the Navy SEALs?"

"Of course I've heard of them."

"I'm signing up," I said, "soon as I turn eighteen."

"Ha." Chubbs swiped his wrist across a dribble of spit on his chin.

"That's right," I said. "What do you know?"

"I know you're not tough enough to be a Navy SEAL."

"You know squat."

"Training so tough it makes grown men puke their guts out?" He eyed me up and down and apparently found me wanting.

"My uncle was in the navy," I said. "My daddy's in the army over in 'Nam."

"That ain't nothing like the SEALs."

"Military's in my blood."

"I bet you couldn't make it to the barn and back."

I eyed him with his albino thighs spilling over his chair. "You think you could?"

He raised his chin. "Faster than you."

"You're out of your mind."

"Prove it," Pretty Boy said. He leaned on his stick beside Delilah in the grass. I glared at him. Chubbs snorted.

"Who's going to time us?" I said. "You?"

"Jimmy can count for you. You count for him."

"What if he cheats?" I said. "You couldn't tell."

"I'm no cheater." Chubbs jumped to his feet tumbling the corn from his lap.

"We'll count together," Pretty Boy said. "Race around the barn and back. Hit the cellar door when you finish and I'll stop counting. That'll be your time. You go first."

I glanced at the cellar door and imagined the monster in my dream.

"Stalling?" Chubbs said.

"You want to eat my fist?"

"Cut it out," Pretty Boy said. "Let's settle it like gentlemen."

"Like soldiers," I said.

"Foot on the cellar door." Pretty Boy leaned toward me. "So I hear it. That's your starting point. And your finish."

I stood and left the corn and husks behind me. I touched my foot to the metal door.

"Is he touching it?" Pretty Boy asked Chubbs.

"Yeah," Chubbs said.

Pretty Boy drew a deep breath.

I clenched my fists.

"On your mark."

I leaned into a crouch.

"Get set."

I thrust my shoulders forward.

"Go!"

I took off, skirted the well, and raced toward the barn. Weeds slapped my ankles as I gained momentum and nearly lost control. As I neared the barn, a dark shadow crossed the loft window. What was that? Dark and hairy and hunched over, its long arms hung to its knees. Then it was gone.

I veered left, circled around the back of the barn, glancing up at the window overlooking the open field beyond. I raced beneath it as straw rained on my head. The dark thing disappeared from the window. It was fast. Fast as me. Maybe faster.

The creature had escaped the cellar to the barn. I kicked into high gear and cleared the barn like commies were after me. Pulling up the hill, my lungs burned. I pumped my arms.

I sucked in air. I wind-milled around the well to keep from crashing into it. I hit the cellar door as Pretty Boy shouted, "Forty-seven!"

"I counted forty-nine," Chubbs said.

I dropped to my knees and gulped air. Willie and Delbert were still in the garden, tossing tomatoes at each other.

"You counted too slow," Pretty Boy said. I turned to Chubbs, palms on my knees, sweat trickling down my face.

"Blind boy said forty-seven," I said. "Beat that."

Chubbs scratched his belly beneath his shirt. "Naw." He plucked the corn he'd dumped on the ground and plopped into his chair. "I don't think so."

I stood tall. "You chicken shit."

"Ida Mae doesn't allow that kinda talk." Chubbs hunkered over his corn.

"He's right." Pretty Boy said and dug holes in the dirt with his stick. "She doesn't allow cussing."

"Who cares?" I staggered toward Chubbs. "You're a coward, you fat slob. I bet you couldn't even make it to the barn."

He blinked up at me. "I've got weak ankles. Anyway, what's so great about running around the barn? What does that prove?"

"It proves I can kick your—"

"Lalalalalalala!" Delilah screamed. She scrambled to her feet and ran in circles, covering her ears.

"Shut up!" Chubbs hollered.

"Don't yell at her," Pretty Boy said. He stepped toward her, and she knocked him off his feet. He lay on his back, his stick tangled between his legs.

I stared at the fat kid overflowing his chair, the crazy girl running in circles, the blind kid struggling like a giant bug on his back in the grass.

"Jiminy Cricket!" I yelled. "I am so out of here!" And I stalked toward the house.

preacher comes a calling

And that's how I finally named the fat kid. Calling him Chubbs was taking the easy way out. He needed a name to convey exactly how incredibly annoying he truly was.

Ida Mae said his real name was Jimmy Krackauer, but I decided to call him Jiminy Cricket after that stupid, annoying bug. Not the one in the Disney movie. That bug wasn't that bad. But the one in the book—I couldn't stand him.

And like Jiminy Cricket got what he deserved in the book, I wanted to squash the fat kid under my high tops. And I didn't appreciate him having the same name as my daddy, neither.

I plopped onto a rotting log. My daddy was the one who told me about the Navy SEALs' motto. *Nobody gets left behind.*

A few years earlier, we were watching news of the Vietnam War with the protests and the helicopter crashes and a movie star touring over there to aid and abet the enemy.

"If I was a younger man signing up for war," Daddy said from his easy chair, gripping a can of beer, "I'd sign on to be one of them Navy SEALs."

"A seal?" I peered at him as my G.I. Joe held Evel Knievel hostage.

"Navy SEAL, son." He sipped his beer and crossed his

socked feet at the ankles, destroying G.I. Joe's bunker made of empty match boxes. I groaned.

"They came into being right after the Second World War. Didn't know much about 'em back then. I wasn't much more than a kid, myself. But my brother was in the next war. The Korean one. By then, they were training boys pretty regularly."

"What's so great about these Navy SEALs?" I said and restacked my bunker.

"What's so great?" He banged the can onto the metal TV tray beside him. "They go through training so difficult more'n half of 'em drop out the first week."

"What kind of training?"

He slumped in his chair. "Underwater training, assault training, airplane jumping. It ain't called Hell Week for nothing. You got to be army, navy, marine man all rolled into one. You got to hold your breath underwater for, maybe, fifteen minutes."

"Nobody can hold their breath for fifteen minutes," I said. I stopped trussing up Evel Knievel with a piece of fishing line I'd found in Daddy's tackle box. I knew it wasn't fair to pit him against G.I. Joe, seeing as how he was barely half his size. On the other hand, the Viet Cong were small, and they'd been whipping our boys pretty good.

G.I. Joe gave Evel Knievel a whack on the head even though the little guy's arms were tied and couldn't defend himself. I'd have to create some special torture since my prisoner was captured using his motorcycle and superstar power to spy for the enemy. Unfortunately, I hadn't been listening to my daddy. He snorted from his chair.

"What'd you say?" I lashed Evel Knievel to a silver candlestick I'd found in the bookshelf. It wasn't real silver because we weren't the kind of people who owned real silver. But it was still tarnished gray.

"I said they can do things no ordinary men can do."

"They can't walk on water." I fixed G.I. Joe's pistol in his fist. It was to be the firing squad, then.

"Wouldn't be surprised," Daddy mumbled.

"Surprised about what?"

With his beer to his lips, he tilted his head back. Frowning, he gave the can a jiggle and then peered one-eyed into it. He sighed and said, "You ever hear of no man getting left behind?"

"No." I returned to my war game.

"It's their motto. No man gets left behind."

"Whose motto?" I replaced the fallen pistol into Joe's stiff grip.

"The Navy SEALs for crying out loud. What've we been talking about?"

"You don't have to get sore about it." I plucked the revolver that fell out of Joe's hand and thought about gluing it in. Or maybe he should stab the enemy with his bayonet.

I fumbled underneath me for the weapon. "I don't believe it," I said, spying the sharp point under the sofa.

"Believe what?" Daddy's head was thrown back on the cushion. He closed his eyes and massaged the wrinkles on his forehead.

"The part about no man being left behind. I mean, you're telling me no Navy SEAL ever gets blown apart six different ways so they can't even find all the pieces?"

"That's what I'm telling you."

"Nobody's been taken prisoner?"

"Nobody."

"Not ever?"

"Never."

"I don't believe it."

"You can't make something your motto if it ain't true."

I shook my head.

He peered at me then. His eyes were red and puffy. "Just because you don't believe something," he said, "doesn't mean it's not true."

I shrugged.

His feet hit the floor. "Look it up."

"Maybe I will." I turned my back on him as he staggered to the kitchen, crumpling his beer can along the way. I stared at Evel Knievel. G.I. Joe stabbed him with the bayonet once, twice. Knievel slumped against his post.

"No man left behind," I muttered. "That's ridiculous. People get left behind all the time."

Just when I thought the day at Ida Mae's couldn't get any longer and was wondering how I was going to survive an entire summer, a shiny black Monte Carlo roared along the driveway, chewing dust and spitting gravel. I stood on the front porch with a stick I hadn't figured out what to do with as the car screeched to a halt in front of me. The driver's door flung open, exposing a blood-red interior like the devil's own ride.

The man who climbed out was as shiny and slick as his car. His hair, too black to be natural, was swept in a pompadour and bounced as he stalked toward us.

He wore a fancy suit, the kind most folks in these parts didn't own until they were buried in it. And on his puffy hand he wore a gold chunk of a ring. The round black stone in the center of it winked like an evil eye in the sunlight.

He approached me, wiggling his fingers at his sides like a gunslinger. But as he drew closer, he took to twisting the ring around and around his finger. The black eye could see me, then it couldn't. Then it could. Then it couldn't. I leaned against the porch column and tapped my stick against my thigh.

"You're new." He stopped at the bottom of the steps. Up close, the wrinkles mapping his face put his age closer to Ida Mae's than his dyed hair implied. Small dark eyes squinted at me. "Where's Ida Mae?"

"Who're you?" I eased the stick over my shoulder and scratched my neck with it.

"Somebody who knows bad manners when he hears 'em." He propped a shiny black wingtip on the bottom step. "Now, where's Ida Mae?"

I continued scratching my neck with the stick. I enjoyed the tingling of it, and the man seemed annoyed by it. So I kept at it.

"Maybe she's in the barn," I said.

His slick brows shot up. "Well is she, or isn't she?"

I shrugged.

"Boy," he propped his hands on his hips, "I don't have time..."

The screen door squealed open behind me and Ida Mae stepped out onto the porch, wiping her knuckles on a raggedy old dishrag.

"The barn, huh?" He glared at me.

I shrugged and scratched the stick further down my back.

"What is it, Rhubarb?" Ida Mae gave the man the same flinty glare she usually reserved for me. "I'm cooking supper."

Rhubarb? I snorted.

Veggie Man shot me a look. "Why don't you teach these young'uns some manners, Ida Mae?"

"This is Jimmy and Martha June's boy," she said.

"Oh yeah?" He eyed me up and down.

"This is Rhubarb Muler," she said to me. "He's the preacher over at First Church of Haley. Say hello, Flynn."

"Hello, Flynn." I smiled sweetly at the man.

He scowled. "How old are you, boy?"

"Old enough. You didn't say hello back."

"Old enough to know better than to disrespect your betters?" he asked.

I was about to ask him what made him think he was better than me. But Ida Mae's glare kept me quiet.

"Jimmy's boy, huh?" The man scratched his dimpled chin with a thumbnail. "I guess I can see it."

"What'd you want?" Ida Mae slung the dishtowel over her shoulder and crossed her arms.

"I brought you something. Hey, how's Jimmy, anyway? Haven't seen that boy in years."

"He signed up for the war," she said. "What'd you bring me? I'm busy."

He frowned. "That boy's a little late to the game and way too old for such shenanigans," he said. "He could've sat this one out. What'd he wanna go over there for, anyway? Heard some horrible stories about the goings on."

Ida Mae kept quiet.

An awkward silence ensued.

"Well, where's Martha June?" he said, finally. "I want to say hey."

"*M.J.* is gallivanting around the state, entering her girl in beauty pageants," Ida Mae said. She pressed her lips together to keep from saying more.

"Beauty pageants!" the man exploded. "Vanity of the devil.

Couldn't you talk some sense into the woman? With her husband off at war?"

"Didn't try."

"Her baby girl couldn't be no more than what? Nine? Maybe ten?"

"Eight."

"Eight years old. What is this world coming to when an eight-year-old is judged on beauty? Ain't all little girls beautiful? Didn't the good Lord say all little children are precious? And then we go and trash that natural beauty with lipstick and rouge. Why, I've seen those girls dressed like tarts. Doesn't Martha June know there's a killer running loose?"

"What was it you came for?" Ida Mae raised her brows along with her voice and inclined her head toward me.

He frowned. "I came to deliver the prescription you forgot to pick up at the drugstore." He patted his coat pocket. "Doc Baker says—"

"I didn't forget nothing," Ida Mae said. "And I'm not taking it. You take it right back where you got it."

"What's going on, Ida Mae?" he said. "Exactly how sick are you?"

"None of your business," she said, "and even if it was, I'm not talking about it in front of the young'uns. I got responsibilities here, and these kids depend on me."

"Ida Mae, you know you can't keep a secret in a town like this."

"I said I ain't saying nothing else about it." She ground her teeth.

The preacher's oily gaze followed the tilt of her head. He squinted at me and swiped a dribble of spit off his chin. He swung back to her. "You missed church yesterday."

She rolled her eyes. "Not that again."

"And the Sunday before. And the Sunday before that. You could've come yesterday. Brought Flynn here, and the rest of your young'uns."

"The Lord says Sunday is a day of rest. So, we rested."

"Listen, girlie—"

Her nails dug into her arms. "Don't you *girlie* me."

His jaw clenched. "Woman, if you don't ever set foot in a church you're headed straight for—"

"Stop!" Ida Mae snatched the towel from her shoulder and fisted it on her hip. "Going to church never got anybody into heaven. So, worry about your own salvation, Brother Muler. And I promise, I'll worry about mine."

"You got no salvation, Ida Mae, unless you accept you're a sinner."

"That's between the Lord and me." She slapped the dish-towel against her faded jeans as she stalked to the edge of the porch. She stopped to peer down at him. "It's none of your dang business."

Brother Muler removed his foot from the porch step. "Is this still about Marshall?" he said. "Hasn't it been long enough you've been blaming God for something that wasn't His fault?"

She crossed her arms and glared at him.

"I'm worried about you, Ida Mae. You and these young'uns. You don't want to spend eternity in an everlasting pit of fire. You don't want these young'uns to follow you along the well-paved road to hell."

"Tell you what I don't want," she stabbed a bony finger at him, the dishtowel jerking with each jab. "I don't want you spouting this fire and brimstone garbage on my property in front of these young'uns. I'll come to church when I'm good and ready."

"Well, when's that going to be?"

"When you get rid of all them gossipy, backstabbing hypocrites sitting in your pews every dang Sunday."

"Woman!"

She jabbed her finger again and descended the steps. "We don't need your church, here, nor your blasted fiery pit."

"Ida Mae," he stumbled downward with each jab, "one of these days..."

"Git," she growled halfway down the steps, "before I fetch my shotgun."

"Sister, you are going to regret this one day." He pointed his pudgy finger at her. "Mark my words. You're going to run out of time. And I won't be able to save you then."

She drew herself up to her formidable height of five feet four and said, "You never were able to save me. And tell Brother Kaine to stop coming around, giving candy to the kids. He appears to be up to no good, and I don't need the dental bills. Now git, before I turn the hogs loose on you."

Shaking his head, he beat a hasty retreat to his car. "You're a hard woman, Ida Mae," he called before sliding behind the wheel and slamming the door.

"At least I'm not a hypocrite," she muttered and thumped her way back up the steps.

The black car spun in the gravel before growling onto the main road.

"Ida Mae?"

She hesitated inside the screen door, a palm propping it open.

"Why'd that preacher call you *sister*?"

She let the door hiss shut between us. "Because I have the great misfortune of being kin."

By the time the black car disappeared around the bend, the smell of bacon and cornbread drifted toward me on the soft evening breeze.

monster games

After dinner, I decided to stay awake all night to discover if the monster could sneak into our room without Willie and me hearing it. But right before bedtime, Ida Mae offered us a special treat. Chocolate chip cookies hot out of the oven. And warm milk.

I wouldn't realize until later how rare this treat would be. Ida Mae wasn't exactly the sort of grandma who offered up cookies and milk on any kind of a regular basis. At the time, I didn't give it much thought. I gobbled three cookies the size of my fist and drank an entire glass of milk. When we finished, Willie and I managed to ease the dresser in front of the window, the suitcase with the chair on top of it in front of one door, the desk blocking the other.

I crawled into bed and lay clutching my newfound stick in one hand, my knife in the other, and stared at the ceiling. I struggled to stay awake. I focused on the bare bulb staring back at me, but my eyelids weighed as heavy as my belly, and the room was powerfully warm.

Shaking myself, I squirmed to a sitting position. The bars of the iron headboard bit through the pillow into my shoulders so I stared out the strip of window visible above the dresser. The jagged branches of a tree, maybe one of the fig trees, dipped and swayed as the quarter moon glowed beyond.

Willie's snoring caused my eyes to droop again, and my fingers loosened the grip on my stick and my army knife. My head dropped to my shoulder, and I snatched awake. I pinched the skin along my arms so hard it looked like I had chicken pox. I thought of the milk I'd drunk with the cookies. Warm and soothing. The chocolate chips, dark and rich. The way Ida Mae studied us from the corner by the sink, waiting. Waiting.

I slumped into my pillow, my palm resting on the stick, feeling so tired, so sleepy, so...

My eyes fluttered open. The moon outside had disappeared. The room was as gray as the light outside. It was morning. Early morning.

I rubbed the back of my aching neck as I straightened from the slumped position I'd slept in. The dresser was in its place next to the window. The suitcase, desk, and chair back where they belonged. Ida Mae had struck again. Like maybe she was trying to clear a path for the monster to get us.

But something else was wrong. I patted the covers. Then snatched them upward to peer underneath. I inspected under the bed as Willie rustled in his sleep. I leaned over and poked in and around him. He groaned.

My heart *ka-thumped*. My stick was gone.

The screen on the back door squealed open, then banged shut. I hopped out of bed and raced along the hallway, hurtling into the warm summer morning. The grass was wet and slick with dew as I ran barefooted to the cellar.

I yanked on the handle. It was locked. I spied Ida Mae's shovel propped against the back door. She was mighty particular about her tools, but somebody had forgotten to put it away.

I grabbed the shovel and ran back to bang on the cellar door. *Wham, wham, wham!* The ground growled beneath me. I hammered the door. The cellar rumbled.

"What in the sam hill are you doing?" Ida Mae said. She was at the back door, already dressed, her hair coiled in her neat bun.

"It took my stick," I said, sweating and shaking. I lowered the shovel to the ground. "It took me hours to find the perfect stick. And it stole it."

Ida Mae stalked toward me and yanked the shovel out of my grip. "It's five o'clock in the morning," she said. "You've probably woken the entire neighborhood."

I glanced around. There wasn't another house in sight. "It took my stick," I said.

"I heard."

Jiminy Cricket, Pretty Boy, and Delbert crowded in the back doorway, watching.

"Long as you're up," she called to them, "best get your clothes on and go slop the hogs. And you," she turned to me, "maybe you need to get a little more shut eye. You're obviously still dreaming."

"I'm not dreaming. I got plenty of sleep." And then I stopped. Why did I get so much sleep? I had attempted to stay awake all night, but didn't make it past a few minutes.

The cookies. Milk. Ida Mae's special treat. Or was it?

"Get on in the house, anyway." She swung the shovel over her shoulder and headed toward the shed. "There's plenty of chores to go around."

With a last glare and a kick at the cellar door, I stomped back to the house and banged through the back door. I passed the other bedroom doorway and glanced in.

Jiminy Cricket and Delbert crowded around Pretty Boy, who held my stick.

"My stick." I shoved Delbert aside and snatched it from Pretty Boy. "You're the one. What a weenie. Snuck in like a thief in the middle of the—"

"I didn't take your stick," Pretty Boy said.

"Like heck, you didn't. It's in your dirty, rotten paws. How do you explain that?"

"I came in here to get my shoes and found it lying under my bed."

"A likely story."

"No, really."

"Well, which one of you bozos took it and hid it under his bed?" I glanced between Jiminy Cricket and Delbert. They looked at each other, then back at me. "I mean it." I raised the stick like I was going to start cracking skulls. "Who took it?"

Willie appeared in the doorway. He was dressed, but his hair stuck out like a hedgehog's. I moved toward him. "You know who took it?"

"Of course not," he scratched behind his ear, "I was sleeping."

"Who was it?" I whirled and shook the stick at them.

"What's going on now?" Ida Mae stuck her head in the doorway. "Flynn, drop that stick before you hurt somebody."

"Somebody took it!"

"Well, you got it back now, so stop yelling."

I gritted my teeth. "But somebody took it."

"Any of you boys take Flynn's stick?"

"No, ma'am."

"No, ma'am."

"Not me."

"There," she said. "It's obviously some mistake."

"It's no mistake."

"You got it back, so drop it."

I glared at the four of them. Jiminy Cricket shrugged his shoulders.

"All right, boys," Ida Mae said. "Make your beds and straighten this room. After breakfast, slop the hogs." She stalked to the kitchen.

"That's it?" I followed her. "Aren't you going to do anything?"

She banged a frying pan onto the stove. She opened the refrigerator and plucked a handful of eggs from it. The door swooshed shut. She rattled a bowl onto the counter and commenced to cracking eggs.

"Like punish them?" I said.

"You see anybody take it?"

"No."

"You got any proof they took it?"

"No."

"You get punished for anything you've done since you been here?"

I gripped my stick and clenched my teeth.

"Now, get along." She commenced to scrambling the eggs with a fork.

I stomped out of the kitchen and into my bedroom. Willie had already made his side of the bed. I stood at the window and stared out, leaning my forehead against the cool glass. Something was horribly wrong. And the sooner I figured out how to trap that monster, the safer we'd be.

disaster at the a&p

The next morning, Ida Mae sent me to town for groceries. I took off in a hurry, glad to be away from her crazy farm, her watchful eye, and the nutty kids staring at me. But mostly I was glad to escape the thing in the cellar.

I was still mad at Mama enough for Willie and me both, so I worked on a plan to track her down. I knew she and Sunny were cutting a path through a string of small towns to get to the big one, Torrence City, up north Alabama. I might not know where she was at the moment, but I dang well knew where she had to end up.

The road to town was newly-paved, and tar oozed, black and bubbly, in the hot sun. A ravine ran along both sides of the road with a steep bank leading up into the woods. Most of the trees were tall, spiky pines. But a smattering of mimosas was scattered throughout, their pink, fluffy halos the only color in a wash of green.

Kudzu covered everything. Big, heart-shaped leaves gobbled the ditch, the embankment, bushes, and low-lying trees. Vines licked their way upward to strangle even the taller pines.

I imagined falling into a swamp of kudzu, never to be seen again. It would slurp me up and swallow me slow. There'd be nothing left to do but blink from beneath the ropy vines and stare at the cloud-spotted sky and watch the world go by.

I'd be Kudzu Man, Superhero! With super-duper camouflaging skills. I could see you, but you couldn't see me. I'd attack and destroy enemies at will. I'd slice and dice a few of those commies over in 'Nam. Yeah, that's what I'd do.

Before I knew it, I was on the edge of town. Stevie's Stop 'N Go appeared around the corner on my right with its lone gas pump and a low red Coca-Cola cooler sweating outside the front door.

A bottle of cola sure sounded swell, but I didn't have any extra money. Ida Mae had given me just enough for the groceries. She counted the bills carefully onto the kitchen counter, and I'd stuck them in my back pocket as I pushed my way out the front door. I caught the back of my jeans on a loose wire on the screen as I spied Willie plowing through the garden. He yelled and waved. But he was with the Delbert kid, so I yanked myself free from the door and hollered, "Later!"

The First Church of Haley appeared on my left. It was an important-looking building with a bazillion steps leading to its massive front doors. A fat white steeple squatted on the roof, appearing to sprawl on its earthly foundation more than it stretched toward the heavens.

A sign on the front lawn announced Sunday's service in crooked black letters. Some wise guy had removed the 'r' from Brother Muler, so it read, "with Brother Rhubarb Mule leading the worship service." As I passed, I heard the squealing of children as two men conversed at a side door.

One was Brother Muler in his slick black suit. The other man was taller and younger and jacketless, his white shirt sleeves rolled to his elbows. His tie hung loose and crooked.

Brother Muler said something, and the young man straightened his tie and ran fingers through his hair, the color of ripe peaches.

Back home, Mama took Willie and me to church now and again. Maybe Easter and Christmas, and anytime Mama got a new dress or a new hat she wanted to show off. We did a fairly regular stint when Sunny was born, as Mama toted her around on a little satin pillow like the Hope Diamond.

Willie and I trailed behind them as little old ladies stopped to coo over our sister, going on and on about how pretty she was. Once in a while, Willie and I suffered a trembly pat on the head. I didn't blame Sunny for stealing the show back then. Because not only was she the most beautiful baby in Peach City, she was the sweetest, too.

I stood in line at the A&P with my arms full of groceries, including one six pack of toilet tissue, which I tried to hide behind the bread and sugar. A smooth voice behind me said, "You're Ida Mae Bolenn's grandson, aren't you?"

I peered over my shoulder. The man standing outside the church with Brother Muler towered over me with an easy grin and a face full of freckles. His tie hung crooked again.

"Yeah." I nodded. "Flynn."

"I'm Braxton Kaine," he said. "I work over at First Church."

"Yeah, I saw you out front." His aw-shucks wholesomeness contrasted with Brother Muler's greasy black hair and the ring with the black eye twisting around his finger.

"Appears you got an armload, Flynn."

"Yeah." I shifted the items before turning my back on him.

A hunchbacked gnome of a woman stood in line in front of me. She took each item out of her cart and held it to the sputtering fluorescent light overhead. She squinted as if she'd never seen it before, then placed it on the crawling conveyor belt.

There went a can of tomato soup. There went a can of black-eyed peas. There went a can of cat food. Nope, she raised it and peered at the grinning cat on the label. Yep, she placed it alongside the peas.

"You enjoying Haley, Flynn?" the preacher man said.

I turned to stare at the can of tuna, pack of crackers, carton of milk, and extension cord resting in his folded arms. "No," I said. And then thinking maybe that sounded rude, I added, "Haven't seen much of it. Ida Mae keeps us pretty busy."

"She's a hard worker."

"You could say that." I studied the conveyor belt. The woman finally emptied her cart and fumbled with a ragged black change purse for money.

"Wish we could channel some of Ida Mae's energy into the church," the man said over my shoulder. I turned as he shifted his items into the crook of his arm and pulled a tube of Chapstick out of his pocket. He ran it around his flat lips. It smelled of mint.

"I don't reckon there's much chance of that," I said. The pony-tailed cashier smacked hard on a wad of gum and shoved the woman's items toward the bag boy, a brawny linebacker with a Three Stooges haircut.

"Oh, Brother Kaine," a little old lady behind the preacher tugged on his shirt sleeve, "I sure do appreciate you stopping by Sarah Jane's. My sister doesn't get out much, but she nearly jawed my ear off telling me how much she enjoyed your visit. And the apple pie, too. Lordy, who knew a bachelor such as yourself could bake?"

"I didn't bake it, ma'am." Brother Kaine's cheeks flooded

pink, and he stuffed his Chapstick into his pocket, nearly dropping his can of tuna. He caught me staring and winked. "Mrs. Ledbetter baked the pie," he said. "I just delivered it."

"Well, aren't you the sweetest thing. The very sweetest one," she said. "I can't believe some young woman in Haley hasn't snagged you yet. We've got some real lookers in town." She fluttered her lashes and nudged him with a sharp elbow. "Amanda Louise Parker for one."

"Yes, ma'am." Brother Kaine studied the items in his arms, maybe wishing he was someplace else. He gave me a crooked grin.

I turned to find the woman in front of me still rummaging in her purse, placing each coin carefully onto the counter. A nickel, a dime. She dug around and produced a quarter.

I rolled my eyes and sighed. I dropped my load onto the conveyor belt that had stopped rolling and stared at the toilet tissue. With a huff, I tried to camouflage it by piling the other items on top.

The old biddy behind Brother Kaine leaned around his shoulder to frown at me. The woman in front of me never glanced up. She slid the coins and a few crumpled bills toward the clerk.

The woman behind Brother Kaine whispered loudly, "Didn't you say that's Ida Mae Bolenn's grandson?"

"Yes," he said softly.

"It's a wonder his mother allows him to visit, given what that old woman's already put her family through."

"I believe Ida Mae was found innocent," Brother Kaine said.

The old woman sniffed. "You never know."

I shifted my weight from left to right, right to left. I blew air out of my cheeks. I studied the sputtering lights overhead.

The cash register dinged, and the clerk, snapping and crackling her gum, handed the old lady her receipt. The woman
folded it like an accordion, then in half, and slipped it into
her purse. Her hand trembled. So did the smile she gave me.

Good grief, I thought. *Move it, sister.*

With a palm braced on the counter, she shuffled out the
door behind the bag boy who hefted her bag of groceries
easily onto his broad shoulder. The cashier slid my bacon
along the conveyor belt.

"You ought to stop by the church sometime," Brother Kaine
said to me as my groceries slid by. "We've got Vacation Bible
School coming up. And a potluck supper Wednesday evenings."

"I don't think so." I fumbled in my back pocket for the
money. The back of my neck tingled as my fingers found the
hole there. "Ida Mae doesn't go to church."

The cashier slid the last item toward the end of the counter.
The cash register dinged.

"Thirteen fifty-two," she said and bagged the groceries herself. I fumbled in both back pockets for the money. Nothing.

"You can come by yourself." Brother Kaine rested a hip
against the counter. "Bring your brother."

"We don't do church, neither." I dug into my left front
pocket, ignoring the pack of gum I'd stolen, as the nosy old
blue hair leaned around the preacher to glare at me. *Oh, sure,*
now *she's in a hurry.* The cashier smacked her gum and picked
at a thumbnail. She sucked on an oozing drop of blood. I
checked my right front pocket, refusing to give in to my
awful dawning.

"Don't your parents take you to church?" Brother Kaine
said as he placed his items on the counter next to mine.

"Some." I started over again with the back pocket. "Mostly

just Christmas and Easter." My ears burned. *And whenever Daddy hadn't gone out and tied one on.* The blue hair sniffed her pinched nose in the air. I yanked my right front pocket inside out sending the pocketknife Daddy gave me skittering along the sticky linoleum.

Preacher Kaine moved to pluck it from the floor. "Nice army knife." He handed it to me.

"Thanks." I rubbed my thumb over a spot of rust on it.

"Hell-*oooo*." The clerk leaned between us. "It's thirteen fifty-two."

"Yeah, uh," I jammed the knife back in my pocket. "I seemed to have, uh—"

"Oh, for heaven's sake," the blue hair huffed.

"You got the money or not?" The cashier frowned. She stopped smacking her gum and glanced over my shoulder. I turned to see the store manager behind a glass booth staring at us. I pivoted back to her.

"Of course I've got it. I mean, who would try to buy groceries without any money?"

"Then where is it?"

The bag boy reentered the store and stopped at the end of the counter to press beefy knuckles into it.

"It's just," my head itched so bad it was all I could do to keep from scratching it. "Well, it's that I don't appear to actually have it on me. You see, there's a hole in my back pocket."

"What am I supposed to do about that?" The cashier folded her arms over her flat chest.

My groceries sat bagged at the end of the counter. My gaze shifted to the door. I eyed the cashier. She cocked a brow.

I peered over my shoulder at the store manager. I was fast enough to snatch the bag and make it out the door. I was sure of it. And I was pretty sure once I'd cleared the doorway, they'd never catch me. I sidled closer to the bag. One more step and Kudzu Man would blend into the wind.

I lunged for the bag as a fist grabbed me and yanked me backward.

"No problem, son." Brother Kaine's grip tightened on my shoulder. "I'll spot you the money for the groceries," his hand slid away, "and the gum."

"Gum?"

He leaned close to my ear. "Left front pocket." His breath was warm and minty. Straightening, he pulled out a neatly folded wad of money. "I'm sure Ida Mae's good for it."

The cashier glared at me, and I had no choice but to dig the pack of Juicy Fruit out of my jeans and plop it onto the counter.

The preacher peeled a twenty off the stack and handed it to her.

She took the bill, gave me a dirty look, and jammed the cash into the register before yanking out the change. My ears burned as if somebody lit a match to them, and I wanted to smack her. The bag boy slid the sack of groceries toward me with a smirk. I wanted to punch him, too.

"Uh, thanks, preacher," I said, fixing my attention on the toilet tissue sticking out of the top of the bag.

The blue hair behind us grabbed Brother Kaine's arm. "You're an absolute angel," she said. "I tell my sister that all the time."

And while they were blabbing, I grabbed the bag and the gum and busted out the door with the old lady's voice shrilling after me into the white-hot sunshine.

a fine howdy do

The government lady appeared right after breakfast the next morning. Her Volkswagen beetle, the color of soggy spinach, chugged along the driveway, churning dust before coming to a shuddering, sputtering halt in front of the porch. Maybe Brother Kaine sent her to spy on me after the grocery store incident. I couldn't say for sure.

Willie and I watched her as we headed from the side yard toward the front steps. The first thing I saw of her was her clunky brown shoes. Daddy would've called them sensible. Mama would've called them godawful ugly.

The lady stepped out of the car, appearing exactly as you'd expect a lady working for the government to look. Her mousy brown hair was pulled into a bun at her neck. Her nubby brown suit was entirely too hot for the summer. And her chestnut eyes behind thick black glasses were as dull as her suit.

She pulled a clipboard from the front seat and clicked a pen with her thumb as she stalked toward us, taking notes even before she said hello. She stopped just shy of plowing into us. "Ida Mae here?" she asked, her focus on her clipboard.

Willie and I had been jousting with some willow branches that we'd stripped bare. We were supposed to be picking blackberries below the barn, but that's where we found the willow tree.

"She's at the barn," Willie said, and I glared at him. No giving aid to the enemy.

With a sharp finger, the lady slid her glasses down her pointy nose and stared over the rim at us. "You're new. Who're you?"

"I'm Willie."

I jabbed him in the ribs, and he yelped and scooted away. I glared at him. He glared back.

She scribbled furiously on her legal pad. Then she stopped and peered at me. "Who are you?"

I stared at her, and Willie punched me in the arm. I punched him back. "None of your beeswax," I said. "Who are you?"

She tilted her nose in the air. "I'm Miss Indie Walker. I work for the government, son. And I don't answer to you." Fingers trembling, she pushed her glasses back up. She tucked a strand of hair behind her ear. It slipped out, and she tucked it again. It refused to stay put, and she pressed it hard to her head.

"Well," I said, "I don't work for the government, but I don't answer to you, neither. Come on, Willie." I tugged on my brother's sleeve. He hesitated, then followed me to the back of the house.

The government lady pursued us. "You tell Ida Mae I need to see her," she called.

"Tell her yourself!" I hollered back, eyeing the cellar door as I skirted it. I thought I heard a grunt.

I let the screen door slam shut and hurried to the kitchen window to watch the woman continue to scribble on her clipboard. She surveyed her surroundings, and I wondered if she knew about the monster beneath her feet.

She picked her way through the scraggly yard as if she were crossing a swamp full of gators. She didn't pay any particular attention to the cellar as she passed, but that was where Delilah appeared and attempted to give her a sloppy hug. The woman fended her off, and Delilah shrugged and fell in step behind her, her ridiculous bell tinkling with every step.

I moved to the back porch as they headed toward the barn. Delilah was three steps behind and picking up her feet exactly like Miss Walker. Jiminy Cricket and Willie joined me, and we watched them all the way to the barn. At the barn entrance, the government lady called, and Ida Mae came out to meet her, shielding her eyes from the sun.

They stared up the hill to where we were standing, and I knew they were talking about us. The government lady scribbled more on her pad, which didn't appear to make Ida Mae too happy, her lips pressed into a thin line. Finally, she waved the woman away and disappeared into the barn.

The woman climbed the hill with Delilah on her heels, pretending to scribble on her own imaginary paper. The government lady kept turning to frown at her, which caused Delilah to bump into her again and again.

By the time they stopped at the well, Miss Walker's forehead was shiny with sweat. She tucked a strand of hair behind her ear and asked for a drink of water. We stared at her.

"Lilah get it." Delilah clapped and pushed past us into the kitchen. She returned with a child's tin cup, dented around the lip.

"Lilah get Miss Walker water." She approached the metal bucket suspended over the well by way of a rope pulley. Miss Walker eased the heavy, square board that covered the mouth of the well into the grass, and within a few attempts, Delilah managed to lower the bucket into the well and bring up water. Miss Walker sighed as Delilah handed her the cup.

"Thank you, Delilah," she said. She laid her clipboard and pen in the grass at the base of the well and dipped the cup into the bucket.

I knew from experience that the water tasted metallic and was so cold it made your teeth ache. Miss Walker dipped the cup into the bucket again and drank and drank and drank.

"Lilah want drink," Delilah said as Miss Walker dabbed her wet lips with her thumb.

"You'll need another cup."

"Lilah want shiny cup." Delilah pointed to the cup Miss Walker held.

"No, Delilah." Miss Walker pulled it out of reach. "This cup is dirty now. I drank out of it. You must get another."

"No." The girl stood nearly eye to eye with Miss Walker. "Lilah want that one."

"Fine," Miss Walker said. "You'll have to wash it first." She handed Delilah the cup.

"No wash." Delilah pushed past Miss Walker toward the bucket, and Miss Walker grabbed her arm, knocking the bucket into the well. One, two, three long seconds passed. Then there was a clunk, but no splash.

"See what you've done," Miss Walker said. "Go wash the cup, and I'll raise the bucket again."

"No wash."

"Then no cup." Miss Walker snatched the cup out of Delilah's grip.

"My cup! My cup! My cup!" Delilah screamed and flapped her arms like she was about to flee the coop.

"Calm down," Miss Walker said. Her face flushed pink as she dabbed the back of her wrist against the sweat beading her upper lip. Ida Mae trudged up the hill, swinging the hogs' empty slop bucket.

"Cup! Cup! Cup!" Delilah shrieked.

"Just give her the cup," I said. Her caterwauling made the hair on my arms tingle.

"It's dirty," Miss Walker said. "It has my germs on it. And she's dirty enough as it is."

Before I could even ponder what dangerous germs the government lady might be carrying, Ida Mae reached us. "What's going on?" she said. "Delilah, stop screaming."

Delilah fell silent.

Miss Walker opened her mouth, but before she could utter a word, Delilah snatched her clipboard off the ground and tossed it into the black hole of the well. There was shocked silence, a clunk, another clunk, and then nothing.

a big splash with the government

No one moved. We stared stupidly at the well.

"Wha... what..." Miss Walker's face flamed clear to her dull brown roots. "You, you little... Ida Mae!"

Delilah twisted her body from side to side, twirling her thumb in the hem of her dress. The tin cup glinted at her feet in the sunlight.

"Holy moly," Jiminy Cricket said.

Ida Mae dropped the wooden slop bucket and stood with her fists on her hips staring into the well. "Maybe the bucket caught it before it hit the water. Otherwise, it's a goner."

She strode to the pulley handle and attempted to crank it, but it wouldn't turn. "Must be stuck." She leaned over to study the black hole. Finally, she retrieved the slop bucket and strolled toward the tool shed.

"Do something!" Miss Walker wailed, her fingers laced on top of her head, her jacket stretched tight across her back.

Ida Mae returned with a coil of rope.

Miss Walker straightened and tugged on the hem of her jacket, struggling to regain some sense of dignity. "You're not planning on lassoing my notebook with that are you?"

Ida Mae uncoiled the rope and said to me, "You're the strongest. You'll be the one."

"The one what?" I stared back at her.

She indicated the well where the black hole yawned its dark maw.

"Not on your life," I said. "I don't care if the Holy Grail's been dropped in there. I ain't going after it."

"You'll have to climb down the bucket rope," Ida Mae said.

"No way."

"It's strong. It'll hold."

"No."

"We'll tie this rope around your waist just in case."

"Not a chance."

Jiminy Cricket flashed his fat teeth at me. "I thought you were training to be some hot shot Navy SEAL. Chicken?"

I bared my teeth at him.

"Ida Mae," Miss Walker pushed her glasses along her nose, "I can't imagine it'd be safe to drop that boy—"

"You want your notes?"

"Well, yes, I—"

"Got any better ideas?"

"Um, maybe the fire department?"

"Honey, by the time those boys got here, your notes would be mush. We either get 'em now, or we might as well not bother."

I raised my hand. "I vote for not bothering."

Ida Mae stepped close. "You're the oldest."

"Not by four months," Jiminy Cricket chimed in.

"Shut up," I said.

Ida Mae's voice was low. "These young'uns depend on me, and we all depend on Miss Walker's reports."

"So, I'm supposed to sacrifice myself for this bunch of freaks?"

Delbert and Pretty Boy had been attracted by the hollering.

Delilah squatted in a patch of scrub grass picking at her grubby bare toes. Willie chewed on a thumbnail outside the back door.

"Whether or not these young'uns have a place to stay may depend on us getting Miss Walker's notes back." Ida Mae's gaze bored through me. "She's already upset about our recent increase in numbers."

I rolled my eyes to the salty sky. A bird soared high above us, too far to tell if it was a hawk or some other bird of prey. I shook my head and sighed.

Ida Mae motioned for Jiminy Cricket to help. Delilah sprawled her legs in the grass, humming some stupid song that sounded like, *The Bear Went Over the Mountain*. I wanted to knock her into the well, as well.

"The bucket's stuck," Ida Mae said, "hopefully the clipboard's with it. Climb down and loosen it." She wrapped the rope around my waist and double knotted it.

I peered into the hole that reeked of darkness and death. "Don't I need a flashlight? Or a weapon?"

"A weapon?" She tied the other end of the rope around her waist. "Don't be ridiculous. You're wasting time."

With her hand beneath my elbow, she eased me onto the lip of the well, barely wider than my foot. For somebody who never seemed to be in a hurry about anything, she appeared mighty quick to toss me into that murky pit. Holding onto one of the wooden beams propping up the tin roof, I hesitated.

She braced her wiry body against the well's stone wall. With her free hand, she held onto the leg of my jeans as I perched there.

Being a little smaller than me, I didn't expect there was any way we weren't both going to end up at the bottom of the icy water. But she nodded, and with a deep breath, I leaned out to grab hold of the rope.

Jiminy Cricket braced his fat body against the pulley so it wouldn't unravel further. Miss Walker muttered something behind me.

I stared into the darkness and thought it would serve Mama right if I drowned in a stupid well. Maybe she'd finally feel bad about leaving us.

With the blood pounding in my ears strong as an ocean's surf, I gripped the bristly rope. I kicked away from the wall and wrapped myself around my lifeline. Swinging crazily, I closed my eyes and held tight.

The rope bit into my palms. The one around my waist squeezed me tight enough to nearly cut off my breath. I peered back at Ida Mae, and she nodded. She eased a little slack into the rope and lowered me into the abyss.

Exactly like a training mission, I told myself. A rescue mission in 'Nam. Perfect for a Navy SEAL. Get in. Retrieve the object. Get out. Simple as that.

Through slimy walls, cool air, panther darkness, I slid into the belly of the great creature. Gripping the rope, my hands were on fire, and my knees trembled.

Ida Mae's gray head blocked the halo of light above me. "Holler when you touch water." Her voice broke into pieces and bounced off the walls around me. And then there was no sound at all except for a soft *thump, thump, thump*.

Was it the heart of the beast? Had the creature moved from the cellar to the well? Did Ida Mae send me down to get devoured? Was everybody in on it? Miss Walker, too? Was this how it ended for the other unsuspecting kids?

Mama was sure going to be sorry when she found out

I'd died from drowning or being eaten alive by some giant creature. It would be all her fault. And I hoped she'd bawl like a baby when she finally realized she didn't have me to kick to the curb anymore.

The soft thumping prickled my skin. I was about to scramble back up the rope when a cold wetness seeped into my sneaker.

It was the creature's giant slurping tongue. I tried to claw back up the rope, but my toe bumped something hard and floating. It pinged against the wall.

I paused long enough to catch my breath and think. What was the sound? I hunkered and brushed fingertips along my leg, to my foot, until I found the cold metal of the bucket.

I couldn't see anything except the small circle of light above me and when I peered up and away, I saw nothing but a bright white ring in the inky blackness.

Fingering in and around the bucket, I found the edges of the clipboard. It appeared to have dinged the bucket and was now wedged partly in the bucket, partly in a crack in the stone wall. I tugged the edge of it, but the soggy paper slipped out of my grasp. My shoulders burned. The paper ripped.

I inched my fingers around the board until I found the metal clasp and tugged so hard it slipped free, banging my shoulder into the wall behind me. The bucket rebounded, clunking my shin.

Hugging the clipboard, I tugged on the rope. "Pull me up!" I yelled.

At first, I simply swung in limbo. But finally, the rope groaned upward inch by inch, the circle of light growing bigger and bigger until I finally grasped the lip of the well and dragged myself over.

A cheer erupted from Willie and Pretty Boy. Delilah wrapped her arms around her thin body and pouted. Ida Mae unfurled the rope from around her waist as Jiminy Cricket wiped his sweaty cheeks against his shirt sleeve. Delbert observed everything with his big, brown eyes.

Miss Walker leaned over to pluck the sopping clipboard from the ground where I'd dropped it. The paper hung in shreds. Pinched between finger and thumb, she held the dripping mess away from her body.

"Might be able to save some of it," Ida Mae said.

"This will have to go in my report," Miss Walker replied.

The smiles on the faces around us faded.

"All of it."

I rubbed my chilled arms and peered around the group. Apparently, a fresh report from the government lady did not bode well for any of us.

just your average neighborhood freaks

Pretty Boy told me Miss Walker wasn't the first government lady to handle Ida Mae's case, as we sat on the front porch steps before dinner. He stared somewhere past the dusty lane holding a chunk of a stick in one hand, a pocketknife in the other. "It wasn't even a lady before," he said. "It was a man. Mr. Willet Boushay. He drove all the way from Birmingham once a month to check on us."

Eyeing him suspiciously, I hefted my stick, which was about as long as my forearm, and scraped off pieces of bark with my thumbnail.

"He was a small man," Pretty Boy said. "Thin and wiry."

"How could you tell?"

He shook his head and smiled like he'd explained this before. He sheared off a sliver of wood. "It was in his voice."

"His voice?"

"He talked big, like he was some hot shot from Birmingham. Some muscle man."

"How'd you reckon it wasn't true?"

"Generally speaking," Pretty Boy thumbed the edge of his stick, "when people work so hard to convince you of something, they're the least likely to be believed."

"He could've been those things."

With a flick of his knife, Pretty Boy sailed a chunk of wood into the air and I half expected a bloody thumb to go with it. "He could've," he said, "but then, every time he came to see us the last year, he developed an awful hacking cough. Generally speaking, tough guys don't suffer a hacking cough." Another chunk of wood flew by.

"Maybe he was just a small man with a bad cough who liked to talk about himself."

"He was sickly." Pretty Boy thumbed the smooth wood. "I shook his hand once. Soft as a girl's. That is, until he started washing them so often."

"Girls?" I didn't want to witness the possible shredding of fingers, but I couldn't manage to look away.

"Hands, dummy. Five or six times a visit. Soon as he arrived in his big silver Cadillac."

"There is no way you could tell it was a Cadillac," I said. "Or silver."

"Jimmy told me. Anyhow, soon as he arrived, he'd head for the kitchen and wash his hands. Then he'd follow us around, asking questions about how Ida Mae was treating us. Then he'd go to the bathroom and wash again."

A few quick nicks with the knife stalled my breath. "Delilah was always tugging on his coat pockets, thinking he'd brought her candy."

"Why'd she think that?" I watched the knife fly, my own piece of wood forgotten.

"Some man stopped by the farm right after she was brought here and gave her candy. Now every time somebody stops by, she thinks they've got Tootsie Rolls, or taffy, or Bit-O-Honey."

"Who was the man?"

"Mr. Boushay?"

"No. The one with the candy."

Pretty Boy shrugged. He stopped slicing. He cocked his head, listening. Then he commenced to carving again. "Ida Mae says it might've been Delilah's daddy or an uncle."

"Why?"

"After he gave her candy, he asked a bunch of questions about her mama, her family, until Delilah got so confused, she commenced to doing that 'lalala' business. Then the man slapped her hard. To get her to stop, you know."

Another series of quick movements left a little pile of shavings between his knees. "Ida Mae ran him off with a shotgun. She fired once over his head and then lowered it straight at his ticker. He didn't wait around, I can tell you that."

"But you didn't see any of it." I wanted to see the thing in his hands, but his knife moved so fast it was a blur.

"Jimmy told me."

"And you believed him?"

"I heard most of it for myself. Jimmy just filled in the details. Anyway, Mr. Boushay washed so often he got to where he spent more time in the bathroom or at the kitchen sink than asking questions." The knife stilled as he fondled the wood. "Right before Miss Walker arrived, we heard he'd cracked up and got locked away in some crazy hospital near Tuscaloosa. Then we got Miss Walker."

"She's kinda jumpy," I said, peering around his fist.

"Yeah, but not as jumpy as old Boushay." Pretty Boy uncurled his palm and in it lay a perfectly carved mallard duck.

"How'd you do that?" I plucked it from his palm.

"Delbert taught me. You can have it."

He stood.

"But how do you even know what a mallard looks like?" I compared the bird to my own shredded stick.

"Jimmy told me. He reads to me. Describes things. And then I carve what I see in my head. Delbert and I are going to live in New York City and be artists."

"You? In New York City?" I nearly choked on my spit. "You wouldn't survive a minute."

"Why not? What makes you so sure you can be a Navy SEAL, but Delbert and I can't be artists?"

"Maybe because I can see?"

"You only think you see," Pretty Boy said. He hefted his cane and tapped his way to the front door, leaving me to stare after him.

~

"What'd you know about being a Navy SEAL anyway?" Jiminy Cricket said. I wandered into the backyard with the carved duck in my pocket. He leaned a hip against the well, arms folded over his bulging belly. He was jealous because Ida Mae asked me to fetch Miss Walker's notebook instead of him. His expression said it all. "You've got to be fearless to be a SEAL."

"What makes you think I'm not?" I could've bumped him off the well, but I didn't want to get too close to his blubbery belly.

"The fact that you sleep with your baby brother."

I wanted to knock his teeth down his throat. Instead, I strolled to the rope swing hanging from the ancient oak and tugged on it. Made of sturdy cotton, it was as thick as my fist, with a knot tied for a seat at the end of it. Worn to a grimy gray, it didn't look like much. But it was tight and strong.

I wrapped my legs around the knot. Lifting my feet, I swung forward a few feet. Jiminy Cricket followed me, which I knew he would. He propped one foot on the cellar door.

I hopped off the swing and dragged it back, back, back. The Cricket's beady eyes followed me. His thumb inched into his nose. With a sprint, I hopped on the swing and whooshed forward, stumbling him backward. He didn't fall, but he stopped picking his nose.

"Anyway," I said sailing past him again, "I have to sleep with Willie because Ida Mae said so. There ain't no place else to sleep."

"Yeah." He wiped his thumb on the hem of his shirt. "But she didn't say you had to cry like a baby and holler out in your sleep, did she?"

"Where'd you hear that?" I sailed away from him.

"Your brother. Talking about your crazy nightmares." I swung closer, and he stepped back. "He squealed on you as loud as Ida Mae's pigs. We got a big laugh out of it."

I launched myself through the air and landed on top of him, pounding him to the ground. I barely got my breath back before I kicked and punched his squishy body, soft as a lumpy pillow. I was nearly blinded by all the dust we kicked up.

I thought I heard a grunt and a squeal before I was yanked backward. I spat out dirt as I struggled against the steel claw at my neck. I glared at the blubbering idiot rolling on the ground. He'd thrown an arm over his face, and a knee protected his privates. I'm pretty sure he didn't even get a punch in.

"I do not have time for this," Ida Mae growled in my ear. "No cussing, no fighting."

"He started it."

She shook my collar. "If you boys got enough energy for fighting, you got enough for cleaning the barn."

"But..."

She squeezed the back of my neck with her talon, making me forget what I was about to say.

"After that," she said, "there's another bag of corn to be shucked at the back door."

Jiminy Cricket crawled to his knees, sniffling and smearing spit and snot and crybaby tears over his fat cheeks with the back of his hand.

"He st...started it," he said.

"That's a lie!" I lunged forward, but Ida Mae yanked me backward.

"I don't care who started it." Her icy stare bored into both of us. Her nails dug into my neck. "It's over now, and you best get going before I add more chores before supper."

"I ain't going nowhere with him." I stared at his blubbering, quivering belly.

"Jimmy, go on to the barn." Ida Mae nodded toward it. "Flynn will be along directly." Fatso staggered to his feet, hitched his jeans to cover his crack, then stumbled toward the barn. His jeans sagged again, revealing his huge white butt.

Ida Mae released me and moved to block my way.

I rubbed the back of my neck and stared at hers, wrinkled as a chicken's, her jaw muscles working. I wasn't much bigger than her and I could probably take her if... my eyes met hers and... well... I decided to concentrate on her pointy chin.

She sighed and shoved her fists into her worn-out jeans, "I didn't ask for you to be here."

"You've made that perfectly clear."

She flashed a palm to stop me, and there was a blister, raw

and oozing, at the base of her ring finger, below a simple, gold band. I shoved my hands in my pockets and stared at the rows of corn.

"You didn't ask to be here, neither," she said. "I understand." We both stared at the cellar door. "But here we are, and somehow we've got to make it work. I'll give you a roof over your head and food in your belly and enough work to keep you from being bored."

I snorted. She stared at me, and I glared back.

"But I've already taken on more than you and your brother."

"A bunch of rejects."

Her eyes lit bright and her cheeks held a spot of red. "A bunch of young'uns who got nowhere else to go," she said. "They're different," she lowered her voice. "They've got obstacles to overcome. But you," I stared at her, "it's time for you start using your brain for some good around here."

She moved closer. "You think you're the only kid in the world who's got problems?" Her chin nearly touched mine. "Look around. You can't spit without hitting somebody worse off than you. Now get to that barn and muck out Loulou's stall before Jimmy has to do his job and yours, too."

We stared at each other. We were so close I could map out the wrinkles crinkling her face. I may've been the first to look away, but I wasn't the first to walk away.

I watched her turn and stride stiff-legged to the back-screen door. She reached for it and rested a palm on the doorframe. I thought she was going to say more, but she just pressed a spot above her left hip. Her eyes fluttered closed for a second as her knuckles bled white on the doorknob. She finally stiffened her back, yanked the door open, and stepped inside.

And I couldn't wait to find my stupid, lying brother and pound him to a bloody pulp.

why daddy couldn't help but join up

Sometimes Ida Mae seemed like a ghost. You never saw much of her, but you sure knew she was around. She had a habit of sneaking up on a fella while he was trying to figure things out instead of doing his chores.

I was shelling peas by the back door. But mostly, I was puzzling over why Mama was so hell-bent on taking Sunny to them beauty pageants. I don't reckon it was because of the money, like she said. In fact, I bet she spent more money on them fancy dresses Sunny wore than she'd ever earn from winning. I believe it was because of something I overheard between her and Daddy, right before he left for 'Nam.

Daddy didn't have to go to war. He didn't even get a hankering for it until he lost his job at the mobile home plant, and his buddy got his leg blown off in his first tour. It was then that Daddy took it upon himself to make this grand sacrifice.

I tried to understand. But Mama did not. They fought about it nonstop. It was sixty some odd days from the day Daddy signed up until he actually headed out.

That didn't give Mama much time to change his mind, but it didn't slow her down none from doing what she wanted to, either.

More than Daddy going to war, they fought about Sunny's

beauty pageant dresses to the point that I wasn't sure if Mama cared more about Daddy getting blown up, or Sunny winning a crown.

The last time I heard 'em argue was three days before Daddy packed a bag and headed out.

They were in their bedroom with the door half closed. Willie, Sunny, and I were playing outside with a worn, grayed tennis ball we'd found. I'd gone inside to ask Daddy if we could use his old wooden tennis racket from high school. But then I heard voices, low and angry. I crept behind the door and listened.

Daddy said, "You're spending too much dang money on them dresses, Martha June. She ain't never gonna have a place to wear them things. She's got a different color for every day. Why can't she wear the same dress? These contests are in different towns. Nobody'll ever see one twice."

"Don't be stupid, Jimmy," Mama said. "I'd see it twice. And how's she gonna compete with them other girls when she's wearing the same old, worn-out dress? Lorene Stanley says she has Louellen's dresses handmade, and she's a puny six-year-old. Sunny's dresses are store bought. Everybody can tell that right off the bat."

"What in tarnation is wrong with store bought?" Daddy said. I peered through the crack in the door. He sat on the edge of the bed shaking a fistful of ruffles. "There ain't a girl in the world who has a use for this many dresses." He gave them a last shake. "Including the Queen of England."

Mama moved so she was out of sight, but I imagined her with her fists on her hips. "You don't seem to realize Sunny has a gift."

"A gift," Daddy snorted. "I'm not saying she ain't pretty." He tossed the fistful of dresses away. "But that's all it is. Good looks. And that'll change eventually."

"That some wisecrack about me?" Mama came into view, her face twisted red.

He scrubbed a hand through his hair that was already tugged wild. "I'm saying she's eight years old. Of course she's pretty. They all are."

"Oh yeah?" Mama said. "You ever watch her compete? Half of them girls look like a dog gave birth to 'em."

"Martha June!"

"It's the truth. They are some of the ugliest girls you've ever seen. I can't imagine what their mamas are thinking."

"Probably the same as you, that their daughters are as pretty as anybody."

"They'd be wrong."

Daddy sighed. His chin sagged more than usual. "The truth is, Martha June, we just don't have the money for these fancy things. I'm waiting to get called up any day now. A grunt's wages ain't going to cover much. And we've got two growing boys."

"Honey, babe." Mama plopped onto the bed beside him, squashing the frilly dresses. She patted his thigh. "Sunny's gonna make all this money back. Some of the pageants pay the winner a thousand dollars. They give college scholarships."

"She's only eight."

"It's never too early to start thinking about college."

"What about the boys?" he said. "What about their college? Flynn's good in football. Willie loves science."

"The boys are fine," she said. "They'll go to work like they're supposed to. You wouldn't have gone to college except for the money the navy gave your mama for your brother's death."

Daddy went quiet. "I don't think this is about Sunny at all," he said finally.

And then the room grew so quiet I could hear the clock on the mantel in the den ticking. It always was a loud ticker. But what can you expect when you win a clock in a church raffle? A loud ticker, that's what.

"What're you saying, Jimmy?" Mama removed her palm from his leg.

Daddy stared straight ahead. Then he glanced at the door. I slipped behind it.

"I'm saying maybe you're hauling Sunny around to these beauty contests for you."

"For me?"

"You enjoy the attention, Martha June. Admit it. I ain't saying that's bad—"

"You think I'm doing this for me?" Mama's voice rose. "I worked my fingers to the bone at that grabby-hands doctor's office five days a week until he realized I wouldn't play that way and fired me. Now I do hair on the back porch for hours. Then, on the weekends, I haul these young'uns around so we can earn a little extra money or a scholarship for my babies. And you just up and signed onto a war half the country doesn't even believe in. All them other soldiers are half your age. You didn't have to do it. You were already exempt. What were you thinking? Not about us, I can tell you that, mister."

The bed squeaked, and her voice moved away. "I am the only one earning any money around here right now. How's this for me?"

"Forget it," Daddy said.

"No. You tell me. How's this for me?"

"You were the reigning Miss Watermelon Queen when I met you. You can't tell me you don't miss the attention."

"And why was it I had to relinquish my crown before finishing out the year?" she said. "Hmmm? Why was it old fat Principal Parker called Mama and said she'd heard rumors, and I had to give up my crown 'cause I was *that* kind of girl, the ones who have to get married—"

"Hush." The bed squealed, and the room fell silent. I peered through the crack, but they were out of view.

"Damn, Martha June." Daddy appeared, shaking his hand, blood dripping through his fingers. "Look what you've done!"

"Next time you slap a hand over my mouth, Walter Jemison Bolenn, you'll be lucky not to lose a finger."

Daddy sucked on the edge of his hand, staring at her like she'd gone bananas.

"Don't you ever try to silence me again, Jimmy. You are bailing on this family. Admit it. And next time, I'll flat take your arm off."

"I heard you the first time," Daddy mumbled. Wrapping his bloody hand in the hem of his work shirt, he stalked toward me. I barely had time to jump out of the way before he slammed the door against the wall and disappeared along the hallway to the bathroom.

I stood in the doorway and watched Mama stack Sunny's fancy dresses one atop the other, smoothing out the ruffles, straightening the hems.

"What is it, sugar?" Without looking at me, she continued stroking and fixing ruffles and poufy sleeves.

I don't remember what I said after that. At the time, I couldn't remember what I'd been after when they started fighting. I don't even remember if I returned to Willie and Sunny waiting outside.

Daddy wasn't in 'Nam three months before he realized his mistake. We got his letters long after he sent 'em, even after he went missing.

He was old for his unit, the average age of an army grunt being about twenty-two. But he thought he was being noble. And I appreciated that. Especially after his older brother, Marshall died in the Korean War.

But Mama thought he was just being selfish. And even after he went missing, she didn't soften her position much.

She said she felt the full weight of the family on her and it was her responsibility to keep us together. And that's why it made absolutely no sense to dump Willie and me on Ida Mae's farm for the summer.

Anyway, that was what I was thinking when Ida Mae snuck up behind me and said, "Them beans ain't gonna shell themselves."

I nearly fell off my stool.

"Keep your mind on your chores," she said. "You'll get done faster."

"Back home we didn't have chores." Running a thumb through the split purple hull, I scraped the peas into a bowl. It was barely a quarter full.

"I ain't surprised." She stared into my bowl. I scowled alongside her at the meager amount of peas. "But around here," she said, "you don't work, you don't eat."

I slit another hull. The peas fell atop the others. I tossed the empty hull in a paper bag. "Maybe I'd rather not eat if I have to work for it."

I said it so low I didn't expect her to hear me. But one thing I learned pretty quick about Ida Mae, was she had the ears of a bird dog.

"That'll be no problem," she said.

I turned to see if she was kidding, but all that was visible was her wiry gray bun disappearing toward the barn.

church and me don't geehaw

Ida Mae had me picking figs and blackberries for preserves until my fingers turned purple from the juice. Nearly every surface in the kitchen was lined with glass jars and metal lids. Fat juicy berries soaked through newspapers and plump figs simmered in pots on the stove. Each stove eye was covered with a tin pot nearly half as big as me. Ida Mae's white shirt was stained with purple splotches, and she sported a nasty red welt on the back of her hand where she'd been burned by the boiling, splattering juice.

Delilah sat on a stool in the corner, her skirt riding over her long legs, bare feet propped on a top rung, an old faded apron tied around her waist. She scraped blackberry innards out of a cooled pot and licked the ladle clean, with her silver bell tinkling. Purple juice stained her mouth, turning her into a crazed circus clown.

I couldn't stomach the girl grinning like an idiot on her stool with that stupid bell, so I suggested to Ida Mae that I go to town to return the money Brother Kaine loaned me. She frowned as she thought it over, probably thinking of more torturous things she could have me attend to.

"Money's over there," she said finally, nodding at a pink ceramic cookie jar in the shape of a circus elephant.

With a fistful of money, I ran out the door in a flash and searched for Willie. I was still mad at him for telling Jiminy Cricket about my bad dreams, but he was infinitely better than the rest of those losers.

I found him and Delbert sitting under the big oak tree with their heads together. Delbert propped a pad of paper against knobby knees. Willie pointed at something on the paper.

"Come on Willie," I said. "Let's go to town. Get away from this crazy place."

"You go," Willie said without glancing up. "Delbert's showing me how to draw horses."

"Who cares about stupid horses?" I said. "You can do that later."

Delbert stopped drawing and glanced up.

"I'll go another time," Willie said. He and Delbert returned to their drawing like I wasn't even standing there.

"Fine," I said. "But I won't ask you again." I stalked along the lane, kicking rocks out of my way. What's so great about drawing stupid horses, anyway? I kicked a rock in the shape of Indiana. Horses got a head, a tail, four legs. How hard could it be?

I stomped along the road and sucked in the scent of freshly mowed grass mixed with the sting of pine. I stopped to pluck a rock from the ground and hauled it at a pine tree along the top of the ravine. I missed. Who cared about throwing stupid rocks, anyway? I picked another rock, made a steadier aim with one eye shut, and let loose. It missed wide right.

"I hate rocks," I said. "I hate horses. I hate idiots." I spent the next thirty minutes strutting along the blistering road, thinking of all the things I hated. "And I hate this stupid hick town," I muttered as the pointy white steeple of the First Church of Haley rose above the trees.

I found the church office through a side door to the left of the sanctuary. A sign announced the Little Lamb Daycare and I got a glimpse of dull silver monkey bars around the corner of the building.

The office was dark compared to the bright sunshine, and hot. It took me a few seconds to find the church secretary behind a cluttered desk. "I need to see the preacher," I said, hovering in front of Lucille Ledbetter.

"Who're you?" she demanded.

I told her.

The woman was thin and sat so rigid in her chair it was like something had stung her spine. With a frown, she buzzed a brown box next to her coffee cup of finely sharpened No. 2 pencils and spoke into it. She gave me the once over while we waited.

A fan hummed in the corner of the room and ruffled the papers on her desk every ten seconds. I picked at a loose piece of skin in the corner of my thumbnail and worked to tear it off with my teeth until Mrs. Ledbetter skewered me with a glare. Then she bent over an ancient manual typewriter that appeared to weigh a thousand pounds. "Now why isn't that letter striking?" She peered at the paper.

"You know they got electric typewriters now, don't you?"

She glared at me, and I commenced to chewing my thumb. "He going to be much longer?" I said, as the skin oozed blood. I sucked on it.

"You in a hurry?" She peered at me like I was a cockroach crawled in from outside. "Brother Muler is an extremely busy man."

"I wasn't looking for Brother Muler." My thumb stung, and I pressed it against my thigh. "I need Brother Kaine."

"You said the preacher."

"Well, how many you got?"

She huffed. "Brother Kaine is an assistant pastor." She said it like she was talking about the janitor. "Anything you need to tell him can be told to Brother Muler. He's the senior pastor here."

"But it was Brother Kaine who loaned me the money."

"Brother Kaine is out on visitation. If you leave the money with me, I'll make sure he gets it."

Just then, Brother Muler appeared in the doorway, saving me from telling Mrs. Lucille Ledbetter that I trusted her with Ida Mae's money about as much as I appreciated her stuck-up attitude.

"Who're you?" Brother Muler frowned from the doorway. His forehead was shiny, his cheeks pink.

"The Bolenn young'un," Mrs. Ledbetter said. "Off of Ida Mae's farm."

"Yeah, yeah. Jimmy and Martha June's boy." He wiped his palms on a handkerchief before stretching a hand toward me. I stared at it. He consulted his secretary. She shrugged and continued typing.

He dropped his hand and stepped into the hallway. "Come on in, Floyd."

"Flynn," I said.

"Right. Flynn."

I followed him through the darkened hallway that smelled of new carpet, to a set of stairs curving up and around and into another room. His outer office was well lit and fancier than the one downstairs. A deep purple sofa lined one wall with a pile of fabric samples thrown over the arm and a stack of wallpaper books on the floor.

We passed an open window where the screams and laughter of children drifted toward us, through another doorway, and into his inner sanctum. His private office was dark wood and deep red, the color of wine. Or blood. Like the inside of his fancy car.

"Come on in, son." He strode toward a massive desk strewn with stacks of papers, books, and two shiny gold pens in a fancy leather box. The front of his desk was carved with angels. "Have a seat," he said, but I stayed in the doorway.

Facing his desk were two leather chairs, their backs high and stiff. Behind the desk was an entire wall of bookshelves. I'd never seen so many books in one place in my life, except maybe the public library.

"You enjoy reading, Wynn?" Brother Muler asked as he eased himself into a chair big enough to swallow him whole.

"Flynn."

"Right, Flynn. I'm just messing with you. You like to read, Flynn?" He swiveled his head toward the books behind him. "I got some I can let you borrow."

I stood in the doorway, scratching one foot with the other. "Not so much."

"Let's see. Books on the apostles. Life of Jesus." He pushed himself out of the chair and studied the bookshelf.

"I don't read much sir," I said. "No time, anyway, seeing as how Ida Mae keeps us busy."

"Hmmmm." The man pressed a finger to his swollen lips. "Peter. Paul. You appear to be a Peter man to me."

"No, thanks."

"Peter as a boy. Peter the fisherman. Peter meets Jesus. There's a good one." He tilted the book out with a finger and dusted off the front cover.

He brought it to his desk. "I always enjoyed this one." He tapped a forefinger against the book. His black-eyed ring stared at me from his fleshy hand. "I was about your age when I first met Jesus." He riffled through the pages. "But Peter was a man full grown. Did you know that?"

"Yes, sir."

"You'd appreciate the story, anyway. You enjoy fishing, son?"

"Sir, I just need to return some money Brother Kaine let me borrow." I came a little way into the room, reached into my pocket, and pulled out the wad of money Ida Mae gave me. A quarter flipped onto the floor with a clink and rolled under his desk.

"Yes. Brother Kaine." Pastor Muler dropped to his knees, as did I. We peered at each other beneath the desk.

"It's closer to you," I said.

"So it is." By the time he fetched the quarter and plopped back into his chair, he was sweating. He mopped his face with his handkerchief.

"Boy, crank that fan on by the window before we roast in here."

I found the fan propped in the far window hooked to a brown extension cord stretching along the wall. When I clicked it on, it made a soft whirring sound.

"Where were we?" Brother Muler slammed the quarter onto his desk.

"Brother Kaine and the money," I said with the wad of bills still in my fist.

"Brother Kaine." He leaned back against his chair, and it groaned beneath his weight. "Out on visitation. Fine young man." He frowned. "Got a lot to learn. Bit on the soft side. But then, he's seen more than his share of tragedy."

I blinked at that bit of news.

"I don't like to talk about my staff," Brother Muler said. "Gossip in this town is something awful. But I try to keep Brother Kaine busy. His sister died recently after being in a coma for fifteen years. Then his mama died soon after, and his daddy just got out of prison and was spotted in these here parts. So, visitation is good for him. Gets his mind off his troubles."

I didn't know what to say to that. So, I said, "Here's the money." And dropped it onto a clean spot on his desk. "It's all there." The preacher frowned at the sweaty ball and the rest of the change. "Except for the quarter," I said, "which you already got."

He blinked at me, "Yeah, the quarter," and slid it across the desk to the pile of money.

A brown box near his hand squawked. Leaning into it, he pushed a button. "What is it, Lucille?" I peered over his desk as he slipped a folded newspaper beneath a stack of papers.

"It's Lounelle's mother, Imogene."

"What's she want?"

"Protection. For her daughter."

"From what?"

"The killer running loose."

"Lord Almighty." Brother Muler huffed. "Lounelle is thirty-seven years old."

"I told her that already."

"Alright, alright." With a push of the button he cut his secretary off and picked up the phone.

"Mrs. Graham? Yes, I've heard," he huffed. "Ma'am, Lounelle is thirty-seven years old. Yes, I'm aware she won the Haley City Auto Worker's contest back in high school. Yes, ma'am," he said, "but this feller's going around murdering little girls. No, I don't reckon I need to go check on her. She's a woman full grown. Why, yes, ma'am. I got my sister's grandson in my office right now." He studied me. "Now, Imogene Graham, you know Ida Mae was absolved of all that business."

I turned away and pretended to study the spot of paint peeling on the windowsill.

"I don't imagine you, nor Lounelle, are in any danger," he said. "Yes, ma'am. I'll keep praying for you, ma'am. Thank you, ma'am." He slammed the receiver into its cradle with a heavy sigh.

"Where were we?" he said. I opened my mouth as the box squawked again.

"Problem..." Lucille Ledbetter's voice came through broken and garbled... "daycare. Carrie Sue Kitchen's four-year-old...insane. Kicking...screaming...stealing."

"Stealing? Oh, bother," Brother Muler said. "Why can't Carrie Sue ever handle these things? Oh, never mind, I'll be right there." He patted his poufy hair into place before pushing out of his chair. "Sorry about this," he said. "Afraid you'll have to excuse me a sec."

Coming around his desk, he tapped the Peter book with a finger. "Take a gander at this while I'm gone. You'll like it." And he left the office, straightening his fancy silk tie.

As soon as he disappeared, I sidled to the open window and peered down at the playground below. Boys and girls ran willy-nilly, screaming and laughing. They hung like monkeys from a tower of metal bars. One little girl shoved another girl out of a swing, sending her howling.

As I watched, Brother Kaine strolled into view. He worked his way to the swing set, patting kids on the head, picking up a toddler who'd fallen and setting him back on his feet.

He stopped behind the little girl who had bullied her way onto the swing. She squealed as he gave her a good push, sending her higher. She held on tight and pushed her chubby cheeks forward into the rushing air. She hung there for a second before falling back, her shiny black Mary Janes wiggling in the air.

"Higher," she squealed, and he laughed and gave her a stronger shove. Too strong, because the swing shot forward, nearly unseating her. It swung crazily and hung in the air fifteen feet off the ground. I held my breath.

But she held on.

As Brother Kaine caught her against his chest, he staggered beneath the force of her little body. She laughed at him, their fair heads blending together.

I retreated from the window and strolled to Brother Muler's desk. I didn't care about the Peter book. My objective was to get in and get out. I had accomplished my mission.

The book was the color of spruce, and the cover was blank except for the title in shiny gold letters—*Hooked by Jesus, the Story of the Apostle Peter*, by Leon Larensky.

Bor-ing. I flipped through the pages. They were stiff and some of them stuck together as if they'd never been turned at all.

I picked up the book and continued to flip through it. Lots of words, no pictures. Like I said, boring. I thunked it onto the desk. Not for me, thanks.

The corner of a yellowed newspaper peeked from beneath a stack of papers. I poked at the expensive stationary scattered on top. The top paper was typewritten with the title, *Lust of the Spirit*, which appeared to be a sermon.

I slid the paper aside with a finger, then the next page, and the next, until I got to the newspaper article. I gasped at the photograph circled in red. Staring at me in a grainy black and white photo was Sunny, in a ruffled dress, her fingertips curved over its lacy edges, her smile frozen.

"Bite-sized Beauty" read the headline. I skimmed the page.

Sunny Beaulynn will be vying for the crown of Little Miss Fig Festival tonight, along with sixteen lovely contestants, at the Etawah County Fair. Her talent is singing and dancing. She has sung and tap danced her way throughout the state of Alabama and will enter the final stages of the contest tonight.

What in the heck was Brother Muler doing with a picture of my sister? Another newspaper lay folded beneath it.

Ten-year-old Regina Muldeen of Bay Bridge, Ala., was found strangled in a ravine a few miles from town. Missing since Friday, she was believed to be walking home from school, barely a block from the Bay Bridge Baptist Church, when she was abducted. She is the second young girl to be abducted and murdered in this county in a month.

Footsteps thudded on the stairs and I snatched the book and plopped into a chair as if I'd been reading the whole time. Brother Muler strolled into the room.

"Oh, good." He grinned. "You're interested after all. I'm telling you, it was one of my favorites." He stopped beside his desk and frowned at it. His finger tapped its way around the sharp corner of wood as he eased into his chair.

"Where were we?" He frowned at the newspaper in front of him for a few seconds before sliding it beneath the other papers. Propping his elbows on his desk and steepling his sausage fingers, he and his black ring eyed me.

"You know how to get to Torrence City?" I said. My

sweating palms slid along the book, and I nearly dropped it. I pressed it into my thighs.

He studied me as he pressed his fingertips together. "Sure I do," he said, and then rested his steepled fingers against his lips. "That's a college town fifty miles north of here. Where your daddy went to school. You got business there?"

"Mama's headed there." I gripped the edges of the book. "Eventually."

"That so?" He tapped his fingers against his lips. He appeared unsettled, like maybe he wanted to take another gander at the newspaper article.

"I thought I might track her down. I mean, get in touch with her."

"You know where she's staying?"

"Not exactly."

"Ain't Ida Mae treating you right?" he said. "You've only been there a week or so. You already cutting out?"

I leaned in to tell him about the monster in the cellar, but the words stuck in my throat. Instead I blurted out, "I need to talk to my mama."

"Well, sure." He gripped the arms of his chair and leaned back. "But a big boy like you's got to learn to break away from his mama sometime."

"It's Willie," I said, "he's been crying most nights."

"He has, huh?" Brother Muler plucked a fancy gold pen from its leather box and tapped it on his desk. "That's a shame."

"Yeah." The pen *tap, tap, tapped*. "Nobody's getting any sleep," I said.

"That so?"

I wanted to tell him about the monster in the cellar. I wanted to tell him maybe Ida Mae had committed a lot bigger sins than not coming to church. A clock ticked somewhere in the bookshelf. A bird twittered outside the window. The pen *tap, tap, tapped*.

"How you planning on getting to Torrence City?" Brother Muler said. His chair squealed as he shifted his weight.

I glanced out the window. "I haven't actually gotten that far. Maybe hitch a ride?"

Brother Muler stopped tapping his pen and studied it, running a finger along its sleek body. "If you were to find out where your mama and your sister were, maybe I could run you and your brother up there. Got a brand spanking new Monte Carlo sitting out in the church parking lot."

"You'd drive us to Torrence City?"

"Sure." He grinned real big, running the pen under his nose like he was sniffing a good cigar. "I've never met your sister. Sunny, is it? And it's been a while since I've seen Martha June. I got business there sometimes. Pastor over at Lakeside Baptist is a friend of mine. His church isn't as big as ours, mind you, but it's respectable." And in a blink, even with the fan whirring, the room seemed a mite too warm. Brother Muler grinned at me over his gold writing cigar as kids squealed outside.

"I've got to go." I stood and the book in my lap tumbled to the floor.

"Don't forget your book." Brother Muler leaned over his desk. The book lay splayed like a wounded bird.

"I'm not sure when I can return it." I stared at it. And picking up that book was the very last thing I wanted to do.

"That's alright. Take your time." He continued to grin big as a fat cat stuffed full of cream. I didn't see any choice but to retrieve it. The cover was rough and awkward to hold.

"Alright, run along now." Brother Muler raised a stack of papers from his desk and shuffled them.

"You gonna make sure Brother Kaine gets his money?" I said.

The preacher turned and pretended to search his bookshelves. "Say hello to Ida Mae for me, you hear?"

Dismissed, I left the office with the stupid book. Lucille Ledbetter barely glanced my way as I passed her desk and fled the church.

I strolled to the gas station across the street, wishing I'd kept enough money for an Orange Crush. Good grief, it was hot. I stared in the big glass window.

The sight of a tan sheriff's uniform inside caused me to wipe my sweaty palms on my jeans. I hopped on the curb as the young man in uniform exited the store with a co-cola in one hand, a pack of Marlboros in the other.

He tapped out a cigarette and struck a match to it. Flicking the match into the gravel, he took a puff, blew out the smoke, then took a swig of his drink.

Too young to be the sheriff, I figured. He glanced my way, and I dropped to one knee and pretended to tie my shoelace. The rusted red newspaper stand caught his attention. He stopped in front of it, hunched over, and squinted through the smoke of the cigarette dangling from his lips.

"Shh-iiiiit," he said. Clenching the cigarette between his teeth, he fumbled into his back pocket, produced a dime, and dropped it into the machine. Snatching a paper off the top, he hesitated, then grabbed another without adding more money. The metal door clanged shut and he stared at the front page.

He folded the papers under his arm and fumbled for his car keys. He tossed the papers onto the front seat of his cruiser, slid behind the wheel, and sped out of the parking lot in a flurry of gravel.

I strolled to the newspaper stand. The headline read, "*Third Victim Claimed by Beauty Killer.*" The picture of the young girl beneath the headline was so like Sunny my heart stopped a beat before blood pounded my ears.

May Nelle Young, an eleven-year-old from Beulah, Ala., is the third girl in a month to be found strangled to death in North Alabama this summer. A former winner of the Little Miss Franklin County Fair pageant, Young's body was found in a ravine five miles from her home after a two-week search. Her clothing was in disarray, with her jeans missing, and her hair had been cut.

The county coroner reported the girl was strangled with some type of heavy wire or cord, and mutilated in the same manner as the last two victims. Her eyes were missing. Family and law enforcement officials refused to provide further details.

Young is the third victim since April to disappear and be murdered in such a savage way. The sheriff of Franklin County and other law enforcement officials are asking for anyone with information concerning these brutal murders to come forward immediately.

The only connection among the victims at this time appears to be that all three girls were beauty pageant winners within the last two years. Meanwhile, pageant officials in Winston County are considering canceling the Little Miss Winston County Pageant until the killer is caught.

I pressed the book into my gut until it hurt.

"Hey, Flynn!" a voice called from behind me. I pivoted to find Brother Kaine waving at me from the edge of the church lawn. He crossed the street. "How you doing?"

"Good, I guess."

"Ida Mae still working you hard?" He planted his feet, as sure as a sea captain on a rolling deck. His white shirt sleeves were rolled to his elbows and his khaki pants were rumpled. His tie was missing.

"I left your money with Brother Muler," I said. "Paying you back for the A&P. Brother Muler said he'd get it to you."

"Oh, sure." He glanced over his shoulder at the church. I followed his gaze up to a window on the second floor where Brother Muler stood staring at us. Even from where I stood, I could tell he wasn't happy. Then, he was gone.

Brother Kaine smiled. "You in a hurry to get back to the farm?"

I shrugged.

"Thought maybe you'd care for an ice cream. I'm heading there now." Something behind me caught his eye, and he stopped smiling. I followed his gaze to the newspaper stand. "The coldness, uh, goes to my head," he said. "Helps me think better." He perked up. "And I'm not scheduled to be in a meeting for another hour. You in? My treat."

I frowned in the direction of the farm. "I guess Ida Mae won't mind."

"We won't be long." He clapped my shoulder and squeezed. And then he strolled toward Main Street at such a pace I had to trot to keep up.

We turned at the corner of the church and passed the courthouse directly behind it. Two men stood on the steps in khaki uniforms. The younger one I recognized from the gas station. I thought I heard him say Ida Mae's name. The other man was taller and rounder, with sparse graying hair and heavy jowls. He shushed the young man as we passed.

"Deputy." Brother Kaine nodded in their direction. "Sheriff."

The older man raised a hand, but the deputy scowled and slapped the newspaper against his boss's ribs.

"What's his problem?" I asked Brother Kaine.

He laughed. "Dale Dawkins? He's probably still sore at the sheriff. Heard he got caught napping on the job last week and got stuck repainting a stretch of Highway 52. Hot work I bet." He laughed again.

"I saw him at the gas station," I said. "He took two newspapers but only paid for one."

Brother Kaine stopped laughing.

"You'd reckon he'd be out there trying to find the killer murdering them girls," I said.

Brother Kaine cocked his head. "What do you know about that?"

I shrugged. "It was in the newspaper. The sheriff," I said, "what kind of man is he?"

"What'd you mean?"

"Is he the believing-in-monsters kind of man?"

Brother Kaine's head snapped back, and I thought he might think I was as crazy as the foster kids on Ida Mae's farm. So, I quickly changed gears. "Hey, is that the ice cream parlor over there?" I pointed across the street.

Past the post office and the library and across the street from the Dixie Theater was a sliver of a building with an ice cream sundae painted on the window. A green canvas awning stretched over white parlor chairs and tables on the sidewalk.

"Why, yes, it is."

We crossed the street and I pulled ahead, my palms sticky against the book. Brother Kaine's long legs caught me easily.

"Read much, Flynn?" he said as we strolled past the library.

"Not much." I stared down at the book forced upon me.

"Brother Muler pushed this dumb old book on me about some lame apostle—" Brother Kaine's snort of laughter stopped me short. "I mean—"

"Book of Peter, right? The one about fishing for men?" Brother Kaine shook his head. "He's tried to unload that book on every young'un who strays near his office."

"Great." I scowled and slouched into my shoulders. "I guess I'm the only one dumb enough to fall for it."

Brother Kaine clapped me on the back. "You could do worse." We stopped in front of the ice cream window. "You're a good fella, Flynn Bolenn. Read it if you've got the time. You might enjoy it." He opened the jingling door. "You appear to be a Peter-kind-of-man to me."

"That's what Brother Muler said." I frowned at the man's broad shoulders as I followed him inside.

ice cream and cold facts

"I know your Daddy's missing in the war," Brother Kaine said, "and that's got to be tough on you."

"Yeah, I guess." We slurped ice cream outside at a table beneath the green awning. He'd bought me a chocolate-covered sundae and an orange soda, even though I insisted a single cone would do.

"Mama got awful sore at him when he signed up. But when our care packages started getting returned and the army wouldn't tell us anything, she got really scared. Then we finally got the visit from some army men. They tried to come in, but she wouldn't have none of it. And when she broke down hysterical-like, that's when Willie and me found out he'd gone missing."

There was an awkward silence as we slurped ice cream.

"Tell me about your sister," Brother Kaine changed the subject. "I saw her photograph in a newspaper on Brother Muler's desk."

"What's to tell?" I shoveled in as much chocolate sauce as I could scrape onto my spoon. Then I flipped the spoon and licked it clean.

"What's she like?"

"Real sweet. And pretty, like Mama. Maybe prettier. More

like an angel." I hesitated at how corny I sounded. "Mama says she sings better than Shirley Temple. But I don't get to hear her sing much since Mama's been hauling her all over creation to be in those stupid beauty contests."

I told him how Sunny's pageant days got started as early as the hospital.

Sunny's real name is Sondra LaShay Bolenn, but she's always been Sunny to me. When Mama first entered her in beauty pageants, she changed her name to Beaulynn. She said it appeared more French. And to Mama, anything French was a step in the right direction.

But that's Mama. Always wanting to make everything fancier than it really is, including Sunny. When she brought her home from the hospital, she kept telling Willie and me her name was Sondra LaShay. But it took one peek over the bassinet at our squirmy sister to name her Sunny.

"It's Sondra LaShay!" Mama stomped her red-painted toes.

"Sunny." I stuck a grubby finger at the baby. She wrapped her tiny fist around it and held on.

Mama said it happened differently. She said once she realized Willie and I were too immature to say Sondra LaShay, she changed it to Sunny. Mama was good at changing history to suit her. But from the first morning Sunny blinked her baby blues at all the faces pressed against the window of the hospital nursery, my baby sister was pronounced the most beautiful baby in Sumpter County.

She was barely eight months old when Mama entered her in Peach City's Prettiest Baby Contest at the local Piggly Wiggly. Polaroids of each baby were thumb-tacked to a bulletin board inside the front door of the grocery store. Everybody who came in the store got to vote on the prettiest one.

One baby's face looked like a squashed pumpkin. One was bawling. One sported a red birthmark the size of Texas. Then there was Sunny, right smack in the middle. She was all smiles with wisps of blonde hair curling against her chubby cheeks. She got every vote in town, except for the mamas of the other babies entered.

Mama continued to enter Sunny in contests and beauty pageants throughout the state. She was barely four years old when Mama entered her in the Little Miss Priss Pageant held in the Rainbow City Recreational Center.

We sat on the bleachers of the basketball court with grungy, gray nets sagging over our heads. A little wooden stage barely a foot off the ground was covered with green Astroturf.

The pageant girls were barely able to cross the platform by themselves. If they weren't sucking a thumb, they were hopping off the stage and running to their mamas who'd drag them back, kicking and screaming. But not Sunny.

She strutted onto the stage in a ruffled blue dress that matched her eyes, her fat ringlets bouncing against rouged cheeks. With her fingertips curled around the edge of her skirt like Mama practiced with her, she posed for the judges and gave everybody a sweet smile.

They placed the tiny sparkly crown on her head, and I thought Mama was going to expire from sheer joy. As we rode home after the show, Sunny pulled the crown off.

"Hurts," she told Mama from the back seat. "Hurts Sunny."

"You put that crown back on your head, missy," Mama said. "Being beautiful and having everybody love you for it ain't gonna hurt nearly as bad as being ignored. If a little pain is the price you pay for being better'n everybody else, so be it."

There were so many other pageants, I can't recall them all.

But the Miss Dixie Pageant in Torrence City was the biggie. It was an all-day affair. And while I couldn't care less about traveling around to those stupid pageants, watching dumb girls strutting around on a dumb stage (Sunny being the obvious exception) I sure didn't cotton to the idea of being dumped on some stinking farm with a crazy grandmother and her own personal freak show.

Brother Kaine brought my attention back to him. "Why do you call them stupid?" he said. "The pageants, I mean."

I shrugged and shoveled in ice cream and let it slide down my throat. "I mean, what's it all for? Prancing around in front of a bunch of people who don't even care about you? Why can't Sunny believe she's pretty no matter what anybody thinks?"

Brother Kaine said, "My sister was in a pageant once. Won Miss Russell Shoals. She thought she was going to be Miss America. She was pretty, too. And blonde."

A voice sang behind me, "Oh, Brother Kaine, there you are."

He smiled past my shoulder. "Here I am," he said, and scraped his chair backward to stand, his head nearly touching the awning. "How are you Mrs. Jeffries?"

"Why, I'm fine, thank you."

I turned to find a thin woman in white gloves crushing a straw hat onto her gray curls. Pheasant feathers sprouted from the band long enough to graze her shoulder. She waved for the preacher to sit.

"Would you care to join us?" Brother Kaine asked. "I can pull up another chair."

"No, thank you." She eyed me. "I was on my way to the cinema. The dollar matinee, you know."

"Yes, ma'am." Brother Kaine stretched a palm toward me.

"This is Flynn Bolenn. Ida Mae's grandson just come to town."

"Yes." She frowned at me, clutching her straw pocketbook for protection. "I've heard." Her expression led me to believe that whatever she'd heard hadn't been good.

"It's all the talk at the Cut and Curl. Well, that and the serial killer running loose. Not exactly the best time for a visit, hmmmm? Say," she brightened at the preacher, "didn't I see you over in Beulah a few weeks ago? I was visiting my husband's sister in the nursing home and there you were, on the street corner, bigger than life. I called and waved, but you appeared in a mighty big hurry."

Brother Kaine smiled and blinked at her. "Beulah? Could've been. Brother Muler keeps me mighty busy with these visitations."

"Why, the good lord, yes," Mrs. Jeffries agreed. "But all the way to Beulah? No wonder you haven't settled down with some fine young woman in town. Brother Muler has you hopping throughout the county."

"Yes, ma'am." The preacher rustled around in his pocket. He pulled out his Chapstick, swiped his lips, fiddled with the cap a bit before snapping it back on. "He even has me picking up his laundry and taking his ring to the jeweler to be fixed. But we sure don't want you to miss your matinee, do we, Flynn?" He eyed me meaningfully.

"No, sir, we sure don't."

"Oh my." The woman checked her watch. "You are absolutely right. I've barely got enough time for popcorn. It was lovely seeing you, preacher." She held out her gloved hand, and he took it gently. "Flynn," she gave me the briefest nod before hurrying on.

"Whew." Brother Kaine dropped into his chair and grinned

at me. "That was close." He lifted his spoon. "Now, where were we?"

I stirred my ice cream.

He pointed his spoon at me. "Beauty pageants," he said.

My spoon clattered against my bowl and I took a swig of soda.

He dug into his sloppy mound of vanilla. "But you didn't agree to join me to talk about beauty pageants, did you, Flynn?"

"Sir?" I nearly choked as the bubbles from the Orange Crush burned my chest.

"You appear to have something else on your mind."

I eased the bottle to the table.

"You want to ask me something? I can see it circling around in your brain. Shoot." He spooned in a mouthful of vanilla and leaned back, waiting.

I raised my spoon again and swirled it around the cherry I'd left in the center. "It's just, with Brother Muler being kin and all..."

"You wanted to ask me about Brother Muler?"

I wanted to ask him why Brother Muler had a picture of Sunny on his desk when, far as I knew, he'd never seen her before. I wanted to ask him about this killer going around carving up little girls. I wanted to ask him about the thing in Ida Mae's cellar.

"Well," I said, "I guess it's about Ida Mae and him. They don't appear to get along too well."

"Not since I've known them."

"How come? I mean, them being brother and sister. Families are supposed to stick together, aren't they?"

"Are they?"

I pushed my ice cream away. "What turned them against

each other? I can't imagine Willie and me acting thataway." And then I remembered Willie and Delbert bent over their drawings, heads together. How Willie chose that dumb kid over me.

"Hmmm." Brother Kaine studied me as he tapped his spoon against the inside of his bowl.

"I mean, the way they speak to each other," I said.

Brother Kaine laid his spoon onto the table. He pulled out his Chapstick and ran it around his lips. This time it left a white, waxy film. He capped it and pocketed it.

He leaned forward and lowered his voice. "You may not believe this, but your grandmother, Ida Mae, was once as pretty as Sunny."

I snorted.

He smiled. "It's true. Brother Muler told me. She was also one headstrong young woman. She came from a family who made a fortune in the lumber business and was the first woman in her family to attend college. She was on her way to becoming the first female veterinarian in three counties."

I shrugged and shuffled my feet beneath the table. I slurped a spoonful of melted ice cream.

"In college, she met a young man."

The story was pretty lame as far as stories go, but Brother Goode didn't appear to care that he was boring the heck out of me.

"The young man was from somewhere up north. Connecticut, I believe. And was what you might call a dandy back then. Within a few weeks, he and Ida Mae fell in love and eloped."

"Eloped?"

"Ran off and got married."

The ice cream took a tumble in my belly, and my spoon clattered in the bowl.

"When the young man's family found out about the elope-ment, they took the first train south and met with the couple to try talking them into an annulment."

"What's an annulment?"

"Canceling out the marriage before God and man. But Ida Mae and William Flynn Bolenn refused, and his family returned up north. Far as I know, they were never heard from again."

I stared at my bowl.

"There was nothing left for Ida Mae's family to do but help them out as best they could. Ida Mae dropped out of school, and her parents bought them a small plot of land with a house and a barn. Ida Mae and William planted crops and raised chickens, along with a few horses and cows.

"Things were fine for the first three or four years. Their oldest child, Marshall, was born. Your uncle."

"Daddy doesn't talk about him."

"I heard he died in the Korean War. On a navy destroyer somewhere in the Pacific."

"His picture's hanging above the fireplace in Ida Mae's den."

He nodded. "Your daddy was sixteen or seventeen when his brother died. Marshall was only twenty-one. So, you can imagine his death broke your grandma's heart." A slight breeze ruffled my hair and goose pimpled my arms.

"After Marshall's death, Ida Mae turned her attention to the farm. Long before your uncle died, it was struggling. With a few years of drought, and your granddaddy's aversion to work, Ida Mae kept it afloat as best she could."

"Where does Brother Muler come in?" I said. "How'd they end up hating each other if her family just wanted to help?"

"I'm not sure exactly. Brother Muler wasn't much more

than a teenager himself, when Ida Mae got married. And his mama, Mrs. Irene, sure doted on him. After Ida Mae dropped out of college, Irene Muler was determined her only boy was going to finish seminary.

"Meanwhile, the harder Ida Mae worked, and the less her husband did around the farm, the less she'd let anybody help. Finally, she refused family visits altogether. Or so Brother Muler says.

"He finished seminary, like his mama wanted. And his daddy ran off with his secretary at the lumber company. So, then it was just Rhubarb and his mama. And he's been trying to reach out to Ida Mae ever since."

"When'd she start taking in them crazy young'uns?"

Brother Kaine stirred the ice cream around in his bowl. "Sometime after your daddy left for college. She was determined that he finish since she never did."

"Mama said something about Daddy getting to go to college because of his brother's death. It upset him something awful."

"I don't want to be spreading gossip," Brother Kaine said, "but there's a rumor your uncle died under mysterious circumstances. Maybe he didn't fall through the ship hatch like they said. Maybe he was thrown."

"But why?"

Brother Kaine shrugged. "One of Marshall's buddies on the ship visited Ida Mae after his death. Let her know about the possibility. The navy settled with her for some sum of money. Maybe that's how your dad could afford college. Some might feel guilty about taking advantage of the situation."

"Guilty enough to sign up for war though he's way too old?"

Brother Kaine shrugged.

We sat for a minute in silence. I didn't want to talk about

Daddy any more. It made my stomach hurt to not have any idea where he was.

"When I was little," I said, "we visited Ida Mae a few times. There weren't any kids then."

"There was an incident early on with one of the boys Ida Mae took in."

"What kind of incident?"

"He disappeared."

"How?"

"They think maybe he wandered into the woods and a wild animal got him." He stopped and stirred his ice cream. He seemed to be pondering something mighty hard.

"Do you think that's what happened?" I prodded.

He bit his lip and swirled his ice cream. "I shouldn't say." He lifted his spoon and let the ice cream drip from it. "Shouldn't stir up more gossip."

I leaned in. "You can trust me." Was he finally going to reveal Ida Mae as the monster's keeper?

"William Bolenn had a hunting cabin deep in the woods," he said. "My daddy built it for him. He had some extra features put in, like an attic and running water. Pretty fancy for a hunting cabin in those days. But that was William Bolenn. Caviar taste on a burnt-toast budget. But I've said too much about that. Flynn, you've got a way of encouraging a fella to talk more than he should. You know that?

"Anyway, after Mr. Bolenn died, I believe it mostly sat empty. Some thought maybe the boy wandered off to find it. Or maybe his mama came and took him away. The authorities conducted an investigation. In the end, they couldn't find any wrongdoing on Ida Mae's part. That was years ago, and hardly anybody remembers the cabin, or if it's even still standing."

He dropped his spoon and scraped his bowl across the table with his fingertips. "There were lots of rumors swirling around," he said. "It soured her on the whole idea of fostering kids for a while." He clasped his fingers and leaned toward me. "And then somebody brought her a little boy. And she said he was the most beautiful child she'd ever seen."

"Pretty Boy."

"That's what the ladies at the orphanage called him. They found him, barely old enough to sit on their front steps one day. He was four or five, but appeared much younger, due to neglect and malnutrition. He'd been beaten by his mama or daddy, who knows, to the point of blindness. The ladies at the orphanage took him in and eventually brought him to Ida Mae."

"And then the others came."

"Then the others came."

"How do you know so much about Ida Mae and her brother, anyway?" I said.

"My daddy told me some of it when he worked for Mr. Bolenn. And Brother Muler likes to talk." He shrugged. "It's a small town. People are prone to gossip."

I leaned back and attempted to sort it out in my head. But there was one thing I still couldn't get a handle on. "So why is Ida Mae still mad at Brother Muler if he was just trying to help?"

Brother Kaine rattled his spoon against his bowl. "Brother Muler's got a good heart," he said, "but sometimes his passion for the church gets in the way. And sometimes it's harder to accept help than it is to give it. Especially from family."

We squinted at the traffic rolling by. We studied our ice cream melting. We watched clouds float overhead.

"And sometimes," Brother Kaine stared at his fingers, long and freckled against the white table, "we can't help but destroy the things we hold most dear."

speaking of monsters

We were back to shucking corn beneath the oak tree near the cellar door. The silky white threads stuck to my fingers and reminded me of the girl on the front page of the newspaper. And of Sunny.

"You know Brother Kaine?" I asked Pretty Boy.

"He comes around." He didn't glance up. "He brings us tootsie pops. Delilah, especially, likes that." He sat in a metal chair behind me. I folded my legs, Indian-style, on the ground. Jiminy Cricket sprawled opposite me with his back against the tree, picking his nose as much as he picked silk out of corn.

Delilah sat in the grass, not far from the cellar door stringing Fruit Loops from a bowl in her lap onto a piece of yarn. Her face was hidden, with only her halo of fuzzy blonde hair visible.

"Besides that, you like him?" I said. "He appears to be a regular sort of guy, doesn't he?"

"What d'you mean?"

"Talks to you regular-like," I said, "not preachy, not about crazy church business."

"What's so crazy about church?" Pretty Boy said.

"You know, like Brother Muler." I picked at the corn. "Always talking about going to church and if you don't, you're going to hell."

"Don't you believe in hell?" Jiminy Cricket said.

I scowled at him for butting in. "I think there's plenty of hell right here on earth without having to go searching for it," I replied. I'd heard some soldier say that about 'Nam. 'We don't need to go underground to find hell,' he'd said.

I turned to Pretty Boy. "You heard about them girls being murdered?"

"No." He glanced up. "Sometimes Ida Mae reads me bits from the Sunday paper she gets delivered. But she didn't read me that."

"I heard about it," Jiminy Cricket said. "Last week we were in town, and I overheard the cashier at the A&P telling Ida Mae."

"What'd Ida Mae say?"

"She said the cashier ought to learn to keep her mouth shut."

"That it?"

"Yeah." Jiminy Cricket chucked the corn cob onto the newspaper folded next to him.

"You missed some," Pretty Boy said.

"How do you know?" Jiminy leaned over and peered at it.

"'Cause you always do. I always get the ones you've shucked and have to spend hours picking threads out of my teeth." He laughed and tapped me on the shoulder with a cob. I took it from him. It was picked clean.

Jiminy scowled and scraped at the cob with his dirty fingernails. I rolled mine between my palms, clearing off more silk that way.

"Anyway," Jiminy Cricket said, showing us his newly-cleaned corn, "I read a story about it in the newspaper. Had to dig it out of the trash. It said there'd been four girls murdered so far. Called him the Beauty Killer."

"It said three." I rubbed at the hair prickling the back of my neck. Delilah continued stringing her necklace. I couldn't tell if she understood anything we were saying, but lowered my voice anyway. "Who'd go around killing little girls?"

"Somebody crazy," Pretty Boy said.

"A monster." Jiminy Cricket tossed the corn at my feet. I ignored it and stared at the cellar door.

"You got a sister, don't you?" Pretty Boy asked me.

"Yeah." I stripped threads.

"Isn't she entering those contests?"

"Yeah." I concentrated on my corn.

"I had a sister," Jiminy Cricket said.

Pretty Boy and I paused to stare at him. He crossed his arms and buried his hands in his armpits. We waited expectantly.

"She died in the crash with Mom and Pops."

"I didn't know that," Pretty Boy said.

"A car crash wiped out your entire family?" I said. "Holy cow."

"Everybody but me."

"How'd you get out alive?"

Pretty Boy squeezed my shoulder to stop me. "Jimmy, you don't have to," he said.

Jiminy shrugged and stared toward the woods. "We were on our way to Sarah's ballet recital. A car hit us head on. In our lane. We landed upside down." He raised an ear of corn to pluck at the husk. "Sarah was in the backseat with me, blood in her hair. Mom leaned against the window. She wasn't moving. Pops was pinned beneath the steering wheel. Pops said, 'Jimmy, I smell gasoline. You okay? You've got to go for help.'

'What about Mom and Sis?'

'They'll be okay. You've got to go. Now.'

So, I wiggled out a broken window."

I couldn't help but eye his belly.

"I was skinnier then." He sniffed. "As soon as I wiggled clear, he told me to run for help, so I took off running and then..."

I leaned forward, shrugging off Pretty Boy's grip. "What?"

"Flynn." Pretty Boy fumbled for me.

"What?" I turned on him. He frowned and shook his head.

The birds had gone quiet overhead, but Delilah hummed to herself. *Come, come, come to the church in the wild-wood. Oh, come to the church in the dell...*

"Kaplooey!" Jiminy Cricket hurled the corn cob against the cellar door. "The car exploded." The corn banged its way to the ground and rested in the dirt. He hunkered over his knees and dug the heels of his hands into his eye sockets.

"Holy moly," I breathed. The air around me burned with the image of the exploding car.

Jiminy swiped at his eyes.

I imagined Sunny or Willie trapped in a burning car with me on the outside. "What'd you do?" I said.

"Flynn." Pretty Boy made a grab for me, but I lunged out of reach.

Jiminy sniffled. "I," his shoulders quivered, "I don't remember. The explosion threw me to the ground, and I remember tasting dirt and blood, but I don't remember much else after that. I awoke in a hospital, and everybody was gone."

"Ho-ly moly."

Jiminy Cricket wiped his nose on his sleeve and lifted another ear of corn. I stared at the silky strands stuck to my fingers. Long, blonde strands. I imagined them bursting into flames. How long would it take for a flame to lick the length of it?

I should've tossed the strands into the paper sack with the other trash. But I didn't. I let them flutter to the ground to float free.

"How old was she?" I pulled another strand off the corn and stared at it.

"Huh?" Jiminy Cricket sniffled.

"Your sister," I said. "How old?" I rolled the silk between my fingers.

He sniffed. "Six." He stared at the corn in his lap. "She was wearing her pink tutu when she..." He stood and lurched past us toward the barn. Pretty Boy frowned at me, or at least in my direction.

"I told you," I said. "Hell on earth."

He sighed and shook his head. Laying his corn aside, he stood, and ignoring his cane leaning against the chair, stretched out a hand and followed Jiminy to the barn.

In the fading sunlight, Delilah raised her string of brightly-colored loops. They slid off the string and into her lap. She had forgotten to knot the end. She stared at the scattered cereal for a long time before taking the string and starting over.

As I watched her, I wondered if you were sometimes better off not knowing too much. I bent over my work and finished stripping corn.

country folk come to town

We'd been at the farm a week when Ida Mae hauled us into town in the back of her rusty pickup truck. I didn't want to go anywhere with her raggedy bunch. So I begged to stay at the farm by myself. I'd even take on the monster in the cellar not to be seen with those idiots.

Ida Mae said no. She couldn't leave one behind. And she needed my help with the others. I didn't imagine I'd be of much help, seeing as how I didn't plan on being no stinking babysitter.

Delilah rode in the cab with Ida Mae. As soon as we left the driveway, she hung out the window waving like crazy to everybody we passed. I rolled my eyes. Good grief. What a goober. But I didn't mind riding in the back so much. The wind ruffled my hair and cooled the sweat on my sunburned face.

As we drove through town, people stared, some with their mouths open. The fact that Ida Mae ran a red light and cut off a woman in a blue sedan didn't help.

A plump woman overfilling a navy polka dot dress and hanging onto a young girl stopped to stare.

"Ain't you never seen a truckload of young'uns?" I shouted.

She grabbed the back of her pillbox hat and the girl's hand

as if we were some sort of crazies escaped from the funny farm and dragged her little girl into a store.

From the truck cab, Ida Mae eyed me in the rearview mirror. Her mouth twisted nearly into a grin, but then worked itself straight before she turned to glance out the window.

Our first stop was the lumber yard, where Ida Mae spent a good long while talking to some man about two-by-fours to patch a hole in the barn loft. They yakked on and on about plywood and other kinds of wood while the rest of us climbed over stacks of lumber and kicked our way through piles of sawdust.

A small fort was off to one side as a display, I suppose. We played pirates for a few minutes until Delilah commenced to muttering. We said girls couldn't be pirates, but we'd let her be our captive slave. She covered her ears and chanted 'lalala,' getting louder by the minute. Jiminy Cricket ran to get Ida Mae.

By the time she reached us, Delilah was going full force. Ida Mae stuffed her, kicking and hollering, into the truck cab, which made her howling mad. We climbed into the back as people shook their heads and grumbled. At least one man muttered "Crazy young'uns."

Hey, I wanted to yell back. *I ain't crazy, or weird, or nothing. I'm as normal as anybody. My only sin's having a mama who don't care nothing for me and a daddy who's gone missing in Vietnam.* Instead, I climbed into the truck bed and pressed my face into my forearm.

Delilah continued her howling until Ida Mae stopped at the Dairy Queen and got us all ice cream cones. The Dairy Queen out on Highway 52 wasn't as nice as the ice cream parlor downtown. And I only got a single cone, a rippled mound of chocolate swirled to a curly-cue on top.

We ate in the back of the truck. And it almost made up for

Delilah's hollering and the dirty looks we'd gotten back at the lumber yard. By the time Delilah finished her ice cream, and hung her head out the window, I could tell she wore most of it on her chin and the front of her dress.

As we sat there, a couple of fellas rode up on shiny new black racers with a girl following close behind. Baseball gloves dangled from the boys' handlebars. The girl's bike sported a white wicker basket with plastic daisies and pink and gold streamers fluttering in the breeze.

She smiled when she caught me staring. Her hair was blonde, like Sunny's, but darker, with some silver glints lit by the sun. I swiped my sticky chin and hunched over to study my ice cream. I concentrated on making sure it'd been licked good and even all the way around.

They parked their bikes and stood at the window to order. The screen door over the counter slid open with a whoosh. "What'ch ya'll want?" The lady behind the counter waved at a fly buzzing around her gray head. She appeared to be missing more than one tooth.

They ordered, and she slammed the window shut. As they waited, one of the boys tipped his baseball cap back on his head and called to us, "How you all doing?"

Willie and Pretty Boy stopped talking and glanced up. "Is he talking to us?" Pretty Boy said.

"I said, how you all doing?" The boy said louder, his grin fading. "You retarded or something? Can't you talk?"

"Maybe they ain't retarded," the other boy nudged his buddy in the ribs. "Maybe they're just stuck up."

"Be nice," the girl said.

"There ain't nothing wrong with us," I said, the ice cream turning sour in my belly.

The counter window slid open, and two banana splits in plastic yellow boats were shoved toward the boys. The girl took the chocolate Dilly Bar handed to her. The window slid shut.

"Well, I say," the first boy shoved a mouthful of ice cream into his mouth, "since you ain't too friendly, there must be something wrong with you. Hey, I know you." He pointed his spoon at Delbert and strolled toward us. "You were in school last year, but had to drop out 'cause you can't talk."

A man and woman stepped out of the diner, staring at us as the boy pointed. They hurried to their car.

"Maybe you ain't a retard after all," the boy said to me. "Maybe you just hang out with one."

"Bevell, hush," the girl nudged him from behind. He whirled on her and then busted out laughing at the chunk of chocolate clinging to her lower lip.

"You better watch out," Bevell said to her, "or that dang Beauty Killer will come for you." She frowned as her pink tongue flicked the chocolate away.

"Delbert isn't retarded," Pretty Boy said, the only one of us who wasn't sticky with ice cream. He dabbed at his mouth with his paper napkin, his blank stare directed somewhere behind the kids' heads.

Holding his boat of ice cream, Bevell glanced behind him and grinned at us. "So, you got one who can't talk," he nodded at Delbert, "and one who can't see. It appears you got a regular freak show going here. What's wrong with you?" He nodded his chin at Willie. "You dain bramaged, too?"

"No, I ain't," Willie said, wearing a vanilla mustache. The two boys howled. The girl moved to stand by her bike with her back to us, vanilla ice cream dripping down her wrist.

"You got any idea why creepy Ida Mae Bolenn's collecting so many idiots?" Bevell asked.

Ida Mae cranked the truck and it sputtered to life. It roared backward, forcing me to grab the side of the bed to keep from being dumped off my perch. We barely missed Bevell as he stumbled backward and stopped laughing.

He watched us shoot forward in an arc around the gravel parking lot, and then hauled his banana split at us. A chunk of banana landed at my feet as vanilla ice cream and red sauce splattered me and Pretty Boy. Pretty Boy thumbed the glob of red off his cheek and licked it.

"Mmmmmm," he said, "strawberry."

As the three of them watched us rumble away, I dropped my half-eaten cone over the side of the truck, the pleasure of it ruined. It splattered on the pavement, before a passing truck squashed it into the ground. "I hate strawberry," I said. I hunkered in the bed of the truck and stared miserably at the trees blurring by as we headed out of town, thinking about how much I hated my life.

where there's smoke

The sky the next morning was yellow, with the air so sticky and still it made me jumpy. Bees stopped buzzing. The birds had gone quiet. It was as if we were all holding our breath, waiting.

Ida Mae puttered around outside, pulling weeds in the vegetable garden, clipping vines along the edge of the woods. But even she didn't stray far from the house.

It was Willie's idea to hide in the barn.

"Are you crazy?" I'd last seen the creature there. I eyed the wooden rungs leading to the hayloft. The ladder was rotten and gnawed by mice and who knows what else. "We'll kill ourselves." I tested one slat with my toe. "We'll bust right through the floor." I stared at the hay poking over the edge and scratched the back of my head, wondering if the monster was up there hiding, waiting for us.

"I'll go first." Willie pushed past me to grab hold of a rung and swing himself up. But I couldn't stand him being braver than me.

"I'll go first," I said and pulled at the back pocket of his jeans. But he kicked at me with his high tops, and I backed away, thumbs hooked through my belt loops.

"Fine," I said. "Be the first one to fall through the floor and

126

land in the emergency room. I bet Ida Mae won't even take you. And anyway, it'll be a lot easier to feed you to the monster with only one good leg." I kicked at the straw floating to my feet as Willie's head disappeared into the loft.

He shuffled across the floor, kicking more straw through the cracks in the floor boards. "Man, you got to see this." His voice was muffled, but I could tell by the creaking boards he was somewhere over Loulou's stall.

I grabbed a rung and hauled myself up, rung by rung. I snagged my jeans on a rusty nail as I scrambled over the edge. The floor was covered in straw, an inch thick in some places. There were a few bales of hay clumped against the back wall and a few by the window overlooking the back pasture and woods. Willie was on his knees beside a wicked contraption of rusted metal bars and jagged teeth.

"What's that?" I walked my hands along the slanted beams overhead, testing the boards with each step, and sidled next to him. The metal cage was as long as my arm. I took it from Willie and it was so heavy, I nearly dropped it. I lowered it to the ground and knelt beside my brother.

"Is this where you found it?"

"Yeah."

"Right here?" I patted the boards covered with a smattering of straw. I brushed the straw aside.

"That's what I said. So what?"

"There's blood on the floor." I showed him the splatter, bigger than my hand. I brushed more straw away and found another bloody smear.

"Maybe it's paint." Willie scrambled to his feet.

"Maybe it's blood, like I said it was."

"Well, it appears to be some kind of trap." He nudged

the awful thing with his toe. "It's probably animal blood. Maybe Ida Mae caught a fox or a squirrel." He shuddered. "Or a rabbit."

"That's a lot of blood for a dang rabbit." I fingered the dried stain and then sniffed my fingers like the detectives did on *Hawaii Five-O.* I only smelled dirt. I wiped my hand on my jeans.

I stood with Willie, staring at the trap, and tried to imagine some good reason Ida Mae would be trapping rabbits. Maybe to keep them out of the garden? But why hide the trap in the loft where nobody was allowed anyway?

"Hey, look at this." Willie stood at the back window. Across the pasture and through the woods, a curl of smoke rose above the trees.

I stood behind him and watched the smoke stretch lazy fingers upward through the yellow sky. It was warm already, and it wasn't even noon. Who would light a fire on such a hot day?

"Maybe it's a forest fire," Willie said.

"There'd be more smoke."

"Maybe somebody's burning leaves or something."

"It hasn't rained since we've been here," I said. "It'd be too dangerous." I headed back to the ladder. "And anyway, leaves fall in the fall."

"Where are you going?" Willie didn't move from the window as I backed down the rickety rungs.

"I'm going to find out what it is." My feet hit the ground with a thud.

"Are you crazy?" Willie's head appeared above the ladder. "You've got no idea how to get there."

"I'm about to find out."

One of the hogs, Janine or Ed, grunted as I passed them

on my way out of the barn. I gave their stall a swift kick, and they grunted and snuffled away. No time for porkers today. I trotted toward the pasture.

Willie caught me halfway to the woods. "You can't run off through the woods without telling anybody." He grabbed my arm. "How're you gonna keep from getting lost?"

I slowed to a walk as the weeds slapped my knees. "If I ask Ida Mae, she'll say no."

"You don't even know where you're going."

"I'll keep walking in that direction until I get there. It's a straight shot. I'll check it out and then come back."

"It'll be lunch soon. You're gonna starve."

I stopped to stare at him. "What do you care? If you don't want to come, don't come. Go hang out with your freak friends and stop worrying about me." I stalked away, and Willie stayed put, frowning into the sun. I growled toward the woods. "You get more like them every day, you know that?"

I wasn't sure if he heard me, but when I reached the edge of the trees, I turned to find him heading back to the house, fists stuffed in his pockets, shoulders hunched. I stared into the woods. They appeared cool and quiet and full of shadows.

When Willie reached the house, he stood beside the cellar door, talking to Pretty Boy leaning on his stick. They glanced my way. I turned my back on them. Didn't Brother Kaine say something about a hunting cabin in the woods? I skirted along the edge of the tall pines, looking for a hint of a trail, even a break in the line of trees.

When I had no luck finding a trail, and Willie had obviously disappeared into the house, I abandoned the shelter of the trees and loped after him. Surely my quest could wait until after lunch.

It was nearly suppertime before I found my grandmother alone. "Ida Mae, what's out yonder in the woods?" I stood in the doorway to the kitchen, eyeing a red apple in the basket on the counter.

"Yonder where?" She took the boiling pot of potatoes off the stove and emptied the water into the sink. A *whoosh* of steam sweated her face. She dumped the steaming potatoes into a bowl. I leaned against the door-jamb, watching her.

"You know," I said, "the woods past the barn." My back itched under my shirt so I scratched it against the edge of the door. The wood dug sharply between my shoulder blades.

"There ain't nothing in the woods. Just Haley beyond." She halved a stick of butter and dropped it into the potatoes.

"Whose land is it?"

She eyed me over her shoulder. "What'd you care?"

"Just wondering. Pretty Boy says it's yours."

She poured fresh milk into the bowl. Then she took a potato masher, rusted around the edges, and smashed the potatoes. She didn't answer.

"Smoke was coming out of the woods earlier." I eased my back along the sharp edge of wood. "I saw it from the loft."

"You don't need to be rooting around in the barn loft." She banged the masher against the bowl.

"Maybe the woods are on fire."

"The woods ain't on fire."

"I saw the smoke. So did Willie."

She stopped working the bowl, but didn't turn. "When?"

"Right before lunch."

She turned to me, and I stopped scratching my back. "Forget it," she said, and turned back to the potatoes. "Probably the lumber mill burning trash."

"It wasn't in that direction. We should call the sheriff."

She dumped the other half of the butter into the bowl. She blinked at the bowl for a few seconds. Then sighed and fished the unmelted butter out with the spoon and dropped the mess onto the counter.

"If it was a forest fire, we'd smell the smoke," she said. "You smell any smoke?"

"No."

"Me neither."

"But the sheriff—"

"I don't need that man nosing around my property. I already got enough government people poking into my business." She poured more milk into the potatoes and then snorted. I guess she'd forgotten she'd already added that, too.

She spooned milk out of the bowl and dumped it in an empty cup. The spoon clattered onto the counter. Bracing her arms on both sides of the sink, her head sunk into her shoulders. "Why don't you run along and tell everybody to wash up for supper?"

"You okay?"

She stayed that way for a minute, then said, "I'm fine." She straightened and banged the bowl onto the counter, splattering mashed potatoes over the sides. Snatching the spoon, she whipped them furiously.

"But the sheriff... say, what's that smell?"

Ida Mae yelped and stalked to the oven. She snatched the door open, and smoke poured out. With a grunt, she grabbed a dishtowel, then the pan of scorched biscuits and flung it on top of the stove. "Do what you're told," she growled over her shoulder and stomped back to the sink. Grasping the porcelain edges, she held on like she might crack it in two.

"Supper'll be ready in fifteen minutes," she said without turning. "Tell the others." She sucked in a deep breath. "Please."

I stomped outside to stare at the barn and beyond. The smoke from the woods had disappeared into the sky, which was already fading to gray. I clenched my fists in the pockets of my jeans. Tomorrow, I'd find out exactly what Ida Mae was intent on hiding.

A creaking noise jerked my head around. The cellar door eased open.

"Hey!" I started toward it, but it slammed shut. As I reached it, the lock slid into place.

Jiminy Cricket banged out the back door. "Ida Mae said you're supposed to be calling everybody to supper." He surveyed the empty yard. "Well?"

I kicked at the cellar door. Something growled, and I jumped back. I skirted the mound of dirt toward him. "You're so smart," I said, "you call 'em."

He narrowed his pig eyes in the gloom. "Do what you're told," he said, "or Ida Mae'll tan your hide."

"Ida Mae'll tan your hide," I mimicked. "I'd like to see her try."

Jiminy Cricket slammed back inside the house. Good riddance. I spit into the grass and caught a movement out of the corner of my eye.

I turned to find Ida Mae staring at me from the kitchen window.

patrolling for monsters

Soon as Ida Mae headed to the barn the next morning to slop the hogs, I raided the kitchen. I swiped two red apples off the counter, a can of Vienna sausages out of the pantry, and a couple of fried chicken legs wrapped in paper napkins left over from dinner. I stuffed the food in my army knapsack.

Willie offered a chocolate moon pie for the trip. Where it came from, I didn't ask.

By the clock on the kitchen stove it was five after nine when we eased out the back door. Willie got word from Pretty Boy the night before there was a rumor of a path cutting clear through the woods, all the way to Haley. The story said the trail led to William Bolenn's old hunting cabin, the same one Brother Kaine mentioned.

No one on the farm had seen it. And Ida Mae refused to confirm it. But if it was true, it might explain the smoke in the middle of the woods. As usual, I glanced at the cellar door, which was closed and quiet.

Willie and I headed to the barn and skirted along the edge of the woods toward the house in search of the trail. By the time we worked our way to the cornfield, we were about to run out of woods. "It's got to be here somewhere," I said.

Willie found a stick, a prong really, shaped like deer antlers. "What's got to be here?" he said.

"The trail, dummy. You've forgotten what we're doing already? What's that?"

Willie fingered the stick's two points. "I suppose I'll give it to Pretty Boy."

"Can't you forget those losers for one minute and help me find this trail?"

"They're not losers." Willie tapped the stick against his thigh. "Pretty Boy and Delbert are super creative."

I rolled my eyes and snatched the stick from him. "Gimme that."

"Hey!"

"I left mine at the house." I actually had destroyed it trying to secretly carve something into it like Pretty Boy did. I poked the stick in the brush among the trees, pushing aside thorny, tangled vines and weeds. "It's got to be here." I turned to find Willie disappearing into the cornstalks. I growled and stalked away from him to the edge of the woods, peering into the shadowy gloom.

A crash behind me whirled me around. Willie staggered out of the corn, his hair wild with flecks of chaff. "Ida Mae's coming," he said. "Up the hill banging her slop bucket. She might've seen me."

"What'd you go back for?" I grabbed the front of his shirt and yanked him toward the woods. "You're bound to get us caught."

"I was searching for another stick."

"You think those woods don't have plenty of sticks? Idiot."

"Am not. And I'm sick of you calling everybody names. Daddy would kick your butt."

"Daddy ain't here."

"Flynn!" Ida Mae called.

"Shhhhhh." I jerked Willie to a crouch. "Trail or no trail, we're going in." I dragged him behind me as we waddled into the woods.

"Flynn! Willie!"

I shoved my brother's head behind a pile of underbrush and crouched beside him. "Don't move," I hissed.

Ida Mae's head appeared through the corn. "Boys?"

My fingers dug into Willie's arm, daring him to breathe. I peered through a gap in the underbrush as Ida Mae stared into the woods. I held my breath as a mosquito buzzed my ear. Something pinched my neck, but I didn't dare move. That stupid mosquito could've drained me dry, and I wouldn't have budged. Ida Mae's gray bun disappeared back through the corn.

Willie moved to stand, but I held him down. "Wait."

"For what?"

"They always come back."

But she didn't come back, and we finally stood and stretched our knees. I shook my foot to get the feeling back. "We better get going before one of those morons finds us," I said.

Willie moved a few steps into the woods and stopped. "What's that?"

I followed his pointing finger to a red scrap of fabric tied to a tree.

I shrugged. "Probably the marking of the property line or something."

"The trees are thinner through there." Willie eased toward the red cloth.

"Hey, you're going to get lost." With my stick, I pushed slithering vines out of the way to follow.

"I think it's the trail." Willie stared at the marked tree.

"Don't be silly. If I couldn't find it, you sure couldn't find it."

I stared after him as he shuffled through pine straw to the next tree and the next. It was the path, and nearly wide enough for two people to walk side by side.

"Let me lead." I pushed past him.

"I found it."

"I'm the oldest."

"That doesn't work for everything."

"Yes, it does."

"How do you know this'll lead us to the cabin?"

"I don't." I tapped the stick along the path, "but it leads somewhere. Which is better than here."

"Ida Mae's going to get mad if we just run off." Willie stopped to grab another stick, as big around as his wrist. He scraped the bark with his thumbnail, and it crumbled to pieces. He chunked it at a tree.

"She won't even miss us," I said.

"I bet she will. I bet she calls the sheriff."

"And tell him what? She let her two grandsons run away?" I snorted. "Not likely. Especially after that other kid—"

"What other kid?"

"Nothing. Never mind." Now was not the time for that particular revelation. "You scared?"

"'Course not. I just don't want to get into trouble."

"Trouble? What's she going to do? Call Mama?"

"She could send us to jail."

"First of all, they don't send kids to jail for exploring. Or even running away. Secondly, she's not going to call the sheriff. You saw how she ran off her own brother. She sure doesn't want the sheriff nosing around. And thirdly, that government lady wouldn't take too kindly to her letting two more kids run off."

"I don't want her to get in trouble with the government," Willie said.

"She won't get in trouble if nobody tells."

"I want to show Pretty Boy my stick. Give it back."

"No way. He can't see it, anyway."

"He can feel it."

"Whatever. You coming or not?"

"We don't have a flashlight."

"Flashlight? It's daylight, for crying out loud."

"Well..."

"Forget it." I stomped further into the woods and called over my shoulder, "You're going to miss out on the best adventure you ever had. But you go back and play sticks with your spastic little friends."

"They're not spastic." He caught up with me, huffing.

"You don't even know what the word means," I said without slowing down.

"It means something like retarded. And they aren't that, either. It isn't right, you calling them bad names."

"Who are you, the dang pope? What'd you care what I call them?"

"They're my friends." He jogged to keep up.

"You keep hanging out with those losers and people will start calling you names."

"They wouldn't."

"Sure, they would. You hang out with retards, people will talk."

"Stop calling them that."

"Oh, drop it will you?" I couldn't seem to shake him of his

weird fixation on those kids. This adventure would be good for him. A little time away from those nutcases and he'd see them the way I did.

We pushed our way through the woods. It grew darker as the sun peeked in and out of the clouds above the tall, rigid pines, which smelled like freshly-scrubbed floors.

The ground was dry and hard as we crunched through leaves and pine needles. Now and then, we stumbled over a rotten log crumbling with white, squirming maggots, slithering centipedes, and once, a feisty scorpion, his tail cocked with poison.

I had no idea how long we traipsed through the woods, rolling logs and poking into the underbrush. But as the day warmed, my belly grumbled.

"Maybe we ought to stop for a snack," I said. We found a large flat rock, big enough to sit on, close to the trail.

Willie dropped onto it with a heavy sigh. His hair was wet with sweat around his ears, and he grabbed for my knapsack.

I swung it out of reach. "I'm in charge of the food."

"Hurry up, then." He snatched at the chicken leg I gave him. We popped the can of Vienna sausages and ate those, too. We saved the apples for later.

Back on the trail, it seemed another hour passed before we reached a clearing in the woods. And smack dab in the middle of the clearing squatted a small log cabin.

It was covered with ivy. Big, leafy vines twisted and snaked along the walls, over the roof, in and around the windows and doors, as if the woods were determined to swallow it whole. The only thing left uncovered was a small square window over the front door.

The house appeared as lonely as the witch's cottage in

Hansel and Gretel. No road led in and none led out. And no smoke rose from the chimney.

We skirted the edge of the clearing, staying hidden by the trees, and watched the house. Something wasn't right.

"Okay," Willie said after a while, "we've seen the cabin, let's go." He headed back the way we came. I yanked him back to a crouch beside me in the bushes.

"Shhh." I held a finger to my lips. "Wait and see."

"See what?" he hissed back. "I've seen the cabin, and I'm not going in. I'm going to hightail it back to Ida Mae's because I'm so thirsty I could drain the Saugahatchee River. And anyway, what yahoo goes exploring and doesn't bring water?"

"I didn't come all this way to not lay eyes on the inside of that cabin," I hissed back at him. "We're going in."

"Not me." Willie's loud whisper rustled a chipmunk a few feet away. It scampered through the leaves, chattering furiously. "If somebody's been here starting fires on property that isn't theirs, they might not take too kindly to being discovered."

"When we get back to Ida Mae's, those losers are going to want to know what we found on our big exploration. You're going to tell them you were too scared to even go inside the cabin?" I surveyed the clearing. "Not me. I'm going in."

I circled to the other side of the house, seeing nary a movement from inside. I couldn't come up with a single good reason why somebody would come all the way into the middle of the woods just to burn something. Or how they'd even find the clearing.

But I was sure of one thing.

I didn't like it. Not one little bit.

cabin secrets

From our hiding place, I hollered, "Hey, you in there, come on out!" with the intention of hightailing it back through the woods should a murdering monster appear.

When there was no response, I snuck across the clearing and sidled to the front door. It was flanked by two bare windows nearly choked in vines. I waited a few seconds, rapped on the door, then flattened myself against the ivy wall. "Get ready to run," I said as Willie pressed against the wall beside me.

It was quiet except for the crickets thrumming in the tall weeds and our heavy breathing. I knocked louder. We waited. The brass knob on the door had tarnished green, and I grabbed it with the hem of my shirt. The door creaked open, and I stuck my head into the dusty gloom.

"Anybody here?" I dropped my knapsack outside the door and clutched the pronged stick. Willie's breath was thick on the back of my neck.

The room was a den of sorts, smaller than the one on the farm. A sofa sagged against one wall, its nubby fabric eaten away in patches. Twigs and pine straw nestled into the foam stuffing. The fireplace opposite it was cold and dark. I eased into the room.

A wooden chair missing a leg tilted in a corner. Next to it

stood a low, rustic table, not much more than a few wooden planks hammered together.

I fumbled for a light switch, but couldn't find one. I eased further into the room. An old oil lamp lay broken at the edge of the sofa, the oil long since bled out. A doorway led to another room.

"Appears nobody's been here in a while," Willie said.

"Maybe." I listened for movement, but heard nothing but the blood drumming in my ears. Something on the ground caught my eye.

I eased the door wider to allow more light. A layer of dust blanketed the raw plank floor, except for a path where it appeared as if someone scraped the table over the floor. The path ran from the den to the front door.

"Looks like something's been dragged in," I said.

"Or dragged out." Willie peered over my shoulder. I looked at him. He blinked at me.

Vines snuck in through the windows and up the walls, as creepy as long green fingers reclaiming a lost toy.

I shivered.

"Anybody here?" My voice boomed too loud in the silence. Something rustled in the next room.

"I told you we should've brought a flashlight," Willie said. He hovered near the front door.

I crossed the room fumbling in my pocket for my knife. But dang, apparently, I'd left it in my knapsack. I raised my stick and stuck my head through the next doorway. The room was smaller than the first and just as bare. Tattered gray fabric hung from the windows.

On the floor, shoved against the far wall, lay a bald mattress. I stalked over to study it. It was soiled with dark stains that appeared sinister, especially in the gloom. And it reeked of something sweet and rotten.

"We should go," Willie called from the front door. "If somebody's staying here they might come back."

I backed away from the mattress and pushed aside a strip of fabric to peer out the window. "The cabin looks too dirty for anybody to be staying here." I stared at a circle of burned grass in a clearing out back and the pile of ashes in the center of it. I thought I saw a wisp of smoke. "But somebody's definitely been here."

"Then we better go."

I moved to the next doorway that led to a tiny bathroom with a stained porcelain sink, a rickety toilet, and a bathtub, one of those free-standing jobs with claw feet. Rust stains bled into the drains, and the toilet seat barely hung by a bolt.

I edged closer to the tub and thumbed a small dark stain. Probably rust, too. I scraped at it with my thumbnail. It seemed etched into the porcelain. I turned the faucet, and it groaned, then sputtered, then there was nothing, and then a splash of rusted water spewed in fits and spurts.

"Turn it off," Willie said from the bathroom door. He backed away, staring at the faucet like it was a living thing.

"It's just water stuck in the pipes." I wiped my wet hand on my jeans. "Wonder why the water's still turned on. If nobody's been here in years."

"Maybe when Grandaddy died, they just forgot to turn it off," Willie said.

"That's dumb." I scowled at him.

"Well, let's wonder about it on our way back to Ida Mae's." He backed all the way into the bedroom. "This place gives me the creeps. It feels bad."

"Brother Kaine said it was used as a hunting cabin." I followed him into the bedroom. "Animals were probably killed here, or at least stored." I thought of the thing in Ida Mae's cellar. I tried to shrug it off as we moved through the bedroom and out the front door. "I want to check out something before we go."

I stalked around to the back of the cabin and studied the pile of ashes. I knelt and fingered the soft, gray fluff.

The ashes were cool, but smelled freshly burned. I poked my stick among the cinders. I uncovered a charred bit of denim cloth and a few pieces of charred paper. I raised a smidge of parchment the size of a matchbook and studied it. It was fancier than the bits of paper Delbert drew on, and somehow familiar.

"What'd you think they were doing?" Willie hovered over me. I let the charred piece flutter to the ground and stood.

"Beats me. Why would anybody come all the way out here to burn some old clothes and fancy writing paper?"

"What's this?" Willie plucked something from the edge of the burn and held it for me to see.

"Maybe a hunk of hair?" I took it from him. It was light in color and singed along the edges.

"Animal hair?" Willie peered over my arm. "They're cooking animals out here?"

I glanced around. "There aren't any signs of bones or utensils or anything. And it appears more like..." I bit my lip.

"What?"

"Never mind."

"What?" Willie leaned into me, and I pushed him away.

"Forget it." I headed to the front of the house, rubbing the tuft of hair between my fingers.

"Tell me what." Willie grabbed my arm and jerked me backward, making me drop it, and it floated away on a puff of breeze.

"Nothing. If I tell you, you'll get all creeped out."

"I won't."

"Sure you will, you big baby. You won't even talk about the monster in the cellar."

"That's because there isn't one."

"Then how do you explain the growling? And banging and snarling?"

"Pretty Boy would've told me if there was."

"He's blind. What does he know?"

"He can still hear."

"Apparently, he can't. You think I'm imagining it?"

"Well, I'm not the one whimpering like a baby in the middle of the night, Mr. Hot Shot Navy SEAL."

"Oh yeah? I meant to beat the tar out of you for that. Thanks for reminding me." We arrived at the front of the cabin as a flash of something in the window over the door caught my eye. "If I ever hear of you telling that lie to anybody else..."

"It's not a lie."

"I'm going to make you wish you'd never been—"

"What?" Willie banged into the back of me. "What are you staring at?"

"The window, dummy. Shut up."

"What's so great about the window? It's too high to reach."

"So, it seems."

"Let's go, I'm thirsty."

But I headed for the front door. Inside, I crept through the house, searching.

"What are you doing?" Willie said.

"Looking for the way up."

"The way up where?"

"To the window. There has to be an attic. Brother Kaine said so. If there's a window, there's a way to it."

I found it on my third time through. It was in the corner of the bedroom wall closest to the den. The ceiling was made of strips of wood, and I noticed a loose board. I jumped as high as I could and jabbed it with my stick. It banged into place. I jumped higher and poked it again and slid it over so that I stared into a dark, gaping hole.

Willie and I scraped the table from the other room and positioned it beneath the hole. The table wobbled as I climbed onto it, and I prayed it wouldn't collapse. But I still wasn't tall enough to see inside. We searched the cabin again and found an old oaken barrel out back, near a small stack of rotting firewood.

The barrel smelled of something dead. We carried it inside and struggled to set it atop the table. I climbed onto the table, then the barrel. It wobbled, but held. I grabbed the edges of the wood with my fingertips.

"You've got to hold it steady," I said.

Willie climbed onto the table, and it lurched. He wrapped his arms around the barrel. "It stinks," he said and buried his nose in his sleeve.

I stood on tiptoe and struggled to pull myself up by my fingertips. "Hold still," I growled as the barrel wobbled beneath me.

"You're too heavy."

"Keep it from moving."

Willie hugged the barrel tight. I jumped to give myself a boost and nearly busted my head on the wall. Willie staggered out from under me, and the barrel nearly overturned.

"Stop moving."

"You're too heavy." Willie panted, sweat trickling down his forehead. "And what do we care what's up there, anyway? Probably a bunch of rats. They'll probably bite your nose off and give you rabies."

"Oh brother." I rolled my eyes. But once the thought was planted, I couldn't shake the image of a horde of beady red eyes staring at me as I pulled myself up through the hole.

I was almost eye level with the attic floor when Willie whispered, "I hear something."

I lowered myself, my heels landing on the barrel. "What?"

"A rustling outside the window."

"Probably an animal. A chipmunk. Or a squirrel."

"I thought I saw a head. A hairy head."

"Animals have heads."

"No. A human head. But hairy."

"One of the kids followed us."

But I was already climbing off the barrel. I landed with a thud on the floor and grabbed the stick where I'd dropped it. I sidled to the window to peer out.

"It wasn't any of the kids," Willie said, his bottom lip quivering.

"Probably a deer or a—"

A crash rattled the windowpane and before I could stop him, Willie charged through the house and out the front door.

"Wait!" I yelled after him. "What if it's the monster?"

By the time I got to the front door, he was running along the path as fast as his stubby legs could carry him. I barely had time to snatch my knapsack up as I bounded out the front door after him.

For a second, something caught my eye in a sprawl of moss

near the front step, something round and shiny and black. But I had no time to dwell on it. Willie was racing pell-mell through the woods with no weapon and a monster on his heels. I ran after him and thought, *if we ever get out of this thing alive, I'm going to kill my stupid brother.*

the monster's lair

By the time we returned to the farm, everything was quiet and the yard was empty. I stood at the cellar door and massaged the pain stabbing my side. Willie tore into the house, and I didn't stop him. I studied the metal door, my lungs burning, side aching. I wasn't worried the monster would come out. It was somewhere back in the woods. I was sure of it.

The door was a dull, corrugated metal, eaten with rust. I locked my fingers around the worn skin of the handle, and that's when I noticed the bloody smear. A handprint. I clearly made out the imprint of fingers wrapping around the door's edge. I fingered the stain. It was dry.

I eased the door open. It was as dark as a cave. I flung the door wide, and it groaned against its hinges before banging the ground in a puff of dirt.

Even with the afternoon sun flooding in, the cellar wasn't any less creepy. The walls were musty and dark and smelled of moldy earth. Against the right wall were four or five shelves stacked with all sorts of jars.

I stepped closer, bracing myself to discover a wall of pickled fingers and toes and lord knows what other hacked off body parts. I descended the rickety stairs to find pickles, fig preserves, blackberry jam, apple butter. The fading labels were written in Ida Mae's small, slanted handwriting.

Past the shelves, the earth ceiling angled sharply toward the ground. And in the small, cramped space lay a pale, lumpy heap. I eased closer and nudged the lump with my toe. It was a blanket, a pale blue one, ragged around the edges. And underneath was an old stained mattress. Like the one in the cabin.

So, the creature enjoyed his comforts, too. Another lump lay beneath the blanket. I studied it for a few seconds before taking my stick, snagging the cloth, and flinging it aside.

I blinked at a stuffed rabbit, a little bigger than my hand, with one ear half chewed and missing a black button eye. I snatched it from the ground. Most of its stuffing was missing, leaving it more flat than fluff. I wondered if it belonged to one of the dead girls.

My name was called, and I dropped the toy onto the blanket. I climbed the steps and poked my head out of the ground to find Jiminy Cricket plodding down the hill toward the barn, his hands cupped around his mouth, hollering my name. What a numbskull. Didn't he notice the cellar door wide open?

I hopped out and eased the door shut while his back was turned. Shouldering my knapsack, I headed for the sprawling mimosa tree at the edge of the front porch to climb and lounge among its branches and pretend I'd been there all morning.

now we're smoking

I waited until everybody was tucked into bed. The moon was high and bright. But I couldn't help that. I had to count on the monster being safe in his lair among his victims' things. The Viet Cong, I'd heard, kept souvenirs, too.

I thought of Sunny's blue eyes, sweeter and kinder than Ida Mae's. But still, I was beginning to see my grandmother in my vision of them.

I eased my knapsack from beneath my bed. I had peeked in on Ida Mae earlier. She'd fallen asleep in front of the television again with her head thrown back, her mouth slack, the half-sewn hem of one of Delilah's tattered dresses on her lap.

The evening news flickered with black and white pictures of Vietnam. Airstrikes and soldiers burying themselves into the marsh of the jungle, covering their ears. The poor, scraggly South Vietnamese children who appeared as likely to kill you as the Viet Cong. And the small, scruffy puppy some soldier adopted.

At the time, we thought it was a sweet story in the middle of another patch of hell. We'd learn later that the soldier strapped a grenade to the pup's back and sent it into a hooch just for fun. The horror was never-ending.

I peeked into the living room again. Now it was dark. The

television was silent. I passed Ida Mae's bedroom. Her door was closed, but I heard her snoring behind it.

I carried my fistful of cherry bombs and a half-soggy pack of matches to the cellar. It was time to see this monster for myself.

A brief summer shower earlier in the day left the ground soft and mushy beneath my bare feet. It didn't take long for the mosquitoes to find me and buzz relentlessly around my ears.

I pulled the bloodied animal trap from the shed where I'd hidden it and dragged it to the mouth of the cellar. I tugged on the door handle. It groaned, but the door held. As usual, it was locked. I studied the door, then slid my fingers around the edges. Close to my foot, I found enough give in the thin metal to poke in a cherry bomb.

I slid the trap in front of the door. The moon seemed determined to hide behind a fluff of dark clouds. Better, I thought, for what I intended.

My fingers trembled as I tore off a match and struck it. It crumpled beneath my fingertips. I swore under my breath and tore off another. It bent in two.

I gritted my teeth, pressed a thumb to the match tip and scraped it along the strip. It flared to life and died. I groaned. Something moved inside the cellar. *Crap.* I scraped a match. It tore. Shaking, I struck another. Nothing but the smell of sulfur. Panic bubbled inside me.

Footsteps thudded on the cellar stairs. Growling rumbled beneath the door. Something scraped metal.

I pressed my thumb into the match against the flint and it flared bright. I fumbled for the small cherry bomb at my feet, lit it, and shoved it between the edges of metal. It hissed, and then there was dead silence, and then *pow!*

I lit another and stuffed it through the crack. And then another and another, before hightailing it back to the house.

My plan was to watch from the kitchen window, but Ida Mae's bedroom light flicked on, so I ducked into my bedroom to pretend I was asleep. I was already in bed when the unholy howling began. I flopped onto my belly as doors banged along the hallway.

The door to my room opened, and my light flipped on.

"Wha...?" I raised my head groggily and blinked at the bright light. Willie moaned beside me.

Grumbling erupted further along the hall. My light was switched off, and I buried my face in my pillow. The howling turned unworldly and seemed to stretch to the moon and back and spread to the stars and hang for a breath in the limbs of the trees outside my window. By the time the back-screen door slammed and Ida Mae made her way to the cellar, wails dripped like Spanish moss from the trees.

The others grumbled, and I wondered how Willie never even woke up. Good grief, I rolled over and stared at him nestled beside me. How does he note every moan and cry of mine, but he can't hear the gosh-awful screaming outside?

I wondered if the trap had taken off a foot, a claw, a paw. I slid out of bed and crept to the kitchen window and peered above the window ledge.

Ida Mae hunched over the creature. Her loose braid fell over one shoulder, and the hem of her gown skimmed the ground. She appeared to be freeing the thing from the trap. A flash of white, or maybe pale blue, was caught in the contraption's teeth and she yanked furiously. And just as quickly, she turned to the window, and I got a flash of eyes of blue chipped ice before I ducked and crept back to bed.

The screen door slammed and slammed again and I imagined the others were gathering around the creature. I realized for the first time, I was truly alone. As I studied Willie in his sleep, all slobbering innocence, I couldn't even count on him. My heart cracked into pieces and fell away to bury itself somewhere inside my body, down to the lowest pit of my belly, my feet, my toes. But destroyed, nonetheless.

I awoke early the next morning, the light pearly outside my window. Someone shuffled in the kitchen, then along the hall. I rolled out of bed and hesitated in the doorway.

Ida Mae was on her knees in the hallway, the flowers of her light, cotton gown so faded as to be a blur, as she scrubbed the floor. Swishing a dirty dishrag back and forth, she scooted along on all fours, erasing a muddy trail until she reached the back door.

"What're you doing?" I said.

Her head popped up and I got a small pleasure from seeing her startled for once.

"Never mind," she said. "Go back to bed."

Erasing the monster's slimy trail? I wanted to ask. But I didn't need to. It was obvious. If he had left muddy prints inside, he'd survived the trap.

And what was equally obvious, was that Willie and I had to get out of there. We couldn't help Daddy wherever he was, but we could find Mama. And save her and Sunny from the Beauty Killer or monster running amok and maybe heading their way.

investigating

"Ida Mae." I eased behind her where she stood at the kitchen sink, scraping and slicing carrots for supper. "What's in the cellar?"

"I told you. Nothing for you to worry about." She bent over the sink.

"Noises are coming from there."

"Your imagination. Now run along."

"It's not my imagination. You're keeping something in there. I deserve to know what it is."

"I ain't keeping nothing nowhere." She stopped scraping long enough to scratch her eyebrow with the thumb holding the knife. She stared at the half-peeled carrot before returning the blade to it.

"I can't keep anything out of the cellar that's determined to be in there," she said. "Now, I said it before, if it's in there, it ain't bothering you. So, stop worrying about it." The glare she gave me shriveled the rest of the questions in my throat.

With this line of questioning going nowhere, I tried another. "Uh, Ida Mae, I was wondering if you could possibly loan me ten cents for a newspaper."

"Newspaper?" she said. "What'd you want with a newspaper?"

"It's a school project."

"In the summer?"

"Yeah, crazy, huh?"

"Yeah." She commenced to peeling.

"It's a report on Alabama."

"I got books on Alabama," she said. "Under the cabinet in the den."

"It's a current events thing. Like real current."

"I get the Sunday paper here."

"I'd really like to start on it today. You know, so I'm not working on Sunday."

"You just went to town. Why didn't you get it then?"

"I didn't have any extra money."

She stayed quiet a long time. "I guess I could spare a dime. In the cookie jar." She nodded in the direction of the ceramic elephant. Lifting its head, I rummaged inside.

I waded through a stash of bills and wondered exactly how much money Ida Mae saved in the jar. She glanced at me as I pulled out a handful of change and plucked out a dime real quick. Scraping the lid back into place, I returned the jar under the shelf.

"I'll be going, then." I pocketed the dime and left the kitchen, feeling Ida Mae's stare burning through my back.

I jogged along the familiar road. By the time I reached the gas station, my palms were sweaty and my heart tripping. I headed straight to the newspaper stand, dropped in my dime, and snatched out a paper. No headlines screamed murder. That was good.

I took the newspaper and plopped onto the curb with it, spreading it onto the grease-stained pavement at my feet. Nothing important on page one except for some business about President Nixon, and the local old folks' home adding twenty more beds. I scrolled page two. In the middle, under Our Community, I read the headline, *Girl Still Missing from VBS.*

Greysville. A small town about fifteen miles north of Haley. A nine-year-old girl went missing from the Greysville Community Church after failing to return home from the church's Vacation Bible School program earlier in the day.

Didn't these mamas understand there was killer on the loose?

Loralee Roby was last seen at the church around 11:30 a.m., right before the closing ceremony. She never returned home. Sarah Roby, the girl's mother, said she walked to the church, not four blocks from their home, and was expected to return right after the program ended.

"I thought maybe she'd gone home with a friend," a tearful Mrs. Roby said. "When she didn't arrive an hour or so later, I called around. Then I called the sheriff. Her daddy got out in the car and went searching for her."

The young girl has been missing for a week, but the Winston County Sheriff's department says it's too early to speculate as to whether this case is connected to the other three missing girls who were later found dead. Loralee Roby was the winner of the Miss Greysville Elementary School Contest earlier this year.

If you have any information concerning the disappearance of Loralee Roby, please contact the Winston County Sheriff's office immediately.

I scanned the rest of the paper. The only other item of interest was an advertisement at the bottom of page six for the Miss Franklin County Fair pageant on Friday, July 14. The pageant was open to all girls, ages six to eighteen.

That was only two weeks away. Mama would've entered

Sunny, I was sure of it. And the county fair was in Weaverton, about twenty or thirty miles from Haley.

I ripped the ad from the paper, as well as the article on the missing girl, folded them, and stuffed them in my back pocket. I tossed the rest of the paper into the trash can. I had planning to do.

the girl, the sheriff, and me

With Sunny and the missing girl on my mind, I wandered past the First Church of Haley, took a left and passed the sheriff's office and city hall. I turned right onto Main Street and passed the sewing store, the dress shop, and the Dixie Theater, and stopped at Elmore's Five and Dime. I slunk to the back of the store and read the comics I couldn't afford to buy.

I read through *Richie Rich*, *Superman*, and *Batman*, before the owner shooed me away. On my way out of the store, I ran into the bicycle girl from the Dairy Queen. Literally. She banged into me, her nose stuck in a tiny change purse in the shape of a cat.

"Oh." She glanced up. But only after her thick, fat head banged into my chin.

"Watch where you're going." I rubbed the sharp pain, then studied my palm. At least I wasn't bleeding.

"Sorry." She frowned and cocked her head. "You're the boy from the Dairy Queen."

"So what?" I meant to push past her, my chin stinging something awful.

"I just meant, hey, I'm sorry Bevell was so rough on you. He's my stupid cousin from Weaverton. My mom makes me

158

hang out with him and his goofy friend when they come to visit."

"Whatever." I quickened my pace to leave her behind, but she caught up with me. We passed her bike, leaning against the brick wall.

"You alright?" She peered under my chin.

"Fine." I raised a shoulder to block her. "Don't let me slow you down."

"Oh, I was just going into the dime store for popcorn and a co-cola." She skipped alongside me. "And to read the comics."

I slowed. "They don't like you to read the comics without paying."

"Oh, I know." She laughed. "Mr. Elmore shoos me out every time. I could pay for them," she crossed her arms, "but it seems a waste of money when you can stand there and read them for free."

"Yeah."

Up close, she didn't appear as fancy as she did the first time I saw her. Her ruffled shirt was frayed along the edges, and a safety pin peeked out from the waist of her denim skirt. I glanced away.

"You're Ida Mae Bolenn's grandson, aren't you?" she said.

"You're mighty chatty, aren't you?"

She shrugged. "Just being friendly. Heard you're staying for the summer. Thought maybe you hadn't met many people yet."

I stopped walking and studied her from her dishwater blonde ponytail to her saddle oxford toes. She wasn't too bad, I guess. For a girl.

"My mama dumped me and my brother at Ida Mae's while she carts my sister around to some stupid beauty pageants."

The girl fingered the tip of her ponytail brushing her

shoulder. "Why didn't she take you along? Not to be nosy, but your grandmother's got a bit of a reputation in town for being, what's the word..."

"Scary?"

She studied the white sky for a few seconds. "Eccentric, I'd say."

"So, you don't believe the story about her killing off some kid?

"Of course not."

"You appear to be the only one in town."

"Oh, most of the townspeople aren't bad," she said. "Maybe a little jumpy about this killer running loose. You might expect that sort of thing in San Francisco or Los Angeles. But not in North Alabama." We continued strolling. She eyed me. "I've been in pageants before, too. It's kind of boring. Especially if you're doing nothing but watching. You'd probably hate it."

"At least I'd be with my family."

"Where's your dad?"

I glanced away.

"I'm prying, aren't I?" She lowered her lashes.

"What sort of pageants were you in?" I said.

"Oh," she waved, "one of those goofy little miss whatevers. It was last year."

"How'd you do?"

"Pretty good, actually."

"You win?"

She tossed her ponytail over her shoulder and plucked at a string on her cat purse. "Just a crown. And a trophy. It was silly, like I said."

"Mama doesn't think it's silly. She's expecting Sunny to win a lot of money. Maybe even a college scholarship."

"That's not until you're older," she said. "In the big pageants, high school and stuff. How old's your sister?"

"Eight."

She shook her head. "At her age, she's basically getting a crown and a trophy. And most of the trophies are plastic. By the time I got home, my name plate had fallen off. Nothing but cheap plastic. My name's Cara. What's yours?"

"Flynn."

"As long as your sister's having fun," she said, "that's what's important."

"Yeah, as long as she's having fun. Say, aren't you worried about the killer coming after you?"

"He couldn't possibly get to every pageant winner in the area," she said with a smile that pitied my stupidity. "There's like a bazillion in each county. Anyway," she flipped her ponytail, "hanging out with Bevell's taught me one thing."

"What's that?"

"How to fend for myself."

I thought of Sunny. No way she could take care of herself.

"I've got to go," I said.

She glanced back at the dime store and then at me. "Nice meeting you, Flynn."

"Yeah." I shoved my fists in my pockets and strolled away. When I turned back, the sidewalk was empty, except for her bicycle still leaning against the wall.

I wandered back past the theater, the dress store and the sewing shop. I crossed the street as the sheriff exited City Hall and headed my way. I hesitated, causing a car to swerve and blare its horn. By the time my foot hit the curb, the sheriff was on me.

"Son, I'd be careful crossing that street." He attempted to

hitch up his pants, but his belly got in the way. "Sometimes cars don't slow down for young'uns."

"Yes, sir."

He was a tall man, taller than Daddy, with the appearance of an athlete gone to pot. "You're new in town, aren't you?" He chewed a toothpick like it was his last meal on earth. He took it out of his mouth. "Don't guess I've seen you around."

"Yes, sir. Flynn Bolenn. I'm staying with my grandmother."

"Bolenn. Bolenn. Knew a Jimbo Bolenn in high school. Mighty fine football player."

"My daddy's name is Jimmy."

"That'd make you Ida Mae's grandson. I'll be dadgum. Jimbo Bolenn's son. Who'd he marry?" He snapped his fingers and pointed at me. "Mary Dean."

"Martha June," I said.

He shook his head. "No, not Mary Dean. Mary Jean." He searched the sky. "No, Martha Jean." His face lit up and he snapped and pointed at me again. "Martha June. Martha June Sullivan."

"Yes, sir."

"How about that?" He splayed massive hands on his hips, and I eyed the shiny black revolver in the holster behind his right pinkie. "Jimbo Bolenn's son back in Haley. How in the world is your daddy?"

"I don't know." I studied the laces on my shoes. They were untied and muddy. I jumped when the church bell chimed the hour. "He joined the army and is over in 'Nam."

"That so?" The sheriff squinted at me. "He's mighty old to be called up."

"He volunteered, sir."

"You don't say."

"Yes, sir. After his buddy got his leg blown off, sir. But he's gone missing, and nobody can tell us where he is."

"Lordamercy," the sheriff said. "Probably got himself an invitation to the Hanoi Hilton. What was he thinking?"

"He was thinking it'd be the right thing to do, sir."

The sheriff scratched his cheek. "Don't see as how that worked out for him if he's missing, buddy."

I stared back at him.

He shook his head. "He was a mighty fine football player. Mighty fine. Might work out to his favor." He stuck the toothpick in his mouth, and I wondered how to broach the subject of the thing in Ida Mae's cellar.

"Next time you hear from your daddy, tell him Earl Pickens said 'hey.' You do that for me?"

"Yes, sir."

"Good boy." He dropped a heavy hand on my shoulder, and before I managed to get the words right in my head, he strolled away, picking at his teeth and whistling.

you can't count on anything

"I'm worried Sunny's in trouble," I said to Willie. He lay cradled in the branches of the mimosa tree in front of the house. I sat against the whitened tree trunk and waved mosquitoes away with a feathery branch.

"What makes you say that?" Willie didn't appear interested, so I told him what I'd read in the newspaper and reached up and handed him the article.

"What makes you think he'd go after Sunny?" He let the slip of paper flutter back to me. I told him about the newspapers on Brother Muler's desk. "What does Brother Muler have to do with it?" He slid out of the tree and flopped beside me.

"I don't rightly know. But it was circled in red."

"What was?"

"Sunny's picture. Some pageant close to here. Fig Festival. Something similar."

"They're bound to have moved on by now," he said. "You reckon Brother Muler's after Sunny?"

I shrugged.

"You imagine he's mixed in with this Beauty Killer?"

"I've got no idea."

"Why don't we tell Ida Mae, and she'll call the sheriff, and he'll handle it."

I stared at him like he'd sprouted wings. "Tell Ida Mae her brother's going around killing little girls? She's liable to get rid of us."

"She wouldn't get rid of us."

"We start causing problems and she might feed us to the creature in the cellar."

"What?"

I lowered my voice. "The thing in the cellar." A lizard shimmied along the porch step, green with a bright blue tail. It slithered into the bushes.

"You still think there's something in the cellar?"

"Of course there's something in the cellar. Every time I pass by, I hear noises. Growling, scraping."

"A wild animal."

"Does a wild animal keep toy rabbits? Does a wild animal find its way into our room and steal sticks?"

"It was a practical joke. One of the other kids."

"And there was a bloody handprint on the cellar door."

"Maybe Ida Mae cut herself."

"I caught her cleaning muddy footprints in the hallway the other morning before anybody was awake."

"So?"

"So, who made the tracks?"

"Maybe she did."

"You ever see Ida Mae make a mess of anything? That woman doesn't let the door slam. How many times did she make us clean our room before we got it right?"

"So, you reckon the monster came into the house?"

"Yes."

"Why?"

"Looking for something to eat."

"Like what?"

I let that sit between us. I shredded the dangling green bean things off of my mimosa branch, then stripped the ruffled leaves one by one.

"If the monster wanted to eat us, it would've eaten us by now," Willie said.

"That's comforting. Maybe it's working with Brother Muler to kill those girls. Heck, maybe Brother Muler, the monster, and Ida Mae are all in on it together. Any way you dice it, we've got to get away and warn Mama."

"I don't know."

"What d'you mean, you don't know?" I wanted to slap him with my branch.

"I mean, how're we going to warn her? We've got no idea where she is. We don't even have a phone number."

"We'll have to find her."

"How?"

"Hike to Weaverton. Hitch a ride."

He frowned.

I slapped the branch against my thigh. "What?"

"I kinda like it here."

I glanced at the house, then back to him. "Mama dumped us here because it was the only place she could think of. How could you possibly like it?"

"I just do." He scrambled to his feet, his chin jutted, refusing to look at me. He studied the driveway instead.

"Spill it," I said.

"What?"

"Whatever it is you're holding back."

"No."

"Out with it."

"You'll make fun of me."

"When did that ever stop you?"

He stomped away. "I got friends to play with here," he said, keeping his back to me.

"Kids to play with? You got kids to play with back home."

"Not like Pretty Boy and Delbert and Jimmy."

"You mean retarded?"

"They're not retarded." He whirled around. "Pretty Boy is smart. Maybe as smart as you."

"He's blind."

"He can't help it. You don't know what his mama did to him. And Delbert's smart too. He just don't talk because he was traumatized or something. But he can draw pictures better than anybody. Better than some of them fancy artists in museums, I bet."

"So what? What about the girl?" I said. "You gonna tell me she's a rocket scientist? Because I just can't tell with all the *goo goo gaga lalala* she's always spouting."

"She can't help it, neither." Willie's cheeks flamed pink. "Her mama and daddy did something so awful to her it made her go back to acting like a child."

"I guess none of it's anybody's fault, huh?" I jumped to my feet. "Just bad luck they turned out like that?"

"Not bad luck." Willie hunched his shoulders. "Bad mamas and daddies."

Ida Mae called from the barn.

"I guess the fat kid had a bad mama, too, for dying, huh?"

Willie hung his head. "I'm gonna go see what Ida Mae wants." With his head low and his fists stuffed in his pockets, he trudged toward the barn.

"Good riddance," I muttered as I watched him go. I slapped

the willowy branch against the tree and cursed Mama and
her stupid ideas.

if you can't beat 'em, lock 'em up

That night I waited until everybody was asleep. Gripping my pocketknife, I slipped out of bed in my underwear and a t-shirt and crept outside on bare feet. I was going to get at least one good night's sleep without worrying about that dang monster.

I found the barrel right where I rolled it earlier, by the door to the shed. It smelled rank, like the one at the cabin. Too heavy for me to lift, I laid my knife in the grass near the mouth of the cellar door and half walked, half rolled the barrel to the cellar.

It creaked and groaned. I stopped more than once to listen for footsteps. But there were no sounds, save the whirring of katydids and crickets and all the other creepy crawlies of the night.

The moon wasn't half full, but it was enough for me to get by, and the cellar door glowed silver in the darkness. I would've asked Willie for help, but I had a strong suspicion I couldn't count on him anymore.

A few feet from the door, I leaned on the barrel to wipe the sweat with the hem of my shirt. Even close to midnight, it was too warm for work. I stared at the cellar door. If it had opened at that moment, I might've peed in my underwear.

My shoulders ached as I finished walking the barrel to the door. But, how to make sure the monster was inside? I scooped up a few acorns scattered at the base of the oak tree.

With my knee pressed against the door, I rested my ear on cool metal. There was a snuffling, a soft whistling. Pressing with my heel, I dropped the first acorn on the door. It pinged. Then there was silence.

I waited.

I threw the second acorn at the door. *Kathunk.* There was a grunt from underground. I dropped the rest of the acorns into the grass and eased the barrel to rest against the door with barely a groan of metal.

I raced back to the house and slipped into bed. Willie was asleep, curled on his side away from me. I lay staring at the bare bulb, pale in the dark room, waiting for some move from the monster. The longer I stared at the bulb, the more it looked like a giant eye glaring back at me. A huge, unblinking eye.

Eventually the eye blurred as my eyelids began to droop. I yawned and widened my eyes, but the room was warm, too warm. I yawned again and thought, I'll just rest my eyes a second, before I stand watch. I yawned again, my eyes watering, and then I closed them for the briefest second.

The huge, unblinking eye glowed yellow. And then it winked. A Cyclops winking at me. The ceiling melted away, and I stared at the stars, twinkling behind the cyclops' head. The creature was as dark as the night, and hairy. And in the middle of the hairiness and below the big, yellow winking eye, yawned a cave of sharp, pointy stalactites and stalagmites like we'd studied in science.

A cave on the ceiling. I struggled to see the formations better, each as glittering and sparkling as the stars, but I was frozen. I tried to speak, but I couldn't open my mouth.

Then the cave fell toward me, yawning wider and so close I realized too late it wasn't a cave at all. It was the creature's mouth, and those weren't formations. They were teeth. And they were chomping, stabbing at me. But I couldn't scream.

The creature let loose a howl, rattling the house. Mirrors, dishes, pictures, crashed to the ground. The picture above the bed, the rider in the storm, rattled and jiggled and danced. As I stared at it, the howling shattered the glass, and it rained upon me. I couldn't raise my arms to protect myself, so I shut my eyes tight so I wouldn't be blinded by the jagged pieces. And with a last burst of strength, I sprang up in bed.

I blinked in the darkness as everything stopped falling. I palmed the covers for broken glass. There wasn't any. Willie lay curled on his side, his pillow over his head.

The picture still hung on the wall. The ceiling was back to normal. The monster was gone.

I scrubbed my damp face. Another bad dream. A door opened, and feet shuffled in the hallway. I tried to remember what woke me. The monster blinking, no, winking at me. No, it was the howling.

A roar shook the walls. The roar of the monster.

"Make it stop," Willie's voice was muffled beneath his pillow. The back-screen door squealed open.

I checked under my pillow for my pocketknife. Gone. *Dang.* I'd left it at the cellar door.

I threw off my covers and dropped to the ground. I crept through the darkness across the hall to the kitchen window. Ida Mae stood at the cellar door, wearing an old plaid work shirt over her granny gown. Her long, silver braid in the moonlight made her appear young and small.

She tugged at the cider barrel until she rolled it off the

door. She yanked the door open and with a glance at the kitchen window, stared right at me before she disappeared into the cellar.

The howling stopped. The blade of my knife glinted in the moonlight. Could I risk running outside and grabbing it? Ida Mae would know for sure it was me who set the monster off. I'd have to wait until morning.

I wiped a shaky hand across my mouth. Delbert and Jiminy Cricket stood in the doorway to their room. Jiminy's hair stood as stiff as straw, and he swayed on his feet.

"What is it?" He yawned.

"Nothing," I said. "Go back to bed." Delbert stared at me with his big brown eyes. "Go to bed," I said and stomped back to my room, wondering if my knife would still be there in the morning, and how long it would take for Ida Mae to come and tan my hide.

help could be right around the corner

As it turned out, Ida Mae did not tan my hide. She didn't say anything at all, which actually felt worse. Because I had no idea what she was thinking. Or plotting.

"Sheriff, I got to talk to you." I stopped Sheriff Pickens outside his office behind the church. He chewed a toothpick, hopefully not the same one as before.

"Yeah, son?" His hand fell heavy on my shoulder. I wanted to shrug it off, but I didn't dare.

"It's about the monster."

"It's terrible." He removed his toothpick and stared at it. "What sorry son of a gun goes around murdering little girls?"

"No, sir, I mean—"

"Son," he squeezed hard, "you ain't got nothing to worry about. First off, his M.O., that's modus operandi for you lay folks, is he only appears to be after young girls. Which you clearly ain't. Got it from a police psychologist in Huntsville yesterday. They said there's some fool out in California killing young ladies the same way." He hitched up his pants. "Second off, there ain't no reason to believe he's anywhere—"

"Sir, I wasn't talking about the Beauty Killer." I side-stepped so his hand was forced to slide off my shoulder. "I'm talking about Ida Mae's farm."

He shook his head, which was mostly shiny forehead with a sparse amount of hair combed over. "There ain't no way the killer is on your grandma's farm, son. I know there's a girl out there, Della, Delia, what's-her-name. But Ida Mae Bolenn's a better shot with a shotgun than I am. There's no way the killer would risk that."

"Sir, I'm talking about the thing in the cellar."

"The cellar."

"Yes, sir."

"There's something in the cellar?"

"Yes, sir." I wished to high heaven he'd stop repeating me. "An animal, a creature, growling, howling."

"Son, there ain't no telling what kind of wild critters get trapped in your grandma's dang root cellar. I told Ida Mae that cellar's so old it's going to cave in on her one day. Or she's going to trip down them rickety stairs and won't be found until it's too late."

"It's not a trapped animal, sir." My jaw clenched. "It lives there. And it comes out at night and goes back in before sunup. And it left," I lowered my voice, "a bloody handprint on the door."

"Probably mud. A muddy print."

"It was blood, I tell you."

"Whoa, there, chief." He grabbed my shoulder and squeezed. "You're letting your imagination get away from you. Lord, if you ain't just like your daddy. He always was one for fanciful tales. I remember this one time he and Betty Sue Bobbitt—"

"Sir!"

He frowned at me.

"I'm not imagining this." I lowered my voice. "There is something dangerous in that cellar."

"Son." He gripped my shoulder. "If there is one thing I can say for certain about Ida Mae Bolenn, it's that she don't allow anything on her property she don't want there. Not a preacher, nor a sheriff, nor some creature of the night." He pointed his toothpick at me. "That you can count on."

"That's what I'm afraid of," I muttered and shoved my fists in my pockets.

The sheriff held his toothpick aloft. "You want me to talk to her? That'll make you feel better? Okay, dadgum, that's what I'll do."

"Thanks," I said, with absolutely no enthusiasm.

"What?" He splayed his palms wide. "What is it?"

"Can you do it now?"

"Lordamercy, if you ain't your daddy made over. Always in a hurry." He checked his watch. "I got to check on some ruckus going on at the church. That's where I was headed. Want to come? Give you a ride to the farm afterwards."

"No, thanks," I flexed my sore shoulder. "I've experienced all the churching I can stand." Plus, I didn't want to come riding onto the farm with the sheriff so Ida Mae would know I was the one who ratted out her monster.

"Suit yourself," he said. "I'll head out there soon as I'm done." He chomped on his toothpick and strolled away, whistling, "she'll be coming 'round the mountain when she comes."

sometimes monsters win, too

Nothing much came of the sheriff's visit later that day. He talked to Ida Mae. He ducked into the cellar. He strolled to the barn.

I followed him around while Ida Mae stood at the well, arms folded. She kept studying me. Not like she was mad exactly, but maybe disappointed.

"Everything checks out fine," Sheriff Pickens said to me with one foot in his patrol car.

"What about the cellar?" I said. Earlier that morning, I'd checked the grass around the door for my knife, but couldn't find it. I would've asked the others if they found it, but then they'd know I was the one provoking the monster.

"Nothing appears amiss."

"What about the mattress, the blanket, the stuffed rabbit?"

"Kids using it for a playhouse."

"Nobody's using it for a playhouse," I said. "I haven't seen Pretty Boy, or Delbert, or any of the others go in there."

"Son," the man made a clicking sound in his jaw, "I've checked it out. I got other things to tend to." He slid behind the wheel and slammed the door. He leaned his head out the open window. "Now stop worrying, kid. Ida Mae'll take good care of you, I promise."

And then he was gone in a cloud of dust.

When the government lady arrived later the same day, I tried to tell her about the monster. "Do you know what's in the cellar?"

She frowned at me, appearing to weigh me, judge me, looking like maybe she wanted to say something. Instead, she said, "Roots, vegetables? I think Ida Mae makes her own preserves."

"No, I mean the thing in there making noises. The growling, the—"

"Ida Mae!" she yelled. "You don't have a dog on the property, do you?"

I shrunk into my shoulders when Ida Mae turned her gaze on me from the backyard. "No, Miss Walker, just the hogs and cow."

She's lying, I wanted to say. *It's there. It's real.* But Ida Mae stared at me so hard the words dried in my throat.

Miss Walker jotted something on her pad. She made a big sweep around Delilah, who was sprawled in the dirt, her long legs stretched in front of her, clapping quietly to a song she hummed. Miss Walker stopped in front of Ida Mae. "Now, why was it I needed to make a special trip out?"

They headed to the barn, and I meant to follow them, but Ida Mae stopped me. "Stay here and watch after the young'uns, Flynn. Make sure Delilah doesn't get in the well."

I didn't want to babysit, and I didn't appreciate her brushing me off. Then it occurred to me. There was something in the barn Ida Mae didn't want me to see. The thing. The thing in the cellar was now in the barn. And Miss Walker was in on it.

Maybe her job was to supply food to the creature by way of foster kids. What could be easier? According to Jiminy Cricket, there always seemed to be a fresh supply.

I waited until Ida Mae and Miss Walker disappeared into the barn before busting it down the hill. I skulked along the backside of the building and stopped near the back door. Voices murmured above the grunting of hogs. Ida Mae and Miss Walker were in the loft.

I slipped inside the first stall. I knew they were right above my head due to the sprinkling of straw floating through the floorboards. I sucked in a sneeze.

"So, he's doing better?" Miss Walker said. "You doing better?" The thing grumbled.

"I can't manage to keep him fed," Ida Mae said. "He's growing so. And the light..."

Feet shuffled. More straw drifted downward.

"I know it's a burden," Miss Walker said. "We're working on relocation. But for now..."

"I'll be alright," Ida Mae said as the ladder groaned, "we'll make do the best we can." I pressed myself into the shadows. "The other young'uns help. But I'm worried about Flynn. He's a bright boy. If he knew…"

"Flynn's the least of our worries," Miss Walker said. "If the field office finds out, we're both going to be in more trouble than we can get ourselves out of. Maybe if I sent you more—" but the rest of her words were cut off by the squealing of hogs as Ida Mae dropped to the ground. Through a slat in the stall, I watched her lean over and pat Janine on her rough, gray head.

Miss Walker followed Ida Mae out as something shuffled above my head. I crept along the stalls to the ladder. The hogs rooted and grunted and snuffled their flat noses. I peeked out the front doorway, blinking into the sunlight. Ida Mae and Miss Walker had almost reached the well.

This might be my last chance to see the thing for myself. Heart pounding blood in my ears, I climbed the rungs of the ladder, pausing halfway. Soft, grunting noises came from the loft, not unlike the grunting of pigs.

I hesitated. Did I actually need to eyeball it? Couldn't Willie and I leave this place, never actually laying eyes on the thing?

No. I had to know. To prove to myself it was real.

I inched the rest of the way up. Fingertips digging into wood, I peered over the edge of the loft like a crocodile breaking the surface of a muddy Vietnamese river. I detected no movement among the bales of hay.

Sunlight streamed through the back window, but the corners of the loft remained shadowy. Scuffling came from the corner to the left of the window, a whisper, a hiss through the straw as I stared into the shadows, struggling to make out the dark lump hunkered there.

The creature.

It was still, and only its deformed, hunched shape and the glow of its yellow eyes were visible. We waited, staring at each other. Then a guttural growl erupted.

I fumbled for the next rung down as the chunk of darkness detached itself from the shadows and rumbled toward me, a black devil with the speed and roar of a freight train. With a pitchfork in its claws and its pointy teeth bared, it barreled straight for my head.

With a horrified yelp, I let go of the ledge and hung for one long, awful second, fighting air. And then gravity slammed me to the ground. I hit with such a whack I thought my lungs were knocked clear out of me. I lay there, too stunned to breathe.

I was weightless as the roof wavered. A dark head appeared above the ladder, and I blinked at it before it disappeared, sharp nails scrabbling over the floor.

I lay with arms splayed like Jesus on the cross, struggling to breathe. The barn shimmered around me before falling away, and hogs grunted somewhere in the darkness.

The inky blackness burned to gray and I heard shouting from the house. Someone called. It was Willie.

"Here," I croaked. I wondered why the creature hadn't eaten me already. Maybe the shouting scared him away. Willie appeared in the doorway of the barn with Jiminy Cricket peering over his shoulder.

"What'ch you doing laying on the ground?" Willie said. "Ida Mae wants us for supper."

The mere thought of collard greens and ham hocks rolled me onto my side as I retched into the dusty hay.

"Hey." Willie crept closer. "You sick? Jimmy, get Ida Mae. Something's wrong with Flynn." Jiminy trotted off, and I rolled onto my stomach and attempted to pull to my knees. The best I could manage was to roll my head away from the vomit and whimper.

I had no idea how long I lay there. Maybe I blacked out again. Because the next thing I knew, Ida Mae was kneeling beside me, poking my back and ribs.

I groaned.

She probed the back of my head with bony fingers. I groaned louder.

"You ain't bleeding," she said. "But you got a goose egg on the back of your head. Boys, help me get him to the house."

Jiminy Cricket grabbed one arm, and Ida Mae grabbed the other. "Willie," she said, "grab him around the waist. Ease him up gentle."

Pain shot through my side as Delilah and Delbert hovered in the doorway. I moaned in agony.

"Ain't no use carrying on until we know what we got," Ida Mae said. "We'll get you to the house and see what's what."

"Doctor," I muttered, my feet scraping the dirt as they half carried, half dragged me out of the barn and toward the house.

"That old quack?" Ida Mae snorted. "I wouldn't let him tend my hogs. Probably just some bruised ribs."

Someone murmured behind me. One of the kids.

"Took a fall from the loft, huh?" Ida Mae said. "Didn't I tell you boys not to go up there?"

I wanted to shake my head, but it was too heavy. "Monster. Dark. Tried to kill me."

Ida Mae glanced at Jiminy Cricket over my head.

"Ida Mae," Jiminy said, "if they find out…"

With a defiant shake of her head, Ida Mae said, "There's nothing to find out." And there was no other sound but our feet swishing in the grass.

They laid me on the sofa in the den, and Ida Mae commenced to investigating every inch of my body. "This hurt?" She poked my thigh.

"Yeah."

She leaned over my shin. "This hurt?"

"Yeah."

Her fingers slid over my ankle, back to my side, which raised me off the sofa in incredible pain. Then she pressed my chest, my back, my neck.

"Yeah. Yeah. Yeah!"

"Anything don't hurt?" Her look was flinty.

My eyes stung, and I turned my head into the sofa cushions.

She straightened up. "Best I figure, you got some cracked ribs. Bruised at least. But there's nothing to be done about it."

I picked at the wetness in the corners of my eyes. "I think we ought to call Mama," I said into the sofa.

"Son, I don't have any idea where your mama is right now." She stood over me. "She didn't tell me where she was going, nor when she'd be back."

"I just want to rest then." My throat was so thick I struggled to get the words out. "I'll be alright. I just need to rest."

"Everybody in the kitchen," she said to the others, "we need to talk." Footsteps clomped out of the room and along the hallway. I heard murmurings in the kitchen. Willie's voice was low, asking questions, but I couldn't make anything out. I wondered what in the world it was that they couldn't tell me. And I'd never felt so alone in my life.

Hugging my chest, I wanted to holler. To kick something. But I held it in, too tired to do much else as the shadows grew long around me and pitched me and the room into twilight.

no time for fools

Brother Muler appeared the next morning. He climbed out of his car in a gray suit, slick as sharkskin. He struggled up the slope, hauling a plump, green watermelon under one arm.

"Where's Ida Mae?" he said as I perched on the top step of the porch, favoring my sore ribs, a stick between my knees.

Pretty Boy was attempting to teach me how to whittle. I had tried to get him to tell me what the kitchen meeting was about the night before, but he clammed up, and I couldn't seem to budge him on the matter. At least the whittling gave me something to do while I recovered and worked out my plan of escape. Chunks of bark littered my feet.

Brother Muler hesitated at the bottom of the stairs and propped a polished, pointy wingtip on the bottom step. He balanced the watermelon on his knee and swiped his shiny forehead. "Tell your grandmother I'm here."

"Ida Mae!" I hollered over my shoulder. "Your brother's here!"

"I could've done that. Go get her."

My ribs throbbed too much to make unnecessary movements. "Where's Brother Kaine?" I said and rested the knife blade against the pad of my thumb. It was one I pilfered from a kitchen drawer and so dull it didn't even break the skin.

"Back at church."

"Why didn't he come?" I pressed the blade harder into my thumb. It left a dent.

"He has work to do." Brother Muler tapped his toes on the step.

"What kind of work?"

"Running errands. Church work. What d'you think?" He swiped his brow. "He's got more important things to do than run around buying ice cream for pestering young'uns and visiting a bunch of ill-mannered kids."

That stung. Especially after I accepted his stinking book. I jabbed the blade into the stick and ripped out a chunk. "Well, you're here." I stared at my stick.

"Huh?"

I frowned at him. "Don't you have any more important things to do?"

"I'm visiting Ida Mae." His foot thunked the hollow step. "And it *is* important. Go get her."

The screen door squealed open and banged shut. "What in the sam hill is all this hollering?" Ida Mae asked, crossing the porch with a tarnished door knob in one hand and a screwdriver in the other. "What d'you want, Rhube?" She stopped so close behind me I felt her breath on the back of my neck.

"When you going to teach these young'uns some manners?" he said.

"When are you going to stop appearing unannounced?"

I tucked my chin into my shirt, fighting back laughter, and studied my stick.

"When I finally get you to send some of them young'uns back to the state." Brother Muler thunked the watermelon onto the step beside his foot. He rested a polished wingtip on it to keep it from rolling. "Dang it, Ida Mae. You got two more young'uns now, and it's two too many. With your sickness eating away at you—"

"I'm fine," Ida Mae said, "and it's none of your dang business."

"If you're so fine," he rested his forearm on his propped knee, his all-seeing eye ring missing, "how come you're always favoring the spot on your side? How come sometimes you can't even move but for the pain?"

"You spying on me now?"

"It doesn't take much to see you clearly aren't well."

"Well enough."

"Doc Baker says—"

"Doc Baker!" Ida Mae's spray of spittle hit the back of my neck. "That quack? I wouldn't trust him to poke a cat. That all you came for? Because I've got work to do." She reached for the door.

Brother Muler slicked down his poufy hair. "I brought you a watermelon for the Fourth. Got it over at the Curb Market." He nudged the lopsided melon with his foot. "And I wanted to talk to you about the girl."

Ida Mae hesitated. "Delilah?"

"Your granddaughter."

"What about her?"

"It's not right, what her mama's doing, dragging her all over creation showing her off in them beauty contests."

I tucked my chin over my whittling and kept my fingers moving even though I wasn't paying attention to the stick.

"I reckon it's a bad idea myself," Ida Mae said. "But what am I supposed to do about it?"

"You got to stop it," Brother Muler said. "It's downright unchristian. It's the devil's own work, dressing them girls as harlots and parading them around a stage."

"I wouldn't go that far."

Brother Muler studied his bare finger. "I've seen them pageants myself, them little girls whoring it up. And with the Beauty Killer on the loose…"

My head snapped up. Brother Muler stared toward the woods. "I'm telling you, Ida Mae," he commenced to twisting his finger, as if the ring was still there, "something bad's going to happen if you don't stop it."

I should've agreed with him. I should've told him about my plan to get to Weaverton and stop Mama and Sunny. Maybe he would've even driven me. Instead, I blurted out, "What d'you care?"

He squinted at me, and there was nothing to do but keep going. "You don't know my sister. You've got no relationship with us. What d'you care what happens to our family? Every day, Willie and I live with, I mean, right over there, in the cellar is a—"

Ida Mae's grip on the back of my neck stopped me.

"There's nothing I can do about Sunny," she said. "She's with her mama, and I have no idea where they are. And with Jimmy missing…"

The sound of Daddy's name was sharp as a knife jab to my gut.

"I tried to tell you that boy was going to turn out to be nothing but trouble," the preacher said. "Who leaves their wife and young'uns to go traipsing off to war if they don't have to?"

An honorable man, I thought.

"Well, maybe when you birth young'uns of your own you can lecture me, and I'll listen," Ida Mae said, her bony fingers digging into my neck. "But right now, I got work to do." She released me and moved away. The screen door groaned, then thumped behind me. "And take that watermelon with you," she said inside the door. "We don't need your charity."

The man's gaze rested on the top of my head. I wanted to tell him exactly what I thought of his criticism of my daddy, but I kept my eyes lowered. He grunted and left the melon where it was. I didn't look up until his car door slammed and the engine rumbled and gravel crunched as he wheeled away.

I watched his car shrink to nothing as it sped toward town. I kept my fingers moving, and when I finally remembered the stick in my hands, I studied it.

I stared at the thing I'd created. It was crude, no doubt about it. But there was no mistaking what I carved into the center of my stick. Brother Muler's all-seeing eye.

if only he could talk

After dinner, I lay on the sofa, watching the flickering gray television. *Hawaii Five-O* ended, and the evening news was next. Lamps at my head and feet glowed orange. The house was quiet.

Ida Mae was outside shelling peas while the others played hide and seek in the shadowy twilight. A movement above my head drew my attention. My bedroom door was open.

I sat up and hissed as pain jabbed my side. Two white eyes glowed from the darkness of the bedroom, and my gut flinched before Delbert stepped into the light. He held a drawing pad and pencil.

"Great," I said. I stretched out on the sofa again, gritting my teeth against the stabbing pain. He hovered in the doorway, staring at me. "Git," I said. "Go play with the others."

I ignored him and had nearly drifted to sleep when a picture of a young girl flashed on the television screen with the word **MISSING** in big black letters. It was the girl from the Dairy Queen. What was her name? Sarah? Cara.

Still in the doorway, Delbert worked his mouth.

"You ain't gonna spit on me, are you?" I glared at him. "'Cause if you do, I'll beat the tar out of you." He slid toward me and slipped a white sheet of paper under my nose.

"What's this?" I stared at it. It was a dark blob of a drawing. He shook the paper at me.

"I don't want it," I said and flicked it away. He snatched it up and floated it onto my lap.

The blob was dark and hairy with tentacles coming out of its head. I swished the paper around. It was a creature with arms and legs and pitchforks for hands standing in a field of straw. I tilted my head. No, the hayloft.

"What's this," I said, "the monster?"

He nodded, his eyes big, his expression, solemn.

"You've seen it?" I pushed up and sucked in my breath as I held my side. He nodded again.

"Up close?" I rattled the paper at him. "I mean, you drew this from seeing it up close?"

He nodded.

"Why doesn't somebody do something?" I exploded off the sofa and groaned, nearly doubling over. "I mean, you got this... this," I rattled the paper, "this *thing* living in the cellar, the barn. It's gonna hurt somebody. It's already hurt somebody." A picture of four girls flickered onto the screen. One was Loralee Roby. They must've found her body.

All four girls were blonde, smiling, pretty little things with their tiaras tucked onto shiny heads.

Delbert shook his head furiously.

"What? Why're you shaking your head? The creature's after these girls, right?"

Delbert frowned and shook his head hard.

"So, Ida Mae's killing the girls and bringing them to him? Their eyeballs are missing, for crying out loud. She's feeding their eyeballs to the monster?"

The boy scrubbed the top of his head. With a bare foot

propped on the sofa and the pad resting on his knee, he scribbled and scratched, his fist moving faster than I could follow.

"What is it?"

His hunched shoulder blocked the paper.

"For heaven's sake." I stalked to the TV to crank up the volume. They were going to commercial.

"More at the ten o'clock news." The newswoman's smile was as fake as a three-dollar bill as she straightened her ruffled suit.

I said to Delbert, "Let me see," and snatched the pad from him. "Why don't you spit it out? Why don't you..." I stared at the drawing. It was of a boy. But it wasn't anyone on the farm.

"The creature's killing boys, too?" I frowned at Delbert. He shook his head and stabbed his pencil first at the picture of the creature and then the picture of the boy.

"I don't understand." I scratched my head hard. The tingling helped me think. The back-screen door banged.

"Boys," Ida Mae called from the hallway, "best get your baths and get ready for bed."

I crumpled the paper and shoved the pad into Delbert's belly as Ida Mae's head appeared in the doorway. "You hear me, boys?"

"Yeah." I crunched the wad of paper behind my back.

Delbert nodded.

"Okay." She entered the kitchen and clanged pots and pans.

The other kids banged through the back door, complaining, fussing, making a lot of noise.

I pointed my balled fist at Delbert. "I'll talk to you about this later," I said. In my bedroom, I shut the doors and spread out the crumpled paper as water ran in the bathroom.

I stared at the picture of the monster, no longer a figment of my imagination. It was a real, breathing, solid thing.

Delbert confirmed it. But why would he be after pageant girls when he had a whole farm full of young'uns right here? Something just didn't seem right. Unless he was in cahoots with someone else.

As I stared at the picture, my mind tripped to Mama and Sunny and the pageant Friday night. If Sunny won one title, just one, she might be the monster's next victim.

betrayed again

The Fourth of July came and went with nary a firecracker or cherry bomb or sissy sparkler to celebrate. My daddy could always be counted on for all sorts of dangerous whirligigs and screaming streamers for the Fourth, and Mama was always fit to be tied, hating them all.

But Daddy was missing, and my gut clenched every time I thought of him shot up in the jungle or in the Hanoi Hilton. Or…worse.

Pretty Boy and Willie finally talked Ida Mae into letting us eat the watermelon Brother Muler left. It was cold, crisp, and sweet. And as we gobbled it up, there was no mention of the preacher. I laid low and made plans.

The next day dawned yellow and warm. The kind of morning, especially in the South, that brings nothing but doom. The entire day, it was as if ants crawled under my skin.

I made my plans, easing around the house, my ribs no less sore. The others played outside as if nothing had happened, and there wasn't a monster in the cellar. Or was it back in the barn? I had no idea. I only knew it was getting bolder and moving more freely every day.

The time had come, and there was no way clear of it. Somebody had to warn Sunny. Willie and me would keep to the side roads. And maybe once we were out of Haley, we'd hitch a ride to Weaverton.

Sunny was competing the next Friday night. If we left the day before and walked all day and nearly another full day to find the fairgrounds, that'd give us plenty of time. I winced as I moved, the pain a punch I kept forgetting was coming.

I saw little of Ida Mae. She wasn't much of a nurse, and for once I was thankful for the lack of attention. Moving from window to window, I spent the day searching the yard for the monster's dark shadow.

I wanted to keep my eye on Willie, too, but he and Delbert kept moving out of sight. I attempted to keep him inside the house, but his expression was like I was the one who'd gone crazy. Which was a different punch to the gut.

A lunch of ham sandwiches and cold milk interrupted my planning. But it gave me a chance to talk to my brother.

We were the last ones at the table, and I scraped my chair closer to his. "I'm planning our escape," I said, keeping my voice low as I glanced around the empty room. "I'm stashing enough stuff to take off next Wednesday night while everybody's asleep."

"That's only a week away. And why do you have to leave at night?"

I wiped a sweaty palm on my jeans. "If we leave at night, we'll get a good head start, and Ida Mae won't know anything until we're too far gone."

"I don't know," Willie picked at the crust of sandwich left on his plate.

"Don't know what?"

"If I want to go."

"What d'you mean?"

"I *mean*," Willie studied his crust, pinching off bits of bread, rolling them into balls, and making a little pile of snow. "It's scary out there in the dark. You've got no idea where you're going."

"It's scary here, with a dang monster running loose."

"There's no monster."

"I saw it," I said, louder than I meant to and lowered my voice, "in the barn." I scraped my chair closer. "How d'you reckon I fell? It probably pushed me with its pitchfork. Why are you shaking your head? You don't believe me?"

"Ida Mae...I mean...Pretty Boy says there isn't any monster."

"How would he know? He can't see nothing. We've been over this."

"He's been here longer than anybody. He'd know if there was a monster. Ida Mae said—"

"I don't want to hear any more about it." The sound of tools clattered against the back door. I lowered my voice. "I've seen it, Willie, and the pain in my ribs proves it." I rubbed my side. "And Delbert's drawn a picture of it. So, whether there is or is not a monster on this farm is no longer in question. And either it, or something just as bad, is going after Sunny if she wins a contest. We've got to warn her."

"You can't be sure it'll go after Sunny. There's lots of pageants going on this summer."

"You willing to take that chance? You willing to just wait and see? Mama is hell-bent on Sunny winning one of them crowns."

"You aren't supposed to say hell."

"Shut up. You'd rather stay here than protect your baby sister?"

"Pretty Boy never tells me to shut up," he said. "Neither does Delbert."

"Delbert doesn't tell nobody nothing, for crying out loud."

"Neither does Jimmy."

"So, you'd rather stay here with those losers?"

"They're not losers."

"Barely a month ago, you were bawling like a baby on Ida Mae's front lawn."

"I was scared," he said. "Of Ida Mae. The foster kids. But they're not scary anymore. In fact, they're a lot like us."

I snorted. "Like heck they are. How in tarnation do you imagine they're like us?"

"They got no family."

"We got a family," I nearly shouted.

"No, we don't," Willie said. "Our daddy's gone. We have no idea where he is. He may be dead for all we know. Just like Jimmy's."

"No!" I yelled. "He's coming back! He's gonna come back. He told me. He said I was just in charge for a little while and then he'd be back. He said so!"

"He could've stayed," Willie said. "He didn't have to leave us."

I lowered my head and glared at my brother. "He was trying to do the right thing. But Mama, she didn't have to dump us here."

Willie swiped a finger under his nose. "She just wants a little attention for herself 'cause nobody pays her any mind."

"She's selfish," I yelled. "She cares more about herself than she does her own kids. And Sunny—"

"What about Sunny?" he challenged.

I clenched my fists, wrestled myself back from punching him, and fell dead silent. "You're right," I said finally, "she cares plenty about Sunny."

"Well Sunny can't help it."

"Nobody said she could."

"Why are you so sore?"

"You're making me want to hit something."

"Me? You want to hit me?" His look was one I hadn't seen since my dream about the boy-faced dog. Like he was scared of me.

But I didn't unclench my fists. I studied the kitchen for something to punch, the refrigerator, the table, the tire swing outside the window and Jiminy Cricket's fat bleached whale belly on it. He jumped off it and headed toward the house.

"Pretty Boy made you a duck," Willie said.

"Big fat hairy deal. He can whittle a bird. You care more about some blind kid who cuts stuff out of wood than your own brother and sister?"

"I didn't say that."

"Who kept Daddy from tanning your hide when you broke the strings on his guitar?"

"It was a dulcimer."

"Whatever. Who got you out of that scrape?"

Willie pressed his lips together. The back door squealed open.

"Who covered for you at the end of school when you ate the entire strawberry pie Mama made for stupid Principal Hecke, who wanted to suspend you for cheating?"

"I didn't cheat."

"That ain't the point. You were upchucking strawberries all over the place, and I told Mama we had spaghetti for lunch and that's the only way you got out of that mess. Principal Hecke thought the lunchroom had poisoned you. You gonna hang a brother out to dry who's always watching out for you?"

"I ain't hanging nobody out to dry."

I banged the table with my fist. "You going with me or not?"

He picked at the tiny snowballs of bread I'd scattered with my pounding. He stared out the window. He stared at the fridge. Everywhere but me.

"Well?"

"I'm thinking."

"What's to *think* about?" He looked like he was about to cry, but I didn't care. "Forget it." I scraped my chair away from him. "I don't want you to hurt yourself *thinking*. I'll go, and I'll go alone. I'm used to everybody bailing on me, anyway. You stay here with your stupid friends. I don't need you. I don't need anybody."

I stood and winced at another jab to my side. I stared at his bent head. "But if you tell Ida Mae or any of them losers I'm leaving or where I'm going, I'm gonna beat the ever-loving tar out of you. You understand?"

His lower lip quivered, but I was so mad I kicked the chair on my way out of the kitchen and got another jab in my side in return. I stormed through the hallway, passing fat Jiminy Cricket. Had he been eavesdropping? My shoulder caught his and drove him backward into the wall.

"Hey, watch where you're going, mister," he said as he bounced off the plaster. I slammed out the back door and nearly tripped over Ida Mae's shovel, propped next to the doorframe. Dark, fresh dirt clung to it. I kicked it, and it clattered to the ground, flicking dirt onto my sneakers.

I stalked to the cellar door and stared at it. Squatting, I wrestled the handle. It didn't budge.

"Hey." I banged the metal with the heel of my hand. "Hey, you in there, come on out!" *Bang, bang, bang.* I glanced up to find Delilah and Delbert staring at me with their mouths hung open from where they dug in the dirt beneath the oak tree. *Great. Two looney birds staring at me like I'm nutty.*

I stormed to the cornfield, losing myself in the tall green stalks. I'd have to rethink my escape plan without Willie. Something rustled behind me. I whirled around to find nothing but corn. The rustling moved further to my right.

"Who's there?" The rustling stopped. I peered through the stalks toward the house. Delbert and Delilah had returned to digging in the dirt. "You better show yourself before I come over there and kick your butt." A bird twittered overhead. I stared at the sickly yellow sky, wishing to the good Lord I had my knife.

The rustling moved closer, and I crashed out of the corn into the backyard. The two village idiots barely glanced my way as I stalked around them toward the front porch.

I climbed the old mimosa tree, which was the safest place I knew. At least I could see anything coming at me from there. I hid among the branches and waited. And watched.

dreams of the damned

While my dreams, or nightmares I guess you'd call them, were never particularly prophetic, the one that night was too scary to ignore.

Willie and I swam in the river back home. It was the Saugahatchee, the one we waded through Lawson's Creek to get to. I held my breath underwater, practicing for my future military training while Willie splashed along the shore.

We were fully dressed, and my jeans were heavy, weighing me down. I'd been underwater so long my lungs burned. The water was clear enough to see minnows swimming and rusted beer cans half buried in the muddy riverbed. My clothes dragged me so far down that Willie was no longer visible.

I thought I'd better surface, seeing as how my lungs hurt and Willie had disappeared. I kicked in his direction, and then I saw it.

A white arm.

One pale arm floating toward me, palm up, the wrist fragile, fingers beckoning. The rest of the body was hidden by a tree, toppled into the water with its roots still grasping at shore.

Wow, I thought, somebody else can stay underwater as long as me. I was about to kick my way to the surface to tell Willie he ought to get a load of this, when something stopped me. It was the fluttering of pink fringe beneath the submerged tree.

The last time I'd seen pink fringe was on Sunny, the day she said goodbye, waving like crazy in her sassy cowgirl suit. How funny, I thought, swimming toward the arm and the pink fluttering fringe, that Sunny would be here, with Willie and me, when we clearly saw her drive away.

I reached the outstretched arm, but the fringe was snagged beneath a bony branch of the tree. I tugged on the arm. It was soft and squishy. I let it go. I tugged on the fringe and it came free, and the body with it. It floated upward.

As it brushed against me, I caught a glimpse of pale cheek and blonde hair feathering over it. And then it was gone, drifting up, up, up.

Willie! I screamed, clawing through the water, but my jeans held me down.

I kicked, I screamed, but never made a sound. My mouth and nose filled with water. Willie. Don't look. Don't look at her. I'm coming.

I kicked and clawed as the water filled me, choking me. I gasped, and more water flooded in. Finally, I yanked my leg and realized the lace of my shoe was caught on a tree branch. I stomped the limb, smashing it clear of the tree corpse and floated upward, light as a bubble.

I broke the surface gasping for air, but it was too late. Willie had dragged the body ashore and stood over it, staring.

The body lay on its back, one arm thrown awkwardly over its head, blonde hair tangled over its face. The pink fringed vest peeled off in decayed ruin. I crawled onto the muddy shore next to it and reached over to gently clear away the tangled mess of hair.

Willie screamed, and I wanted to gag into the mud. It was Sunny. Sunny's mouth in perpetual surprise. Sunny's sweet face with two gaping, gouged-out holes for eyes.

the smell of desperation

Ida Mae crackled the newspaper at the kitchen table. The others had already eaten breakfast and skedaddled outside to play since it was Sunday, and there were no chores.

"You let me sleep late." I stood in the doorway and stretched an elbow over my head, wincing at the pain.

"Thought you needed it." Her nose remained buried in the paper.

I stared around the kitchen. Cold biscuits were on the counter. I plucked two from the plate and leaned against the counter to nibble one.

"Milk's in the ice box." She snapped open another page.

I poured myself a half a glass of milk and slid into the chair opposite her. I stared at the paper in front of me and chewed biscuits.

The front-page headline was *Drought Dries Up Summer*. Below it, was a picture of Cara, still missing.

Caraline Borden, of Haley, was last seen on Friday, June 30, around noon, near the Weaverton First Church on Main Street in Weaverton, Alabama. The thirteen-year-old had been visiting relatives in the area when she was reported missing.

The Franklin County Sheriff's office, as well as friends and family, continue to comb the area in a desperate attempt to find her.

She was crowned Little Miss Winston County a year ago, as well as Haley's Little Miss, before dropping out of the pageant circuit to pursue an interest in horseback riding.

I placed my half-eaten biscuit on the table next to my glass of milk. "Ida Mae?"

"Yeah?" The newspaper crackled.

"Why do you think the mamas and daddies of those girls keep letting them go out by themselves when there's a killer on the loose? Why let 'em go out alone? I mean, I know many of them were going to or coming from church activities. Do they think church is going to somehow magically protect them?"

And then I thought, *Who's tied to churches more than preachers?*

Ida Mae glanced up. "Maybe the parents are just too busy or too scared to acknowledge what's going on. There's a powerful lot of people who wanna stick their head in the sand concerning evil."

"You sure you've got no idea how to get in touch with Mama?" I said.

Ida Mae laid the paper face down on the table, her thumb saving her place. "Why?"

"I'm worried about Sunny."

"What about her?"

"I'm just worried's all."

Ida Mae peered at the photo of Cara.

"She's not much older than Sunny," I said. "The paper says she disappeared in Weaverton. That's where Mama's entering Sunny in the fair."

"Your mama can take care of Sunny," Ida Mae said. "If there's one thing I'm convinced about Martha June, it's that she takes care of her own."

"You mean like me?"

Our eyes locked. Somewhere outside the window, Delilah giggled. The biscuit lay heavy as a stone in my gut.

"Just because your mama dumped you here for the summer doesn't mean she doesn't love you."

I stared at her and folded my arms. The glass of milk warmed on the table. She snapped the paper open and commenced to reading. Jiminy Cricket gave a shout from the yard, and Delilah squealed.

"Just because you don't cotton to something," she said, "doesn't mean it's not the truth."

I ignored the fact that my daddy had once told me the same thing. I said, "Like them kids out yonder? My mama loves me like their mamas loved them? Is that how it is?"

She laid the paper on the table. "It's not the same. Their mamas are in no position to ever come back for them." She rested a palm on the paper, and I stared out the window at the clear blue sky. The top of Willie's head was barely visible as he whizzed by. They were playing some game. Probably tag.

"Drink your milk," Ida Mae said, "before it gets warm." She snapped the paper back to life.

"The kidnappings are coming closer together," I said.

She didn't stop reading.

I sipped the milk, but it was too late. It slid down my throat and turned sour by the time it hit my belly.

In the living room, rummaging through the bookshelf, I found a half set of encyclopedias. I pulled out the one for Alabama, tucked it under my shirt, slipped into my bedroom, and shut the door. I slid my suitcase to block one door, propped the chair beneath the doorknob of the other. Sprawled on the rug, I found a map of the state.

With a pencil, I traced my route from Haley to Weaverton. It was nearly a straight line north and passed through a few smaller towns. Good. I'd be able to stop and get provisions. And then I thought of something.

I drew a star at each town where a girl had been murdered. Twin Creek, Bay Bridge, Beulah, Greysville, then Haley. I drew a line connecting the towns, but something was wrong. I studied the map. I'd drawn nearly a complete circle until I got to Haley.

I stared at the collection of towns. Then I remembered that Cara didn't disappear from Haley. She disappeared from Weaverton. I drew a star there. The circle was three quarters complete. There was only one town still unconnected in the circle. Torrence City. And the one town smack dab in the center of the circle was Haley.

the gift

"What's that?" I glared at Pretty Boy from my perch in the mimosa tree, arms folded. It was two days before the pageant, and I was nearly out of time. I'd been sitting there stewing over my predicament so long my backside was numb.

"A sword," he said. He held it outstretched, balancing it on his fingertips as if he was presenting Excalibur to King Arthur. It was too short for a sword, more of a dagger, about as long as my arm from fingertip to elbow. "It should be longer," he said. "But I ran out of wood. It was the leftover piece from patching the hayloft."

I shrugged. "It's alright." But truth was, it was more than alright. It was a real beauty. One sleek piece of wood, finely honed to a piercing point. Swirling vines and squirming snakes were carved into the handle. I'd never seen anything as fine in my whole life. "What's it for?"

"You. Take it."

I settled into the tree and faked a yawn and said, "Why're you giving it to me?"

"You seem scared. I thought you needed protection since you lost your knife. And a Navy SEAL needs a weapon."

"I have a stick," I said, "and I ain't scared." I dropped out of the tree and landed soft as a cat in front of him. "Where'd you get the dumb idea I was scared?" Barely an inch from the point of the blade, I stuffed my fists in my pockets.

"You bar your bedroom door at night," he said. And he didn't waver, even though I stood practically on top of him.

"How do you reckon?"

"I hear you moving things around."

"So?"

"Willie told me why."

The snitch. I glared toward the house. "What else did the little snot say?"

Pretty Boy ran fingers along the satiny blade. Behind him, a hummingbird hovered over a patch of bright pink lantana, vibrating the air with its wings. Then it was gone.

"What else did he say?"

"You know what else he said." Pretty Boy tapped the blade against his thigh. "You've already heard it from Jimmy."

"It's a lie. A dirty, filthy lie." I was glad he couldn't see how bad my face burned. "What a worm. What a lowlife, telling lies about his own brother."

I stalked away, my fists deep in my pockets. I stopped and whirled around. "How's he guess what I'm dreaming if he's asleep?"

Pretty Boy pressed his lips together. A bee buzzed between us. "You want the sword or not?" he said.

"I don't have any money."

"I don't want any. I'm giving it to you."

It was a trick. Nobody goes to that much trouble for some-body else. "Why didn't you make it for Willie? You two are thick as thieves."

"He didn't need it." His shoulders drooped and the sword quivered in his fist. "Want it or not? Last chance."

"You're just going to give it to me?"

"Yes."

"Just like that."

"Yep."

"No strings attached?"

He stabbed it into the ground, where it shivered, Excalibur back in its stone.

"Take it or don't," he said and strode away.

I stared at his back, his shoulder blades sharp beneath his thin t-shirt. I stared at the sword quivering in the dirt. I glanced around to see if anyone was watching. I was alone.

I stepped forward to finger the hilt of the sword. It was as smooth and silky as it appeared. I grasped the handle and thought, for one horrible second, what if I couldn't pull it clear? And then it whooshed upward with such force I staggered backward.

I eased it one way, then another in the fading light. I fondled its beveled blade and gently brushed off the dirt. I fingered the wicked point. Not in a million years had I ever owned anything so fine. I swished it in the air, slicing up oxygen with a few quick jabs.

I turned toward the house and thought I saw a flutter of curtains in Ida Mae's bedroom. I skirted the front porch and raced to the back of the barn where I spent the rest of the dying day jousting with the weeds and slicing and dicing wicked preachers and evil monsters.

Who had time to worry about the Viet Cong when monsters lurked in your own back yard?

i hate delays

That night, the thunderstorm that rolled in was so violent, by dawn it was still dumping buckets. My view from the back door was gloomy; the rain, unrelenting.

"What're you doing awake so early?" Ida Mae snuck up behind me, causing me to nearly jump out of my pajamas.

"Nothing. Couldn't sleep."

"I wonder if I kept you boys busier, you'd sleep better."

"The howling woke me." I stared at the rain lashing the roof of the well. "Thought it was a dream." I left the doorway to follow her into the kitchen.

"Nothing to worry about." She plugged the percolator in and filled it with water for coffee. "We need the rain." The machine vibrated and hummed.

The smell reminded me of Daddy sitting at the kitchen table on Sunday mornings, nose buried in the newspaper, sipping black coffee from a Jack Daniels mug.

"Where do you think Daddy is?" I said. "Why don't they tell us anything?"

She banged a cup onto the counter and paused to stare out the kitchen window at the rain pelting the trees. "I don't know."

"What if they have word of his whereabouts and they come

to our house like before to tell us, but there ain't nobody there 'cause we're here and Mama's gallivanting all over creation?"

She sighed and ran tap water into her cup to rinse it out. She dried it with a towel. "We'll just have to wait," she said, "and pray."

Pray, I scoffed. *When has that ever done me any good?*

⁓

After lunch, tires crunched the gravel driveway as I pinned wet undershirts to the clothesline Ida Mae strung behind the house. The rain left the ground a mushy, muddy mess. Mosquitoes hummed. The air was sticky warm, and I thought it was a poor time to be hanging out the wash. But nobody asked me.

Delilah sprawled in the grass at my feet, handing me wooden clothespins. I shooed her away, but she stayed underfoot, chunks of wet grass sticking to her bare legs, her bell jingling merrily.

I admit, I liked the sticky, squeaking sound the wooden clips made when she popped them open and handed them to me. Other than that, she wasn't of much use sitting there, grinning, getting soaked from the bottom up and smelling of soggy animal crackers.

At the sound of the car, I dropped the pin she handed me. Could it be Mama? Or finally word about Daddy? I ran around the house to find Miss Walker already out of her Volkswagen. She strode toward the front porch, fanning her shiny face with her clipboard. She'd left her jacket thrown over the front seat of her car, and her milk-pale arms were bare.

"You there," she paused at the edge of the grass and shielded her eyes, "which one are you?"

"Flynn."

"Where's Ida Mae?"

I shoved my fists in my pockets. "How come you're here again? I thought you weren't supposed to come back for another month."

"Something's come up." She continued to fan herself. "I need to talk to Ida Mae."

"You appear awful hot."

"My air conditioner took out on me again. Where's your grandmother?"

"What's come up?"

"She in the house?" Miss Walker strode toward the porch.

"Tell me what's come up." I pinched my thigh through my pocket wishing I had my sword.

"Nothing I can discuss with you." She fanned like crazy.

"Just tell me," I said, "and I'll tell you where she is."

"Ida Mae!" she called as she climbed the porch steps.

I let her get all the way to the top step before I said, "She's out at the barn, I reckon."

"Why didn't you say so?" She pivoted on her ugly brown shoes and clomped back down the stairs. By the time I raced to the barn and slunk around the back side of it, she'd disappeared inside.

Ida Mae tossed leftover corncobs to Janine and Ed. They grunted, pushing and jostling for their snack. Miss Walker fanned herself furiously, and jerked the front of her white blouse away from her skin.

"There's nothing I can do, Ida Mae," she said. "Somebody's got to go. I'm sorry."

Ida Mae's back was to me, her head low over the slop bucket. I couldn't hear her over the grunting of the hogs.

"It doesn't matter who's kin and who's not," Miss Walker huffed. "It doesn't matter if they just got dumped on you. There are rules we have to follow. And one of those rules..."

I needed to get closer to hear. I slipped into the last stall, ankle deep in hay, and peered through a crack in the slats.

"I know you take good care of them," Miss Walker said. "Of course they're well fed." She dabbed her thumb at her upper lip. "You're one of the best foster parents I've got. I wish you could see—" she pressed a palm to her forehead, "never mind."

Ida Mae murmured something.

"If they found out what's really going on...the cellar..." Miss Walker stared out the doorway "...you'd lose the others for sure." She turned back to Ida Mae. "Unless you can come up with a drastic solution, there's nothing I can do for you." She commenced to fanning. "I'm sorry. I truly am." And with her lips pressed tight, she did look like she was about to commence to bawling.

Ida Mae held onto the hog pen for so long, head bowed, I wondered if she was alright. Miss Walker frowned at the grunting hogs.

Finally, Ida Mae straightened and left the barn, shaking her head. The bucket banged against her thin, blue-jeaned thigh. Miss Walker trudged behind her toward the house.

I sank into the straw and the coolness of the barn. Loulou the cow blinked from the opposite stall before dropping her head to munch hay.

Somebody's got to go. I leaned my head against the empty stall that used to house the horse. Who'd it be?

Pretty Boy had been there the longest. Delilah next. Jiminy Cricket was an orphan. And who'd take on moody Delbert?

Then there was Willie and me. Ida Mae wouldn't give us up, being family. Or would she?

Actually, Willie appeared to fit into Ida Mae's crazy family just fine. The only one who didn't belong was me.

I struggled to my feet and hefted the pitchfork resting against the wall. I scratched the ground with it. Wasn't I leaving, anyway? Wasn't I desperate to warn Mama and Sunny about the Beauty Killer?

I didn't need to wait for anybody to kick me out. The metal teeth scraped long gouges in the dirt. The time had come. Rain or not, there was no use putting it off any longer. I slammed the handle against the stall and quit the barn.

Blinking into the bright sunshine, I found Delilah dancing around the clothesline with a pair of Ida Mae's panties on her head, the back of her dress mud-stained. Willie rolled around her feet laughing, while Pretty Boy smiled into the distance.

Swallowing the hot ball in my throat, I raced to the other side of the house, slipping unseen among the fig trees.

trouble comes in pairs

Brother Muler pulled into the driveway about the time Miss Walker's dull green bug disappeared around the edge of woods heading toward town. I had retrieved my sword from under the porch where I'd hidden it and stood near the steps, waiting as the preacher bellied out of his black sedan. He caught Ida Mae crossing the front yard.

"I ain't got time for you now," Ida Mae said with a dismissive wave. She kept going.

"Ida Mae, hang on a dang minute." Brother Muler was already red-faced and huffing. Brother Kaine climbed out of the other side of the car. He stood in a nice sport coat instead of his rolled-up shirtsleeves for a change. And I wondered if maybe Brother Muler had finally worn off on him. For some reason, I felt a mite disappointed at the thought. He stretched his arms, fingers clasped, over the roof of the car.

"I said I ain't got time." Ida Mae whirled around, the slop bucket swinging wildly.

"I got to talk to you, woman."

"God almighty!" she yelled.

He pointed a fat finger at her. "Don't you take the Lord's name in vain in front of me, girlie."

"This is not the time, Rhubarb." She said it like she was

chewing glass. "I got the Walker woman breathing down my neck. And I got the government wanting to take my kids away."

"That's what I want to talk to you about." Brother Muler swiped his jaw where the sweat trickled. He stared at his damp palm for a second before fumbling in his pocket.

Ida Mae cocked her head. "How'd you know about that?"

He pulled out a handkerchief, and I thought I caught a bit of lace before he mopped his brow with it. "There ain't no secrets in this town, Ida Mae. They came to see me first."

"You?" She squinted at him. "You sicced them on me? You tell them I needed to get rid of young'uns?"

"Look around, Ida Mae." He threw his arms wide. "You ain't got the money to take care of them kids. Especially since Martha June dropped her two young'uns on your doorstep. You ain't young anymore. And you're sick. Real sick. I talked to Doc Baker."

Ida Mae lowered her head and stalked toward him. "You've got no right. I already told you it's none of your business." She hauled the bucket at him, and it barely missed. Banging the ground, it splattered bits of carrots and lettuce and slime onto his fancy pants.

"Ida Mae." He jumped back and stared at his pant cuffs. "I paid two hundred dollars for this suit. And I've got a meeting with the Tubervilles in an hour. They're buying new robes for the choir." He brushed at the garbage stains. "I can't go visiting like this."

"Your suit alone could've bought a truckload of food for starving kids," Ida Mae said.

"What am I supposed to do?" He glanced at her. "Stroll around in sackcloth and ashes? What'll my congregation think?"

"They might think you actually care more about them than yourself, duding yourself up and riding around in fancy cars."

"They gave me that car."

"You could've refused."

"How would I visit shut-ins?"

"In something less flashy."

"You've got no right telling me what to do with my church."

"I thought it was God's church. And you've got no right butting into my business, neither."

"Choir robes for every single member, Ida Mae. Do you have any idea how many that is? For the little ones, too."

"You're talking new choir robes, and I'm telling you some of my young'uns are about to be without a home. You reckon just anybody's going to take these kids?"

Brother Kaine left the car and strolled toward me. "What'cha got there, Flynn?"

I flexed my fingers, gripping the handle of the sword and held it stiffly by my side.

Brother Muler slapped at his pants with his handkerchief. "You are quite possibly the most stubborn woman I ever knew." His poof of hair bobbed over his forehead. "You believe every bit of life revolves around these young'uns? Good works ain't going to get you into heaven, Ida Mae."

"And you are the most pig-headed hypocrite I ever knew." Ida Mae stomped to the slop bucket and snatched it from the ground. Brother Muler jerked away from her. "All you ever talk about is your precious church and winning souls to heaven, and you ignore the starving mouths right under your nose."

Brother Kaine said to me, "Looks like a sword. Can I see it?" I let him pluck it from my fingers. He raised it to the sunlight. "Mighty fine." He ran a finger along the beveled blade. "Where'd you get it?"

"Pretty Boy made it."

Delilah, Pretty Boy and Delbert crowded the edge of the bushes at the corner of the house.

"I'm simply thinking of you, Ida Mae." Brother Muler frowned at his soiled handkerchief. "With your can... er, health issues, you can't keep going like this. This never-ending work."

"Don't talk to me about health issues," Ida Mae said. "You've never been concerned about nothing but your precious church. Everything else is just for show."

"That ain't true." The preacher passed the handkerchief between his palms as if it was a hot potato. "I care plenty."

I leaned against the porch railing and hugged a paint-peeling column.

"Pretty Boy," Brother Kaine said, "the blind kid?"

"Yeah."

"I forgot," Ida Mae said. She straightened her shoulders. "You care about our mother. You care about her plenty. In fact, you care about each other so much there's not much room left to care about anybody else."

"That ain't fair." Brother Muler searched around, as if scouting a place to get rid of his soiled handkerchief. "Mama begged to help you. You and William both, in the beginning."

"Pretty Boy," Brother Kaine fondled my sword, "he carve it himself?"

"Yeah."

"He does good work. In fact, I'd say he's quite an artist."

"Doesn't matter now," Ida Mae said. "I've got my own problems, and they don't concern neither of you. Just leave me in peace." She climbed the porch steps and stomped past Brother Kaine and me. She frowned in his direction. "Brother Kaine."

"Ida Mae." He nodded at her rigid back.

The front door slammed.

"That woman." Brother Muler stomped halfway up the steps and stared.

"Get a load of this, Pastor," Brother Kaine showed him my sword.

"What?" Brother Muler eyed the sword as if it was a hissing snake.

"One of the kids here made it." Brother Kaine glanced to where Delbert, Pretty Boy, and Delilah huddled together. His gaze lingered on Delilah as she twirled a finger in her downy hair.

He jerked back around. "The workmanship's mighty good, don't you think?" He gave the sword a swish, then held it toward the preacher.

Brother Muler took it, still staring at the front door. "Yeah, it's good," he said without even looking at it. "Real good."

I snatched it from him.

"Let's go," Brother Muler said. Shaking his head, he descended the steps. "I ain't never seen anybody more stubborn in all my born days." He stalked toward his car.

"See you around, Flynn." Brother Kaine squeezed my shoulder. "Take good care of her," he nodded at the sword and hustled down the stairs.

"Brother Kaine," I caught him at the bottom.

"Yeah, son?"

"You got any idea how to get to Weaverton from here?" I wanted to make sure my map wasn't too old to be counted on.

"You planning a trip?"

"No." My cheeks flamed. But it sure wasn't the first time I'd lied to a preacher. "My Mama and sister are headed thataway. I was just wondering which direction they might take."

"Well," he cocked his head, "Weaverton is north of here. Highway 52 takes you right to it. It runs along the railroad tracks the whole way."

"How many miles, you reckon?"

Brother Kaine stretched his chin and scratched. "About twenty or so. Maybe thirty." I wanted to ask him how long it might take to hoof it. But I didn't.

"Thanks," I said. Brother Muler rumbled his car to life and peered over the steering wheel, drumming his fingers. "You better go," I said. "Brother Muler appears mighty steamed."

"Yeah, I better." Braxton Kaine grinned back at me. "Take care, Flynn." He gave me a salute.

He'd helped me out at the A&P. He bought me ice cream. He talked to me like I wasn't some stupid kid. And I wondered, not for the first time, why he couldn't be kin as he strolled around the black sedan and slid into the front seat next to his boss. Brother Muler peeled out in a splash of mud before rumbling along the lane.

After supper, I spent the rest of the evening in my room, working out strategies. The others laughed and carried on somewhere on the other side of my closed door.

I checked the items in my knapsack. Food. Water in an old army canteen I found in the bottom of the chest of drawers in our room. Daddy must've missed it when he cleared out his brother's gear. Flashlight. I clicked it on and off a few times to make sure it worked. My sword. And a few bills I pilfered from Ida Mae's elephant jar.

At the last minute, I slipped a clean pair of socks into my knapsack, remembering something Daddy said about his buddy in Vietnam never having dry socks and always getting some kind of foot fungus or disease.

I stuffed my knapsack under the bed as Willie came in from his bath. His hair was wet, his feet bare, and he was already in his pajamas. He might as well have been five years old.

We didn't speak, but he kept glancing my way, and I knew he wanted to say something. We climbed into bed, and I was the first to roll away and stare at the wall long after we switched off the light.

send me on my way

The moon was on the wane and retreating from my bedroom window when I pulled my knapsack from beneath the bed. It was no use sleeping. I laid on my back and counted the minutes ticking by and listened to the sounds of the house gradually falling into silence. I waited an hour or so, listening to the crickets chirping or a distant owl hooting, and then eased out of bed.

I crept along the darkened hallway as Ida Mae snored behind her closed bedroom door. I had practiced my route, so I knew which creaking floorboards to avoid. Keeping close to the wall, I passed the other bedroom and slipped out the back.

Crossing the yard, I realized the cellar door was open. The monster was on the loose. I scanned the yard, the cornfield's dark shadows, the moonlit patches for any movement. Maybe it was inside the house. I thought of Willie sleeping peacefully in bed. I pivoted to go back, then stopped. Maybe it was in the barn.

With moonlight splattering the yard, I almost talked myself out of the idea of a monster on a dilapidated farm in north Alabama. I tugged my knapsack closer. I mean, what a crazy idea. A monster on a beat-up, hollowed-out farm with a bunch of crazy kids?

Willie was probably right. Whatever I thought, whatever

I'd seen in the barn was probably my imagination, a misunderstanding. I shrugged, but the twinge in my ribs reminded me it was, in fact, quite real.

I gripped my sword and crept across the yard toward the woods. If I followed the path past the hunting cabin, it would eventually dump me on the other side of town. I could probably cut twenty minutes off my travel time and avoid being seen on the road.

I skirted the cornfield and hesitated at the edge of the woods. It was darker, with the trees blocking the moonlight. If the monster wasn't in the cellar, he might be hiding in the woods. He might be watching me where I stood.

The sword slipped in my sweaty palm, and I gripped it tighter. I inched forward and stopped. What was that sound? A crackling of leaves? I fumbled in my knapsack for the flashlight. I flicked it on and flashed it behind me. Its beam was miniscule compared to the army of pines looming overhead. The pinpoint of light revealed nothing moving.

I swiveled toward the road. I might be able to jog along it and make up the extra time. But I'd still run the risk of being seen. And how was I going to explain trodding along the road by myself so early in the morning? Somebody'd be bound to call the sheriff.

It had to be the woods. With a deep breath, I plunged into darkness as something grabbed me from behind. I whirled around, my light held high, ready to plunge my sword into the monster's black heart.

Willie's face was pale as he raised a hand to block the beam of light.

"What're you doing?" I hissed and clicked off the light. "Go back to bed."

"I'm going with you." Shivering, he rubbed his bare arm, even though the night was warm.

"Forget it." I waved the flashlight at him. "And lower your voice. You'll ruin everything."

He stared at me. "I'm going."

"You and your buddies have a fight?"

"Families stick together." He scuffed a toe in an arc in the grass. "Ida Mae said so."

"Well, I didn't bring enough food for the both of us."

He raised a plastic bag full of orange lumps.

"What's that?"

"Circus peanuts."

"What?"

"You know, those little orange marshmallowy—"

"I know what they are. Where'd you get 'em?"

"I found them in the trash. Ida Mae threw them away. She said Brother Kaine had given her a couple of bags, but she didn't want that junk rotting our teeth." He jiggled the bag. "I kept them all. I can fetch more."

My nose scrunched at the thought of Willie digging through Ida Mae's trash. But then, beggars couldn't be choosers. "Too risky," I said. "It'll have to do." I was still mad at him, but the weight pressing my shoulders toward the ground crumbled off like crusty old armor. "Come on." I clicked on the flashlight, and we slipped through the trees.

"Why are we going through the woods?" he said. "Wouldn't the road be easier?"

"You going to question everything I do?" I held a branch out of his way until he caught it.

"The road's got to be easier."

"Too risky. If somebody saw us, they might alert the sheriff."

"What if we get lost in the woods?"

"We've been this way before. Ida Mae said it's a straight shot to town."

"We've never been past the cabin."

A twig snapped behind him. I whirled and flashed the light over his shoulder. "You see anything?"

Willie peered into the darkness behind him. "No."

"You notice the cellar door open when you passed through the yard?"

"Yeah."

"Keep moving." We hurried through the trees, stumbling over fallen logs, tangling ourselves in snarled vines. Tree limbs as knobby as skeleton fingers snatched at our clothes, our hair.

A branch crashed behind us. Willie plowed into me, nearly knocking me to the ground.

"What was that?" He clung to me.

I pushed him off. "Probably a squirrel or a chipmunk." I gripped the sword and worked the flashlight ahead of us and behind. The crackling and snapping of twigs and tree limbs followed us. But each time we whirled around, nothing was there. When we finally broke into the cabin clearing, the house was dark.

"Let's keep going," Willie said.

I crept to the front door and stared through a dusty window. I flashed the light around inside. Everything appeared as we'd left it. The door creaked open, and we hesitated, staring at each other before slipping inside. I clicked off the flashlight and moved to the edge of the window to peer out. I motioned for Willie to do the same at the bedroom window.

"I'm not going in there by myself," he whispered.

"Then get out of sight and stay there."

After a few minutes of watching the clearing with Willie flattened against the opposite wall, he whispered, "what're we doing?"

I rolled my eyes. "We're waiting to discover if whatever was following us will show itself. Or it might've gone around back. But I can only watch one window at a time."

"Then give me the light."

"No way."

After a few minutes with no movement from the shadows or bushes or trees, I flicked on the flashlight, and we slipped through the house into the bedroom. As I passed the bedroom window, a movement drew my attention. I pressed myself against the wall and clicked off the light.

"Shhhhhhh." I snatched Willie to the other side of me, slamming him against the wall. I peeked out the corner of the window. The moonlight pooled on a bare patch of grass.

"Too dark," Willie said. "I don't like it."

"Quiet. Something's out there." I peered out again. The clearing was still. Not even a tree branch rustled.

"What is it?"

I searched the yard, but not a twig or a leaf appeared out of place.

"It's your imagination," Willie said.

"Maybe." I pushed past him into the bathroom and peeked out of the window there. Nothing. "We better get going before it gets light. We've got to be out of Haley before Ida Mae wakes up and finds us gone."

I shut the door to the cabin and flashed my light around the clearing. The trail had to pick up somewhere opposite of the direction we'd come. There it was. A red marker tied to a tree. Easier than Hansel and Gretel following breadcrumbs.

It wasn't long before the sound of twigs snapped behind us again. With a hand bracing the bottom of my knapsack and the flashlight bouncing along the path, I slow-trotted with Willie, who struggled to keep pace.

"Come on," I called over my shoulder. "We've got to get to the road. I have no idea what's back there, but we don't appear to be losing it."

We finally broke through the trees into the graying dawn. I stumbled down a muddy embankment onto a road I remembered from our trip to the Dairy Queen. On the other side of the road was a gas station, Joe's Filler-Up. It was closed.

If we followed the road past the gas station, it dead ended at Highway 52, which would take us to Weaverton. I turned to tell Willie, but he was nowhere to be seen.

"Willie," I hissed from the bottom of the ditch. I heard rustling and saw a speck of white in the stripe of Willie's shirt. I cupped my hands around my mouth and called, "Willie, come on!" He moved through the trees, stopping every few seconds, then moving on.

"What are you doing?" I said as he finally slid down the embankment. He stuffed a white handkerchief in his pocket. "Can you please keep up?" I said.

We trudged along the road a few minutes until we reached Highway 52. We headed right and by the time we reached the Dairy Queen, it was light enough to flick off my flashlight and slip it into my knapsack.

We had crossed the empty parking lot and headed for the railroad tracks running behind it when something crashed behind the building.

"What the—"

Jiminy Cricket stumbled out from behind the gray brick

wall. Delbert followed, leading Pretty Boy. And Delilah trailed behind, wearing a simple, white cotton dress and hacked-off house slippers.

"What are you idiots doing?" I gripped my sword and protected my knapsack.

"We're going with you," Pretty Boy said, holding onto Delbert's shoulder and grasping the knob of his walking stick. Delbert clutched a pad of paper and pen to his chest.

"On your adventure," Jiminy Cricket said, swiping at his already sweaty brow.

"Lilah want to go home," Delilah said. She stared around the parking lot, her hands twisting the hem of her dress, her bell jangling loudly in the early morning air.

"This ain't an adventure," I said. "This is serious business, and you can't come. Now, go home," I shooed them with my sword, "before Ida Mae finds you missing."

"We can't go back now," Jiminy Cricket said. "She'll tan our hides."

"Well, you're not going with me." I scooped up a handful of gravel.

Willie stepped between me and the others, eyeing my fistful of rocks. "You're not going to hurt them, Flynn."

"Not if they get going like I told 'em. Did you tell them where I was going? You tell them they could come?"

"I didn't tell nobody nothing. I thought they were asleep."

"I heard you talking," Pretty Boy said. "At lunch the other day. Delbert and I decided to go with you. We thought we might help."

"Help? From a blind kid?" I snorted. "Hardly."

"Don't be mean," Willie said.

I glared at him.

"We were already in the woods," Pretty Boy said, "when we realized Jimmy and Delilah were following us."

"How did Delilah even get out?" I said. "She sleeps on a cot in Ida Mae's room for crying out loud."

"She can be pretty sneaky when she wants to be," Jiminy said.

"And how did she get dressed without Ida Mae hearing?"

"Sometimes Ida Mae lets her sleep in her clothes," Jiminy said, scratching his fat, white belly. "It's a lot simpler that way."

"She's not even wearing real shoes."

"They were all I could find," Jiminy said. "They were Ida Mae's. She cut off the toes to fit Delilah. They'll be okay."

I stared at Delilah's grubby toes hanging over the edges. "She'll never make it like that."

"She'll be fine," Pretty Boy said. "She's tougher than she looks."

"Great." I squeezed the rocks so hard the sharp edges dug into my palm. "Just great. I don't need any help, thank you. I can do this by myself. So, go back before Ida Mae finds you gone and goes berserk."

"It's too late," Pretty Boy said. "She's already awake by now and searching for us. She'll be awful sore."

"She's going to be a whole lot sorer," I said, "if you don't come back at all."

"Lilah want to go home," Delilah said. She squatted in the gravel, twisting the hem of her dress over her knees revealing tattered white panties.

"It's going to be hard enough getting Willie and me to Weaverton," I said. "It's going to be dang near impossible to get you all there without being seen. Now, go home."

"Actually," Jiminy Cricket butted in, "Ida Mae's not the only one to worry about."

"What'd you mean?" Pretty Boy said.

"If Miss Walker finds us gone," he said, "Ida Mae might be in a heap of trouble."

"How's that?" I asked.

"Miss Walker was supposed to pick some of us up today to take back to the children's home. If she found out Ida Mae let us run off, the government's liable to put Ida Mae in jail. Then they'd dump us all in the orphanage."

"Not me," I tapped the sword against my thigh, "I'm no stinking orphan. I've got family."

Jiminy Cricket bellied his way toward me. "You mean the mama who ran off and left you?"

"She's coming back."

"How do you know?"

"I just do."

"Then why go chasing after her?"

I shoved him, and he stumbled backward, landing in the gravel in an awkward heap.

"You don't have to be so hateful." He flicked a piece of rotten banana off his jeans. "It's not my fault your mama left you."

Everybody stared at me, even Willie. He bent to help Jiminy Cricket to his feet.

"Go back," I growled. "You don't want Ida Mae to go to jail, do you?"

"It's too late," Pretty Boy said. "Miss Walker's meeting Ida Mae first thing this morning. We'd never make it back in time."

"Try."

"Lilah want to go home!" Delilah wailed.

"Will somebody please take her back?" I said. "She'll never make it."

"I'm not going back," Pretty Boy said. He held onto Delbert's shoulder, and Delbert shook his head and crossed his arms, hugging his pad of paper.

"Go back," I ordered, as a car's headlights appeared in the distance, "or I'm going to beat the ever-loving crap out of you."

They stared back at me.

"Crap, crap, crap, crap." Delilah rocked back and forth on her heels, shoulders hunched, arms wrapped around her knees.

"Let them go with us," Willie said.

"No."

The car cruised along the road. It was a shiny black sedan, its headlights searching in the pale dawn light as stealthy as a pair of yellow cat eyes. "I can't take care of you all on the road. I didn't bring enough food or money."

"I got a Mars bar," Jiminy Cricket said and pulled a rumpled candy bar from his pocket.

"I have thirty-seven dollars," Pretty Boy added.

"Thirty-seven dollars?" I said as the car stalked toward us. "Where'd you get thirty-seven dollars?"

"Saved it."

"Doing what?"

"Singing at a little black church in the country. Where we found Delbert."

"You got it with you?"

"Of course."

The car slowed, close enough for me to realize the front passenger window was rolled down. Only one person I knew drove a fancy black car with a blood-red interior. "Quick, everybody behind the Dairy Queen."

"What?" Willie jumped as if he'd been pinched.

"Move it."

Jiminy Cricket grabbed Delilah by the back of her dress and dragged her as we scrambled around the back of the building.

"What's going on?" Pretty Boy said.

"Stay here." I crept along the edge of the low, square building to peer around the corner.

The car stopped along the curb in front. I couldn't see the driver. The engine continued to idle, but no one got out. The smell of sour milk and rotting fruit was nearly more than I could stand.

"We've got to get out of here," I said. "Maybe somebody's seen us. Ida Mae will probably get the sheriff out searching for us."

"I'm not so sure," Pretty Boy said. "If the sheriff knew we were gone, he'd release us over to Miss Walker. Ida Mae wouldn't call the sheriff. She'd call somebody else."

"Brother Muler?"

"Maybe."

"It might be him sitting out front." I clutched my sword. "He's waiting for us to come out." I stared at each kid in front of me. "But we're going to make a run for the railroad tracks. They'll lead us to Weaverton where we'll catch back up with Highway 52.

A car door slammed.

"We've got to go now. On the count of three, we're going to hightail it to the dumpster over there and then slip through the woods until we get to the tracks. Ready?"

"Lilah go home," Delilah said, her bottom lip quivering, her bell jingling.

"Too late now, Tinkerbell."

Footsteps crunched gravel on the other side of the building. I raised my fingers. "One. Two. Three. Go!" And I took off running like my butt was on fire. I reached the bin first, with Willie right behind me. Delbert pulled up with Pretty Boy, as Jiminy Cricket arrived huffing and puffing, red-faced, with Delilah dragging her stupid heels.

"She's going to get us caught," I hissed at Willie. We were barely able to squeeze behind the dumpster, even huddled together, without being seen. I peered around the corner of it. The back of the Dairy Queen lot was empty. Had I imagined footsteps?

A dark figure darted to my left, a blur, and then it was gone. Maybe my eyes were playing tricks in the early morning gloom. The stench of sour milk was overwhelming behind the dumpster. Flies buzzed our ears.

"Go," I said, and we ran toward the line of pine trees separating the railroad tracks from the road. "Stay low." I used my sword to cut through the weeds. "And blend in. At least until we get out of town." Hunkered close to the ground, we stumbled our way through fallen pinecones and broken tree limbs toward Weaverton.

hot on mama's trail

A few miles out of Haley, we left the protection of the trees to hike along the edge of the railroad tracks, our feet shuffling through dusty gravel. Brother Muler probably couldn't see us from the road. But the going was slow.

Pretty Boy kept tripping over railroad ties and loose rocks, even with his stick tapping ahead and Delbert guiding him. Delilah kept wandering off to chase butterflies and dragonflies. As we ground up miles, the slow pace chewed my insides.

"Lilah hungry," Delilah said. The sun had burned away the last of the night's fever, leaving the sky pale and cloudless.

"Later," I said.

"Lilah hungry." She pushed past Jiminy Cricket to grab my knapsack.

"Hey." I snatched it from her. "Cut it out."

"You should probably give her something to eat," Pretty Boy said. He wiped at the sweat trickling along his jaw. "Ida Mae has her on a pretty strict schedule."

"Well there's no schedule here except mine." I slapped at her groping hand. "I didn't ask her to come, and I ain't stopping every time one of you yahoos gets the urge. I'm trying to get someplace important, and I can't afford to spend the livelong day doing it."

We trekked along with the crickets thrumming in the weeds filling the silence. Something tugged on my knapsack.

"Get away, will you?" I pushed Delilah's chest. She stumbled into Jiminy Cricket, but he continued walking, head down. She didn't cotton to that.

"Meanie Lynn hurt Lilah." She rubbed her chest. "Lilah tell Ida Mae."

"It's not Lynn, it's Flynn," I said. "And Ida Mae can't do nothing for you now." I hugged the knapsack to my chest, feeling the hard edge of my sword inside it. "Tell whoever you want. Flag down the sheriff. He'll send you back to the orphan home."

"Stop it," Pretty Boy said. "You'll scare her."

Her lip quivered, and her eyes filled with tears.

"She started it."

"She's just hungry." Pretty Boy stared past me. "Can't you give her something to eat?"

"No. Because I said no. If I changed my mind and said yes, she'd realize she could get away with anything." A crow cawed overhead. It flapped its black wings and soared from a tree branch to rest on the telephone line. "I'm the leader." I squinted along the train tracks. "And I say we press on. Anybody who doesn't want to follow me can go back. Hike to the Dairy Queen and call Ida Mae. She'll come and get you. I'll give you the money to call."

Delilah sniffled. Everyone else remained silent.

"Then we'll keep going," I said. "We're never going to get there if I'm forced to keep stopping and lecturing you people."

As I whirled around, a movement in the trees past Pretty Boy's head caught my eye. It was big enough to be an animal. Maybe a deer. Or a person.

"Any of you yahoos tell anybody where we're going?" I asked. They stopped and stared at me.

"We don't even know where we're going," Pretty Boy said.

"Why?" Willie swiped at a buzzing fly.

I studied the trees behind us. "You keep going. I'm going to hang back a little."

"What's wrong?" Willie dropped back, sidling next to me. The others tramped ahead. Only Pretty Boy glanced backward.

"Nothing," I said. "Something keeps popping out of the corner of my eye."

"A bird? An animal?"

"Something big and dark. Maybe a deer. I've been having this crazy feeling we're being followed."

"We were being followed. By them." He nodded at the others.

"Yeah, but I've still got the feeling. Prickles on the back of my neck. Tingling in my arms. I had it at the Dairy Queen, and I've still got it." I tugged my knapsack closer around me and fumbled for the hard edge of my sword. "Go on ahead." I nodded. "Lead the others. I'll stay back and keep an eye on things. And Willie..."

He turned. "Yeah?"

"Keep them moving, okay?"

He frowned, but pushed his way to the front of the pack.

I held back for thirty minutes, trying to catch a glimpse of whatever was following us. I didn't catch hide nor hair of anything out of the ordinary. When I caught up with the rest of them they were plodded along, slapping at mosquitoes and tripping over railroad ties. The grumbling was never-ending.

"I'm hot."

"I'm tired."

"I'm hungry."

"When are we going to be there?"

"I'm thirsty. I gotta pee."

"How can you be thirsty and have to pee at the same time?" I asked, suspecting they just enjoyed complaining.

We finally found a spot in the shade along a strip of trees between the road and the railroad tracks. I dropped onto a tree stump, and they dropped to their knees in front of me, as if awaiting manna from heaven. I rifled through my knapsack and brought out the canteen. Delilah licked her lips and swayed on her knees like a snake being charmed.

"Listen," I said, "everybody gets a small sip. We've got to make it all the way around at least once." I locked eyes with each one in turn. "I have no idea when we'll come upon a gas station or a store. We've got to make it last."

I handed the canteen to Willie on my right. He took a swig, swiped his mouth, and passed it to Delbert. Delilah clapped fast until the canteen reached her, and Jiminy Cricket had to yank it from her before she nearly gulped it dry.

"I told you." I glared at her.

She stuck out her tongue.

"Keep it up, Tinkerbell. You won't be getting any food," I said.

She dropped her head and hugged herself. "Lilah want food."

"You bet you do. Now, I've got three slices of bacon. There are six of us. Everybody gets a half."

"Only a half?" Willie said.

"Stop bellyaching. I only planned for me. But I also have three biscuits. Three get tops, three get bottoms." By the time the last biscuit was handed out, the food was gone.

"We need more food," Pretty Boy said as we packed our things.

"Yeah," I said. "But we've got to get somewhere first."

As we lumbered along the train tracks in the wet, sweltering heat, something lay dead somewhere. I couldn't see it, but I sure smelled it. Dead and rotten and stinky.

But the shadows of the woods surrounding us were alive with the chirping, humming, strumming of insects and birds. It was as if the grass, the weeds, the wildflowers thrummed to life. Some of the smell was fresh and green and weedy, the smell of summer, sweet as freshly-mowed grass. But something else lurked, too, something dead and dark and decayed.

A bird rustled in a tree overhead, shimmering the leaves. Or maybe it was a squirrel. The buzzing of bees, horseflies, and dragonflies filled my head. A faint crunch of bark was stripped from a tree. The dry spring had left the leaves of the maples splotched brown.

The air was still. The sun, white enough to blind. I saw nothing but a glow of green when I glanced away from it.

Weeds and wheat stalks with feathery heads brushed our shins. Delilah insisted on touching each one, her fingertips trailing along their downy heads, maybe recognizing her own kin. What was she, anyway, but a stalk, a weed, with nothing but fluff filling her head?

She couldn't manage to keep pace. She lagged behind, bending to pluck a purple flower, finger a stalk, study a rusty leaf.

"They're just weeds," I called to her.

"Pretty." She twirled a sprig of tiny purple flowers between nail-bitten fingers. A dragonfly, bottle green, flitted against my cheek. I shooed it away.

"You know," Jiminy Cricket said, "dragonflies don't live for more than twenty-four hours." He tugged his shirt over his white belly. It rode up again.

"How d'you know?" Willie said. He jumped to catch the dragonfly, but it darted back to me.

"Read it in a book."

"That's stupid." I swiped at it, humming in front of my nose, and missed. "Why would God make something that didn't live more than a day? That's plain mean."

"It's cool," Pretty Boy said. He cocked his head toward the whir of its wings. "Think about it. You have twenty-four hours to live. You wouldn't waste it on anything stupid or unimportant."

"You mean like flitting around and bothering the heck out of somebody who might squash you hours before your blip of time ends?" I swatted at the insect. It zigzagged between us before darting away. Pretty Boy turned away.

"Lilah love pretty flies," Delilah said as a blue one lit on her shoulder. It flexed its wings. She blew softly on it, and it zipped away.

"Stupid dragonflies," I muttered and trudged on. The sun scorched our heads as the curve of the train tracks shimmered in the distance. I swiped at the sweat trickling into my ear. Before long, the grumbling commenced.

"I'm hot."

"My feet hurt."

"Can't we rest?"

"No, we can't rest." I slapped at a mosquito buzzing my ear. "We already rested. How are we going to get anywhere if we keep stopping?"

"I wish I'd never come," Jiminy Cricket said. He slapped a mosquito dead on his fat white arm, leaving a red welt and a smear of blood.

"You can still go back," I said. "It's not too late." I swatted as a mosquito buzzed my head. "Nobody asked you to come. You could be swatting mosquitoes back at the clothesline or in the cornfield, having so much fun doing chores and every blame thing Ida Mae tells you to." Our feet clomped along the side of the railroad tracks.

"Go ahead," I said. "Go back. You haven't come too far."

"Leave him be," Pretty Boy said. "He's just hot. We're all hot."

"I'm hot, too," I said. "And I'm the one carrying all the weight." I shifted the backpack on my shoulders. "And I'm the one who's got to feed you people and figure out where we're going."

As everybody stumbled along, eyes down, I remembered the awful camping trip Daddy took us on one summer. Mama complained the whole time. It rained day and night, so we had to sleep in damp sleeping bags. The fish we caught after Willie's line got tangled with Daddy's never got done, so we ate raw catfish over a soggy campfire. By the time we returned home, nobody was speaking to nobody. I sighed.

"We've got to be getting to Piney Grove soon," I said. "It's twenty miles from Haley, and I figure we've gone at least eighteen."

"I bet it's twelve o'clock," Jiminy Cricket said. "I can tell by the position of the sun in the sky." He stared hard at the white ball, shielding his eyes. Then, the idiot, blinded by the glare, staggered into Willie, who banged into Pretty Boy. And the whole troop nearly toppled like dominoes.

"I can tell by the grumbling in my belly," Willie said, pushing Jiminy Cricket off of him. "We've got to get somewhere soon," he said to me. "You sure you ain't got more food?"

"What about you?" I said. "You got a bag of circus peanuts." Everybody swiveled to stare at him.

"I'm saving them." He clutched his stomach protectively where he'd hidden them inside his shirt. "Until after lunch."

"Give 'em up," Jiminy Cricket said.

Everybody crowded around, greedy fingers grabbing, until Willie cried out, "Hey, get off my foot. Stop shoving."

As it turned out, a bag of circus peanuts doesn't go as far as you'd expect, especially with six mouths to feed. We each got four, and we drew blades of grass for the last one. Jiminy Cricket won it, but Delilah snatched it out of his hand and crammed it in her mouth before anyone could stop her.

"No fair!" I cried and jabbed my finger into her bony shoulder. "You play by the rules, Tinkerbell, or so help me, I'll flag down Brother Muler and turn you in myself."

She commenced to bawling, and orange slobber oozed out of her mouth and smeared her chin. Delbert dabbed at it with his handkerchief.

Her wailing ended in hiccups, which caused her to drink what little was left of the water in the canteen. And after watching orange slobber trickling into the canteen, I wanted to chuck it anyway.

"That's it." I crammed the empty canteen into my knapsack. "We've got to find a gas station soon." They shrugged and stared into the distance, making me want to slap every last one of them, including Willie.

a real pig of a place

Twenty miles out of Haley, so parched we could barely talk, we entered the city limits of Piney Grove, population 675. The town appeared to consist of one gas station, Moe's Quick-n-Go, a barbecue joint called The Rusty Pig, and a few houses lining the road. They were shacks, really, ones that could've been built sometime during the Civil War.

The Rusty Pig wasn't much more than a cement block of a building with a crooked sign with the 'i' missing. I guess it might've as easily been named The Rusty Pug. We stepped inside the diner, which was cool and dark and smoky.

Past the checkout counter to our right, three men at the lunch counter in trucker hats pulled low and bellies hanging over their workpants hunkered over piles of shredded pork and greasy fries. The man closest to me sopped barbecue sauce with a piece of loaf bread and crammed it into his grizzly mouth. A few customers glanced our way.

Beyond the lunch counter, meat roasted on a grill, flames licking pink flesh and charring it black. A man hunched over the flames in a splattered apron. When he straightened to stare at us, he was so tall his head nearly touched the ceiling. The sleeves of his t-shirt were rolled to reveal a dragon tattoo on a bicep nearly as big around as Delbert.

A gum-chomping waitress wearing a black hairnet and a frown slid toward us. Heavy black gunk lined her eyes, giving her the appearance of a sad raccoon. "What'ch you young'uns want?" she said.

Her attention landed on Delbert as she fumbled in her uniform pocket for a pad of paper. She peered over her shoulder at the cook, now coming toward us clutching a pair of crusty tongs.

"Lunch," I said. Watching him approach, I backed away and bumped into Willie as the man towered behind the woman.

"Not today." He stared at Delbert, his tongs dripping grease onto the sawdust floor.

"But we're hungry," I said. "We've got money."

He squinted as he pressed a meaty palm into the checkout counter next to the register. "I said not today."

"Ern," the woman worked her jaw, popping and cracking her gum. "They's just kids." She tapped a ballpoint pen against her pad of paper. "Let's let 'em eat, real quick-like."

"Why can't we eat?" I glanced between the two of them. "I said we've got money."

"I already seen what you got," the cook lowered his nose to mine to reveal the bloodshot meanness in his eyes. "You got some of the wrong kind with you, that's what you got. The kind we don't serve here."

Smoke hovered in the air, and the sound of forks and spoons stopped scraping plates. It appeared as if everyone in the room paused to listen.

"The wrong kind?" I snorted. The smoke watered my eyes and Delilah whimpered behind me. "They're harmless," I said. I turned to study our raggedy band of misfits.

Pretty Boy, Delilah, Jiminy Cricket, and Willie, huddled

close to the door, their bodies limp from the heat. Delilah, known to pitch a mean fit, rested her head on Pretty Boy's shoulder.

"We won't cause any trouble." I faced the cook. "We'll eat and then go." I thumbed the sweat trickling down my jaw.

The barbecue roasted. Fat dripped and spit on the open flame. I could practically taste the smoky flavor hanging in the air. I wanted barbecue so bad I licked my lips just smelling it.

"You're already causing trouble." The cook jutted his chin over my head. "Bringing him in with you." He folded his arms over his grease-splattered chest.

"Ern," the waitress scooted behind the counter, "just this once. There ain't no need…"

I didn't hear the rest of what she said. I followed his glare behind me to find Delbert staring out the window, then studying his feet, his paper and pen clutched in his fist. In the silence, he started scribbling on the paper.

"Him?" I snorted at the kid who was little more than half my size and scrawny as a newborn colt. "You reckon Delbert's going to cause trouble?"

"He is trouble," the man said, "like all his kind."

"Ern…" the waitress pleaded from behind the cash register.

Angry, staccato sounds erupted behind me. Then scratching on paper.

I glanced around the man to survey the room and realized for the first time every face watching us, or pretending to study their food, was as white as the day was hot.

"He doesn't even talk," I said and blinked at the big man.

"There's some divine justice." He glared back at me. "Like I said, he's a problem. And I don't like repeating myself. You better go, and I mean now."

Delbert stood, hunkered over the pad of paper, scratching, clawing, scrabbling out words. Angry words. Thick, black words lined and underlined. A page covered with ink fluttered to the ground.

LEEVE ME ALONE

leeve me alone

LEEVE ME ALONE

OR ELSE!!!

Pretty Boy tugged on my sleeve, but I shook him off. I refused to concede I was going to miss out on lunch because of some skinny black kid.

"You retarded, boy?" The cook bumped me backward with his big belly. "Didn't you hear what I said?" I stumbled into the group and Delilah muttered some strange, high-pitched nonsense.

"Let's go," Pretty Boy hissed in my ear. "We'll find someplace else."

"You bet your scrawny butts you'll find someplace else." The man's head pumped on his bull neck. "This is my restaurant. My daddy built it and give it to me. And I say who eats here and who don't. And we don't let no ash-faced, nappy-haired—"

Papers fluttered at my feet. "Are you kidding me?" My voice came out louder and shriller than I'd meant. Perhaps the hunger and smoke clouded my head. Grease hissed and spit into the fire. The waitress popped her gum and clicked her pen furiously. Delbert scratched feverishly behind me.

"This is the 1970s, mister," I said, "in case you haven't noticed. You can't keep black folks out of businesses. It ain't legal. It ain't right."

"Boy," the man thundered, "I can do whatever the hell I

want. You don't like it, go find the sheriff. He'll run you riffraff out of town so fast..."

"Riffraff!" I strangled my fists at my sides.

"Flynn," Pretty Boy fumbled for my sleeve, "let's go." Delilah mewled behind us.

"And take your bunch of freaks with you!" the man thundered.

"Ernie," the waitress said, "your heart, your blood pressure." She sunk so far behind the counter you couldn't see much more of her than her dark eyes and the top of her head. She turned those sad, bleeding, vampire eyes on me. "Boys, you best go."

Delilah flinched away from Delbert's flying pages. He scrawled like mad, the anger so full inside of him it appeared his blood bubbled just beneath his dark skin. Veins bulged in his neck. His hand scratched fast over the paper.

Paper flew. And flew. Splattering in every direction, limp doves sliding to the ground, tumbling at our feet. Page after page.

I plucked a few from the floor. They repeated the same thing. HATE HATE HATE HATE

Delbert's little body was wound tight, one fist curled and bearing down on the pad, the other wrapped around the pen moving in a blur.

"What's he doing?" Pretty Boy said.

I raised a sheet. "Writing."

"Writing what?"

"Hate. Over and over again." I bent to retrieve another. *"BACK OFF OR ELSE!"*

"Or else what?" Willie said. He'd gone wide-eyed as he stared at Delbert's flying fist covering the page with pure, raw emotion.

"He ever done this before?" I asked.

Pretty Boy shook his head. "He just draws pictures. He's an artist."

"He's a nut." Jiminy Cricket looked like he was about to hurl.

A white page fluttered at my feet. I stared at the heavy black words.

you crazy bich! I kill you iswearkill you kill kill kill

I blinked at the words. They weren't Delbert's words. His hand had slowed so that his marks were deep, heavy, gouging through the paper, ripping it.

"What'd you say happened to his mama?" I whispered to Pretty Boy as a page floated and landed in front of me.

WONT LEEVE ME

YOU AND YOUR RETARD KID

kill kill kill kill

"Pow!" Delbert shouted. And I jumped backward. We stood, stunned. It was the first sound to erupt from his mouth all summer.

My cheeks burned from the smoke, or the heat, or the stares boring into me. "What the—"

"Out!" The owner's voice rattled the dishes. The man at the end of the counter jumped, knocking the ketchup bottle off the counter, and it shattered on the floor.

I didn't wait to watch him sop up the bloody mess because somebody grabbed my collar and hauled me out the door. "And take your crazy coon friend with you!" the man roared as I stumbled into the sweltering air.

The man snatched the papers from the floor and tossed them out the door after us. They fluttered to the gravel where the hot breeze skittered them across the parking lot.

"We got to find the sheriff." I glared at the door jangling behind us. "He can't treat us thataway. We've got rights."

"Forget it," Pretty Boy said. "We'll get something else to eat. The gas station."

My neck burned, my lips burned, my eyes watered. I headed back to the door, but Pretty Boy grabbed my sleeve.

"Let go," I said and struggled against him. And then a thought stopped me. "Okay, you're right. Maybe we can sneak around the back and steal some sandwiches. At least some French fries. That'd teach him a lesson. He can't treat people thataway."

"Where's Delbert?" Pretty Boy said.

I yanked my arm free. Maybe we could slip through an open window, or a back door. I'm Kudzu Man. I'd use my most secretive, covert operations to sneak in and—

"Where's Delbert?" Pretty Boy yanked my arm hard enough to bring my head around.

I glanced around. "Over there." I jerked a thumb at the boy chasing papers across the parking lot as cars whizzed by.

"Where?" Pretty Boy stared past me.

I huffed. "There. Trying to catch the papers that jerk tossed out."

"How close is he to the road?"

I eyed the gas station across the highway. It was probably better than nothing. But my mouth sure was watering for a nice, juicy—

"How close?" Pretty Boy's bark snapped my head around.

"What? I don't know. A couple of feet."

Jiminy Cricket and Willie attempted to calm Delilah, who fluttered her hands like bird wings and mumbled, "hungry, hungry, hungry."

Pretty Boy tapped his stick toward Delbert. It caught in an empty cardboard drink carton, and he stumbled, barely catching himself before he fell.

"Wait," I said. But he kept going.

"Tell him to stop," Pretty Boy said as he staggered toward Delbert.

"What?" I stalked after him.

"Stop him."

A car whizzed by, but Delbert ignored it as his papers scattered across the road. I grabbed ahold of Pretty Boy's arm. He jerked away from me. The next car was little more than a speck on the straight stretch of road.

"Grab him," Pretty Boy said, his fingers outstretched as he staggered forward.

"Grab what?"

"Anything. Just get a hand on him."

"What for?"

The car grew bigger, shiny and black. A four-door sedan. For a second, I thought it might be Brother Muler barreling toward us. Delbert headed for the fluttering papers in the middle of the road. I glanced at Pretty Boy. He was as close to the road as Delbert.

"Step back," he said to Delbert.

Delbert paused, fixated on his papers now lying still in the center of the lane. Pretty Boy stumbled toward him, but he was nearly to the road. Delbert ignored him. The car sped toward us.

"Stop," I told Pretty Boy. "You're too close to the road." But he continued as if he was going to stumble right out in front of the car. Sunlight flashed off its shiny chrome grill.

Delbert clutched his pad of paper in one hand, a fistful of

crumpled sheets in the other, his skinny arms so tight the veins bulged. The car was coming fast. Too fast. He ignored it, his focus solely on his lost emotions, soon to be splattered in the middle of the road.

Pretty Boy lunged, and I had no time to do anything but snag the back of his shirt and yank hard. "Let gooooooooo!" he hollered as he fell backward. And the rest was in slow motion, like a Polaroid picture where the photograph is green and blurry, then everything bleeds into place.

Pretty Boy lay in the dust as Delbert stood on the edge of the road, balancing on his toes. And I realized what he was about to do. Desperate to take back the raw emotions he'd spewed, he was crazy enough to think he could rescue and stuff them back inside.

The car roared closer, but he lunged anyway. I dove for him as he sailed toward the blur of black metal.

My stomach and right shoulder took the shock of asphalt and gravel and tangled legs. The car blared its horn as I rolled over and over, Delbert's knees scraping my chest, his shoe popping me hard in the mouth. I lay on my back, tasting dirt and rocks, shoe leather, and blood.

"Holy crap!" somebody yelled. But I was too afraid to open my eyes. At the scuffling above my head, I rolled onto my side, not sure where I was. The pain in my ribs sucked the breath from me. When I opened my eyes, all I saw was feet. Willie's high tops, Jiminy Cricket's worn out tennies, Delilah's dirty toes. I spit grit and blood onto the side of the road.

Nobody screamed, which was a good sign. Delbert crawled into the shade of a parked Buick, hugging his pad of paper as he rested his head onto a mud-splattered fender. His jeans were torn. One knee was scraped and bleeding.

I rolled onto my knees, and pain shot through my belly. I sucked in air as I lifted my shirt. The scrape against my ribs was raw and oozing blood.

"You alright?" On his knees, Pretty Boy reached for me and grabbed my ankle.

"Yeah." I slid my foot out of reach.

"Delbert?"

I peered at the kid. He stared at his bloody knee.

"He's alright. I think."

I groaned as I struggled for footing. I grabbed Pretty Boy's elbow and helped him up.

"You're hurt," he said.

"A scrape." But my knees were so wobbly and my hand shaking so bad I couldn't manage more than to push him in the direction of the stupid kid who almost got us killed. "Help him."

"Freaking far out," Jiminy Cricket said, staring after the car where it disappeared along the strip of road. Willie studied my scrape. And Delilah rocked on her heels, arms wrapped tight around her, having been finally, successfully, shut up.

snakes alive

We entered the gas station, and I sighed at the air conditioner perched in a window roaring at maximum speed. It helped clear the smoke clinging to us. We bought saltine crackers and Vienna sausages and bottled co-colas.

While the others hunched on the curb and wolfed down their lunch, I rinsed circus peanut drool out of the canteen and filled it with water from the outside faucet.

Then we filled our glass soda bottles. There'd be no waste this time around.

The way I figured it, it'd taken the entire morning to walk twenty miles. It'd take us another four or five hours to walk fifteen more. But we'd still arrive in Weaverton with plenty of time to find the fairgrounds and Mama and Sunny before the pageant began.

It occurred to me that Brother Muler might not be following us to take us back to Ida Mae. He might be following us so we'd lead him straight to Sunny. So we continued along the railroad tracks, but kept the road in view as best we could.

Traffic after lunch was light and lazy, and I stayed on the lookout for the black sedan and even the sheriff. Brother Kaine might've given us away by now, reporting my questions to the authorities. But mostly the road was clear, except for a pickup truck or two loaded with watermelons or a station wagon with a bunch of kids hanging out the window and hollering at us.

We were a good seven hours out of Haley when I realized the stiffness in my neck had eased, and I hadn't given a single thought to the monster in quite awhile. The scrape on my belly burned, and my ribs throbbed, but for the first time in a long time, I felt free.

"There's a train coming," Pretty Boy said. He stopped and stared behind us.

"I don't hear anything." I peered along the tracks. "Don't see anything, either."

"Feel it." He squatted on the tracks and pressed a palm to a blistering rail. "Close your eyes and feel the tremor."

We squatted on the tracks, and I closed my eyes. The hot metal vibrated, and the faintest sound of a whistle blew in the distance.

I stood. "Everybody off the tracks. I've got no idea how long it'll take the train to get here, and I don't want anybody catching a shoe in the tracks like in the movies. I've got no time for anybody losing a leg today."

Delilah stepped out of her slippers and wiggled her dirty toes. "Now Lilah got no shoes."

"Put those slippers back on," I said. "Everybody off the tracks. Now. Move it."

When the train finally appeared, rumbling along the rails, it was a long dusty line of boxcars. From the shade of the trees, we counted nearly fifty. One from Wisconsin, one from South Carolina, Bridgeport, Maine, and a coal car from Jasper, Alabama. There were more cars the color of red Alabama mud than any other color. We waved at the engineer hanging out of the caboose when he finally rumbled past.

With the train fading into the distance, we strolled along the edge of trees, keeping to the shade. Delilah and Jiminy Cricket were already pink from the sun, and Willie staggered along with a dazed look.

A few miles outside of Philcrest, our protection of trees ran out. We crossed a field and a dirt road and happened upon a junkyard full of rusted, wrecked cars. Empty cans of motor oil and Schlitz malt liquor beer lay scattered among abandoned washing machines. An old timey ice box lay on its side, its door rusted and yawning open. Along the edge of the yard, a shingled gray shack listed to one side.

Willie took off running to inspect one of the cars up close. It had no doors and the foam innards of the front seat spewed out. He slid behind the wheel, and Jiminy Cricket hovered nearby.

I surveyed the area. We were barely off the highway and out in the wide open. "Hey, y'all," I said, "we've got no protection here. Somebody might drive by and catch us."

"Aw, come on," Willie yelled twisting the wheel as hard as a race car driver. "Maybe a few minutes? We haven't had any fun all day."

Without waiting for me to answer, Delbert led Pretty Boy to another car. It was minus tires and doors, and the roof was peeled back like the popped top of a sardine can.

"Maybe a minute," I said as a dump truck rumbled along the road. It passed, and the driver, a boy who didn't appear much older than me, waved. I tugged on the straps of my knapsack and strolled to the abandoned cars as Delilah wandered off to poke around a washing machine.

Delbert slid behind the wheel of the car, and Pretty Boy pushed him aside. "Let me drive."

"You can't drive," Jiminy Cricket said.

"I can drive this one." Pretty Boy grinned as he shot up straight and ran his palms along the dashboard.

"You already crashed," I said. "You took your hands off the wheel."

"Yeah." He squirmed in the seat. "But I'm a race car driver. I'm used to crashing."

"You're never going to be a race car driver," Jiminy Cricket said. "It's stupid to pretend you are."

"What's wrong with pretending?" I said. "Don't you ever pretend you're something you never got a chance of being?"

"Like a Navy SEAL?" Jiminy Cricket pressed his fat face toward mine.

"That's for real." I gripped the straps of my knapsack.

"So you say."

"That's right. I do say."

"What makes you so all fired sure you're gonna be some hot shot Navy SEAL anyway? There's a lot safer ways to get all that glory."

"It ain't about the glory."

"The danger, then."

"It ain't about the danger, neither."

"Then for crying out loud, what's it about?"

I remained mute.

"What's it about?" Pretty Boy said.

I stared at the railroad tracks in the distance.

"What's it about, hot shot?" Jiminy Cricket taunted.

"They don't leave nobody behind," I said.

"What?"

"My daddy left me. My mama left me. At least it's one damn group of somebodies who won't leave me behind."

Jiminy sniffed, his nose in the air. "I used to be gung-ho like you. At my school in Cincinnati, I played baseball. I was going to be a famous first baseman. I was the best batter on the team. Before life gave me one big fat kick in the butt."

I laughed. "Now you've got more butt to kick." But nobody laughed with me. "Anyway," I said, "you're too fat to be a baseball player."

"Am not."

"And you've got weak ankles. You couldn't get to third base if somebody lit your butt on fire."

Jiminy stared at the strip of white belly showing beneath the hem of his shirt. "Maybe I've gained a few pounds." He tugged on his shirt, but it inched its way up again. "I didn't use to be this big. After Mom and Pops died, they just kept bringing food to the house."

"Who?"

He shrugged. "People. People from church. People from Pops' dentist office. Chicken casseroles, and mashed potatoes, and macaroni and cheese, and cakes. Good grief, every woman in church brought a cake. And they kept feeding me. And I guess when I was eating, I didn't miss Mom and Pops so much."

I couldn't imagine how a stupid cake could take the place of Mama or Daddy.

"But when they shipped me south to live with Pops' sister," Jiminy said, "she took one look at me and said she didn't want me. And so I kept on eating. And I didn't feel so sad about nobody wanting me. Then when Ida Mae took me in, she kept feeding me, too."

"Fattening you up," I said.

"Huh?"

"Never mind." I kicked a pebble, and it bounced off a flat tire. I left them at the car, poked around a bit, and kicked some tires. I didn't have a good feeling about hanging around. I studied the sun, high in the sky. We'd wasted too much time already.

"Watch out," I called to Delilah as she wandered into a patch of weeds. "It looks pretty snaky over there."

As she pretended to wash clothes in the old washer, something rustled behind the burned-out car beyond her. I clutched my knapsack and reached out.

"Come out of there," I said. "Now."

With her lower lip poked out, she let me take her arm, and we headed back toward the others. The metal of a car door squealed, then slammed. A gray, grizzled head appeared around the end of a busted Volkswagen missing its rear end.

The man's hair was slicked to his head with sweat, but sticking out behind his ears. His face was red with sagging jaws. His eyes, small, dark, and quick. They squinted at us.

The man's body was wiry with a bit of a pot belly, like a military man too long out of the war. His arms were skinny and burned by the sun with a tattoo of a snake slithering along an upper arm. His undershirt was stained with what appeared to be a week's worth of lunch. His boots were thick and dusty and missing their laces. And wrapped around his wrist was a real-live, diamond-backed snake with a faded orange head.

I shoved Delilah behind me.

"You there," the man said and stabbed a finger at me, "what'ch you young'uns doing on my property?"

"N...nothing," I said. "We just stopped to rest a minute. We're headed to Weaverton." I backed up and tripped over

Delilah. I staggered a few steps. "We didn't mean to trespass. We'll get going."

"Oh, it don't matter." The man waved his free hand. His grin showed two front teeth missing. "This ain't actually my property. I just sleep here with the cars. Keeps the rain off me and my pet boa. He's a constrictor. His name's Luther. Want to pet him?" He stretched his arm with the snake toward us.

"No." I staggered backward dragging Delilah with me. "No, thanks."

He stroked a finger along the snake's body coiled tightly around his arm. Its head rested on his knuckles. "Luther ain't the friendliest pet I ever had. He done bit me two or three times already. Ornery, is what he is."

"That why your fingers' turning black?" I nodded toward the snake-wrapped hand.

He raised his fingers, along with the snake, and squinted at them. "Yeah, I reckon that's where he got me the first time." His breath sounded wheezy, as if he'd run a long distance. "Wanna pet him?" He pushed Luther toward me.

"No. Not right now."

"Yeah, he ain't too friendly. You know my son, Wally?"

"Huh?"

"You said you's headed to Weaverton. Where my son lives. Wally."

"No, I don't know Wally. I don't know anybody there."

"Then why you going?" He stroked the snake, and it hissed and struck at his fingers. He snatched them back just in time. I dug my fingers into Delilah's arm. The snake settled onto the man's wrist. "You gotta be quick," he said. "Or he'll get you for sure."

"I can see that." I searched for the others.

"Lilah don't like snake." Delilah clung to my arm, her bell tinkling.

"We better get going." My gaze fell on the man's free arm. It looked nearly twice as big as the one the snake hugged. And it was an angry red. "How many times you say you've been bit?"

"Oh," he wiped the sweat beading his brow with his thumb, "maybe three or four. You know my son, Wally?"

"No, I don't know your son, remember?"

"He's a hot shot lawyer in Weaverton." The man stared past me toward the road. A car rolled past. "Walton Jefferson Davis," he said. "His mama named him. I call him Wally. Rolls off the tongue a bit easier."

He scratched an eyebrow with his thumb. "Got a mean wife, though. Bratty young'uns. He's not so bad. Big hot shot. Drives a fancy car. You got any water?" One eyelid drooped. "So hot. So thirsty."

"No," I said, feeling mildly guilty about lying. I was still responsible for getting five kids to Weaverton. "We've got to go now." I pulled Delilah along.

"Hey, what's going on?" Jiminy Cricket appeared behind me, then Willie and the others.

"Nothing," I said. "We're going."

"Who's he?" Willie pointed at the old man.

"Some old crazy guy," I said out of the corner of my mouth and jabbed my head toward the road. "Let's go."

"Coleman," the man said to Willie, his voice cracking so it came out "Cole-man."

"Okay, Mr. Cole Man," I said. "Nice to meet you. We'll be going now." I pushed through the middle of the gang, shoving Delilah at Willie.

"You got a snake wrapped around your arm, mister," Willie said. No one moved to follow me.

"Luther," Coleman said, clenching and unclenching his free hand, "my pet boa." He spread his fingers wide and shook them out.

"You alright?" Pretty Boy said with a cock of his head. "You having trouble breathing?"

"I'm alright," Coleman wheezed. "Just thirsty." He smacked his lips. "I been parched all day. Must be the heat."

"Give him some water, Flynn," Pretty Boy said. "I already finished mine and tossed the bottle. We all did."

"We need it." I clenched my teeth hoping the old man couldn't hear me. With a nod to the washed-out shack, I said louder, "What about the house over there? I bet it's got water."

"No water there," Coleman said. He peered at Willie. "You know my son, Wally?"

"No, sir," Willie said. "You appear mighty hot. You want to sit a bit?"

"He's a hot shot lawyer in Weaverton," Coleman said. "Ain't that where you're headed? Nice fella. Wife's mean as a snake, though."

"Yes, sir," Willie said.

"And them boys of his ain't worth shooting. They laugh and spit at me when their daddy ain't looking." He shielded his eyes as he stared in the direction we were headed. His arm seemed bigger than a few minutes before.

"Come on," I said to the others, nodding toward town.

Jiminy Cricket moved closer to the old man. Not close enough to touch, but closer than the rest of us. "Sir," he said, his own puffy fists propped on his hips between sagging britches and the t-shirt riding over his belly, "that ain't no boa constrictor you got there. That there's a copperhead."

With a hiss of breath, we all stumbled backward, except for Jiminy.

"It's my pet boa," Coleman said and ran fingers along the scaly body. The snake hissed, but didn't strike.

"It's a copperhead," Jiminy Cricket said.

"You sure?" I called out.

"I'm sure," he said over his shoulder, but he kept his attention on the snake. "The triangular head? Orangish color?" He nodded at the old man. "Where'd you find him?"

"Over there," Coleman nodded toward the strip of trees in the distance, "hidden in the leaves. We been buddies for near four days now. Maybe a week. I forget." He squinted at the sun. "You got any water?" He peered back at us. "I sure am parched."

"Flynn," Jiminy Cricket said to me, "this man's been bitten by a copperhead. More than once. We've got to get him to a doctor. Now."

I stared at the old man. "There's no time."

"Give him some water," Pretty Boy said.

"He's sweating pretty good," Willie said.

"Lilah want water, too."

"Shut up and let me think." I grabbed a fistful of hair, slick with sweat.

Jiminy Cricket eased closer to me. "He's going to die if we don't get him to a hospital."

"I've got no idea where a hospital is." I yanked on my hair making my head tingle before letting go.

"Give him some water," Pretty Boy insisted.

"Lilah want water too." She stomped her foot, stirring up dust.

I snatched the canteen out of my knapsack and shoved

it at Jiminy Cricket. He unscrewed the cap and jabbed it at the old man who gulped for a full eight seconds. I counted.

"Hey," I cried finally and he handed it back, wiping his swollen hand against a bristly chin.

"Lilah, now." Delilah snatched it from Jiminy before he could even screw the cap back on.

By the time I got the canteen back, it was unbearably light, and I felt my plans slipping away as fast as water down a snake-bitten throat.

"Where are we?" Pretty Boy said. "There's probably a hospital in the next town. Maybe we can hitch a ride."

"All of us?" I watched the old man's eyes half close as he weaved where he stood. "We probably shouldn't move him."

"We need to suck out the venom," Jiminy Cricket said. "There's at least one set of puncture wounds on his other arm."

"I ain't sucking nothing," I said.

"You're supposed to make an incision at the puncture sight." Jiminy said. "Then suck out the venom."

"We don't have any idea how long it's been since he was bitten nor how many times. His fingers are already turning black, and I ain't putting my mouth on any part of that old man to suck out nothing." The snake hissed at me, and I jumped back.

"Wally?" The old man struggled to open his eyes as he leaned into Willie. Willie staggered under his weight, his gaze trained on the snake.

"We've at least got to get the snake off of him," Jiminy said. He turned to Coleman. "You got anything we can put your snake in?"

"Lu...ser?" Coleman rasped. "He's my buddy." He rested his head on the top of Willie's head, his mouth dropping open, showing the gap in his teeth.

"Yes, sir," Jiminy Cricket said. "We want to make sure your buddy doesn't get hurt. You got anything to put him in? A sack? A bag?"

"You got any water?" The old man's eyes fluttered, then closed.

"Yeah, we got water," Jiminy said. "But first, we want to take care of Luther. You got a bag?"

"Got a pillowcase," the old man's eyes fluttered open. He straightened. "Got no pillow, though. Lost the feathers somewhere back along the railroad tracks. But I got a pillowcase."

"It'll do," Jiminy said. "Can you show me where you keep it?"

With Coleman stumbling over beer cans, they disappeared behind the Volkswagen. We waited for the squeal of the car door and then the slam. When he appeared again, Jiminy Cricket carried a pink pillowcase, covered with faded roses.

"Put him in here." Jiminy held the cotton sack as far away from his round belly as possible.

I held my breath as Coleman lowered his arm into the bag and peeled the snake from it. The snake appeared mighty glad to be rid of his buddy, too. With Luther safely inside, Jiminy twisted the sack closed.

"Alright," I said, "let's go. I'll get Mr. Coleman." I took the arm Luther had clung to. There were two fresh puncture wounds on it, and the wrist appeared to be swelling. "Willie, grab his other side."

Mr. Coleman leaned on me and turned to grin in my face. He stunk of canned tuna. Or maybe cat food.

"Quick as we can, fellas," I said, sucking in my breath and turning away.

"You know my son, Wally?" the man said as we staggered from the junk yard.

a desperate detour

We trooped along the road with Coleman staggering between Willie and me. Jiminy Cricket carried the snake. Delbert guided Pretty Boy.

Delilah lagged behind, her bell a sad, discordant jangle. She stopped to pick black-eyed Susans along the side of the road, tearing off the velvety petals one by one. She chased butterflies into the ditch. Delbert was forced to abandon Pretty Boy more than once to fetch her since she wouldn't let Jiminy Cricket anywhere near her with his new bag of tricks.

"Keep up!" I yelled behind me as Coleman lurched into me. After thirty minutes, I was practically carrying him. His breath was wheezy, like wind whistling through a hole in his chest. His eyes fluttered open now and again.

A car passed, then another. We attempted to flag them down, nearly getting run over in the process. I finally gave up after I saw a sign that read *Philcrest city limits*.

"Come on, we're nearly there." My belly rumbled, and lunch seemed a long time ago.

"What time you figure it is?" Willie said. "I'm mighty hungry. My tummy's growling."

"So's mine." I squinted at the sun. "It's probably three or four o'clock. Hang on a little further."

A gas station appeared in the distance—the Top of the Hill Quick Stop. I sent Jiminy Cricket running ahead to discover where the closest hospital was. Lord knows I didn't want to, but there was nobody else to go.

He shoved the bag of snake at Delbert before taking off running, his weak ankles flailing. After a minute, he slowed to a limping lope, pressing a hand to his side.

He arrived at the gas station and disappeared inside. As we drew closer, he came tearing out of it, his face the color of cooked beets.

"Up... on... left," he gasped.

"Give him some water," I said.

He gulped what little was left in the canteen. "Hospital... between here and Weaverton... just a little further."

"You heard him," I called over my shoulder. "Nearly there." They grumbled as we passed the gas station without stopping. I didn't reckon the old man would make it if we slowed down even a little bit.

We finally limped into the Franklin County Medical Center, straggling through the glass door to the emergency room. A woman in a white uniform and cropped brown hair glanced up from a desk. She frowned at us. We dragged Coleman over to stand before her.

"We need medical attention," I said, bracing myself as the old man leaned into me. "Now." His head lolled around to stare at the receptionist, his tongue hanging out.

"Your daddy drunk?" She squinted at me.

"He ain't my daddy." I studied his sunken face. "And I don't believe he's drunk. He's been bitten by a snake." Delbert dangled the pillowcase over her desk. The nurse shoved herself backward, the wheels of her chair squealing across the slick linoleum floor.

"What's that?" She stared at the bag.

"The snake," Jiminy Cricket said.

"What's going on here?" she demanded.

I surveyed the room behind me. A few people lounged in orange plastic chairs staring at us, their magazines forgotten in their laps. One man sported a bandage over one eye, oozing blood. I winced.

"I told you," I turned back to the receptionist and leaned a hip against the desk. Coleman sagged with me. "This man's been bitten by a snake. More than once."

"A copperhead." Jiminy Cricket nudged my shoulder. I frowned at him before pivoting back to the woman.

"We found him on the side of the road," I said. "He's not doing so good."

"Lordamercy." She wheeled toward her desk and waved at Delbert's bag. "Take that thing away." Poking a button on a gray intercom, she leaned in. "I need a doctor out here, stat." Her unpainted mouth was merely inches from the button. "We got a poisonous snake bite."

"Venomous," Jiminy said.

She glared at him.

"It's a venomous snake, not poisonous," he clarified.

She let the button go and leaned back in her chair. She eyed the bag of snake, then pushed the button again, "And the poisonous snake."

She nodded. "You boys take a seat over there. Somebody'll be right out." I turned to go. "You," she stabbed a finger at me, "you got to fill out some paperwork."

"What kind of paperwork?"

"Name, address, insurance."

"My name's Flynn Bolenn."

"Not your name." She stabbed a finger at Coleman. "His name."

She shuffled through a stack of papers, then shoved a white sheet at me with a lot of writing. She held out a pen which I ignored.

"His name's Coleman," I said.

"First and last."

"*Mister* Coleman."

"I got to have more than that." She peered at me, twig fingers clasped on top of her stack of papers.

"I don't know anything more than that."

"Where's he live?"

"At the junkyard, I guess. That's where we found him."

"Junkyard is not a residence. You can't put that." She noticed me staring at her bony fingers and folded her arms and tucked her hands into her armpits. "You got to tell what town."

"I got no idea what town." Coleman was getting mighty heavy. "Somewhere between Piney Grove and here."

"That ain't an address."

"I said I don't know."

"Well, who's his next of kin?"

I shrugged.

"Who's going to pay for his medical treatment? Somebody's got to pay."

"I've hardly got any money left."

"I've got some," Pretty Boy said. He tapped his way toward our voices. The lady frowned at him.

"I've got money in my pocket." He bumped my shoulder and stopped.

"How much you got?" She narrowed her gaze.

"You can't take money from a blind kid," I said.

The lady's lips screwed together in a wrinkled pucker. "Somebody's got to pay."

"I've got thirty-seven dollars," Pretty Boy said.

"You can't spend your money on somebody you don't even know," I said.

He shrugged.

"It shouldn't take more than twenty-five," the nurse said.

"Twenty-five?" The weight of eyes fell upon me. "That'd leave him with, what, twelve dollars?"

The nurse leaned toward me. "What's a blind kid need with thirty-seven dollars?"

"She's right," Pretty Boy said. He straightened his shoulders and pulled a leather pouch from his pocket. "Mr. Coleman needs it more than me."

"But you earned it."

He shook his head.

I counted out the money and handed it over, giving the nurse the meanest glare I could manage. She ignored it.

"Now," she tapped the form I'd dropped onto her desk, "we have to know what to do with this man once we take care of him."

I scratched behind my ear. "He said he's got a son in Weaverton. Wally somebody."

"A president's name," Willie added, "just can't remember which one."

She ignored him. "Wally Coleman?" She arched an eyebrow as if she'd solved the mystery of the pyramids.

"Probably." I shifted Coleman a little. "Can you get somebody out here now? Or you're going to be peeling him off the ground."

She stared at me for a mighty long minute before stabbing

a claw at the squawk box. "I need somebody out here, stat." She snatched the paper from me and began scribbling. "Have a seat," she said, apparently done with us. "Somebody will be here in a minute."

Not likely, I thought, peering around the waiting room. I stared out the window as Willie and I eased Coleman into a chair between us. The sky outside took on a pinkish glow, and my heart sank with the anticipation of the setting sun.

We were sitting in a row against the wall waiting for the doctor when a tall black man in a white orderly's uniform stopped at the receptionist's desk. He leaned over to speak to her. She said something to him, and they both glanced our way.

His shirt stretched tight across massive shoulders and forearms. He was perhaps the largest human being I'd ever seen up close. Even bigger than the owner of the Rusty Pig.

He stalked over to us and stared at Delbert. "That it?" He plucked the pillowcase from the boy.

"Easy," Willie said. "That's Coleman's pet."

"Pet what?" The man's voice was tumbling gravel. He held the bag away from him without looking in it.

"Snake," Willie said.

"It's a copperhead," Jiminy Cricket said.

The man opened the bag and peered inside. He swirled it closed, and in a flash, raised the bag and *wham!* slammed it against the wooden table next to Delbert. We jumped.

He opened the sack, studied it a few seconds, then closed it again. He handed it back to Delbert. "Ain't no copperhead no more," he said, and walked back through the whooshing emergency room door.

It was a few more minutes before another orderly came to fetch Coleman, who gave us a weak wave with a hand that, if you stuck it with a pin, might pop like a balloon, spewing venom onto the floor. In his other fist, twisted in the faded rose pillowcase, he toted what was left of his buddy, Luther.

a fair bit of trouble

We left the hospital at a jog, but before long, were forced to a walk. By the time we reached Weaverton, the sky's rosy glow bled out and bruised to purple twilight. From a mile away, we watched the lights of the Ferris wheel rise and fall above a line of trees.

We found the Franklin County fairgrounds on the outskirts of town in a huge open field. As we drew closer, the tinny organ music of the merry-go-round drifted toward us.

We topped a hill and stared down at it, spread below us with music, lights, spinning rides, and the Ferris wheel looping up and around in the center of it all. The smell of corn dogs and cotton candy filled the air as we descended the hill. We were an hour late as the pageant was scheduled to start at seven o'clock.

We followed a steady stream of cars and trucks easing onto a narrow dirt road. The back of my neck prickled. I glanced behind us and around, but couldn't make out anything but the dark shapes of the vehicles and their glowing yellow lights.

"Listen, gang," I said over the drunken music of the merry-go-round, "stay together. We've got to find Mama and Sunny first. They'll be somewhere in the middle of the pageant."

Delilah tugged on my shirt sleeve. I ignored her.

"Where do we find them?" Willie said. "Where's the pageant?"

People strolled everywhere. Mamas hung onto snotty-nosed kids, teenage boys chased girls to the Ferris wheel, men with slicked hair and slicker smiles strolled in front of their games, hawking shooting galleries, bell ringing, and ring tossing.

Delilah tugged on my arm. She pointed toward the merry-go-round. "Lilah love horses. Lilah ride."

"Not now," I said. "Maybe later."

"Aw, can't we ride something?" Jiminy Cricket said. "We're at the fair, for crying out loud. Maybe the bumper cars or the Tilt-A-Whirl?"

"Maybe later," I said through gritted teeth. "I said we were late."

Delilah stomped her foot. "Now."

"Not now, Tink. We've got more important things to do."

Delbert reached for Delilah's hand, but she jerked away. I ignored them both and stopped a clown carrying balloons. "The Miss Franklin County Pageant," I said, "where is it?"

He pointed a white gloved finger in the direction of a big striped tent rising above the rides at the other end of the strip.

"Balloon, balloon!" Delilah clapped, her bell jingling crazily.

"Not now," I barked at her. "Come on." I pushed my way through the crowd with Willie behind me. We were a few yards from the entrance to the tent when Pretty Boy cried, "Delilah's gone!"

I stopped, and Willie slammed into my back. "What'd you mean she's gone?" I said. "Who was in charge of her?"

"Delbert," Pretty Boy said. "He grabbed her, but somebody bumped into him, and she slipped away."

Delbert was already heading back in the direction we came. Good grief, a kid who couldn't talk running loose in a place like this, and a girl without a lick of sense.

The sign in front of me said the pageant was in progress. I peeked inside. People were already seated. A line of girls in flowy dresses marched around the stage. I turned back to find Delbert nearly out of sight.

"Willie, go find Mama. Oh, forget it." We couldn't split up now. "We'll have to come back after we find Delilah." Delbert disappeared into the crowd of people. "And Delbert."

We pushed past Pretty Boy, who stood with his head cocked. "Come on." I grabbed him, pulling him along. "We can't afford to lose you, too." We stopped at the hot dog stand where we'd last seen Delbert.

"Dang," I said. "We'll never find them in this crowd." Pretty Boy slid a finger beneath my fingertips digging into his arm.

"Sorry." I loosened my grip.

"He headed left." Pretty Boy nodded in that direction and rubbed his arm where my fingers left a mark. I grabbed his wrist.

"How do you know?"

"His smell. Ivory soap. What's in that direction?"

I peered past him. "The Tilt-A-Whirl, a balloon stand, a bunch of trailers. We're near the edge of the fair."

"Let's go that way," he said.

And because I didn't have a better plan, we passed the Tilt-A-Whirl with kids screaming and slamming into each other, then the balloon stand, where a clown filled balloons with helium from a silver tank.

"What's over there?" Pretty Boy nodded.

"The edge of the fairgrounds," I said. "There's a line of

trailers and motor homes. Maybe where the carnival work-
ers stay. It's dark there. No carnival lights. Maybe a few lit
windows in the trailers."

Pretty Boy stared, a palm feeling the air.

"Wait a minute," I called as he pushed past me. "Where
are you going?"

"Delbert came this way."

"But there's nothing over there."

Jiminy Cricket and Willie huffed alongside me.

"Where's he going?" Jiminy said.

"Pretty Boy, slow down," I called. "They wouldn't be over
there." But he kept going.

"Delbert's here," he called over his shoulder. "Delilah, I'm
not sure."

I trotted to him and took his arm. "At least let me—"

A howl rent the air.

I dragged Pretty Boy through the dark field, weeds slap-
ping our ankles. We slid to a halt at the end of the last trailer.
Jiminy Cricket, Willie, and I peered around the corner of it.
Pretty Boy stood still, head cocked, listening.

In a patch of grass lit by an early moon, Delilah struggled
against the arms of a teenage boy not much bigger than her,
his arms wrapped around her thin chest. A beefier boy stood
guard, his arms folded, his feet planted wide.

Another jerk held a red balloon just out of reach, taunt-
ing, threatening to release it into the air. A grin split his
pockmarked face. His dark hair was tucked, limp and greasy,
behind his ears and hung nearly to his shoulders.

His buddies laughed as Delilah squirmed. It took me a few
seconds to find Delbert, crumpled on the ground, pressing
the heel of his hand against his left eye. Towering over him

was a boy bigger than me and Jiminy Cricket put together, wearing a grungy Grateful Dead t-shirt.

"What do you reckon, RayRay," the boy with the balloon said to the one holding Delilah, "should we give the retard a balloon?" He laughed. "Or should we just *give* it to her?"

RayRay slid a hand beneath the hem of her dress, and Delilah squirmed furiously.

Delbert scrabbled over the ground, but the brute beside him grabbed a handful of his collar and yanked him backward. "You ain't going nowhere, Zulu," he said.

"Stop!" Pretty Boy burst from behind the trailer, clenching his cane. He stared into the space between Delbert and Delilah. "Let them go." He worked his fingers open and closed around the stick.

"Who the hell are you?" Balloon Boy said.

Pretty Boy half turned in his direction. "I said, let them go."

"Make us." The boy stepped toward Pretty Boy, and Pretty Boy pivoted toward him. The boy stopped. Pretty Boy stared straight ahead.

"What do you know?" Balloon Boy said. "We got us here a sure enough freak show, fellas. They must be part of the carnival. Bull's got the dumb Zulu midget who can't talk. RayRay's got the girl retard, and now we got the pretty blind boy who might suit us just as well as the girl. Maybe we can dress him in a pretty little dress, too. Any two-headed twins out there? Dog-faced boys? Who else we got out there in the dark?"

There was nothing to do but show ourselves. Jiminy Cricket, Willie, and I stepped into the moonlight.

"Oh, my gawd," Balloon Boy cried. "We got ourselves a full house. Come on over boys, what's our final count? A dumb darkie, a retarded girl, a blind girlie-boy, a fat slob, another midget, and you." He strolled toward me. "What's your problem?"

I remained silent.

"You deaf? Or just the chief freak?"

We outnumbered them, but I couldn't for the life of me figure out how a blind kid, a girl, and Delbert, who was already hurt, were going to help get us out of this.

"Do something," Willie said.

"What do you suggest?" I hissed back at him.

"Something. You're supposed to be the big hot shot military genius."

I stared at Balloon Boy. "We don't want any trouble," I said. "Let 'em go, and we'll forget all about this."

"Oh yeah?" The boy released the balloon, and it drifted into the air. I watched it float toward the moon. "Forget about it?" Balloon Boy brought my attention back to him. "I ain't forgetting shit."

He stepped toward me as Pretty Boy reached for my arm. Bull yanked back on Delbert's head. Delilah grunted against the arms binding her.

I fumbled in my knapsack for my sword, as something zinged through the air and pinged against the metal trailer wall. I searched behind me for the source. Separated as we were from the carnival, nothing but patches of darkness surrounded the open field.

A thud sounded, and Bull yelped. With a grunt, he dropped his hold on Delbert and fingered the side of his head. Pulling his hand away, he rubbed his thumb against fingers.

"I'm bleeding," he said to Balloon Boy and showed us his palm. "Leroy, somebody just—"

Another *kathump*, and Leroy, aka Balloon Boy, staggered a few steps, holding his head. "What the..."

The boy guarding Delilah grunted and fell flat on his back, legs stretched in front of him, eyes closed. RayRay released Delilah, and she dropped to the ground and crawled through the weeds toward the closest trailer. RayRay kneeled beside his buddy.

"Leroy," he glanced up, "T.C.'s out cold." He snagged a rock next to his buddy's head and showed it to Leroy. It was bigger than a walnut.

"Monty," Pretty Boy breathed, whirling toward the dark field.

"What was that? Who's there?" Leroy called.

RayRay slapped his buddy's cheeks. "Wake up, T.C. Get up. We got to get out of here." Bull left Delbert to lumber over to help T.C. They got him to a sitting position, but his head lolled onto his shoulders.

Leroy bent and raised the ankle of his jeans high enough to whip something out. The knife's blade gleamed long in the moonlight.

I yanked my sword out of my knapsack.

"Leroy," RayRay cried, "the tall one's got a knife, too!"

Leroy stalked toward me. Another *zing*, and he yelped and dropped his knife in the grass. He hugged his wrist to his ribs.

"What the hell's out there?" he cried. "RayRay, Bull." He backed toward the two boys staring into the darkness. He didn't bother to retrieve his knife. "Get T.C. on his feet." He kept his attention on the field.

"He won't wake up," Bull cried. "I think he's dead."

"He ain't dead." Leroy dropped to his knees beside him. "He still breathing?" He pressed against his buddy's chest. "He's still breathing."

I stepped toward the huddle.

"Don't come any closer," Leroy said. "We're leaving. We were just funning with you, anyway. You didn't have to hurt nobody." Lowering his voice, he muttered, "Bunch of stinking retards." A rock pinged off the aluminum siding of the trailer right past his head.

"I don't reckon I'd say anything else if I was you," I said.

Bull and RayRay grabbed the unconscious T.C. under his armpits and dragged him between the two trailers.

Once Leroy was in the shelter of the trailers, he called, "You wait, we'll get you spazzes later."

From the darkness surrounding the field, a black piece of ground arose and moved toward us. Dark, hairy, white-fanged, with razored claws.

"The monster." I raised my sword.

Leroy screamed and nearly knocked over his buddies, racing through the parked trailers toward light and laughter and cotton candy.

"Monty," Pretty Boy said beside me. The dark figure circled around us and stopped to retrieve something from the ground. Leroy's knife. He dropped it at Delbert's feet, who hunkered in the dirt, still pressing his eye socket.

The knife stuck in the ground. Delbert stared at it before yanking it out by the handle.

Monty the Monster stalked over to Delilah, who lay curled tight as a baby under one of the trailers. He crouched beside her, but she scooted away. Willie ran to kneel beside Delbert.

"What's he covered with?" I said. Every inch of the creature was dark. The only thing truly visible was the whites of his eyes.

"Dirt most likely," Pretty Boy said. "Or mud. The darker the better."

I stared at him.

"His daddy was in Vietnam, too." Jiminy Cricket scratched his bare belly between his jeans and shirt.

"He was a high-ranking officer in the army. Lost his entire platoon in a raid. Couldn't get over it so they honorably discharged him. He came back all tore up. Kept having flashbacks and nightmares. But he didn't go crazy until Monty's oldest brother, Mitchell, was killed in action. One night he tried to choke Monty to death, mistaking him for the Viet Cong. They locked him up in the psycho ward at the army hospital. After that Monty's mom hung herself in their living room, where Monty found her swinging. His other brother left to join the Black Panthers or some militant group."

"No wonder he's so nutty," I said. "But why's he cover himself with dirt?"

"Camouflage." Pretty Boy cocked an ear toward the monster.

"But why?"

"Ever have your own daddy try to kill you?" he said.

"But his daddy can't get him now."

"He's fascinated with everything Vietnam," Jiminy said, hitching up his sagging britches. "Like you. His daddy told him stories about soldiers smearing mud and paint and whatever else they could find to camouflage themselves in the jungle."

"Devils with green faces."

"Huh?"

"What the Viet Cong call Navy SEALs," I said. "Because of the camouflage. If his daddy's locked away, what's he still need to hide from?"

"Well, without his mama and daddy and brother," Pretty Boy said, "he thinks it's the only way to protect himself."

I squinted into the darkness. "What's that hanging out of his back pocket?"

Jiminy Cricket peered at Monty trying to coax Delilah out. "Probably his rabbit." He'd gone back to scratching his belly. "He doesn't go anywhere without it. It's the only thing he had when he arrived at Ida Mae's." He stopped scratching. "Guess I'll attend to Delbert," he said, and loped away.

"I never heard of a boy his age carrying around a stupid stuffed animal," I said. "Why didn't somebody tell me? Why'd you let me think he was some monster hiding in the cellar?"

"We told you there was no monster," Pretty Boy said.

"You didn't tell me it was a kid."

"Ida Mae made us promise. She thought you'd tattle, and you did. And Monty would be taken away and stuck in an institution. It would kill him after everything he'd been through. When you thought he was a monster you'd hardly go near the cellar. Well, except when you tried to smoke him out."

"He was howling and clawing and banging like a wild animal," I said. "Obviously he has issues."

"Things run a lot better on the farm when nobody bothers him. We thought it best."

"You let me go to the sheriff with a crazy monster story. I asked Miss Walker about it. You made me look like an idiot."

"You did that by yourself," he said. "You wouldn't listen."

The creature coaxed Delilah a little further out from beneath the trailer, but she shook her dandelion head.

"But Delbert showed me a picture."

I watched Jiminy peer at Delbert's right eye, which had quickly swelled shut. Delbert showed Leroy's knife to Jiminy.

"He drew what you'd been describing," Pretty Boy said,

scratching away a mosquito lit on his cheek. "He was probably telling you he understood what you were feeling. But he gets frustrated when people can't understand him."

"Is he ever going to talk?"

Willie snatched Leroy's knife from Jiminy Cricket and sliced and jabbed the air with it. Pretty Boy shrugged.

"They said he was always a slow learner, maybe dyslexic, but he didn't stop talking until they found him alone with his mama's dead body."

"You better be careful," I called to Willie as he stabbed the knife into the darkness, "before you poke out an eye."

Eyes. "Holy crap." I slapped my forehead. "The beauty contest. Sunny."

"What time is it?" Pretty Boy said.

"No idea. Willie!" I yelled. "Come on!"

"Delilah's still not out," Pretty Boy said. "Sometimes it takes, well, you can't make her do something she doesn't want to do."

Willie trotted over. "What?"

"We've got to get to Sunny."

"We can't leave everybody."

"But," I stared between Pretty Boy and Willie, "we've got to."

"Go," Pretty Boy said. "We'll stay here until you get back."

"What if those losers come back?"

"They don't want to face Monty again."

I hesitated. "We should stay together. Splitting up was how we got into this mess to start with."

"It's your sister." Pretty Boy fumbled for my chest. He shoved. "You've got to protect her. We'll be okay until you get back."

Delbert, Jiminy Cricket, Monty, Delilah, Pretty Boy. What a mess.

"Willie should stay with you," I said.

"Take him. You might need help. We'll be fine."

I glanced at Willie. He shrugged.

"Come on." We took off running, and I yelled over my shoulder, "Don't move! We'll be right back." Pretty Boy waved, and Willie and I raced through the crowd.

The Tilt-A-Whirl, merry-go-round, Ferris wheel, and bumper cars blurred past. I knocked a cone of cotton candy out of a woman's hand as she bent to offer it to her crying daughter.

"Hey." She glared at me.

"Sorry!" I yelled. But I didn't slow down. By the time we reached the striped tent, people streamed toward us.

"No," I said, as we ducked through the doorway. Fighting past mamas and daddies and crying babies, we reached the twenty or so rows of metal chairs set in front of a stage lined with big leafy ferns. A black curtain hung behind the stage with a *Miss Franklin County Fair* sign in gold glitter.

"It's over?" I grabbed a woman dragging a little girl by the arm. The child cried all over her frilly dress.

"It's okay, honey," the mother said. "We'll win next year."

"Is it over?" I tugged on her sleeve. She frowned before yanking her arm out of my grasp. "It sure is. And I've never seen such injustice in all my life."

"Who won?" Willie stuck his head around me.

The woman flicked at her sleeve like she was getting rid of my cooties. "Some girl. Sunshine something. She's not even from around here." The little girl threw her head back and wailed. "I don't blame you, sweet pea," the mother said. "It was rigged from the start. Stupid judges." She patted her daughter's wet cheek.

"Where's the winner?" I asked.

She flinched away from me, her lips forming an ugly line. "Making pictures, I guess."

"I want my picture made!" the girl howled.

"Come on," I grabbed Willie. "We've got to hurry. If she's won..."

We fought our way to the stage, dodging howling girls and angry mamas, and daddies who probably just wanted to go home and suck on a beer. By the time we reached the stage, it was empty of everyone except a man with slick black hair and puffy eyes shuffling papers on the podium.

"You know where the winner is?" I stumbled toward him, tripping over a long black cord.

"Gone." He tapped the stack of papers against shiny wood.

"I heard they were making pictures."

"Done already. You might catch somebody backstage in the dressing room."

"Where's that?"

Willie and I fought our way behind the heavy black curtain and descended some rickety wooden stairs.

Another curtain was strung up, and we clawed our way around it. Willie and I burst into the makeshift room to find a woman beside a girl wearing a small crown packing lipstick, hairspray, and nail polish into a traveling case.

"You seen Sunny Bolenn?" I stumbled to a halt.

"Just missed her," the woman said. "Her mama hauled her out of here so fast she hardly had time to pack her belong-ings. Her mama said 'we got bigger fish to fry, baby.' And the poor girl barely had the crown fixed on her head." She snapped the case shut.

"Aaaaaagh!" I snatched the hair nearly out of my head. The

knapsack I'd been hauling around weighed as heavy as a dead body. I shrugged out of it and thumped it to the ground.

"You might still catch her." The woman hefted the case and reached for her daughter. "They left just a minute ago. Might still be in the parking lot."

The little girl grabbed her mother's hand and smiled at her. "Ice cream, Mommy?"

"Sure, sweetie." She patted her daughter's head. "You done good. Real good."

I snatched the bag off the ground. "Come on," I said to Willie, and we struggled our way back out of the curtain.

The parking lot outside the tent was dark and half filled with cars. We zigzagged around pickup trucks and station wagons and motorcycles, searching for a blonde head with a glittering crown. I spied her seconds later as Mama dragged her along, a dress bag thrown over her arm, makeup case in her grip.

"Mama!" I yelled, trying to dodge cars squealing out of the gravel. A pickup truck backed right in front of me, nearly knocking me sideways. "Hey!" I banged the metal bed. The driver screeched to a halt.

"Listen buddy," the man leaned over a young girl with buck teeth, "I nearly ran you over."

"Move it!" I yelled, and waved my arms wildly. "Move! Move!"

Shaking his head, he eased back extra slow. I raced around the cab, but he cut me off.

"Aaaaaaagh!" I threw my knapsack at the truck, and it grazed off the hood as the vehicle roared forward in a cloud of gravel dust.

"You nearly got run over," Willie gasped behind me. By the time the truck rumbled out of sight, there was no sign of Mama. I ran to where I last saw her. Nothing but empty cars and the smell of exhaust in the air.

"Damn. Damn. Damn. Damn. *Damn!*" I hollered, turning around and around in the parking spot she vacated. Willie limped to me, carrying my dusty knapsack.

Pulling hard on my hair, I stared at the stars, wanting to cry. I was so tired. And we were so close.

Thunder rumbled in the distance.

"We know where they're going, right?" Willie said.

I let my fists drop to my sides as the warm summer night settled over my shoulders. Willie stared at me.

"We know where they're going, don't we?" He nudged his elbow into my arm. I stared straight ahead, still seeing stars.

"Yeah," I said.

"We better get the others," Willie said, "before it rains."

Laughter and carnival music lingered in the air behind us.

"Yeah." I took the bag he held out to me and rubbed away the blurriness. We headed back to the carnival as the sky rumbled overhead.

monster in our midst

By the time we found the others, we'd had enough of the Franklin County Fair. I bought everyone corn dogs wrapped in greasy paper, lemonade, and one stick of cotton candy from which everybody but Monty took a pinch.

Lightning flashed in the distance. Thunder continued to rumble. The air around us stilled.

Cars streamed out of the field as we trudged along the dirt road. They didn't slow for us, and we didn't flag them down. We were beaten soldiers, back on the bloody trail.

We made it to the main road and headed toward Torrence City. Monty the Monster jerked each time lightning flashed. But we had to keep going until we found shelter. Pretty Boy asked Monty how he'd found us.

"Followed you from the farm."

"All the way?" I said.

"Yeah."

"It was you on the railroad tracks?"

He stared at me.

"In the junkyard? At the hospital?"

He shuddered as lightning lit the sky.

"It ain't even close," I said. "Just heat lightning."

"There's no such thing," Jiminy Cricket said.

"Is too." I glared at him. "Like when there's no storm brewing, but lightning in the distance. You see any rain?" Good grief, I was tired of him acting like he knew everything.

Monty hunched his shoulders and hugged his wiry body. The dirt, or mud, or whatever plastered to his face streaked his cheeks, making him appear to be some exotic animal.

"So, your daddy was in 'Nam, too, huh? And your brother?"

I got warning looks from the others.

"What?" I said. "I was just wondering because my daddy's missing over there. The last thing he gave me before he left was his buddy's pocket knife. He asked me to take care of it for him, but I lost it outside the cellar door. Maybe you found it?" I asked Monty. My sword twitched in my fist.

Monty snatched something out of his pocket and reared back his arm.

"Take it easy." I eased the sword back by my side. "Never mind. I just wanted it back. It's important to me."

"He doesn't want to talk about it," Jiminy Cricket said.

"No kidding. I was just—"

"He doesn't want to talk at all," Willie said.

"How do you know?" I turned on him.

"Pretty Boy told me."

"You knew the whole time he was the monster, and you didn't tell me?" We passed the Tasty Freeze drive-in and headed out of Weaverton.

"Ida Mae was worried you'd turn him in to the authorities. She was afraid they'd take him away. He'd already been bounced from one foster home to the next. She was his last resort. And we all knew you'd bother him. Like now."

"Bother him? *Bother* him? He nearly took my head off with

a pitchfork and broke my ribs. And you're worried about me bothering him?"

The monster growled.

"That's what we're talking about," Jiminy Cricket said. "He doesn't like—"

"He doesn't like, *he* doesn't like." I stopped walking and faced them. "I am sick to death of what everybody else doesn't like. What about what I don't like? I don't like my Daddy running off to war and then going missing. I don't like being left with a bunch of damaged kids while Mama goes gallivanting all over creation. I don't like having crazy kids follow me with nothing more than a bag of circus peanuts, a melted chocolate bar, a pad of drawing paper, and a stupid stuffed rabbit and then expect me to take care of them on thirty-seven dollars and seventy-six cents."

They glanced at each other and shuffled their feet.

"I don't like spending the entire day attempting to help some crazy old coot who's so stupid he can't tell a copperhead from a bloody boa constrictor even when it's bit him four times. And I don't like—"

Thunder boomed and drowned me out as lightning fractured the sky. Then, as if the lightning ripped a hole through the stars, rain crashed down.

"Run!" I yelled, and we splashed alongside the highway as water hit us so hard it bounced from the ground to slap us again. In the distance, a plain, whitewashed building huddled under a grove of sprawling oaks, with a simple cross on its dark, shingled roof. It had a small covered porch. "Head for the church!"

I shrugged out of my knapsack and swung it over my head. I wasn't sure why I bothered, as I was already soaked through. We reached the church and huddled beneath the porch's sagging roof.

I yanked on the front door. It was locked.

"Why is it," I said, water dripping from my hair, my ears, my eyelashes, my nose, "that every dadgum time you need a church, I mean really need one, they're always closed?"

"I told you there wasn't any such thing as heat lightning," Jiminy Cricket said.

And I wanted to sock him right in his big, fat mouth.

We crowded together on the porch, shoulder to shoulder, backs to the wall, and watched traffic swish by on the slick-ened highway. There was barely enough room for us to sit, legs stretched out, without getting overly wet.

A pickup truck slowed at the entrance of the church as if it wanted to turn in, then rumbled on. I rummaged through my knapsack for anything salvageable. I passed around the soggy bar of chocolate, too exhausted to break off a piece for myself.

I leaned my head against the church door and stared at the wet, pale faces around me, wondering where all the anger in the world came from. The boiling, raging, bubbling, foaming-at-the-mouth kind of anger. The kind that made a mother slap her child silly. Or leave him.

What scared me most? Feelings I couldn't contain?

What was inside of me, anyway, but dark, hopeless, helpless, gutlessness? The fear of being dragged around by my betters. Foot-stomping, stark-raving madness. The kind of anger that carved up leather seats, broke dishes, hurled a cat up a tree. The sly, sickening, squeezing-every-moment-for-all-it's-worth anger rumbling like thunder and rattling the shutters.

Monster Monty sat on the edge of the porch on my left

and buried his head in his knees. He clutched his rabbit in his fists and jerked at each flash of lightning and splash of a car driving by. He trembled, terrified, not much of a monster after all, just a boy afraid of flashing lights and loud noises.

How bad did his daddy scar him black? I wondered. And his mama, killing herself, too? I stared at his dark head, the silver gleam of his daddy's dog tag around his neck. I couldn't fathom why he wore it, except he appeared to be caught in his own private war—him against the whole world.

"Why'd you follow us, anyway?" I asked him. He murmured something against his knees.

"I said how come you followed us if you're scared to be seen? How come you traveled this far in broad daylight to be with us?"

He lifted his head enough for me to hear. "I stayed in the shade."

"But how come?"

"Leave him be," Pretty Boy said. He rested on my right and leaned his head against the whitewashed boards staring straight ahead. Delilah lay curled like a cat between him and Delbert. She sucked her thumb with her eyes closed. My belly rumbled. I hugged my knees and rested my chin on them.

"I wanted to protect Delilah," Monty said. "You don't care nothing about her. And she deserves better."

Delilah shifted away from Pretty Boy to rest her head on Delbert's shoulder. The heaviness of her breathing indicated she was asleep. And even though Delbert's eyes were closed, and he leaned back against the wall, he most definitely was not.

As the rain hammered the roof over our heads, I puzzled over something that had bothered me since we discovered Monty at the fair.

"If Monty the Monster didn't kill those girls and cut out their eyes, who did? We found blood at Ida Mae's cabin. And a bloody handprint on the cellar door." Cars swished along the slick pavement. Delilah slept, her breath barely a sigh. "Ida Mae? It's her cabin, her property."

"Anybody could've used that cabin, and she'd never know," Pretty Boy said. "She hasn't been there since your grandfather died."

"How do you know? She tell you that?"

"I don't imagine she ever went there when he was alive, either," he said. "And she's no killer."

"Maybe she isn't." I scraped a thumbnail at the mud caked on the side of my high tops. "Then again, maybe she is." I mused on that a minute and said, "Then that leaves Brother Muler."

"Brother Muler?" Willie squirmed and bumped my shoulder. "He's a preacher. He can't kill people."

"Don't be stupid." I scraped the mud out from under my thumbnail with the wet hem of my jeans. "Anybody can kill."

"How do you reckon he's the killer?" Jiminy Cricket said, sprawled between Willie and Monty. Even from the other side of Willie, he stank of mildew and sweat and soured wash.

"What makes you think the killer's even from Haley?" Pretty Boy said.

"I found a map of the state."

"Where?"

"In one of Ida Mae's books." My knapsack lay propped between my outstretched legs. I fumbled inside it for the map I'd torn out of the book. "I marked the places where the girls' went missing." I unfolded it and tried to study the circular pattern I'd drawn in the darkness.

Jiminy Cricket gasped. "You tore that out? Ida Mae's gonna have a fit." He leaned over Willie to stare at the map. "She's gonna tan your hide for sure." His breath was warm and as sour as his clothes.

I shifted away from him. "The marks made a circle. And guess what was smack dab in the middle?"

Pretty Boy stared at me. Jiminy shrugged.

"Haley."

"That doesn't mean it's where the killer's from." Jiminy Cricket squirmed.

I glared at him. "It's got to be his base."

"But Brother Muler?" Pretty Boy leaned into me. "Why?"

"I found newspapers on his desk of the killings. And the picture of Sunny from the newspaper a few weeks ago? It was circled in red."

"But why?" Pretty Boy gazed toward the road where cars continued to swish in the rain. "He started the daycare. None of those kids have gone missing."

"That'd be too close, probably. Somebody might suspect him. Maybe it's why he leaves Haley."

"To divert suspicion," Jiminy Cricket said. He frowned past Monty's huddled body toward the direction we'd come.

"Yeah."

"But why little girls?" Pretty Boy insisted. "What's he got against girls?"

"Pageant winners," I said. "Every girl killed has won one of those beauty contests."

"Okay, why kill beauty contest winners?"

The rain slowed to a steady drizzle. Fewer cars passed. I wondered what time it was and glanced at the monster. He pressed his forehead into his knees and turned further away from us.

"Maybe he wanted to be a girl," I said. "And he kills 'em because he's jealous."

"What?" Pretty Boy's snort brought my head around. His face was twisted like he was about to bust out laughing.

"You can't see me," I said, "but I'm the guy giving you a dirty look right now."

He struggled to choke back his laughter.

"There are men," I continued, "I've heard, who want to be girls, so they dress like them. Sometimes they have operations. It's a really big deal out in California."

"You've got to be kidding." Pretty Boy laughed out loud.

"It's true," Jiminy Cricket said. "I've heard it too." He sniffled, closed his eyes and moved away from us.

"You okay, Jiminy?" I said.

"My name's Jimmy." His shoulders shook as the rain continued to patter against the roof.

"What's wrong, Jimmy?" Pretty Boy said.

"Nothing." He pressed his nose into his knees like Monty. "Leave me alone." His voice was muffled against his arms. The rain pinged against the roof and dripped through the trees.

Pretty Boy sighed. "I can't imagine Brother Muler wants to be a girl."

"Why doesn't he have a wife or kids?" I asked him. "That's not natural for a preacher man his age."

"Because he takes care of his mama."

"He told Ida Mae pageants are sinful," I said. "Maybe he's gone berserk, attempting to stamp out sin."

"Why cut out their eyes?" The monster said, lifting his head to stare at me in such a way as to make the back of my neck prickle.

"How'd you know about that?"

He went quiet, staring off in the distance. "I hear things."

"What things?"

His pause was so long I didn't think he was going to answer me.

"Everything," he said.

I thought back to all the times I stood in the yard under the big oak tree, thinking I was alone. I squinted at him. "Maybe he's just..." I shook my head.

"Crazy," Monty said, and rested his forehead back on his knees.

We fell quiet, and the others drifted to sleep. I folded the map and slipped it into my knapsack. I slid my sword out and laid it across my thighs, just in case. I rested my head against the church door.

After awhile it was just Pretty Boy and me awake. As he stared at the starless sky, I wondered what was going on inside his head.

"You remember anything about seeing?" I asked him.

He smiled at the ceiling. "I remember blue," he said. "The color of the sky. And my mother's eyes."

"Doesn't it make you mad?"

"Mad?" He cocked his head, his fingers skimming over his walking stick resting between his outstretched legs.

"Mad at God. That He did this to you."

"God didn't do this to me. My mother did. She got so mad she shook me until she scrambled my brains. Detached my retina, they say. And beat me some, maybe. I don't remember much about it. The nurses at the hospital told me what happened when I came to. But I didn't really understand."

"But why?" I tried to imagine Mama beating me so hard she put me in the hospital. She'd barely even swatted Willie's behind when he poured her fancy perfume down the drain, just to send a message to Captain Kangaroo in its bottle. "What did you do to make her so mad?"

He rested his head against the wall. Delilah stirred and shifted her head onto his shoulder, curling her body against his arm.

"I was maybe three, or four." He stared into the darkness. His fingers flexed against the stick. "The only thing I remember before waking up in the hospital was falling asleep in my new big boy bed and dreaming of wolves. Mother told the nurses I'd wet the bed. She admitted she stood over me yelling, then knocked me to the floor. She said she'd worked two shifts at the hospital that day only to come home and find my good-for-nothing daddy passed out on the sofa. She was exhausted. She said she must've blacked out. She didn't know what she was doing.

"While I was in the hospital, she said she couldn't handle a handicapped child, even if it was her fault. She couldn't pay the hospital bills, either. So she just left town. Soon as I got released from the hospital, Daddy dumped me on the steps of the orphanage with nothing but a note pinned to my shirt. Nobody ever heard from either one of them again."

His palms rested on the stick. "I can tell you though, I never wet the bed again."

The rain stopped, and we listened to it drip through the leaves of the trees. Jiminy Cricket fell against Willie's shoulder, mouth open, snoring. Willie scooted downward so that his head rested against my hip. I slipped my knapsack beneath his head.

"One more thing," I said. "What's your real name? I know your mama didn't name you Pretty Boy. The ladies at the orphanage did that."

He took so long, I didn't think he was going to answer me. "Peter," he said finally, "Peter Boynton."

"Peter," I murmured and had no idea what to say after that.

"When you pray to God," Pretty Boy broke the silence, "what do you pray for?"

"I don't pray for nothing." I fingered the snakes on the handle of my sword. "I don't know nothing about God."

"Nothing?"

"I guess that's not true." I closed my eyes. "I know God's never done anything for me. That's what I know."

"You got a family. That's something. More than most of us got."

I thought for a minute, wondering where my daddy was and would he ever be found. Would I ever see him again? The shape of him was already getting blurry around the edges of my mind. I dug my fingers into my sword. "You've got Ida Mae," I said. The road stretched dark and slick and silent in front of us. "And she at least cares enough about you to fight for you."

"Yeah," Pretty Boy said. "We've got Ida Mae. And each other. That's sort of like a family, isn't it?"

As the rain fell on the porch roof, I thought hard about everything we'd been through. Sure, I'd called them idiots. And worse. But I was wrong. They weren't idiots at all. I was the idiot. Thinking I was some hot shot hero. But I wasn't. And I probably couldn't have gotten this far without them.

I gripped my sword and watched the rain drip from the trees into wide muddy puddles until I heard Pretty Boy's breathing turn heavy and deep beside me.

a fine day for going berserk

We reached Torrence City by lunchtime and crossed a bridge stretching what seemed like a mile over the Tennessee River. Traffic was light, but we stuck close to the railing anyway. My belly lurched as I gazed at the churning water below where a fishing boat was barely a speck. Past the river, we climbed a hill and found ourselves on Main Street.

Torrence City was two, maybe three times as big as Haley. A proper city. Poplars lined the sidewalks in front of two-storied brick buildings. The Bank of Torrence to our left stretched four stories high. A fountain sprayed water nearly to the second floor from a small pool in front.

We trudged three or four blocks, passing department stores, law offices, and a stationer before finally stumbling into a tiny diner tucked at the end of the street.

The dining area was long and narrow. On the right, an old-fashioned soda fountain with a counter and red leather stools ran the length of the room. A man and woman sat at the counter.

We slid into one of the booths opposite them and as far from the other diners as possible. We were a mess from our run through the rain and sleeping outdoors.

My clothes had dried stiff on my body and scratched

296 IDIOT FARM

against my scraped ribs. Besides Delbert's torn jeans, his eye was still swollen shut. Delilah's slippers and bare toes were muddy. And Jiminy Cricket reeked of sour sweat and lord knows what else.

Pretty Boy, Jiminy, and I sat on one side of the booth facing the door. Willie, Delbert, and Delilah clamored opposite us. We left Monty the Monster outside in the narrow alley because he refused to come in.

A woman with teased blonde hair strolled over. She appeared to be close to Mama's age and picked at a loose thread on her pink and white polyester uniform. She carried a pad of paper and a pencil. The name on her uniform was Wanda.

"What'll it be, sweethearts?" She stared at the pad cupped in her palm and waited.

"We'll have co-colas," I said, "and a...how much is a ham sandwich?"

"Two-fifty." She plucked at another string embroidering her name.

"What's your cheapest sandwich?" I asked and pulled the last of my money out of my pocket and counted it onto the table. Two dollars and eighty-two cents.

"I still have a little money left," Pretty Boy said. He wiggled the money out of his jeans and added it to the pile.

"Tuna salad's a dollar ten," Wanda said. "Hey," she glanced up, "where's your mama?"

"Shopping," I said, before anyone had a chance to speak. Delilah's mouth fell open.

"Actually," Jiminy Cricket lifted a finger, "she's—"

I slammed my elbow into his ribs, and his breath whooshed out.

"Ah," he coughed, "shopping. Like he said…" Everyone else studied the table except for Pretty Boy, who stared serenely ahead.

"Shopping, eh? Some of you ain't even wearing real shoes." She squinted under the table. "Can't serve you in house slippers."

"We're headed there next," I lied. "We're meeting Mama to buy shoes. She sent us in for lunch, first."

She swept us with a hard look. Her gaze rested on the bell on Delilah's wrist until Delilah dropped her hands beneath the table.

"You all have the same mama?" Wanda's gaze landed on Delbert.

"Some of us are adopted," I said.

"Adopted." She reared back as if we had chicken pox. "Which ones?"

"Excuse me?"

"Which one of you's adopted?"

Everyone stared at me now, and I fought the urge to wipe my sweating palms on my jeans. "Well, he is," I nodded toward Delbert, "obviously."

"But he's as good as the rest of us," Jiminy added.

"Even better," Pretty Boy said.

"Except he don't talk," Willie said. I kicked him under the table.

"Ow! What'd you do that for?" He glared at me. "It's the truth."

"She doesn't need to know that," I said between clenched teeth. "How much was the tuna sandwich?" I asked Wanda sweetly.

She cocked her head at Delbert.

"Look, Wanda," I gave her my best Sunday school smile. "Our mama's going to be back soon, and she's going to be awful sore if we haven't been fed."

"Lilah don't want tuna," Delilah said from the corner. She hugged herself and rocked back and forth, jingling the bell.

"What's the matter with her?" the waitress said. "Why's she wearing a bell?"

"Older sister," I said. "Gets grumpy when she's hungry. She likes the sound it makes." I stared meaningfully at Delilah and prayed she wouldn't fall apart on us. Wanda stared at her, too.

"We'll take uh, six tuna sandwiches, please," I said. I counted out the money again. "You got anything cheaper than tuna?"

Wanda watched Delilah.

"Wanda?" The situation was about to spin out of control.

"Chicken noodle soup," she said. "Sixty cents a bowl."

"And a bowl of chicken noodle soup." I slammed the last quarter onto the table.

Wanda stomped away without writing anything on her pad. I wiped at the sweat trickling over my ear as she banged behind the counter toward the register.

"We better get out of here," Jiminy Cricket said, tapping the table, "before she goes and calls the cops."

"She ain't gonna call the cops," I said, "as long as you stay calm and don't act crazy."

Willie hunkered in his seat. "I don't want to go to jail."

"Sit up and act right," I said. "Nobody's going to jail. She's got no reason to believe we ain't exactly who I said we were."

"Except we don't have a mama," Jiminy Cricket said.

Willie glanced past my shoulder, his eyes bugged out, and I whirled to find Wanda balancing four sodas. She banged them onto the table without a word and stalked away.

"She's mad," Willie said.

"Who cares?" I reached for a soda. "Calm down and stop acting so scared."

Wanda returned with two more drinks. She banged them onto the table.

"What about Monty?" Pretty Boy asked.

"Uh, Wanda." She turned with a stony expression. "We'll need one of those sandwiches to go." She stomped away.

As she disappeared into the kitchen, I hoped that by the time we finished our lunch, the monster outside would still be exactly where we left him.

We were nearly finished with our sandwiches when all hell broke loose. I gave Delbert his drawing paper and pen I'd been keeping in my knapsack so he could draw while we ate. Jiminy Cricket took out the knife Monty had given Delbert and flicked it open, fiddling with it.

Delilah had finished her soup and before anyone could stop her, snatched half of Delbert's tuna sandwich and chomped on it.

"Hey," I said, "you said you didn't like tuna."

"Lilah hungry."

"Okay, Tinkerbell, but you can't steal Delbert's lunch. I'll get you something else." I was trying to get more money from Pretty Boy when Delbert lunged for his sandwich. Before he could grab it, Delilah crammed the rest of it into her mouth.

"No fair!" I cried.

In the blink of an eye, Delbert slapped Delilah's hand so hard it sent her bell jangling. The table erupted as everyone began arguing.

Delilah's fists hit the table. *Pow!*

"Quiet," I growled, glancing around. The couple at the counter had turned to stare at us.

"Lilah not quiet. Lilah quiet no more. Deebee hurt Lilah." She rubbed the red splotch on the back of her hand. "Lilah tired of being hurt."

"Okay," I said. "He's sorry. You're sorry for hitting her, aren't you, Delbert? Tell her you're sorry."

Delbert shook his head hard and gripped his pen like a dagger, and I thought maybe he meant to stab her with it.

"Listen," I leaned in, "we're gonna get thrown out of here if y'all don't act right. Now, Delbert didn't mean to hit you," I said, "and you shouldn't have stolen his sandwich."

"Hurt Lilah," she said, rubbing the back of her hand, then tugging on the string encircling her wrist.

"You're fine," I said. "It'll stop stinging in a minute, Just—"

"Lilah tired of being hurt. Bad boys hurt Lilah at the fair. Called Lilah a cow. Lilah not a cow." She tugged on the string.

"Nobody thinks you're a cow," I said. "It's kinda sweet, actually, Ida Mae wanting to make sure you're safe."

"Lilah not like bell," she said. "Wear bell no more. Bad people find me."

"Nobody's gonna find you," I said.

"What bad people?" Pretty Boy asked.

"Hurt Lilah," she said. "Touch Lilah in bad places. Make Lilah touch squishy elephant trunk."

"Whaaaaaat?"

"Say Lilah stupid. But Lilah know. Lilah know bad people."

"Who?" Pretty Boy said. "Who are the bad people?"

Jiminy Cricket paused playing with his knife. Willie looked ill.

"Daddy. Mama. Uncles. Bad, bad cousins. Lilah try to hide. Lilah crawl under house. Hide in closet with the stonky shoes. Lilah hide in basement in cabinets with the rats and the stink and the stinky water dripping in Lilah's hair. But they find Lilah. They always find Lilah."

"Stop," I said. "Just stop. I can't hear it."

Pretty Boy's hand covered his mouth.

Jiminy Cricket stared out the window past Willie's head, picking at the corners of his eyes, his knife forgotten. Willie's mouth had fallen open, his face blank, and I wasn't sure how much of Delilah's ramblings he understood.

But Delbert—Delbert stared at me, strangling his paper and pen. Like he understood her perfectly.

Delilah's voice lowered to a growl full of gravel. "Delilah," she said, "go along with Uncle Lenny, now. Mama's got to get her cigarette money."

We sat in stunned silence. The couple at the counter shuffled out the door with a nervous backward glance. Wanda swung through the door from the kitchen and headed our way.

Before we could stop her, Delilah lunged for Jiminy's knife.

the gig is up

Wе exited the diner to find Ida Mae leaning against her dusty pickup truck chewing on a piece of straw. She spit it out when she saw us. She wore her raggedy white tee with a faded blue and white plaid work shirt hanging loose over it, having apparently dressed up for the occasion of our eventual apprehension.

She hooked a thumb through the belt loop of her jeans. "You young'uns need a ride?"

Delilah clapped violently and ran to her, laying her dandelion head on the old woman's shoulder. Ida Mae let her rest there, staring hard at Delilah's bare wrist. Delilah had sliced the bell off with Jiminy's knife before he managed to snatch it back. Monster Monty slipped out of the shadow of the alley.

Ida Mae nodded to him. "Monty."

Studying his feet, he nodded and shoved his fists deep in his pockets. I handed the last tuna sandwich to Willie, who handed it to Delbert, then Jiminy Cricket. Monty took it and slunk back into the shadows. I could barely make out his figure hunkered in the darkness, cramming the sandwich into his mouth.

"Flynn," Ida Mae said, "something you want to tell me?" I glanced around the group. Nobody met my stare. "This your idea? Everybody leaving the farm without telling me?" she asked as Delilah clung to her arm.

"No, ma'am."

"Without leaving a note or anything?"

"Well, no, I mean." I couldn't get anybody to look at me. A car rumbled along the street behind her. "Didn't figure you'd miss me," I said finally.

"You didn't figure?"

"No, ma'am."

"What about the others? You figure I'd miss them?"

"I tried to make them go back. Once I realized they were following us."

"Us?"

"Willie and me."

Ida Mae's mouth disappeared into her frown. We stared at each other. The fountain in front of the bank shot water straight into the sky.

"Get in the truck, then," Ida Mae said. "We're going home."

"No, ma'am," I said. "I'm not going."

She stared at me. "Not going where?"

"Back to the farm. Not yet."

Jiminy Cricket strolled away, his fingers laced atop his red head. Pretty Boy's knuckles bled white on Delbert's arm. Willie's face crumpled as if he was about to cry.

"Where exactly you headed?" Ida Mae asked quietly.

"I'm going to find Mama and Sunny and warn them about the Beauty Killer." I searched for Monty, but the shadows held him hostage. "We tried to stop them at the fair, but we missed, and I'm not leaving until..."

Somehow, in the bright sunshine on a cloudless summer day in the middle of the big city, the whole thing seemed too ridiculous to put into words. It was just a feeling, a real bad one I couldn't shake.

"What exactly is your plan, son?" Ida Mae squinted at me.

"I'm going to find the college campus where the pageant's being held," I said. "Find Mama and Sunny and try to get them to leave before she wins."

"If Sunny already won last night, another crown's not going to matter," Ida Mae said.

"How'd you know she won last night?"

She squinted at the sun, then back to me. "I've been following you."

"Since when?"

"Since I realized yesterday you left and weren't showing up for breakfast."

"Where'd you first spot us?"

"This side of Piney Grove. Rhubarb followed and kept an eye on you until I could get rid of Miss Walker. He called from a gas station across from the Rusty Pig. I don't like having to lie to the government, son." Her stare was piercing.

"Wait!" I cried. "You were at the fair? You let those boys attack Delbert and hurt Delilah?"

She strolled to Delbert and tilted his chin to the sun. He blinked his good eye at her. She rested a palm on the top of his head. "I had to park the truck. By the time I found you, Monty was already handling things."

"You knew Monty was following us the whole time?"

"Of course."

"You let us sleep in the rain last night?" Willie said. "It was awful."

"You appeared okay to me. And there wasn't room for everybody to take shelter in the truck."

"You watched us?" I said. "At the church? The whole night?"

"Pulled in behind the graveyard with my lights off. Kept my eyes on you the whole time. Unfortunately," she leveled her sharp blue gaze on me, "my truck wouldn't start when you took off this morning. Had to flag somebody down to jump start it. But I'm here now. So everybody pile into the back of the truck."

Delilah had one foot in the cab when Ida Mae eased her back and steered her toward the truck bed. "I'm going to let you ride in the back this time, honey. First time. Jimmy, help her in."

Delilah clapped crazily. "Goody, goody. Lilah love riding in truck."

"I know you do." Ida Mae turned to me. "Where's her bell?"

I stared back at her, mutinous.

Pretty Boy dug into his jeans pocket and held his palm out to Ida Mae, revealing Delilah's tarnished bell and tattered string.

"Lilah no cow," Delilah said, "no more."

Ida Mae sighed and scratched her brow. "Get in," she said to me, and flung a palm toward the cab.

"I said I ain't going," I repeated.

"Oh, I'm taking you to your mama," she said. "The school's five or six blocks from here."

"I can walk."

"I said I'll take you."

"I'll sit in the back with the others."

She caught my arm. Her fingers dug in as tight as teeth on a metal trap. "I want you to ride up front with me."

Willie stepped up. "I'll ride in front." Delbert and Jiminy had already helped Pretty Boy and Delilah into the back.

"Maybe on the ride home, son," Ida Mae said. She jerked her head toward the back. "Keep an eye on Delilah for me, will you? Make sure she doesn't stand or lean too far over the side."

With a last glance at me, Willie shuffled toward the back of the truck.

"What about the monster?" I said.

Ida Mae stuck two fingers in her mouth and gave a piercing whistle. Monty appeared at a full trot and practically dove into the bed of the truck. The others shrieked and scrambled out of his way.

"Flynn." She held the door for me. The others were already laughing and pushing and squirming in the back. I had no choice but to slide onto the blistering leather seat as Ida Mae slammed the door behind me.

Climbing behind the wheel, she gunned the engine in reverse, and we lurched backward. We sped along Main Street, and as the traffic light turned yellow, then red, we roared underneath it.

We'd gone no more than a block when Ida Mae said, "So this doesn't have anything to do with your mama leaving you, huh?"

"Of course not." I stared out the open window at gold brick office buildings and dark green awnings. "What do you mean?"

"I mean, you're not chasing after your mama, are you? With your daddy missing, she's all you've got." The light changed green, and she gunned through it, making a left turn to cut off the driver behind us. He blared his horn. She waved without looking back. The fuming driver hunkered over his steering wheel.

"Of course I'm not chasing Mama," I said. "And I got Willie."

I stared out the front window. "And anyway, it wouldn't do any good. I mean, I don't want to be dragged around to those stupid pageants."

"Don't you?" She stared at me so long she nearly rear-ended the Monte Carlo idling at the next light. I slammed my palm against the dashboard and braked with my foot as we were thrown forward and then back as the tires squealed to a stop. The stench of scorched rubber hung in the air.

I turned to find Pretty Boy picking himself off the floor of the truck as Delilah laughed and clapped hard.

"No, I don't," I said as she gunned the engine, and we rumbled through the intersection. "I mean, I want to go home to Peach City. I want to sleep in my own bed. I want them to find my daddy and bring him home. I want all of us," I stared out my window, "to be a family again. But that doesn't appear to be an option right now."

"No," she said as the green rolling lawn of Torrence State University appeared before us. "It doesn't appear so." She peered over the steering wheel. "Your daddy played football here, right out of high school. Where's this thing supposed to be held?"

I sunk into my seat. "I hoped there'd be a sign or something." We passed a few girls hugging books and boys tossing a frisbee on the lawn. A group of students lounged under a shade tree.

"There," I pointed. "There's a sign." A white banner hung over the entrance to the Richard Gayle Auditorium, *Miss Dixie Pageant.*

An empty police car sat out front.

Ida Mae had barely pulled the truck into a parking space when I opened the door and jumped out. "Wait here," I said.

"I'll find them and be right back." I hit the front steps of the building two at a time and yanked on the heavy glass door.

Two women sat behind a table inside the lobby. One counted tickets. The other counted money. They were pretty, with flippy hair and too much makeup. A man in a blue uniform roamed the space beside them murmuring into a walkie talkie, a gun in a holster around his hips.

The woman counting money glanced up and said, "Honey, you better hurry, the pageant's about to start. You got a ticket?"

"No." I skidded to a halt. "I'm not here to watch. I've got to talk to one of the contestants, Sunny Bolenn."

"Not possible." The ticket lady stopped counting. "They're probably on stage by now."

"But I've got to—"

"You'll have to wait until it's over," the money lady said. "Nobody's allowed backstage except for mamas. And you'll need a ticket to get past here."

"How much?"

"Two-fifty."

I dug in my pocket and pulled out a dollar and a dime. I had given Pretty Boy the rest.

Money lady peered into my palm. "Sorry. You'll have to wait outside."

I fisted the money with a groan. "But she's my sister."

"Sorry," money lady shook her head, "even her mama had to pay."

"That's the stupidest thing I ever heard of."

The policeman gave me a long, cold stare before turning and speaking into his walkie talkie.

Ticket lady sniffed. "How do you imagine we pay for those fancy crowns and trophies?"

"Aaaaaaagh." I snatched at my hair and spun around. Maybe Ida Mae would cough up the money. I stalked to the glass door and peered out. The truck was empty. Pushing open the door, I scanned the campus lawn from the steps. No Ida Mae. No kids.

I trotted to the truck. No one was even on the street to ask. I turned to the low, flat building I just left. There had to be more than one way in.

I found a side door hidden behind a clump of scraggly azaleas. It was locked. Trotting around the back, I found a wall of glass doors like the front. A policeman paced the sidewalk, his back to me, talking into a walkie talkie similar to the blue uniform inside. I eased toward the double doors in the center. They were locked. The door to the right was also locked. Without much hope, I tried the last door on the left. It swung open.

I found myself in a similar lobby, but this one was dark and empty. I raced to the door on my right and yanked. A dust mop tumbled out. I shoved it inside and closed the door. Music swelled overhead.

The pageant had started. Where was everybody? Light streamed beneath the next door. I jerked it open to discover a long hallway. I raced along it until I met a young woman in a flowing lime green gown with a sparkling crown on her head.

"Where are the young girls?" I said. "Eight-year-olds?"

"They're on stage. The pageant's already started."

The music swelled louder. "How do I get to the stage?"

"You don't." She fiddled with her crown. "It's off limits to anyone not in the pageant."

"I have to reach my sister." I clenched my jaw so tight my teeth should've cracked.

"You can wait in the dressing room, I guess," she said. "But you'll miss the show."

"Where's the dressing room?"

"Along this hall."

I raced past a door with a small rectangular window papered over from the inside. I pushed it open, stuck my head inside, and was met with a high-pitched squeal.

"No boys allowed." A teenage girl held a dress to her bare chest. Several girls sat in front of mirrors in bras and panties. Some had curlers in their hair. Some put on makeup. Mothers fluffed dresses, brushed out curls.

I shielded my eyes. "Where's the next group? The younger ones, eight to twelve."

"Next door." A girl in nothing but a lacy bra and panties hauled a hairbrush at me, and I shut the door in time for it to clatter to the floor. I knocked on the next door. No response.

"Hey." I banged on the door. "Sunny in there? Sunny Bolenn?" The music was so loud from the auditorium I didn't reckon I could hear an answer anyway. I eased the door open. The room was empty.

I stepped inside and stared at the mess. Hair curlers, brushes, and makeup littered the counters. But beneath the next to the last desk, I spied Mama's baby blue makeup case.

I returned to the hallway and caught sight of Delilah's blonde head. A woman gripped her arm.

"What's your name, honey?" the woman said. "Where's your mama?"

"Delilah," I raced toward her, "where is everybody?"

"Lynn." She struggled to pull her arm out of the woman's grasp.

"Well, Delilah Lynn," the woman said, "you better get

changed, or you're going to miss your cue. You remember where your dressing room is, honey? And good gracious, where are your shoes?"

"She isn't, oh, never mind," I said. "Delilah, where's Ida Mae? Where are the others?"

"Lookie here, son," the woman tugged Delilah away from me, "this young lady has to get dressed. Her group's about to go on stage, and she's going to miss her intro. You'll have to wait until the pageant's over to talk to her."

Delilah stared at me over her shoulder as the lady dragged her away.

"But she's not—"

"Son, you're not even supposed to be back here," the lady said. "Now run along before I call security."

"But she's—"

"Lynn!" Delilah called.

"It's Flynn!" I yelled.

"Well, I imagine she knows her own name." The woman shoved Delilah into the last room. "Dear, what are we going to do with your hair?"

A voice boomed overhead, introducing the next group.

"Forget it." I waved in frustration as they disappeared. They'd figure it out soon enough. I commenced to searching for the stage door.

and now, the bad news

I finally found Mama, backstage behind the curtains.

"Flynn." She nearly jumped out of her skin when she saw me. An elderly woman with black cat-eye glasses and a bee-hive of gray hair shushed her. Mama grabbed me. "Sweetie, what're you doing here? How'd you get here from Haley?" She squeezed me to her side and pointed to the brightly-lit stage. "Isn't she beautiful?"

Sunny strutted into view. She prissed her way to the middle of the stage, her pale blonde hair poufy and curly and her fancy blue dress ruffling around her knees. Her lips were painted carmine, and she gave the audience a wide, practiced smile.

"Mama, I've got to talk to you." I wrestled out of her grip.

"Not now, dear." She squeezed me again. Her head bobbed to the music, and she grinned bigger than any contestant on stage.

"Smile, sugar," she called to Sunny. And Sunny grinned big enough to split her rouged cheeks. She sashayed and strutted around the stage like she'd already won. And when she struck her last pose, one hand on a cocked hip, the auditorium erupted.

"That's my girl." Mama laughed and clapped and swiped at

her mascara. She crushed me to her side. "Isn't she something? Isn't she the most gorgeous thing you ever did see?"

"Yeah, Mama, gorgeous. I got to tell you—"

Sunny ran offstage and Mama pushed me aside to catch her in a bear hug. The crowd thundered as Ole Cat Eyes snatched Sunny out of Mama's arms and shoved her back onstage.

Sunny strutted to the middle of the stage and did a slow, deep curtsy thing, dipping her head, then gave the judges in the front row a big wink. The crowd roared.

"You see that?" Mama's face was about to bust open with pride. "She learned it in Pascagoula. Drives the judges crazy."

My sister raced off stage, and Mama caught her again. They laughed and jabbered so much with their heads together, I couldn't get between them. They skipped down the steps and out the stage door. So there was nothing to do but follow. We were in the hallway before I got a chance to grab Mama's arm.

"Mama."

"Oh, Flynn, honey, what is it?" She flicked her hair over her shoulder.

"Flynn." Sunny flung her arms around me. "Did you see me? Did you see how good I did?"

"I saw." I hugged her hard before pulling back. "What I've been trying to tell you is—"

"Flynn," Sunny's hands were on her frilly hips like a miniature Mama, "what are you doing here?"

"I've been trying to tell you."

"Where's Willie?" Sunny searched the hallway. "He saw me, too? What'd he think? Where is he?"

"Somewhere around here." Girls flooded the hallway, pushing around us, a laughing, chattering pack of hyenas.

"Honey, you better get moving." Ole Cat Eyes passed us

and gave Sunny a little shove. "Sportswear's next. You haven't got much time."

"Wait till you see." Sunny grabbed my arm. "I got this cute little cowgirl outfit."

"With pink fringe," I said. "I know. But you aren't a cowgirl."

She pouted at me.

"Cowgirls live out west," I said and scruffed my hair, staring at the giggling girls pushing past. "You live in the south."

"What do you expect her to wear, Flynn?" Mama said. "A cotton-picking mammy dress?"

"Well."

"You're getting an awful lot like your daddy, mister." Mama frowned at me from her clunky platform heels. "And not in a good way."

"I don't want you talking bad about my daddy when he was trying to do the right thing, and it ain't his fault he's gone missing."

"Listen, mister," she said, "he didn't have to go. He didn't even ask me what I thought. Just signed up like we didn't need him or nothing."

"He was trying to do a good thing!"

"If this war is such a good thing," she said, "how come there's so many people protesting? How come so many boys are coming back all shot up or acting crazy? How come your daddy's disappeared, and nobody will tell us nothing?" Tears sparkled her eyes, and she pressed a palm to her powdered forehead. "Flynn, I cannot think about this right now. I just can't. Sunny, run along and get out of your dress. I'll be there in a minute."

I watched my sister skip along the hall. "Mama," I said, "Sunny can't win this contest."

Mama folded her arms and cocked her hip. She wore a new ring on her finger, a square emerald as big as my thumbnail. "And why not?" she said. "She's already won one."

"Yeah, last night. But we've got to get her out of here before—"

"How'd you know she won last night? It's not even in the papers yet."

"I was there."

She squinted at me. "What in the world have you been up to? Ida Mae been dragging you all over tarnation chasing me? Trying to unload—"

"Unload?" I interrupted. "You mean me? Like a load of garbage?" A woman scurried past and shushed us.

"Flynn, honey." Mama placed perfectly manicured fingers on my folded arms. They were as cold as dead fish. "I didn't mean it like that. Of course I didn't."

I jerked away. "Like you unloading me on her?"

"Flynn, sweetie, with your daddy missing, I was thinking of you, what was best for you and Willie."

"No," I said. "You were thinking of what was best for you."

Her head snapped back. "That's a horrible thing to say. I'm trying to keep this family afloat. It's all been left up to me, and I'm trying to create a better life for Sunny, and for you."

"How's this a better life for me, huh? How's being stuck on a farm with a bunch of..." I stopped as my gut hitched. I thought of Delbert's swollen black eye. Jiminy Cricket crying last night. And creepy RayRay's paw sliding along Delilah's thigh. "How's this better for me?"

"Darling," Mama watched other mamas and little girls rush by, "I had no idea you'd be so miserable there. I thought you'd enjoy having boys your own age to play with. It'd be a distraction from all that nasty war business."

"Well."

"Well, what?" The music was loud. "I can't hear you, honey." The hallway filled with people. A mama bumped me, dragging her dolled-up daughter. The girl wasn't more than four or five.

Mama reached out. "Flynn, honey, I've got to go." She sidestepped a battleaxe of a woman bearing down on us with her arms full of ruffled dresses.

"Mama," I said, "it's me who's got to keep this family together. Daddy said so."

"What, honey?"

"He said I've got to hold us together. Not you. Me."

"Lord, honey, I can't hear nothing. And I've got to check on Sunny."

"Mama, Sunny's in danger."

"What?" She cupped an ear toward me.

"I said Sunny's in danger!" I stumbled over her foot as her bare toes crunched beneath my high top.

"Lord, Flynn," she hopped backward on one foot. "It's too crowded here, and *dang...*" She bent and pressed a finger to her toe. "You broke my toenail. Holy Mother of Mary, that hurts."

"Sorry, Mama," I said. "I'm just—"

"Thank goodness. Sunny." Mama snagged my sister as she hustled past us in the press of people, dragging her vest and straightening her skirt. "Honey, you're a mess and your hat's crooked."

Sunny slipped into her vest as Mama righted the pink cowgirl hat and was bumped from behind. "And what in the world did you do to your hair?" she said. "Flynn, honey, we've got to go. Just stay put, and we'll talk after the show. Wish us luck!" She flashed crossed fingers and pushed Sunny toward the stage, limping after her with the rest of the girls.

"Good luck," I said as the hallway emptied again, and the music blared in the auditorium. Where were Willie and the others? I returned to the room where I'd last seen Delilah. It was empty.

I stalked the halls and found lots of girls and more mamas, but no Willie, no Delbert, no Pretty Boy, no Jiminy Cricket. And no Ida Mae.

I waited in the darkened wings of the stage for Sunny to finish and wondered if the Beauty Killer might be somewhere in the audience. There should be more security. One guy in the front and one in the back wasn't going to cut it. The Beauty Killer had proven to be one slippery dude.

Sunny pranced around the stage in her white cowgirl boots and pink hat, shooting her toy guns in the air yelling, "Yee-haw!" The crowd cheered as she ran off stage, and Mama caught her and pushed past me without stopping.

I followed them to a dressing room full of girls. The chattering and squealing were enough to drive anybody out of their mind. The door slammed in my face, so I had to wait in the hallway. Ten or so girls came out before Mama and Sunny finally appeared. Sunny wore a yellow dress so bright I nearly had to shield my eyes.

"Isn't she as beautiful as a sunbeam?" Mama said as Sunny did a little twirl in front of me.

"Yeah, sunbeam. Mama, I need to talk to you."

"Lord, but you're persistent," she said. "You know, son, sometimes that is not an attractive trait. But here," she hustled Sunny toward the stage, "this is the last event. They're going to crown the Little Miss Dixie as soon as the juniors leave the stage. Come on."

I followed her, my head swimming with the giggling and

squealing and the bright colors and loud music. We stood in the shadows as the older girls strutted onto the stage.

And right smack in the middle of the lineup was Delilah, contestant number seven, in a pretty lavender dress, a floating cloud around her knees. Someone had washed her feet and slipped a pair of silver sandals on her, and she glided onto the stage as calm as the others. She greeted the audience with her chin tilted slightly so, her smile, sweet and serene.

"What's she doing out there?" Mama hissed as Delilah glided toward us. The announcer introduced her as contestant number seven, Miss Delilah Lynn."

"Lordamercy," Mama said. "This pageant's gone to pot. They'll take anybody, I swear."

"Mama," a girl said behind us, "isn't that my dress?" The tall redhead pointed at Delilah.

"Don't be silly," her mama said loud enough to earn a shush from Ole Cat Eyes. "Of course it's not your dress. Your dress is hanging in the dressing room. But soon as we get back to Weaverton, I'm gonna give Betty Sue Parker at The Little Red Rooster a piece of my mind. The very idea. She told me your dress was one of a kind."

Ole Cat Eyes shushed her again.

The pageant dragged on for another forty-five minutes, with girls coming and going, last year's winners parading onstage with their crowns, girls singing, and then finally the big announcement.

Sunny won, of course, squealing and clapping on stage, waving to the crowd and blowing kisses to the judges. She jiggled her skinny legs so much they were barely able to pin the crown on her head.

The shocker was that Delilah won, too, and I nearly fell

out backstage. But when they attempted to crown her, she didn't understand and kept shaking her head and scooting away so they finally just handed it to her. She took the roses they gave her and paraded around the stage, as poised as Sunny. She looked positively queenly. Then we were caught in the flow of the crowd and dumped back into the hallway.

"Well, I never," Mama said. "Imagine a girl like that winning a beauty contest. I thought the Miss Dixie Pageant had higher standards." She stared as a gaggle of girls pushed past us. "I'm going to write them a letter. We'll be more discriminating next year, sweet pea." She lifted Sunny's chin to kiss her on the lips. "But we won't think about that now."

"Delilah's just as pretty as those other girls," I said, and both Mama and Sunny turned to stare at me. "I mean, Sunny's pretty, too."

"Honey, they ain't even in the same league," Mama said. "That girl can't even talk right. There's no comparing the two."

"I'm just saying, when it comes to the looks department—"

"Flynn, honey, you simply do not understand beauty contests," Mama said. "It's more than beauty." She stroked Sunny's golden curls. "It's about personality. It's about smarts."

"They didn't even have to speak."

Mama frowned at me. "I said, we're not going to talk about that right now. Are you trying to ruin your sister's big day?"

"Of course not."

"I mean, one minute you're trying to escape those kids and the next you're defending them. Willie, honey." Mama peered past me. "Give your mama a big ole hug." She threw her arms wide and smothered Willie. "How you been, baby?"

Willie's answer was muffled against her chest. He pulled away.

"Did Flynn tell you there's a killer on the loose?" he said.

"Honey, I haven't been able to get a single thing of importance out of Flynn since he got here. You mean the Beauty Killer?" She stroked Willie's head. "Honey, we've heard about him. It's just rumors."

"No, Mama, it's in the newspapers. Tell her, Flynn."

I opened my mouth, then shut it again because Mama wasn't even looking at me.

"Now, Willie, sweetie, we're going to stop this awful talk about killers and such before we ruin Sunny's special day."

"But Mama."

"I was telling your brother I've changed my mind. I'm going to take you boys with us to Mobile. It's the state pageant, the next step for all the Miss Dixie winners. We'll have a hoot of a time. Of course, we'll need to put you boys to work. Won't we, Sunny?" She rested a palm on Sunny's upturned head and then snatched it away.

"Dang, I've chipped a nail." She splayed her fingertips in front of her. "Anyway," she said, "you boys can haul our bags for us."

"What about our stuff?" I said. "It's still at Ida Mae's."

"Where is your grandmother, anyway?" Mama searched the hallway. "I don't understand what you boys are doing, running loose all over creation."

"I don't want to go to Mobile," Willie said. A girl shoved him from behind with a big suitcase. He stumbled into me.

"What do you mean, you don't want to go?" Mama ruffled his hair and frowned at her defective nail resting on top of his head. "That truly looks something awful."

"I want to go back to the farm," Willie said. "Pretty Boy's got this cool collection of animals he's carved out of wood."

"Pretty Boy." Mama snorted. "What kind of dumb name is that?"

"It's not dumb," I said. "If you seen him—"

"Saw, sweetie, not seen," Mama said. "I'm sorry. What about this Pretty Boy? He simple, too?"

"No," I said, "he's actually pretty smart."

"Well, there's definitely something wrong with that girl."

"She's plenty smart, too. It's just some bad people did bad things to her, hurt her—her family; people she trusted. And she got a little messed up in the head on account of she couldn't handle it so she reverted back to being a little kid."

"Whatever. I'm telling you, she ain't right."

"You don't even know them," I said. "And it's not right you talking bad about 'em."

"Sunny Beaulynn," Ole Cat Eyes called from the stage door. "Last call for pictures."

"Mama." Sunny stomped her foot.

"Go on, sweetie, I'll be there in a jiffy." She nudged Sunny toward the stage and turned on me.

"I tell you what's not right, mister." She parked her fists on her hips. "The way you've been sassing me ain't right. And I don't appreciate the bad attitude you picked up at Ida Mae's." Willie crept after Sunny toward the stage.

"Bad attitude? You left me with a monster."

"I don't want to discuss it. You're getting more like your daddy every day. Negativity, all the time. I should've known leaving you with Ida Mae would do that to you."

"He ain't even here to defend his freaking self."

"Watch your mouth, mister."

"In fact," the blood boiled in my ears, "I haven't seen him in six months, since the day he left. And I haven't heard a single thing about where he might be. The Hanoi Hilton? Dead in the jungle somewhere? And I didn't hear nothing from you, neither. What kind of mama runs off and leaves her kids with their daddy already missing and don't ever call or nothing?"

"Are you criticizing me? Your mother?"

"I'm simply asking. How do you go off and not ever call or write or nothing? You got any idea what I've been going through? My daddy's gone. There's a killer running loose. There was a monster in the cellar. I fell out of the barn and nearly cracked open my skull. I definitely cracked some ribs. I traveled fifty miles to get to you. Don't you care?"

She stared along the empty hallway. "You young'uns don't appreciate nothing." She glanced back at me. "You don't appreciate anything anybody attempts to do for you. It's all about you, huh? What you want. What you need. It's never enough, is it?"

She threw up her hands and stomped away. "I can't take it, mister. I can't take this criticism and negative attitude. I'm trying to make a better life for you kids. I've been left holding the bag, and I'm doing the best I can to keep this family from going under." She shook her head. "If you ain't any more appreciative than that, maybe I won't take you to Mobile after all."

"Mama," I grabbed her arm. "I'm trying to keep this family together, too. Daddy said so. It's the last thing he told me. He gave me one job to do, and I aim to do it. Don't you see? I've lost my daddy. I don't want to lose you and Sunny, too."

She frowned and shifted her hip. Then sighed. "Alright." She grabbed my head and pulled me close, smelling like honeysuckle on a hot summer day.

I rested my cheek against her slippery dress and let the badness empty out of me, an uncorked bottle flipped upside down. She hugged me. "Baby, you're shaking. You okay?" She tried to pull away, but I held tight.

"Flynn!" Jiminy Cricket burst into the hallway like a rusted tornado. Delbert and Pretty Boy followed.

"What in tarnation?" Mama said over my head.

I wiped my cheek against her silky dress and pulled away. "What's going on?" I said. "Where've you been?"

"Delilah," Jiminy Cricket was nearly out of breath, "you've seen her?"

"Yeah. She won." I smoothed my mussed hair.

Jiminy waved. "I mean since she won."

"No." The hallway continued to clear of weary mamas with clothes bags dangling over their arms and girls clutching makeup cases. "She must've gone off the other side of the stage."

Pretty Boy advanced toward me. "They took her picture, and she disappeared."

"Mama!" Sunny wailed from the stage door.

"I'll be back." Mama left me and trotted up the steps in her clunky heels. She passed Willie, descending the stairs.

"Where's Ida Mae?" I said.

Jiminy Cricket pressed his side. "Looking for Delilah. It's crazy. She was there one minute, gone the next." He bent over, palms on his knees, working to catch his breath.

"You know how she is," I said, "always wandering off." I thought of the fair and the boys who messed with her. "You don't reckon," but I stopped myself. There was no way those losers had the guts to follow us all the way to Torrence City. And then I thought of something else.

"Reckon what?" Jiminy Cricket straightened to stare at me.

"What is it?" Pretty Boy held Delbert's arm. "You don't think," but he couldn't put it into words, either.

"What?" Jiminy glanced between us. "What is it?"

"Where'd you last see Ida Mae?" I headed along the hall.

"Other direction," Willie said, "talking to a security guard."

"Go through the auditorium," Pretty Boy said, pushing Delbert past me. "It's quicker."

"Where are we going?" Jiminy Cricket fell in line behind Willie. He rubbed the stitch in his side. "Where's Delilah?"

We were halfway through the darkened auditorium when I remembered Mama. She was on the brightly-lit stage, smoothing the ruffles around Sunny's neck and positioning her curls over her shoulders. Sunny pressed her crown to her head with a grimace. Flashbulbs popped.

"Willie," I said, "run tell Mama where we're going. I don't want her to leave without me." Willie took off running along the aisle and jumped the stage. I turned my back on the squawking and complaining, and we hit the lobby doors at a full run.

should we stay or should we go?

We found Ida Mae in the front lobby, staring out the big wall of glass as a man, different than the police officer, in a charcoal uniform stood with his back to her, talking on his walkie talkie. She turned as we reached her.

"I found Mama and Sunny," I said.

"We've been searching for Delilah." Pretty Boy gripped his cane and held onto Delbert.

"You didn't find her?" Ida Mae glanced between us.

"No, ma'am." Pretty Boy clenched and loosened his fist on his cane. "We checked the dressing rooms."

"And the bathrooms," Jiminy Cricket said. "Everywhere we thought she'd be. Broom closet. Back stage."

"Where's Willie?" Ida Mae asked.

"With Mama."

"Where's Monty?"

We exchanged glances. I hadn't given him the first thought.

"Oh, lord, we got two missing now," Jiminy Cricket wailed, his freckles splotching red against pale skin.

Ida Mae frowned. "Don't take the Lord's name in vain, son."

I puzzled things together in my head. "You don't reckon he's, I mean he and Delilah…" I stopped at Ida Mae's fierce expression.

"Monty wouldn't hurt nobody," Ida Mae said. The group fell

silent as we pondered that a minute. "Well," she amended, "he'd never hurt Delilah. She's always sneaking him extra helpings of biscuits and cornbread when she thinks I'm not looking."

I walked to the window and stared out. "Maybe they're somewhere together."

There were now four policemen on the front lawn, and another police car pulled up, lights flashing. Too little, too late.

The walkie talkie squawked over my shoulder, and the security guard faced us. "We've got two men circling the grounds and another questioning the girls as they leave. Too late for any sort of lock down. If he's got her, they're probably long gone. Best we can do is get a description of her to the police. They'll take over the questioning. You people hang tight." The walkie talkie squawked again, and the guard walked away, murmuring into it.

"What're we going to do?" Jiminy Cricket wailed.

"We're going to stay calm," Ida Mae said. "Go get a drink of water and come right back."

"You going to tell the security guard about Monty?" Pretty Boy asked. She stared at the back of the man's head.

"Over and out," he said and strolled back to us. "I got a man stopping people outside the back door. He says somebody saw a girl matching your girl's description leaving the building with a man."

"What man?" I asked.

He frowned at me. "Maybe her daddy?"

"What did he look like?" Ida Mae said. She folded her arms.

"Didn't get a good ID. The lady didn't look too closely at him. She did say he's wearing a nice jacket. A professional. But that doesn't mean anything, really. He could've been dressing up for the occasion. Or to blend in."

"Was there a boy with them?" Ida Mae said. "Dark hair, dark eyes?"

"No mention of a boy." The box squawked again and he strolled away.

Jiminy Cricket joined us, water dribbling down his chin. He swiped it against his shoulder and asked Ida Mae, "Could it be her daddy? Or somebody in her family?"

She rubbed her thumb over her lower lip. "They wouldn't have any way of knowing she'd be here. And Delilah probably wouldn't go with any of them anyway. It'd be someone she trusted, or she'd scream bloody murder."

"Not if he gave her candy," I said.

She studied me.

I shrugged. "How many men could she possibly know? Mr. Boushay's at the funny farm." I stopped at the frown she gave me. "But Brother Muler..." everybody's attention swung to me. And like a puzzle piece clicking into place, I saw the whole thing clearly. The newspaper clippings on his desk. The picture of Sunny. The cabin.

Hold it. What about the cabin? My mind raced back to the day Willie and I were exploring, the day we thought the monster was after us. What was it? What made me remember the cabin in connection with Brother Muler? Something on the ground as I hightailed it out the front door.

Brother Muler's seeing-eye ring. It was laying in the grass, but he never took it off. Except...when he gave it to Brother Kaine to be fixed.

"I know where she is," I said. The blood rushed to my ears, and I stared at Ida Mae. And the tiniest bit of fear flickered in her eyes.

The auditorium doors busted open. "There you are." Mama

sashayed toward us with Sunny in tow. "Flynn, honey, we've got to get going. We've got a long drive ahead of us and barely a few days to get settled. Sunny needs her beauty rest."

"Mama, Delilah's missing, I can't leave yet."

"Sweet pea," she gripped my chin and tilted my face to hers. It was a cold hand. "I'm sure Ida Mae'll find the girl. What are you going to do anyway, except get in the way?"

"I know where she is and I can't leave until I'm sure she's okay."

"Ida Mae will call us." Mama turned to my grandmother. "Won't you?"

Ida Mae studied her. "Sure, I'll call," she said finally. "If you leave me a number this time."

"But Mama," I slid away from her dead fish hand, "I've got to show them where Delilah is."

"Son, if she's lost, you've got to let the police handle this."

"She's not lost," I said. "She's been kidnapped."

"Kidnapped." Mama snorted. "Don't be silly. Who'd want to kidnap her?"

"I've been telling you. It's the Beauty Killer."

"Why on earth would he take her?"

I scrubbed my face. I might as well've been swimming in molasses. "She won, didn't she?"

"Honey," Mama cocked a hip, "Sunny and I do not have time for this. And it sounds like something best left to the police."

She flicked a red-hot curl off her shoulder. "You are barely fourteen years old and I can't imagine what you reckon you're going to do for that child. You wanted to leave the farm. I said you could come with us. Now, you coming or not?"

I glanced at Ida Mae. She turned to stare out the glass at

the sky, quickly fading to gray. I studied Pretty Boy, Delbert, Jiminy Cricket, Willie.

Sunny tugged on Mama's arm. "Can we go now?"

"Well?" Mama cocked her head at me and tapped her painted toes.

"Can't you stay one night?" I begged. "Let me find her?"

"No can do." She tapped the cheap watch on her wrist. "The chicken's a ticking." The circle of fake diamonds glittered under the fluorescent lights.

A door slammed. The security guard's walkie talkie sputtered and crackled.

"Flynn, honey?" Mama's eyebrows slashed upward.

"I can't go with you," I said. And as I said it, a little piece broke off inside of me and quivered, suspended somewhere inside my bloodied gut. Probably the shame of disappointing my daddy. "It's my fault Delilah was here. I should've sent her back, and I didn't. But I know where she is. I can find her."

Mama stared at me. She studied her broken nail. She fiddled with the watch at her wrist. "Suit yourself," she said finally. "Willie, you staying or going?"

"Staying," Willie said.

"Appears it's just us chickees," she said to Sunny. "Grab your makeup case, sweetie. I'll be right behind you." She pulled me close and kissed the top of my head. "You take care, you hear?" She cleared her throat and pulled Willie into our hug. "You, too, bugaboo." She kissed his cheek. "Don't you boys do anything dangerous. Ida Mae," she said over our heads as she tightened her squeeze.

"Martha June," Ida Mae said.

Mama released us and followed Sunny out of the lobby, her heels clunking on the hard tile floor.

"Alrighty, then," Ida Mae said as I thumbed the corner of my eye. "He took her to the cabin, didn't he?"

I choked on the burning in my throat. "Yeah."

"Let's go, then."

"What about the police?" Willie said.

Ida Mae studied me. "We can't wait."

"What about Monty?"

"It'll be dark soon," Willie said. "We can't leave him."

She and I stared at each other. Her nod to me was faint. "He moves best by moonlight, anyway," she said. "Knowing him, he's halfway home."

Loaded in the truck, I studied the trees blurring by in the twilight and realized for the first time, if something happened to Delilah, this time it would be all my fault. She trusted me to look out for her. But even Monty knew I didn't have it in me. I simply didn't care enough.

Yesterday, all I could think about was my mission. But now I knew, if anything happened to Delilah, if the Beauty Killer…well…I couldn't finish the thought. I just knew I'd never forgive myself. But I was stuck in this stupid truck while she was out there somewhere in the dark. So I did the only thing I could think of.

Bouncing along in the front seat of Ida Mae's pickup, I prayed all the way home. I prayed to a God I barely knew that somehow we'd catch the killer before he commenced to plucking out eyes. I prayed for Monster Monty, and Pretty Boy, Delbert and Jiminy Cricket, and Willie, that we'd all be safe. I prayed Ida Mae wouldn't wreck the pickup truck and kill us on that lonely stretch of highway. I prayed Mama and Sunny would finally find what they were searching for in Mobile.

And I prayed, *please God, even though I scarcely know you, let them find my daddy and bring him home.*

long way home

By the time we reached Haley, the sky was bruised and bleeding into the green fields we lumbered past. We passed the Dairy Queen and squealed on two wheels into Joe's Filler-Up. Ida Mae and I clamored out, and I followed her to the truck bed.

"Pretty Boy, you and Delbert stay inside with Joe." She lowered the gate, and they scrambled out. "Call Sheriff Pickens. Tell him to meet us at the cabin." She said to Willie and me, "You boys reckon you can find it from here?"

"I can," Willie said. "I tied cotton strips to the trees."

"What?" I stared at him. "When?"

"When we came through yesterday morning. In case we needed to find our way home."

"Good boy," Ida Mae said. "You stay with the others and wait for the sheriff. Help him find the way. And you," her gaze fell on Jiminy Cricket, "reckon you can keep up with us?"

Jiminy glanced at me. He studied his feet. "I don't know," he said. Even in the pale light, his freckles reddened.

I nudged his arm. "We could use your help," I said. "You can do it."

He hesitated, then nodded. "Alright."

Ida Mae rubbed her palms together. "Then there's no time to waste." We scrambled to our assignments.

We found Willie's white markers easy enough, and I clicked on my flashlight, my knapsack weighing on me as heavy as a sack of cement. We hurried as fast as the woods allowed, trying its best to trip us on a rotten log, or slap us with a bony branch.

My sides burned, and Jiminy wheezed behind me. But Ida Mae moved as purposefully as a bloodhound, sniffing the air, trotting low to the ground.

"I've got to stop," I said finally, pressing the stabbing pain below my ribs. "My side's killing me."

Ida Mae and Jiminy hesitated.

"Go on." I gestured toward them. "I'll catch up."

"You've got the light," Jiminy said.

"Nobody gets left behind," Ida Mae said. "We've lost too many already."

"Please," I handed the flashlight to Jiminy Cricket. "Take it. I can't breathe, my side's burning."

"Come on," Jiminy said. "If I can do it, you can."

"No time. Got to rest. Go." I pressed my palm to my forehead. The trees spun overhead.

"You go," Jiminy said to Ida Mae. "I'll stay with him."

"We all go," Ida Mae stared at the faint trail. "I can't do it alone. Neither can you. Delilah needs us."

I wished a million times I'd gone with Mama and Sunny to Mobile. And yet, I was so mad at her. Mad because she gave me no choice but to do this. Mad because she left me again. Mad because she loved Sunny more than me. Mad because my daddy ran off to war. And mad at Mama for letting him.

"You're right," I finally agreed. I gave the light to her and struggled to my feet. "I'll be right behind you."

"I've got your back." Jiminy said.

We pushed further into the dark, silent trees. When I thought I couldn't stagger another step, we neared the cabin. Ida Mae slowed to a creep. We tiptoed to the clearing and peered at the house from the trees. A faint glow of yellow dipped in the window.

"What's the plan?" I whispered.

"No idea," Ida Mae whispered back.

"We're just going to stroll through the front door and say, 'Give us the girl?'"

"Why not?" She crept forward.

"You crazy?" I hissed. "What if he's got a gun? What if he's on LSD? What if..."

But she was already halfway across the clearing. She pressed her back against the wall beside the door, pulling her loose shirt close around her.

"Oh, lord," I said and drew my sword from my knapsack. I turned to Jiminy. "You got any—"

He raised a familiar blade, winking wickedly in the twilight.

"Where'd you get *my* knife?"

"Monty gave it to me. He felt bad about taking it when you dropped it outside the cellar. And he thought I'd need it. You want it back?"

I hesitated. My dad had given me that knife. It was special. And I sorely missed my dad. But my sword was special, too. Carved just for me. I tightened my grip on it. "Maybe later," I said. "I'm good for now."

I left my knapsack in the grass and followed him toward the house, my sword raised. We flattened ourselves against the wall on the other side of the door from Ida Mae. I breathed over Jiminy's shoulder.

"You hear anything?" Ida Mae mouthed.

I listened. Nothing but crickets and katydids and an owl hooting in the distance. I shook my head.

"Jimmy," she whispered, "go 'round to the back window and holler if you see anything. Flynn, come with me."

She reached out and turned the knob. The door creaked open.

I gripped the sword tight enough to crack my fingers. All other sounds were drowned out by the roar of blood in my ears. My right cheek pulsed with it.

Ida Mae nudged the door open further with the toe of her tennis shoe. She peeked around the door. I thought if she didn't hurry, I might hurl.

A light, an old-fashioned oil lamp, glowed from a small table beside the chewed-up sofa. We stared at it.

"Bedroom," Ida Mae whispered. We crossed the room and pressed ourselves against opposite sides of the door, which was open. I glanced at Ida Mae.

She motioned for me to slip into the room. The sword nearly slipped from my fingers, but I caught it against my thigh and wiped my sweating palm on my jeans. She nodded to me. I slipped into the room and pressed myself against the wall. Where was Jiminy?

I waited for my vision to adjust to the darkness. A shadowy shape passed the window outside, and I melted into the wall. The mattress below it was pale and empty. My sword trembled in my hand.

Something touched my arm and I nearly screamed. It was Ida Mae.

"See anything?" she whispered.

I barely moved my head.

"Hear anything?"

I shook my head. Past the doorway, I crept along the wall toward the bathroom with Ida Mae at my back.

I imagined a bloodied Delilah in the tub. The door stood ajar. The cabin was as quiet as a hallowed grave. I peered into the bathroom. The tub was empty. I scanned the sink, the window. A pale face appeared, and I screamed.

Ida Mae fumbled to turn on the flashlight and beamed it toward the window. The face disappeared. "What was it?" she hissed.

I shook my head and pressed the sword to my quivering heart. "I think I'm going to—"

"Shhhhhhh," Ida Mae grabbed my arm. "Listen."

Something rustled overhead. We stared at each other. "What're we—"

Pressing a finger to my lips, she stared at me and pointed to the ceiling.

I drew in a deep breath and shook my head.

Ida Mae jabbed her bony finger upward.

I wagged my head and hissed, "I ain't going up there."

"If he's got Delilah."

"No. No. No."

She gave me the glare she used for burning children at the stake and said, "Then I'll do it."

Willie and I had left the apple barrel on the table the last time we were there. But as Ida Mae threw a knee onto the scarred plank to boost herself up, she paused and then collapsed forward, resting her forehead on the rough wood.

"Ida Mae?" I struggled to see her face.

"I'm fine." She rested for a few seconds before sitting upright, her face flushed, her eyes watery. "It's just a pain in my side. Comes and goes. Help me get my other knee up."

"Brother Muler says you need medicine. It'll get rid of the pain."

"Son," she stared me square in the eye, "nothing can get rid of this pain except death."

"Ida Mae, you've got to trust the doctors."

"I said I'm fine."

"If you kill yourself," I tugged at her loose shirt, "then where'll we be?"

She stared at me. She stared at the ceiling. Sweat beaded her upper lip. She crawled off the table.

Have mercy on our souls, I thought.

I climbed onto the table, then the barrel, and edged the attic panel aside. She handed me the flashlight. I flashed it through the hole, and the rustling stopped.

Like in the barn loft, I peered over the edge of the opening and whipped the light around the darkness. I was reminded of Monty and his pitchfork. I edged the point of my sword through the hole.

To tell you the truth, at that moment I didn't want to find Delilah. I didn't want to witness fat old Brother Muler plucking out eyeballs. I wanted Daddy with beer on his breath, or even Mama and her sweet smell of honeysuckle.

The thin stream of light bounced off attic walls, the floor, the cobwebbed ceiling. A movement fluttered against the far wall. It might've been a mouse or a squirrel. A few feet away, the light flickered over a bundle.

"Anything?" Ida Mae hissed at my feet.

I poked my sword at what appeared to be a flour sack. I hooked the tip of it into the cloth bag and dragged it toward me.

It was one of those old-fashioned flour bags you could still find in some redneck general stores. Ida Mae saved hers for years and stored all sorts of things in them. I thought maybe even her kitchen curtains were made out of the same faded material. I grabbed the bag and climbed down.

"What is it?" Ida Mae peered around my knees.

My feet thumped the ground. "No idea."

"Take it to the den," she said. "More light there." She took the flashlight from me and I carried the sack to the middle of the room and lowered it to the ground. It made a soft plunk. I sank to my knees beside it.

Sunshine Flour, for fresh Southern biscuits was printed on the side with faded sunflowers blooming in the sun.

Praying mightily it didn't hold a dead rat or some other critter, I eased open the mouth of the sack. I lowered the edges of the bag as Ida Mae splashed light into it.

At first it appeared to be empty. It took me a few seconds of blinking into the opening to figure out exactly what I was seeing. It seemed to be a bag of marbles splashed in mud.

Ida Mae made a gurgling sound behind me and groaned, "Oh, sweet Jesus," before the flashlight stuttered and died.

a cut above your average killer

I yelped, dropped the bag, and spider-crawled backward across the floor. "Oh, gross, oh gross, oh gross."

Ida Mae stared at the bag. I rested my head against the wall muttering, "Holy shit, holy shit, holy shit." A body filled the doorway, and I screamed. Ida Mae jumped.

"Jimmy," she barked, "where've you been?"

Jiminy Cricket stepped inside the door. "I been around the outside of the entire cabin like you said. No sign of anybody."

"There's a sign of somebody here." I pointed at the flour sack.

"What is it?" He stalked over.

"Never mind." Ida Mae made a move for the bag.

Jiminy snatched it before she could get her fist on it. I buried my cold, clammy forehead into my knees and hugged them tight.

"What the—what is *that*?" Jiminy rustled the bag, and I whimpered against my knees.

"Is that—is that..." the sack thumped to the floor. I buried my face further. Jiminy's footsteps stumbled outside the front door, followed by gagging sounds.

"Well," was all Ida Mae said.

I raised my head to find her plucking the bag from the floor and twisting it closed. I swallowed hard.

"Come on." She nodded toward the door. "We best get home and call the sheriff."

"He's probably on his way here."

"Yeah." She hesitated. "We better leave a note. Got any paper?"

I patted my pockets. "Maybe a candy wrapper. No, wait." I scrambled to my feet and ran outside.

Jiminy Cricket rested his forehead against his arm propped on the ivy-covered wall. He reeked of vomit. I found my knapsack along the edge of the trees where I left it.

"You okay?" I called as I rummaged through my bag. He gurgled and started gagging again. Guess not. I found Delbert's paper and pen beneath the clean socks I never used.

"Ida Mae," I called. "Got paper." I flipped through the pad and found a clean sheet.

"I've got no idea where he'd take her," Ida Mae said from the doorway. "The church? It has a basement."

Flipping through the pages in the moonlight I realized how good an artist Delbert truly was. He'd drawn a picture of Willie hiding in the corn. Delilah lying in the grass.

"I mean, he's my brother, and we don't exactly gee haw, but I can't believe he'd...can't imagine he'd..." Ida Mae's voice drifted off on the warm summer breeze.

I stared at a drawing of Pretty Boy's carved swan. And me on top of the cellar door. He'd drawn my head a little fat and my arms sort of puny, but it really wasn't a bad likeness. I flipped the page and stopped. My stomach dropped as if I'd tumbled down a roller coaster. Or the cellar steps. "What'd you say?" I stared at the drawing. I carried it into the moonlight.

"You got any idea where he'd take her?" she said.

"Yeah." I wanted to puke, or cry, or both. "I reckon I do."

Ida Mae crossed the yard to peer over my shoulder. It took her a few seconds to realize what she was seeing. "Sweet Jesus, help us," she said staring at the picture. When she raised her chin to study the pines towering over us, tears squeezed out of the corners of her eyes.

maybe they're behind door number two

We left a note for the sheriff stuck to the door with a wad of Juicy Fruit and raced through the woods.

Ida Mae wasn't sounding so good, wheezing ahead of us. But she didn't say a word, and she didn't slow down. She was careful not to let a loose branch or vine slap me, but I wasn't nearly as careful with Jiminy behind me. I heard an *oof*, and a grunt a few times and called out, "Sorry." But I didn't slow down, either, and I didn't look back.

My knapsack hardly weighed on me anymore, even with the bag of eyeballs added to it. I willed myself not to think about it, or imagine the little girls and whether they were alive or dead when he...I couldn't follow through with the thought. I kept shaking it off, hard as a wet dog wanting to rub against me.

If we met the killer in the woods as we raced along, we'd be done for. I braced my sword in front of me, and Jiminy wielded my knife, but a bullet to the gut would take us out easily.

Ida Mae stopped and pressed her side above her hip. Sweat glazed her forehead. "Pain," she said, gritting her teeth. "Can't go on. You boys, go."

"It's a stitch," I said, knowing I lied. "Like mine. We'll rest."

"It's not a stitch, Flynn." She stared me dead in the eye, and a chill shivered through me. "It can't be fixed except to be cut out of me, and I don't have the time nor the money. We've been through this."

"I ain't leaving you," I said.

"You've got to."

"No man gets left behind."

"I ain't a man."

"You know what I mean."

"I know what you mean." She grimaced. "You've got to get to Delilah."

"What if she's already—"

"Stop wasting time!" she barked. "Go."

"I can't stop the killer by myself."

"Take Jimmy." Her face was silvery in the moonlight.

"No," I said. "He stays with you."

"I'll be fine." She groaned and bent over with a palm pressed to her side, her other hand braced against her knee. "I'll rest a minute." She ground her teeth. When she finally straightened, her eyes were wet.

"I'll carry you." I stepped toward her.

"You'll do no such thing."

Her eyes fluttered closed, and she bore the pain between the lines in her forehead. "Go," she whispered, and then her eyes opened. Her voice was stronger. "We're running out of time. Every second we waste here arguing is another second he—" her groan choked off the rest.

I knew she was right. "Stay with her, Jimmy," I said.

"What'd you call me?"

"Just help her."

"Take this." He held out my knife.

"Keep it. You might need it." I took off running and turned only once as he eased Ida Mae to the ground.

I raced through the trees. They crowded over me, huge hulking demons, their bony branches reaching out to snatch my clothes, my hair. They took turns slapping my cheeks, my neck, my arms. They caught my sleeve and slung me backward. I landed so hard on my back I struggled to breathe. I whimpered, staring at the few stars winking from a sleek, panther sky. I fingered my arm. My sleeve was torn. My skin was warm and sticky. *Don't*, I thought. *Don't even look at it.* It felt like a claw had scraped it to the bone.

I lay, a wounded animal, and thought of Delilah and her white halo of hair against the dark sky. I thought of his expression, ugly and twisted above her, sneering and putting his dirty paws on her.

I thought of Sunny, prissy and perfect in pink fringe, her golden curls bouncing beneath a sparkling crown. I thought of Mama with her greedy red lips and her trembling long nails and Ida Mae hunched over in pain and grief, her gaze lifting, searching for me in the darkness.

"God help me," I whispered. "Help me." I was bone tired. Beat low. I wanted to sleep in a field of red poppies and wake up in my own bed in Peach City, clear of the Land of Oz with its wicked witch and crazy, flying monkeys.

I snatched myself. Did I fall asleep? Did I pass out? I stared around the forest, dark and quiet and smelling of rotting leaves. But I heard something. A whisper. A cry?

I rolled to my knees and knelt while the forest spun around me. When it settled, I staggered to my feet and followed the sound of crying. *Go*, my mind screamed. *Run!*

Breathing raggedly, my chest burned, my feet tripped as I

staggered out of the woods and into long, beautiful rows of golden corn. The stalks waved, dark and willowy, welcoming me home. If Delilah's life wasn't at stake, I might've stopped and hugged them, I was so thrilled to be out of the woods.

The sound of crying guided me out of the corn, and I hesitated at the top of the hill. I half slid, half skittered my way down it, my sword raised, heart pounding.

Moonlight spilled onto the scene before me. The door to the cellar yawned open. A dark figure knelt over a body, lying on the ground. Huddled beneath the oak tree a few feet away, a figure rocked on its knees, crying.

Delilah, with the pale glow of a lantern at her feet.

I approached the kneeling figure as he raised his fist over his head. Monty held a sharp, wicked rock, as big as my foot.

"No!" I yelled and charged toward him, my sword raised. I stumbled to a halt on the other side of the body and pointed the sword at Monty's blackened neck.

His face was dark from mud, or grease, except for the two streaks down his cheeks where tears glistened in the moonlight. At his feet lay a man, stretched on his back, eyes open to the moon, his skin pale, strawberry hair tipped red with fresh, flowing blood.

Brother Kaine.

"Monty," I said, "drop the rock."

"He hurt Delilah." The boy stared at the man. He cocked his arm back, meaning to crush Brother Kaine's skull.

"Drop it, now," I said. "Tell me what happened."

"He hurt her."

Blood seeped into the dirt beneath Brother Kaine's head. I knelt beside him, sword at my side, and rummaged through my knapsack. My fingers brushed the bag of eyeballs. I shuddered and fumbled around and pulled out the pair of clean socks.

"Don't," Monty said, the rock wavering in the air. "Don't help him."

"I'm just going to—"

"No!" Monty's eyes had nearly disappeared into his camouflaged face. "He doesn't deserve it."

"What happened?" Still squatting, I eased closer to the man's head.

"Stop moving," Monty said through his teeth.

"You stop this nonsense right now," I said and popped to my feet to tower over him. "He needs a doctor. So, drop the rock and talk to me. You saved Delilah? You kept her safe?"

"He took her to the cabin," Monty said. "Like the others. But I got her away from him, and we ran. He caught us as we broke through the corn. He wanted to take her to the cellar." He lowered the rock and hugged it, hunkered over, staring at Brother Kaine. "She hates it down there. She's scared of the dark."

"She likes the light," I said.

"That's what I told him." His head snapped toward Delilah, curled beneath the tree. "He wanted to hurt her. Do awful things to her. He made her cry. With the others, I didn't know them—"

"Others?" My own voice seemed far away, traveling through a long tunnel.

"They cried, too." Monty stared at Delilah. "He said it was a game. He asked did I want to play a game."

Brother Kaine made a gurgling noise.

I wanted to bash the man's head in myself. I trusted him. I thought he was the good guy. I finally believed in somebody, and he turned out to be a good-for-nothing murderer.

I squatted and pressed the strip of clean sock beneath his head. His eyes fluttered.

"Don't help him." Monty frowned.

"It's okay, now," I said. "Delilah's safe. You saved her."

"I lit the lantern for her."

"You helped her not be afraid."

Brother Kaine needed a doctor, bad. Blood pooled beneath his head. His eyes opened and rolled away from Monty toward me.

"Why?" I said. "All them girls. So young, so innocent. We talked about it. Over ice cream." I clenched my gut to keep from upchucking. "Tell me why you did it." I pressed the clean sock to his bloodied head. "Tell me why you killed 'em."

He closed his eyes.

"I trusted you," I said. "I told you things."

"I didn't mean to," his eyes fluttered open, "not at first." He choked on the words.

"You tell me why you did it." I leaned over him, pressing the bloodied sock hard into his head. "Why young girls? Pageant winners? Why Delilah? There were lots of winners there."

He half chuckled, half choked. Blood trickled from the corner of his mouth.

"This funny to you?"

"No." He struggled to clear his voice. "Not funny at all. You have a sister. I had a sister."

"So?"

"Your sister's pretty. Saw pictures of her in the paper."

I growled.

He winced. "My sister, Lily. Pretty, too. Just sixteen. In a pageant. My father," he choked, coughed, "forbade her, but

Mama doted on her, worshipped her, helped her sneak out. And she won. Thought she'd be Miss America one day.

"Father found out as she was being crowned. In a swimsuit." He sucked in his breath. "Charged the stage. Knocked her crown off for whoring it up." His eyes fluttered closed. "She landed across the floor in front of all of those people." He coughed and blood bubbled between his lips. "Her head hit the podium. Or something. Ended up in a coma. Father, in prison."

"But why—"

His eyes stuttered open, but he stared past me. "Put her in a home for crazy people. Near Tuscaloosa. Except she wasn't crazy, just asleep. Couldn't wake up. And Mama couldn't let her go."

His pause was so long I thought he was done for. Until his eyes flickered to life. "Mama started dressing me like Lily. Me, not more'n eight years old. Rouge and lipstick and eyeliner. Only in secret. Only when it was her and me. Alone. In Lily's bedroom. At night."

He turned his head and spit blood into the scrub grass. "Couldn't make sense of it. Father. Jail. Me, alone with…Mother."

He coughed, choked, his shoulders rising off the ground before collapsing. "Lily died a year ago. In her sleep. Mama stopped eating. Forty-eight days later…put her in the ground. Forty-eight days. How long it takes a body to starve."

He smiled, showing bloodied teeth.

"A year ago," I said. "That's when the killings started."

He rolled his head to stare me in the eye.

I shivered and asked, "Why the eyes? Why cut out the eyes? And why little girls? Your sister was nearly full grown."

He turned his head and coughed more blood into the

ground. He tried to raise his wrist to swipe at his mouth, but it fell useless at his side.

"Got the job at the church. Mother died. Rage inside me built and built and built until I couldn't stand it. Only release I got was seeing a young girl in the newspaper with a crown on her head. So like Lily. Couldn't help but find where she lived, went to school, church. Just wanted to talk. Maybe get a little of Lily back. But she was scared of me. Not like Lily at all. And I didn't like the look in her eyes. Judging me. Who was she? A child. Didn't she know how much I'd done for everyone? My mother? The church?

"Didn't mean to do it the first time. Just wanted to talk. Give tootsie rolls and pops. But that look. Couldn't stand it. Wrapped my fingers around her neck, fragile, delicate, until it popped like a chicken bone. Her eyes finally closed. I felt such a rush. Sweet release. Then a little shame. But I wanted her family to find her so they could have a proper burial. She deserved that.

"And everything was fine. Good. Until Brother Muler sent me on a visit to a family who'd stopped coming to church. They had a young daughter. Were skipping church to go the pageant route. Saw a photo. Blonde. Like Lily. Crown on her head. The pressure in my head began to build. And build. Until I didn't think I could get out of there before exploding. Managed to tamp it down long enough. Buy an extension cord. Figure out how to get to her without being seen."

"Why Delilah?" I said. "She's already been through more horror than you can imagine. She trusted you, too."

He choked and his back arched as he struggled to clear his throat. "Knew Sunny would win. 'Cause of the papers. But I saw you. In the distance. Couldn't go through with it. Didn't want you to think…bad of me." He coughed hard enough to loosen a lung. "But Delilah. Didn't expect that. Knew she'd go with me. Besides," bloody spit dribbled down his chin, "who'd care about her, anyway?"

"Shut up," Monty said, "shut up talking." He pressed his free hand to his ear.

Brother Kaine gazed at him. "You're guilty," he said, "same as me."

"Shut up!" Monty raised the rock. "I didn't kill nobody!"

Brother Kaine's laugh ended in a coughing fit. "You watched." He smiled at Monty. "You enjoyed it. The game."

"Monty!" I got his attention. "Not yet." I motioned for him to lower his weapon.

"Why the eyes?" I asked Brother Kaine.

He closed his eyes, his smile weak. "Last time I saw Lily, before she fell asleep, she stared at me. With her big green eyes, she begged me, pleaded with me to help her, save her. But I couldn't do it. Couldn't do anything. The eyes of those other girls? The ones I put out of their misery? When they realized their fate, their eyes turned hard. Condemning. Even as young as they were. And I just couldn't have them judging me."

I wanted to hurl. My stomach lurched. But I cupped my palm against my mouth to hold it in. Finally, I lowered my hand and said, "Why involve Monty? He's a kid. He didn't know no better."

"Found me at the cabin." Brother Kaine licked his cracked lips. "Like I said, it was a game. He enjoyed it as much as me."

Monty cried and hugged his rock.

"Only way to keep him from turning me in. Kill him. Or make him an accomplice. And I liked having him join me. My own little sidekick."

Something thrashed in the corn, and I turned to find Jimmy crashing through it with Ida Mae staggering at his side. I closed my eyes as a siren wailed in the distance.

and justice for all?

The Little Lamb Daycare of Haley was shut down. The scandal of having a murdering minister in charge of children was more than even Brother Muler could survive. He had hired the man.

"I don't understand why you have to take all the blame," Ida Mae said. She shucked corn in a rocking chair on her front porch next to her brother. "Nobody else in town knew what he was up to, either."

Brother Muler picked at a silky ear of corn. He tugged a few strands. "I had suspicions," he said. "But it just seemed too horrible, impossible to imagine. So I didn't do anything about it. I got to accept my share of the blame."

Ida Mae shucked in silence. Brother Muler twirled the corn cob between his palms. The sticky strings clung to his fancy suit.

"What're you going to do now?" she asked.

He shrugged. "There's a church group leaving out of Decatur on a missionary trip to South America. Chile, I believe. Thought maybe I'd go along. There's some mighty poor people in Chile." He shook the sticky strings off his fingers. "Mighty poor."

"What about First Church?" Ida Mae handed him the

dishtowel draped over her shoulder. He dropped the corn and wiped his hands clean.

"They'll get along fine without me for a spell. There's a new fella coming in. Married man. Six young'uns."

"You don't say."

They carried on, and I stopped listening to the drone of their voices. I leaned my head against the porch post and closed my eyes.

Laughter floated in the distance, close to the barn. Delilah squealed. Crickets thrummed in the tall grass. Two blue jays fussed in the mimosa tree.

The government lady was still breathing down Ida Mae's throat. But the day before, a man stopped by the farm. He was a lawyer by the name of Coleman. Walter Jefferson Davis Coleman. He asked Ida Mae to call him Wally.

He'd finally tracked us down to thank us for taking care of his daddy. Said his daddy was out of the hospital and doing better. His wife set him up in a room over the garage.

When he found out about the legal trouble Ida Mae was in, having too many kids, then letting them run wild, then having one arrested as an accomplice to murder, he offered to help. He said he shouldn't have any trouble getting all of that mess dismissed or discharged or something.

"In fact," he said, "I believe I can get you some extra money from the government on account of them placing a dangerous sociopath by the name of Montague T. Minor in your home."

"No," Ida Mae said. "I don't want Monty dragged into this. He's got enough trouble already."

It was true. They'd locked him in the children's ward of the mental hospital near Tuscaloosa. Maybe the same one Mr. Boushay was in. Maybe they'd become friends.

Ida Mae said she'd visit him and maybe bring us along. But I couldn't manage to get the bag of eyeballs out of my head, or Brother Kaine's bashed-in skull.

Brother Kaine was transported by ambulance to a fancy hospital in Birmingham and remained in a coma. Same as his sister, which is what you might call ironic. The doctors questioned whether he'd ever come out of it.

Some people thought he escaped justice. I wasn't so sure. Maybe he simply postponed it awhile. I thought one day I might investigate his family further with his daddy out of prison and in the area. Then again, maybe not.

Amazingly enough, I hadn't suffered any bad dreams lately, least not any that'd make me cry in my sleep. I guess if you live through enough nightmares during the day, there's nothing left to dream about at night.

Mama called and said Sunny won the state pageant, so they were traveling on to Nashville. She said they'd be back in time for us to start school back home in Peach City, but I wasn't holding my breath.

We still hadn't heard anything about Daddy's whereabouts. They simply reported him missing in action. And apparently there were quite a few of those. We were referred to something called the National League of Families, who handled such matters, but so far, they hadn't been much help, either.

It was a slow grinding in my gut, the not knowing. But there wasn't much to be done about it, except to keep busy.

I sat on the porch and ripped a chunk out of a stick with my rusted Swiss Army knife Jimmy had returned to me. I cocked my head at my work. It was already looking a little like a swan. I cocked my head the other way. Or maybe more of a chicken.

It didn't matter.
I was just getting started.

acknowledgements

According to Proverbs 27:17, as iron sharpens iron, so one person sharpens another. And truthfully, I have an incredibly creative, passionate team who helps me be a better writer, but more importantly, a better human being.

I'd like to thank my readers, Millie Thomas Gardner, Melissa Gambill, and Kaylen Hamilton, for their insightful critiques and support of this project. Many thanks go to Boo Cole Archer who coaches me with much humor, laughter, hard truths, and more grace than any person I know. A hearty thanks and much appreciation go to my eagle-eye editor, Teresa Kennedy, for her ability to convey what I mean better than me, the courage to be brutally honest in the endeavor to make my fiction the best it can be, and her unfailing encouragement every step of the way. Many thanks also go to my publisher, Mike Parker at WordCrafts Press, whose enthusiasm for this project and timely advice carried me over the finish line.

And I can't express enough love and appreciation for my family. Carly, your creative mind continually inspires me to dream bigger, reach higher, and stretch more than I ever thought possible. Ty, your continual encouragement of my writing and thoughtful advice keeps me going on the most discouraging days, and means more to me than you'll ever know. Tucker, you make me laugh, build me up, call me out, and sharpen me in every single way. The three of you have my whole heart for my whole life.

And I'm eternally grateful for you all.

about the author

Susie Mattox is an author and Alabama native who developed an interest in ghosts and the macabre spending summers in her grandmother's home, which was haunted. She lives in Montgomery, Alabama, with her husband and two dogs, and struggles to keep up with her kids who've flown the coop. When she's not writing, she's competitive ballroom dancing and working on sassying up her samba.

Susie is on Facebook, Twitter @mattox_susie, and Instagram @susiemattoxwrites

Also Available From

WordCrafts Press

House of Madness
by Sara Harris

Muldovah
by Marian Rizzo

Summer on the Black Suwannee
by Jennifer Odom

The 5 Manners of Death
by Darden North

Obedience
by Michael Potts

www.wordcrafts.net

CPSIA information can be obtained
at www.ICGtesting.com
Printed in the USA
FSHW010110230621
82590FS